The Shee

THE SHEE

Joe Donnelly

BCA

LONDON · NEW YORK · SYDNEY · TORONTO

This edition published 1992
by BCA
by arrangement with Random Century Ltd

Copyright © Joe Donnelly 1992

CN 2762

Printed in England by Clays Ltd, St Ives plc

In recollection of Martin Kinney, an old friend and a storyteller

Some place names might be familiar, but Kilgallan, unfortunately, does not exist. Similarly, all the characters are fictitious, except, of course, the *Shee*.

Prologue

There were seven cottages on the edge of Kilgallan. You'll know the kind of cottage if you ever watched John Wayne fight over Maureen O'Hara all across the fields and past the river in *The Quiet Man*.

Parts of the village could have come straight out of the film too: old whin and sandstone houses of one and two storeys nestling together under tired and sagging grey slate roofs, a pub where everyone went of an evening and a hotel to catch the tourists and fertilizer salesmen, and one good road coming in and heading west to peter out way down past lonely Tallabaun Strand, where the sands go on for mile after shifting mile to disappear in the haze at the edge of the ocean.

There was an undertaker's parlour with one hearse that worked fine for funerals, black and polished and as dignified as anyone would want for that last journey to the little churchyard, and another that was hunkered on bricks down the lane for years and is probably still slowly settling into the cobbles. There was one church with a crumbling belltower and an old priest who was well into his seventies and nearly stone-deaf and who doesn't figure too much in this story until near the end.

The cottages squatted on the west side of the village where a shady lane snakes past the trunks of some tall elms and a few well-spread chestnut trees and towering limes. They stood in a haphazard sort of circle a short walk from the raised tor close to the shore. They had whitewashed walls and thatched roofs and even the obligatory cart-wheels leaning nostalgically against their gables. The only difference between them and every other croft on the far west coast was that they were *new* houses, built to look old, in the hope of luring travelling money out to the edge of Mayo, the old kingdom of Connacht.

They hadn't set the bogland ablaze, but then again, they hadn't done too badly. There's good fishing here, and a wealth of seabirds of all sorts picking a living from the sands and from the vast tidal mudflats of Clew Bay. There's also something quite spectacular in the solitude and isolation of that part of the coast, and there are always the few who will seek it, so the cottages did some reasonable business.

Life has been quiet in Kilgallan since the big famine a hundred and fifty years back when thousands of the big westmen of Mayo and their wives and children starved in their crofts or joined the hungry migrations to the States or over the Irish Sea to Scotland. It's even quieter there now on the far west tip at the bottom shore of the bay. Oh, Kilgallan is still a dot on some maps; only some, though there are damn few people living in the cluster of ramshackle houses where the roads meet.

The cottages are gone now. Brambles and nettles tangle and twine on the few places where one stone lies upon another. You can still see the outlined mounds of the seven houses that stood in a rough circle in the lee of the tor where stunted elms bent themselves over, cringing in the face of the cold Atlantic wind.

Donovan's bar is still open for what business it can get. The peeling door of McGavigan's funeral parlour creaks on its hinges. Trade is slack for the moment, but it has been better. *Much better*. The windows of the Tallabaun Inn are boarded over and its rooms gather dust. There has been no buyer since O'Hara died in what he wrongly boasted was the most westerly hotel in all of Ireland with its thousand welcomes in half a dozen languages.

There is no welcome now. The cold, damp wind swirls around the corners and sagging eaves. Apart from the few inches of gloom beyond the green door that shows McGavigan's is open for business, the other doors are closed. There is no-one walking the cobbled street. It is as if the people in Kilgallan have battened themselves down and shut themselves in.

Travellers still pass by, but few stop on their way to the Tallabaun Strand for the fishing, or over the moor and down to Galway Bay. There is no welcome. Even with the windows shut and the heater full on, the *feeling* of the place oozes in. It's a cold feeling, a shivery, uncomfortable feeling. Drivers slow down at the crossroad sign past the bridge and speed up again, hurrying on through.

Kilgallan has shut itself down. It's gone back to being a quiet little place. You could say it's as near dead as a place can be. That's close to the truth.

But there was a time, when the cottages still stood in their round by the tor, that Kilgallan wasn't a quiet place at all. There was life there – of a sort.

It came slinking through the shadows and howling in the wind. It came in all its fury, the way it had in the old days when Ireland still had gods and heroes.

And then there was *death*.

1

Rita Burke followed the road west along the south edge of Clew Bay, round the curve that skirted the mudflats and then past the massive shoulder of towering Croagh Patrick.

It was early evening in high summer, the sun slanting down from the blue west sky ahead. A grey, misty haze, like a pall of smoke shadowing the distant houses, piled up over the village, still a few miles away. It was the only shadow on the whole of the wide bay.

The Dubliners were playing a ribald tune that crackled from the old speakers in Rita's dented car as she trundled it along the winding road. Her thoughts were on home and a nice glass of sherry before dinner. After she left the bank, where she worked as a cashier, she had picked up a good piece of sole at the fishmongers and a dozen Clew Bay oysters. Rita was a widow of indeterminate age who was merry enough to be having another go at marriage. She'd set her sights on Toomy Toner, who cobbled all the shoes on the south side of the bay and was a steady enough wee fellow. He didn't smoke and he drank less than most. He had a good going business all to himself and could be doing with a bit of looking after. Maybe he did look a bit like a leprechaun as he huddled over his last, shoving his awl through the soles of the big ploughmen's boots, but he had a twinkle in his eye, smelled of leather, and he *loved* a good dish of fish.

Rita hummed along with the throaty singing and swung the car at the fork to head into the village. Ahead of her the cloud passed in front of the sun, sending another shadow swelling across the fields in a grey wave. She drove into it, and the crackling of the radio welled louder, drowning out the rough singing voices. Inside the crackling there was a buzzing rasp that tingled in the back of Rita's ears. Without knowing it, she dipped her foot on the brakes just before the hump-backed bridge and slowed the car to a halt on the flat grassy verge that had been cropped by countless sheep. If a passer-by had seen her, they would have thought her deep in contemplation as she sat there in the shade of the cloud that expanded over the village ahead. But no-one passed. The road was empty.

A few moments later, she seemed to shake herself out of a daydream and got out of the car. There was a flash of movement from the other side of the road, just beyond the bridge. A boy was fishing for minnows.

'What are you catching today, Michael Boyle?' Rita called out. 'Trout for your tea, is it?'

The small boy looked round quickly, as if he'd been caught at something, and then smiled when he recognised her.

'No, it's just wee ones here, Aunty Rita,' he called back. 'But they're too quick for me. I only have one of them.'

He bent down and picked up a jar. A piece of string looped round the neck and doubled and tucked to serve as a handle. He held it up. From inside came a small flash of silver as the little fish swam in circles, nosing the glass.

'Now there's a beauty for you, Michael. It'll be the salmon next, just like your father.'

Michael was the youngest of the burgeoning Boyle family who lived next door to Rita on the Killadoon road. She'd babysat them often enough to be an honorary aunty to them all. Michael, the youngest of the pack, was for that reason the favourite.

'Here, let me see it,' she said, walking slowly across the road. The afternoon was quiet. A cool eddy of wind rustled the ripening tips of the grass in the nearby hayfield. There were no other cars on the road. A few clouds dappled a blue sky, and the big grey one blotted out the sun to the west.

A small track, worn by generations of wee boys, led down from the road to the side of the bridge. The old humpback arched over the deep Roonah Water like a rough stone snake. Here there was a grassy bank, and further down a flat, marshy place where dark reeds straggled in the mud as the Roonah meandered to empty out into the bay. Underneath the bridge, the water moved slow and deep with only a few dark whorls on its surface to show that there was a current.

'Let me see your fish now, Mickey,' Rita said. For an instant there was a strange hollow rasp to her voice. The boy looked up quickly, but Aunty Rita smiled widely at him, and the small uncertainty withered.

'It's just a wee stickleback. Look, you can see the spikes on its back.'

'And it's got a red belly too. Looks like it's been drinking blood, the horrible thing.'

'No, they're all that colour,' the boy said, laughing. Aunties never knew anything.

'The water's deep here,' she said. 'I don't think your mother would be wanting you to play down here on your own, now would she?'

The guilty look flitted across the small boy's face. He looked at her earnestly. His reddish hair was dull in the shade and his freckles looked as if they had been painted on against the pale of his skin.

4

'You won't be telling her, would you, Aunty Rita? Only there's nobody to play with today. And Mother said for me to go and not bother her when she's making the tea.'

'Well, just this once I won't say a word, so long as you promise not to come here by yourself.'

Before he could answer, she turned and walked under the bridge where a stone bank left a step-way a few feet above the water surface. Under the broad arch, it was even darker. The stream swirled inky, with hardly a murmur.

'Look here, Mickey. Come and see this,' she said, peering down at the turbid surface.

The boy came forward unhesitatingly, carrying his stick with the loop of wire fixed to the end that bore the foot of a bedraggled nylon stocking for a net.

'Look how deep it is there, young man.' Her voice echoed in a shivery way between the water and the stones. Michael looked. He couldn't see the bottom. In the deep shade, it could have gone down for miles.

'And can you swim now?'

'No. But I've to learn, my mum says.'

'And what would happen if you were to slip and fall in there?'

The boy shrugged his shoulders in the way that boys do when they know the answer and don't want to say.

'You'd drown to death, wouldn't you.'

'Uh-uh,' he said in a small voice.

'Well, we none of us would want that.'

He shook his head, hoping that she wouldn't drive off in her old car and tell his mam.

Rita sat down on one of the big stones that had been rolled up against the bridge wall by shepherds, generations back, who had used the arch as a shelter from the storms. She held her arms out to the boy.

'Come here and I'll tell you something,' she said. The shivery echo seemed to be part of her voice now, but Mickey came forward into Aunty Rita's embrace. She hugged him close.

'Now if anything happened to you while you were down here all by yourself, why nobody would know about it, would they?' She felt him shake his head, in at the top of her shoulder.

'And if you can't swim, there's no saving you, is there?'

Again the shake of his head.

'Now, I won't tell your mother this time, but you need to learn to swim. Do you want me to teach you?'

Mickey nodded. She eased her hug on him. Inside her ears, her own voice was underpinned by a strange insistent ringing. In the shadow, her eyes looked dark and hollow.

'Right, Mickey. Come on then. Put your net down, and I'll show you.' She reached out and grasped the bottom of the boy's mud-smeared tee-shirt and lifted it up past his chin. 'Arms up.'

He raised them, and she slipped it right off. The summer air was still warm, but underneath the arch of the bridge, a cold eddy of air swirled. The boy shivered a little and goose flesh rippled on his arms. She reached down and pulled off his short trousers. He stepped out of them innocently and she slipped off his wet sandshoes, slimed with algae from the edge of the reed bed.

'Sure, you're a fine figure of a man, aren't you?'

Mickey looked up at her trustingly.

Rita stood up, took her jacket off and folded it to lay it on the stone. She unzipped her skirt at the back and shoved it down over her hips and bent to step out of it. Her summer blouse was next, then her white brassiere. She slid the straps over her shoulders then hunched forward to undo the clasp. Straightening, she took it right off and her large white breasts wobbled as they slipped out. She stood there for a moment, savouring the cool air on her skin, while Michael looked on, slightly embarrassed, mightily curious at the strange shape his Aunty Rita had.

She hitched her thumbs on the rim of her tights and pulled them straight down, along with her pants, almost losing her balance as she stepped out of them. Now Michael was agog. Aunty Rita had *hair*. He just stared at it, wondering where the other parts were.

She caught the look and smiled at him as she took the three steps towards him, holding out her hands.

'Now Mickey, we'll make a swimmer out of you.' She took his hands and walked to the edge of the water, then hunkered down and sat on the stone ledge, pulling him to sit with her. The water was cool; she savoured the tingle. It matched the teasing buzz at the back of her head. She put her hands behind and lowered herself down into the deep pool, catching her breath, feeling the cold ease up against her skin.

It *was* deep here. Still holding on with one hand, she let her feet go down until she found the bottom, slick and smooth under her outstretched toes. The cold squeezed at her skin, tautening her nipples. Up above, Mickey watched her. She reached up to him and gently tugged. There was no fear in his eyes and he came down into the water with her. She heard his little gasp for breath as the shock of cold hit his ribs, and hugged him to her. His small body was warm against hers.

Inside her, an ache swelled, though she didn't know what it was. The

6

ringing in her ears was suddenly loud and urgent. Her heart beat faster and blood surged under her skin. Suddenly a wave of *need* coursed right through her like a hot, pulsing stream. She felt it between her legs, and her nipples pulsed, hard and rhythmic, as if they had been squeezed. The sensation tingled and sizzled her nerves and she shivered with the intensity of it.

In the dark under the arch, she hugged Michael between her large breasts and then drew his head down. She squeezed him against herself and then shoved his small tousled head under the water with a swift brutal motion. He squirmed, hard and furious, panicked by the sudden submersion, but she held him under her breasts and against the stone ledge, trapping him with her body. She could feel him kick and struggle, but he was too small. Behind her ears, the tingling rose higher and higher, blotting out the splashing sound as the terrified child thrashed for air. Inside she felt urgency well up in a red-hot flow that shivered through her and took her *hard*, jolting her body on a wave of black pleasure.

The movement under her stopped. A small white arm trailed out from beneath her left breast, waving downstream as the current pushed past. Rita let go her clasp on little Michael. His red hair was dark brown in the dim light, floating like waterfronds above his pale face. His body turned over in the sluggish current. Lifeless eyes stared up at her from the black stream. The flow spun him down and his small frame caught on a dead branch jammed between two rocks.

Rita hauled herself heavily out of the water, panting a little with the effort. The ledge was wet from the splashes the little boy had made as he fought for life, so she made no footprints. Inside, she felt *sated*, wonderfully filled. Yet, in another part of her mind, she walked as if in a dream. Water cascaded from her as she went towards her clothes and began to pull them on, ignoring the damp as they clung to her skin.

A few minutes later she walked out from underneath the bridge, looking down only once to see the pale outline of the little body deep in the shadows. The buzzing in her ears was a shrill crescendo that could not be denied.

Rita crossed the road and got into her car. She sat alone for several minutes as the strange pleasure that had rocked her drained away. She started the engine and reversed out. The big cloud that had floated in passed on its way. She saw the edge of its shadow race across the fields, bringing sunlight in its wake. A ray of the summer evening light reflected back from a wing mirror and speared her eyes.

Instantly the buzzing, chittering sound that had snared the *real* mind of Rita Burke fled from her.

7

And just as instantly came the realisation of what she had done.

The horror of it almost stopped her heart as the terrible deed came back to her in every minute detail. A wave of nausea choked her throat and in that moment, she knew that there could be no forgiveness for the enormity of the foul thing that had happened under the bridge.

No forgiveness, not from old Father Cullen in the fastness of the confessional; none from Sinead Boyle and her brood, who would soon discover, after a frantic search, that they had lost the baby of the house; none from herself, though she could not explain the madness and the hunger that had taken her in a death grip.

To the east of Kilgallan, along the bay road, there is a cut-off track that takes fishermen down to Tiraun Point. Rita Burke, eyes stinging with tears of horror and remorse, shunted the car down that road as if she was making a frantic dash for freedom. The hedges whipped past on either side, unnoticed. At the far end of the road there was a dip that went down to the old stone jetty. She ignored that, revving the car's little engine as hard as it would go, and sped past the turn, keeping a straight line on the top track.

The road petered out, leaving only a flat grassy slope. The old car rattled across it, came to the edge, and continued on and down, in a steep arc. It hit the jagged rocks nose-down a hundred yards below. Rita watched them swoop up to her with something that neared relief.

There was a tearing crack as the car crumpled on the rocks. Rita was catapulted through the shattered windscreen, spun like a doll and smashed onto a stone. There was a small crack as the force of the blow doubled her backwards and her spine snapped. She fell another twenty feet to land face-down on the barnacle-crusted stones that stood right at the edge of the water, crushing her ribs with such devastating pressure that they were forced through the skin of her back. Her head was whipped forward and smashed into the rock.

There was no pain. Rita died instantly.

But the last picture that flashed in the front of her mind on that catastrophic tumbling fall was of little Mickey's body down there in the dark water, and the reflection of herself on the surface as she peered down at the lifeless shape.

Even in that last fleeting second, she saw her reflection change into a face that was long and gnarled and twisted with savage glee.

And the foul face she saw in that reflection, wearing a look of triumph and slaked desire, was not her own.

It was the face of something else.

2

Down in County Clare, on the west coast south of Galway Bay, a special festival takes place every autumn in the village of Lisdoonvarna. It is not unique to Ireland, but is the best known, thanks to some shrewd promotion in recent years. It has gone on for centuries, drawing hopefuls from all over the poor counties.

The marriage festival of Lisdoonvarna is a throwback to land-hungry times, when first sons only married when they inherited the land of their fathers, often at what the Irish call a *good* age. It happens in the autumn, for any crops, barley or turnips or potatoes, have been harvested, and a middle-aged man's thoughts turn to finding someone to share his inheritance and milk the cows.

Sean McCullain found himself bored by it all. Busloads of elderly tourists converged on the village in knees-up fashion for seven days of drinking and seven nights of dancing, while the gnarled men from the boglands gave them what they hoped was a line of blarney and measured them up like prime stock.

The story had been done before, many a time, and not for the first time did Sean wonder what on earth he was doing here. He watched the greying men and saw their hopeful, shameful, hungry eyes and recognised the whole thing for what it was – a testament to Ireland's bleak and battered history, pure and simple. For the tourists, it was a laugh, a joke, a romantic notion. Few if any of the blue-rinsed ladies and their shy, spotty daughters from Scotland and England and Wales would disappear off into the bogs on the back of a rickety cart with one of the fine ould fellas.

Liz Cannon, though, Sean thought, was in her element. She was smart and she was bright, and even her casual city clothes spoke of a culture that was a million miles away from this flat land near the edge of the Atlantic.

Sean watched her, wondering what she was doing here, what *he* was doing here. She *was* smart enough, he reckoned. Yet she wore a veneer of hardness that he suspected was brittle. He also suspected that underneath it was just an up-and-coming girl trying to make her bones in the newspaper world and scared of getting it wrong. He'd seen it before. Hell, he'd *been* it before, but that was a long time ago, and now it was the last thing he needed.

9

What he did need was to get the hell out of Ireland and move back home for a while, back north. Somewhere quiet to get his head sorted out, to take some time to get *himself* sorted out. Somewhere away from the hustle and the trouble where he could breathe again and maybe try to get a night's sleep without the dreams ripping him apart. Somewhere that was a million miles away from here and now. He didn't want to be here, taking set-up pictures that probably wouldn't see the light of day. He needed to be back in his own place, up in the hills, using his camera to paint pictures with light. In his mind's eye, he saw the morning mist blanket a hill loch at dawn, with the sun just a glow in the early air. He saw the tumble of white water in a mountain stream close to home and knew that was where he should be.

Instead, he was here, on a useless, unplanned assignment with a kid who had convinced herself she knew it all, and had some hard lessons ahead.

She had arrived at the office Sean shared with the Belfast bureau men almost, but not quite, unannounced. Sean knew she was coming and could have done without it. He'd been told by the deputy picture editor, standing in for the boss on the desk, to stay on a bit longer and do a couple of easy numbers. David Robertson, who ran the photographers' team with flair born out of many years on the road, wouldn't have allowed it, but his number two didn't have wit or wisdom to think beyond the convenience of having Sean in the right place at the right time.

To McCullain, there was never again going to be right time to be in Ulster. This was his sixth visit in less than a year, and hopefully his last for a while. He wanted a break; time to let the dreams fade away. He'd done a year's stint in the Province, his second spell in the past decade, doing the work he did best: standing on the mean streets of the city and the cobbled lanes of the border towns, recording for the rest of the world a conflict that he could make neither head nor tail of.

His work as a photographer had taken him to other mean streets and other cobbled roads, to dirt tracks and jungle trails, capturing the images of man's continuing inhumanity and bringing them home. Ulster was different. McCullain, a big Scot from Clydeside who had seen at first hand the aggravation of bigotry, knew *that* for a fact. And it became something worse than different on that day, more than a year past when he'd been sent over to cover the burial of the victims who had died at another funeral. That was the one when a gunman had come running into the cemetery and opened fire – all live on worldwide television – at the mourners.

At this second funeral, he had been there when the unmarked car had screeched in, from nowhere, it seemed, and he'd felt the electric shudder of alarm that swept through the crowd.

The thought that had flashed across his mind had been just like theirs: *'Oh no . . . not again!'*

The scene had changed like the dizzy flip into a bad dream. It went from sombre, angry mourning, to flaring madness in the space of seconds, and still the professional part of him worked on automatic. His camera had captured the images on film, *gut-wrenching* images of the last awful moments of the two soldiers who found themselves in the wrong place at the worst possible moment. He'd watched it happen, every freeze-frame instant of it. And like his camera, his eyes had stored up the images too, showing them on the light-board of his mind in a non stop re-run. At night in the small hours, he'd be wrenched out of sleep, drenched in sweat, shaking with emotion as those pictures flitted incessantly back to him: the faces of the two doomed men; the twisted faces of the crowd who killed them.

Even in the darkroom, processing prints, fixing negatives, Sean saw those faces again and again. Now he didn't like the dark any more, though that was *his* secret. He gritted his teeth and printed his pictures and tried to blur his mind against the images that came crowding in from the shadows. Once or twice, he was able to push them away.

Ever since his photographs, close-up and pin-sharp, had shocked the world, Sean had become the property of the British judicial system. He was Witness Number 17 who six times had sat in the oak-panelled box in the old courtroom, shielded from public gaze by a heavy green curtain like the kind they throw around dying men in hospital wards, guaranteed anonymity by the security services who wished to protect their property. Six times he'd had to live it out again, answering the questions, trying to keep his voice flat and emotionless and failing each time. *Yes, I was there. Yes, I took those photographs. Yes. Yes. Yes. I saw the men die.*

Yes, David Robertson would have known he'd be wrung out again at the end of it. Yes, he would have told him to take a break. His deputy only knew that McCullain was in Ireland. Handy and dandy. He'd told him to stay and wait for Liz Cannon.

He had never worked with her before. Big Sean had to concede that she was a fair enough looker when they met, and he'd have gone so far as to admit she could look even better if she could lose the *I'm a magazine writer* attitude that she wore like a badge. Sean had seen them come and seen them go. It didn't matter too much to him. What did matter was

11

getting on with the job and doing it right, and when he heard what the jobs were, he exploded in a fit of professional wrath.

The same old, time-honoured Irish features. *Lisdoonvarna*, for God's sake. The shrine at Knock that had been done to death every two months since the Pope's visit. *The World's First Peat-Fired Power Station.*

And they wanted McCullain to go along with that. The man who'd brought back the firsts from Panama, Colombia and Soweto. He'd called McIntyre at the office and given him a mighty savaging, and then listened to the excuses given by a man promoted higher than his competence should allow. He agreed only because he knew that Robertson would be back in three days, and he was a man you could deal with. Robertson was a gamekeeper who still retained his poacher's soul.

It took Sean less than a day to form the opinion that Liz was a lightweight. He knew she saw him as a hard-arse who didn't rate her, and that put her on the defensive. When he'd laughed at the idea of the Lisdoonvarna feature, she'd been enraged, especially as he'd done it in front of the two bureau men, who would no doubt send the story singing down the wires to head office. One thing was certain, Sean thought: she knew absolutely *nothing* about Ireland. *Ryan's Daughter* country she called it. She expressed what he considered a prurient, sidewalk-gawper's interest in the troubles, and didn't seem to know what it was all about. McCullain didn't know what it was all about, and he was sure nobody ever would, but at least he'd put in the time *trying* to find out.

Her attitude, he knew, was defensive, and he thought he knew why. Sean knew the game. He'd read her stories. They were not bad, some of them showing spark. Yet it seemed she was battling for something, recognition maybe, or even just a better toe-hold in the rough and tumble world. But she had a lot to unlearn, and he wasn't yet in the mood to teach her.

Still – he had pointed her in the right direction at Lisdoonvarna when he could have left her floundering. It had happened in the middle of a job, in full view of a bus-load of ogling tourists, in the middle of the town's main street. He had turned his back on her.

'Don't you *ever* do that to me again, McCullain,' Liz said in a tight voice that scraped past gritted teeth. 'I've never been so embarrassed in my *life*.' She was shaking with anger, body all tight and held in as if she was scared to let go in case it would spring apart.

12

McCullain ignored her. He was standing at the back of the car, bent under the opened tail-gate, putting his gear back into his pack. He studiously wiped the filter on the front of the Nikon, then wrapped the soft chamois scrap around the camera.

'Are you listening to me?'

'I hear what you're saying,' Sean replied, as he continued packing the equipment.

'Well, I want you to go back there and take that picture *right now*.'

'Want all you like. You can *stick* the picture. For two reasons.'

'And what, may I ask, are they?'

McCullain stopped what he was doing, stepped out from under the tailgate and looked directly at her. His eyes could have been mocking, and she wanted to believe that they were, although the expression in them was hard to read.

'First of all, it's crap. Everybody's done it, so it's not new, and then again, it means nothing. Just a bunch of tourists in a line-up.'

'That's what the feature is all about. That's what I'm writing.'

'You at the tail-end of a long line.'

Liz Cannon was stung at the suggestion that she was merely copying other people's ideas, other writers' features. 'And what's the other reason?' she asked grittily.

'That one's simple. I'm not *your* photographer. Never have been, never will be. You have to learn that.' Sean went back to stowing the camera equipment carefully in the case.

'What are you talking about, McCullain? What's that got to do with taking a picture?'

Sean straightened up again and turned back to her. He raised his hand as if he was going to grab her and she involuntarily flinched back. He continued the movement, took a hold of the tail-gate and leaned on it. Her mistaken apprehension infuriated her even more.

'Now I don't mind taking happy snaps, even if they are crap. I can print them up or not, depending on what I choose, and the picture desk only gets what I give them. Generally speaking, I'm prepared to go along with you and take what you think you need, though if you had any sense you'd see there was a better story here anyway.' He paused and looked into her eyes. They were brilliant dark blue and would have been startlingly pretty but for the anger that shone out of them.

'But when you got those people off the bus for your happy snap, you told them I was *your* photographer.'

'Well, what's wrong with that? I'm the reporter.'

'I hear what you say. Keep telling yourself that and it might come

13

true. But just because you happen to be a writer doesn't mean I'm *your* photographer. You call me that, and you take your own pictures.'

'But you just walked *away*. You left me standing there looking like a complete idiot, with all those people waiting to have their picture taken.'

'As I said, you'll learn. There'll be another bus along filled with the same old blue-rinsed grannies out for a spot of fun. If you do it right next time, I'll take your happy snaps. Just remember, though, I'm *my* photographer.' Sean tensed his arm and pulled on the tail-gate. It swung down and closed with a harsh bang, causing Liz to flinch yet again.

'And what's the real story then,' she asked archly.

'Take a wander into that wee pub at the far end of the main street. The men in there aren't tourists. They've come here the way their fathers did, and maybe their grandfathers. They're all old and worn out and now they've got a bit of a croft and want a woman to share it with them. It's not like the old days. There aren't enough young women who want to go tramping over the bogs with a man twice their age, and these poor old souls don't need any of those giggling tourists who think this is *romantic*.'

He turned round to her and she caught that half-mocking, half-sad look on his face again. The expression was so mixed that her temper started to evaporate again. Not for the first time, the thought crossed her mind that there was more to McCullain than his surly distant manner suggested.

'I've taken some shots. Come on down and have a porter with them while you wait for the next bus. They don't mind talking,' he suggested, with a small, tight smile. 'You might get something for your story.'

He locked the car and strolled off. She stood and watched his back for a moment, slightly hunched, his hands stuck deep into the pockets of his faded green thornproof coat. He walked as if he was carrying a weight on his shoulders. After a few moments, she reluctantly followed him along the road.

It was when they crossed into County Sligo, on their way down south from Belfast, that Liz had caught the first glimpse of the *other* Sean McCullain. He had taken the wheel for a spell and unexpectedly hauled the car in a left turn onto a narrower country road. She asked him where he was going and he told her he was making a detour to something he'd always wanted to see.

The road twisted and coiled itself round low sloping hills for a few

14

miles until they came to a broad expanse of water. Sean drove along the road hugging the edge of the water until he came to a flat, open spot that gave a view of the placid loch.

'Where is this place?'

'It's Lough Gill.'

Liz stared across the calm surface towards the green islands far out. Around them the wind soughed through the last of the russet leaves, and small wavelets rippled onto the shingle shore. McCullain got out of the car and stood staring across the water. He was mumbling something.

'. . . I hear lake water lapping with low sounds by the shore; While I stand on the roadway or on the pavement's grey, I hear it in the deep heart's core.'

Something in the words tugged at Liz.

'What's that?'

Sean turned quickly, startled. 'Oh, nothing. I was just trying to remember the words of a poem.'

'Which one?'

'Yeats. "The Lake Isle of Innisfree". He wrote some wonderful words about this place. Water lapping on the shore. He could hear it in his mind, no matter where he went.' He nodded out across the water. 'That's it over there. The Lake Isle. I've always wanted to see it.'

'It's beautiful. But I wouldn't have taken you for a poetry buff,' Liz said. 'Did you learn it at school?'

'No. I learned it a year or so back, when I was trying to find out about this place.'

She pointed across the lake.

'The island?'

'No, Ireland.'

'What, searching for your roots?' she asked flippantly.

'No, just trying to find an answer to it all.'

'I don't understand,' Liz said.

Sean turned to look at her. The grey of the water matched perfectly his eyes, grey under black eyebrows. He stared for a moment and then sauntered back to the car. Once Liz had followed him inside, he started the engine and drove off along the side of Lough Gill. About a quarter of a mile further on, she asked what he had meant.

He kept driving, as if he hadn't heard, then, a few minutes later, after they'd passed a tractor loaded with a swaying tower of late hay, he abruptly started speaking.

'Do you know what I was doing in Belfast?'

'No. Covering a story, I imagine.'

'I wasn't covering a story. I was giving evidence at Crumlin Road Court. Witness Number Seventeen. They collect me at the airport. I've got a pass that gives me another name, and they drive me in a blue Ford Sierra at a hundred miles an hour into Belfast. Then I sit in a smelly old courtroom behind a rig-up of curtains where nobody can see me and tell them what happened.'

'What did happen?'

'I saw two men getting killed.'

'Why?'

'That's what I've been trying to find out ever since. I've listened to all the arguments and I'm no nearer an answer. I've seen men killed before, in other places, but not like this.'

'I didn't know,' Liz said quietly.

'And I *still* don't. Ireland. It should be a beautiful place. My ancestors came from here at some stage of the game, and yours too probably.'

'My grandmother,' Liz put in.

'But it's been ripped apart for hundreds of years, and for what? I've read the books and seen what's happened, and now, no matter what they say in the papers, I just don't know who's right in it all. It's a mess, and it's been a mess for centuries.'

'Does that mean you support the IRA?'

'No, of course it doesn't. What it means is that when you've got a country that's been pillaged and ripped off and plundered down through the years, you're going to have people killing folk. There's no way of stopping it, but there's no point in letting it go on. Ever since I saw those men getting beaten to death, I've tried to puzzle it out, but I can't. All I've done is try and find out how it started, and the more I've read, the more mixed up it becomes.'

He paused and looked out at the water passing them by on the left.

'I only know that this is where one of the great civilisations started. They had a culture here that was ahead of anywhere else in its time, and that's all gone. If they had left it alone, it would have been a wonderful place.'

When they had left the hotel in Belfast, he exchanged his hired car for a Volvo estate which gave him enough room for his gear, his portable process lab and his one rucksack, alng with Liz Cannon's suitcase.

He drove out of the city and onto the motorway that spans Ulster province. At Enniskillen, he stopped by the monument, recalling his

16

assignment there in the bleak aftermath of yet another incomprehensible tragedy. Liz had surprised him by asking his impressions of what had happened, rather than giving the usual loaded and ignorant slant about *Provo atrocity* and *barbarians*. She further surprised him by *not* asking for a picture beside the memorial stone.

West of Enniskillen there is a small border town where a bridge spans a narrow river that marks the great divide between Eire and Ulster. Liz was behind the wheel now, and had stopped on the bridge at the sign which orders drivers to wait for clearance. Through the window of the office near the centre of the bridge, on its downstream side, the customs officer was visible, but he hadn't registered their presence.

Liz reached a hand to put the car into gear. McCullain said: 'What are you doing?'

'If he's going to ignore us, he doesn't deserve our courtesy,' she said hotly.

'Things are a wee bit slower out here,' Sean told her in that calm way that infuriated her.

'Well, we can't wait here all day for them to condescend to even look at us.'

'Do you have your passport?'

'Of course.'

'Then let me have it,' Sean said. He held her gaze until she huffily rummaged in her bag, then handed the passport over.

Sean opened the passenger door and hauled himself out, slowly standing up and stretching his back. He leaned through the open door and said to Liz: 'Now I'd hang around if I was you.'

Liz simply glared at him, and when he'd turned towards the customs hut, she said out loud: 'Patronising *bastard*.' But it wasn't loud enough for him to hear.

Sean ambled towards the hut and went inside. The customs man was reading a book. Maybe he hadn't even noticed them arriving. He was a fat, bald-headed Irishman in a rumpled shirt.

'Can I help you now sir?' His broad west accent was softer than the east Ulster tongue.

'Sure. Two passports. One for me, and the other for the lady over there.'

The official didn't even bother to look. 'Are ye carrying any contraband or the likes?'

'Not today,' Sean said, with a grin. The officer returned it.

'Well, in that case, we'll not be needing to stamp your papers. So have yourself a nice day and a safe journey.'

17

'Do my best,' Sean told him.

Back at the car, Sean hauled himself inside. 'He'd never have noticed if I'd just driven on,' Liz said as she started the car.

'That could be true, but then again, *they* might have.' He jerked his thumb over his left shoulder. Liz screwed round in the seat to look. Behind them, in a small stand of trees, was a concrete enclosure topped with razor wire. She could just make out the camouflaged helmets of the two soldiers watching over the wall.

'It wouldn't be the first time they've made a mistake. I'd rather get the questions over with. That helps stop misunderstandings. Don't you remember what happened here about five years ago?'

Liz shook her head. She pulled the car away from the barrier and crossed to the other side.

'One of the soldiers made a mistake. Just nerves. But a boy the same age as him was walking on the bridge, and he died of it, shot in the back of his neck. Two lives ruined by an accident of place and time. Just because it's a border between the north and the south.'

Liz said nothing. At the far end of the bridge a sign told them in English and Gaelic that they were entering the Free Republic of Eire.

The good road that had continued from Belfast to the end of the bridge stopped abruptly and Liz found herself driving on a track that was pitted and pot-holed and flaking away at the edges. It was as if they had gone from one universe to another, rather than from one political administration to the next on the same small island.

But the difference was palpably evident everywhere. Across Ulster, there had been wide farms and rich fields. Despite the troubles, there were modern ranch-style houses in well-tended gardens, and good road metal going east and west. Then over the border, it was like stepping backwards in time by a hundred years.

Liz eased the car round the first bend, past a scraggly stand of willows that bordered a dark, rush-covered marshy field. Beyond that was a small pasture, headed at the far end by a sway-backed farmhouse and a small, even more dilapidated byre that fought a losing battle with the ropes of ivy strangling its crumbling walls. Through the hedgerow came a flash of white, and when they passed a gap in the hawthorn, Sean saw what it was.

'Stop the car a minute,' he said.

Without thinking, Liz stood on the brake and eased over to the side.

'Look at that,' he said, surprised. 'It's a dead cow.'

In the field, a lone cow was lying on its back, legs stiff and splayed, udders full and pointing to the sky like miniature anti-aircraft guns. Liz pulled a face and revved the engine.

'Hang on a moment. I want a picture of that.'

'You're not serious,' Liz said. 'It's disgusting. What do you want a picture for?'

'Because it's there, and it's dead, and I've never seen this before,' Sean said. He rummaged among his gear and clunked the car boot closed. She watched him in the mirror as he crossed the road and hoisted his leg over the rusted wire fence.

It was only a dead cow, lying forlorn and swollen with gases in a scraggy field. Sean himself didn't quite know why he wanted the picture. There was just something poignant and strange about it, sprawled stupidly in the damp grass. It seemed to show, more radically than the change in the wealth of the farms, the difference between north and south. Here there was independence and a sort of self-determination; and also marked poverty and one dead cow. Somehow, it seemed to fit. Sean took a couple of frames from different angles, filling his viewfinder with the ungainly black and white image against the grey-green of the boggy grass.

When he got back to the car, Liz was drumming her fingers on the wheel. 'Going for the Pulitzer then?' she asked sarcastically.

'What would you know?' Sean replied quietly, almost under his breath. Liz shot him another look and gunned the engine hard.

As they drove on through the poor countryside punctuated by more small, shabby farms, Sean's feelings sagged and flattened out. The depression worsened, although there was no explanation for it. The image of the dead cow in the marshy field came back to him. He tried to shake off the sensation of wrongness that had wormed through him since he crossed the border, but it lingered until he fell asleep, huddled inside his waterproof cotton jacket, and started on the strange journey into and through the dream.

3

The dream *changed* with that familiar, inexplicable lurch of certainty that the sleeper experiences in the halfway house between the conscious and those deeper levels of the mind. The semi-familiar territory of the dreamscape altered and slipped and slid out of true and started going in the wrong direction. If the sleeper had been awake, he would have heard a ringing in his ears of mental alarm bells. If he'd been wired up to electrodes, they would have picked up the change in his breathing and his heart rates as they jumped out of idle and into gear.

Maybe it was the movement of the car, rocking on its springs as it trundled round the narrow bends and over the pot-holes on the road that had narrowed down from a sleek highway to a back route after crossing the bridge. Maybe it was just that the dreams had developed a habit of changing and going in the wrong direction now as a matter of course.

In his dream he had been somewhere else, doing something different, and then it *jumped* as if the camera of his mind had been jostled and suddenly he was back *there* again.

There was a high-pitched singing note oscillating at the back of his head. Around him was noise, a wave of harsh sound. Everything happened very quickly, yet with that underwater torpid slowness that stretched moments out and out and filled them with minute detail. The funeral march had been plodding its way from the church. Two flag-draped coffins were on the shoulders of hard-faced, sombre men, just like that other time. He had been there and now he was here again, *again*, watching the faces, noting the eyes on him, the outsider.

Then the car had come roaring in from nowhere. A rough voice close to his ear said: 'Oh no, not again.' He had swivelled, startled by the tortured screech of brakes, and then it had started. *Oh, it had started all right*.

The dream flipped and flopped from one unreality, a *normal* unreality, into this *real past*.

There was a flash. He knew it was from his camera; the big Nikon zoomed out to eighty-five. Thumb and forefinger powered the focus, and the two faces shadowed behind the windscreen were momentarily caught, surprised expressions fixed. In that instant they were just two men in a car who had taken the wrong turning and found themselves in a one-way street, with the traffic coming against them.

The camera flashed again, twice, this time catching the backs of the heads as the driver and passenger screwed round, reversing fast. Rubber screeched again, hard. The car stopped, blocked by the crowd behind. Then *bedlam*. Shouting of hard voices: '*Who the fu* —' . . . '*Get the ba* —' . . . '*Jesus Chri* —'

He was thumped hard on the arm, the camera jostled aside. He whirled, got his balance, and then swept on with the press of bodies. The car door opened. A man stepped out, something in his hand. A gun? *A gun?*

From the other side came the clattering squeal of a door almost wrenched off its hinges. The camera caught a face upon which flickered surprise, annoyance, maybe a touch of alarm. Then the face disappeared into the swarm. The camera was on reflex. Flash. Click. Whirr. A face, contorted with fear and anger. A hand, fingers hooked, reaching, grasping a lapel. The sounds dopplered down, deepening out. There were words, but they were down on the low register, like tapes slowed beyond comprehension; alien, *eerie*. The scene became a series of frozen images that slammed into the eyes with every click of the shutter.

The starter handle – or was it a wheelbrace? – swung up like an iron shillelagh. There was barely a pause and it came down, fast and vicious. A low crunch. It was only feet away from him now. There was a grunt, and a drop of blood splashed on his left hand. He felt the recoil of revulsion like a fist clenched inside and, distantly, the awareness of extreme danger. But at the top, everything was on automatic. The hand focused on the ring, the finger pushed the button, the flash went off, catching everything.

The metal club went up again and down again, crunching savagely. More blood sprayed. There was a cry of pain. Beside him somebody snarled like an animal and the smell of hot blood was everywhere.

Far off, sirens wailed. Overhead, a helicopter hammered at the air while down on the ground two men were being battered to death. The camera captured all of it: the faces, the blood, the wide, frightened eyes.

A big man reached out a slow hand to grab the camera, face contorted, teeth yellowed behind snarling lips. He pulled back from him. The man was blocked by another, who lunged into the heaving mass of bodies. The crowd parted a fraction, showing him the pulped face of the man who had only moments ago looked surprised and slightly annoyed. There was a crater the size and colour of a rotten-ripe

21

apple on the side of his head. One eye was rolled so far back into the socket that only white showed. The other was blue and gleamed with life. The camera flashed, getting it all in close-up, that living eye in the face of the dying. It stared straight into the lens, and in that tiny moment it looked as if it knew *everything*. Then the face was gone, dragged back into the crowd. Somebody grabbed him by the arm, and the field of vision spun around. He fell and a women fell on top of him and the crowd milled past. He crawled to his knees and got to his feet, helping the woman up. She looked at him with wide panicked eyes and backed away. He turned back to the crowd and saw another hand go up and crash back down. A red piece of flesh spun off. A deep bellow of terrible pain rose over the ringing at the back of his head and the cloying smell of blood came thick again on the air . . .

And then the dream *changed* again.

The singing in his ears soared higher and higher as the scene unexpectedly and inexplicably flipped, for the first time *ever*, and he was out of *that* nightmare. He was somewhere else.

There is blood on the air; familiar blood. There is the roar of the crowd, but this time it is different. He sees an arm raised, this time not with a wheelbrace. The hand clenches an axe with a shining black head. It catches the light flashing up from the water and comes down in a swift arc.

There is no fear, only the high singing sound that is like *power* in his mind. He moves easily, casually, twisting his body away from the strike, turning on one foot and pivoting with his own weapon that whoops in a broad sweep and strikes like a scythe. A grunt of surprise is followed by a splash as the big, wooden-hafted axe tumbles into the shallow water. The man before him falls backwards, arms wide, belly a wet red mess, and crashes against the shingle bank, doomed before he even hits the stones.

There is a roar of approval from behind, a more muted one from ahead. He stands, knee-deep, at the ford, with both his arms raised to the sun. Words, familiar yet incomprehensible, come from his mouth, taunting, challenging. He can feel himself tall and strong and raging with life, his leggings wet and his shoulder hot from the effort. He has a shield of leather on his left arm and a cape of fur around his neck.

He walks forward a few steps, smelling the hot, wild blood, hearing the *song* of his own, and raises the challenge again. The crowds are silent, shifting and ashamed.

Then, out of the lifting mist on the other side comes a big, fair-haired man in a long fur cloak. He wears a leather helmet which bears two

22

rams' horns that curl around the side of his face. His shoulders are wide and in his hand there is a great dark sword.

Now the *sensation* of the dream alters. He can feel it, again on some level aware that he is dreaming, but this is so *real* he can smell the air and hear the soughing of the wind through the reeds on the bank, the far-off cawing of a crow.

There is a feeling of recognition. He *knows* this fair-haired warrior, and he feels a desolate sadness at the certainty that he must fight him. The man lifts his sword in salute and challenge. He responds, but, strangely, they first wade towards each other and embrace. He can feel the muscles ripple under the fur cloak, smell the sour sweat of a man prepared for battle. They back off, and then, without hesitation, they fight.

From the first clatter as the huge swords meet, there is nothing but movement and intense, wild joy as they spin and dance and lunge. He feels strength singing in his blood, powering his arm, and he goes with it, taking the fight forward, beating the big man back to the shingle.

And then, when he has almost forced his opponent onto the bank, something comes at him from the water; something black and swift. It coils around his legs, tripping him backwards, a long, sinewy eel that is more like a snake than a fish. It loops around his calves, spilling his balance, and he crashes into the shallows. His opponent seizes the moment and leaps, sword high, for the kill.

But the singing in the blood alters its note. The eel writhes, looping out of the water, and he sees its red, glaring eye, and knows what it is, what *she* is. That knowledge brings the anger and the anger brings the *change*. The terrible fury comes upon him in an instant, and he can feel his body contort and swell. His blood *sizzles* and his limbs seem to warp out of shape. His hair rises like a hackled mane as he hauls himself from the water. The other warrior moves forward and slices with his broad blade, catching him on his thigh, yet there is no pain. The blade slides off as if it has struck *stone*.

Then it is all over. His arm moves in a blur, faster than the eye can truly follow. He hacks once, driving the metal through fur and skin and bone. Again, a low arc, and the blade bites into a hip. The warrior falls back, and a third blow takes him on the side of the face, crashing through the horn and into the jaw. His opponent, mortally wounded, topples with a heavy thud onto the shingle on his own side of the ford, blood steaming from gaping wounds, the light already fading in his eyes.

It is then that the battle frenzy dissipates, draining away like the flow of the stream, taking with it the heat and the hate. His muscles uncoil

23

and his vision clears. He looks down to the dying man who is also his true-friend, and feels a desolation sweep over him and a burning fury at the eel-shaped monster who has brought on that warped frenzy.

He kneels down at the edge of the water, reaching for the twitching hand of his foe-friend. He raises his eyes to the sun and calls out for his father . . .

4

Tom and Nancy Ducain arrived at their cottage in Kilgallan in the last days of September, a full five days before Sean McCullain turned up with a very reluctant Liz Cannon. This was the final leg of their six-week honeymoon. So far they had enjoyed every day of it, even in rainy London, from where they'd taken the flight to Shannon airport before motoring north in the rented Granada.

It had been Nancy's idea to come to Ireland on the last two weeks of their holiday and Tom had readily agreed, despite the fact that he hadn't been exactly sure whereabouts on the map of the world Ireland actually sat. Six weeks before they'd flown out from Vermont, she had been Nancy Keenan, fourth-generation American but Irish back before that. County Mayo had a romantic ring to it, much more so than the country they found themselves driving through, on the wrong side of the road over the moors north of Connemara. By the time they reached the Mayo boundary, Tom had just about mastered the stick-shift gears, but there was no way he would even try to wrestle with the place names, which were exclusively in Gaelic on every road sign.

Nancy had chattered delightedly every mile of the way ever since they left Shannon, enthusing about everything from the colour of the fields – they were indeed truly *green* – to the quaint little croft homesteads at the side of the roads. To Tom, they looked poor and primitive, and he hadn't seen one sprig of shamrock in more than a hundred miles; but what the hell, Nancy was happy, and if she was happy, he was too.

Tom was two years short of thirty, and as one of three partners in a dental practice in Vermont he had crowned more film-stars' teeth than he cared to count. The money kept rolling in, and the extra two weeks' holiday was just part of his wedding present from his two partners. Nancy was five years younger and she was, in his view, a knockout. If someone ever had to describe an all-American cheerleader, they could have pointed to Nancy Keenan and said: '*That's* what I mean.' She had a mass of fair hair that spilled down over her shoulders, and a wonderful set of naturally white teeth that any star would have killed for, and she was brimming with undiluted enthusiasm about absolutely *everything*.

When she had told him she'd just *love* to spend her honeymoon in a real Irish cottage, Tom had contacted the agent to alter the arrangements. Originally he'd booked a suite in the Tara Hotel in Galway, which would have suited him right down to the ground, but it was difficult not to give Nancy what she wanted, especially when she said it was such a romantic idea. He'd told her that because this was self-catering, it was the first big test of their marriage. He'd find out if she could actually cook.

It was getting after two in the afternoon under a clear blue sky that stretched right across the Atlantic to home territory when they arrived in Kilgallan. Nancy had the road map and the tourist brochure open on her slim knees and was pointing out places of interest on the way west along the south shore of Clew Bay. They passed Croagh Patrick rearing up from the flat shore land, and Nancy read from the booklet.

'It says here that Saint Patrick climbed to the top of the hill and beat his drum and all the snakes came out and threw themselves into the sea.'

'Just like lemmings,' Tom said. 'Except in the Walt Disney film they were pushed.' He jerked his hand on the gear-stick on an approaching bend and the car jolted as the clutch slammed in.

'Yeah, and ever since then, there hasn't been a single snake in all of Ireland. That's amazing, isn't it?'

'Absolutely. Wish they would do the same back home. It would make camping a hell of a lot safer.'

Ten miles on, they came to the fork in the road and Nancy directed Tom to take a right, her navigation spot-on yet again.

The car trundled onto the hump-backed bridge over the Roonah Water and they rolled into town.

'Doesn't look like much of a place,' Tom ventured. 'You think it's maybe out to lunch?'

'Or fallen asleep,' Nancy said. She looked around when he stopped the car past the crossroads, next door to McGavigan's green door. The street was empty. The old stone houses crowded against each other and onto the road. A small dog trotted across the street further ahead, sniffed at a fence post, and disappeared behind a wall.

'It's just like some sleepy hollow,' Nancy observed. 'You could imagine leprechauns living in these little houses.'

'Well, I hope these aren't the cottages we're supposed to stay in. If they are, I'm heading back to Galway.'

Just then, the green door swung open and a tall, gnarled man in a dark suit came out onto the pavement, blinking behind thick-lensed glasses. He noticed the car and gave an Irish kind of little wave, almost knuckling his forehead.

'Good afternoon to you,' he said in a wheezy voice laden with west-coast accent.

'Hello,' Nancy said. 'Could you help us, please? We need some directions.'

'And where is it you're heading after, young lady?' Patsy McGavigan asked back. 'O'Hara's hotel is just down the road a bit further on, if it's a place to stay you're looking for.'

'Well, we have a place to stay, but we don't know exactly where it is,' Tom said, leaning over to talk through the passenger window.

'And where would that be now?'

'Kilgallan Cottages,' Tom said hopefully.

'Well now, you've found the right place all right, and you're not a kick in the shirt tail away from where you'll be staying,' McGavigan told him, and Nancy tried to suppress a smile.

The tall angular undertaker turned round and peered myopically further along the road. He raised a hand and pointed a long, nicotine-stained finger.

'Take yourselves just further along a bit now, and when you get to Donovan's bar on the left, you go right. Now there you'll find the road that takes you right round and you'll find Mrs Gilly, who looks after the places. Just peep your horn outside her gate and she'll come and look after you. Oh, and mind the dogs. She's got two wee terriers that would have the leg off you if they don't know who you are.'

Tom thanked him and Nancy flashed a glimpse of her spectacular teeth. They drove twenty yards at the most and found the lane. Tom nosed the car down between the lime trees and found the place without difficulty. McGavigan had been right. As soon as the horn sounded, two fierce little Scotch terriers came racing out and scrambled up onto the low dry-stone wall, where they barked shrilly at the car until a woman came out to the gate and hushed them up.

'You'll be Mr and Mrs Ducain?'

'That's us, ma'am,' Tom said, still proud of the fact that he had a new wife who had *his* name.

'Well, welcome to you, and we hope you'll be enjoying yourself here,' the small woman in the brightly coloured headscarf said cheerily. 'If you care to follow me, I'll show you where you're staying.' With that, she turned and walked further down the path and round a corner past a privet hedge that obscured the way ahead. Tom looked at Nancy, shrugged, and crunched the car into first gear. As they pulled away, the two little dogs started up their belligerent barking.

The car rounded the corner and the cottages came into view. There

27

were seven of them, scattered about an uneven field, each in its own little patch of ground, whitewashed and thatched.

'Oh, they're lovely,' Nancy said as soon as she saw them. 'They're just like something out of a book.'

'I just hope they have running water,' Tom said with a grin. He put on a thick Irish accent. 'Otherwise you'll be up at the crack of dawn to draw the water for me tea, begorrah.'

'Of course they've got running water. The brochure says they've got everything.'

They followed Mrs Gilly, who was walking at a brisk pace towards the third cottage on the right. It stood on a slight slope that raised it higher than the other six. Tom pulled the car to a stop and they both clambered out to follow her inside.

'*Wow*,' was Nancy's reaction when she looked around. Everything was just *perfect*, the way she'd always imagined it would be. A vast pine farmhouse table, pattered with knots and whorls, stood four-square in the middle of the room. But the dominant feature was the gaping slate fireplace from which a peat fire threw out a ruddy warm blast. On either side were old-fashioned irons, one of which, Mrs Gilly said, was a toasting fork.

'You've never had toast as tasty as when it's done in the peat-reek,' she promised.

Tom whispered to Nancy that he'd only had toast out of a toaster, and the old woman turned immediately and told him that of course there was a toaster, *one of the pop-out kind as well*, in the kitchen. Tom's face went red, and Nancy again had to stifle a giggle.

As soon as Mrs Gilly had shown them all round the place, she left, and when the door closed behind her, both of them burst into laughter.

'One of the pop-out kind as well,' Tom imitated. 'I didn't think she'd heard me.'

'Well, she did,' Nancy said, still choking with laughter. She reached towards the fire and pulled out the long three-tined fork, holding it up to Tom's nose.

'I thought she was going to give you some of this,' she said, waggling the prongs in front of his face. 'That would sure have made you pop out.'

5

'Look . . . *Look*!'

The sudden shout in the quiet car startled Liz Cannon so badly that her hands jerked on the wheel just as she was taking a tight bend. The car veered out from the verge towards the cattle truck taking up most of the road as it rattled towards them like a dirty green monster. A horn bawled a raucous warning as the car skittered past, missing by fractions the high bars jutting from the front of the cab.

'Bloody hell, McCullain! You nearly gave me a heart attack,' Liz shouted, stamping down on the brake pedal and hauling the car off the road onto a grassy verge. Her hands gripped the wheel fiercely, showing white knuckles, and her voice shook in the aftermath of sudden alarm.

McCullain was looking around as if he didn't know where he was or what month of the year he was in. He had woken to the blare of the truck's horn and had seen the flash of green as it scraped past while he was caught between the dream and the present. He still looked blank and bewildered, his face ashen, his eyes wide and bemused.

'What's happening?' His voice was almost as shaky as hers, but still sleep-doped.

'You just about killed us, that's what. Shouting in my ear like that.' Liz Cannon braced her elbows on the wheel and laid her head on her forearms, spilling her thick blonde waves forward so that they hid her face. She let out a long, trembling breath.

Sean McCullain shifted position in the passenger seat to look at her. His expression said he didn't know what she was talking about and cared not a fraction more. He noticed the tremor in her hands, dangling over the curve of the steering wheel. His own were steady, but his whole body felt as if it had been wrung out. The dream had been *vivid*. The memory of it was still up at the front of his mind, though receding at speed into the past the way dreams always do, but the *feeling* was there in his body.

Sean McCullain knew he'd had that recurring dream, the nightmare of Belfast he relived in his sleep again and again – and then relived while awake every time he was hauled back to court to tell the black-gowned old men the same old story. But this time it had *changed*, and that had

29

not happened before. Oh, the second half had been every bit as bloody and brutal as his unfailing memory pictured the first scenes, but it was a *righteous* brutality. That feeling stayed with him as the visual memory of the dream faded under the onslaught of reality.

'I only saw a truck,' he finally said.

'You nearly had that truck down your throat.' Liz raised her head from her arms and turned towards him. 'Just what the hell did you think you were doing?'

'Just what the hell are you talking about?' McCullain whipped back, although his tone was more dry than angry.

'It's bad enough driving on these godforsaken backroads in this damned backwoods of a country with every sign at every crossroads in a foreign language . . .'

'That's Gaelic,' McCullain said matter-of-factly, stretching his arms up behind him and putting his palms against the roof to force sleep further away.

'I know it's Gaelic. What do you take me for?'

McCullain just glanced at her with that annoying black look, everything in it designed to get on her nerves.

'So what were you shouting about?'

'Shouting? I don't remember that.'

'Yes you did. At the top of your voice, just when I was going round the bend. You roared at me to look. Or look out. I don't need you to tell me how to drive.'

'I must have been sleeping,' he said lamely.

'You must be out of your mind. But when I'm driving on these farm tracks in this bloody Third World country, just let me do it, okay?'

'It's your choice to be here, not mine. I'd sooner be back home, that's for sure. So if you want to fix up a few old-hat features that have been done to death a million times, don't complain to me.'

'And don't you tell me how to do my job either, McCullain.'

'Wouldn't dream of it,' he said, looking out of the passenger window. 'Even if I knew what it was,' he muttered under his breath, but not enough to prevent her hearing it.

'What's that supposed to mean?' Liz swivelled round in her seat to glare at him, infuriated by his attitude. Even his posture seemed calculated to be offensive.

'What it means is that if you're going to wangle a couple of weeks in old Ireland doing a few pieces on old stories, then it's your choice. If you don't like the backwoods, why did you bother getting them to send you in the first place?'

'That's got nothing to do with you, McCullain. Just remember, I *did* get the go-ahead. And you're the photographer – what I say goes.'

McCullain looked her straight in the eye, expressionless for a moment. Then he laughed lightly. That infuriated Liz even more. She started up the engine again and prepared to pull out, feeling hot and angry and a little foolish.

'Now, do you want me to drive?' he asked.

'No, I can handle it,' she said moodily. Under her breath she was muttering that McCullain was a hard-arsed chauvinist button-pusher. He heard it and muttered back in the same tone, deliberately mischievous, about her being a tight-arse know-it-all bimbette.

She gritted her teeth angrily and slammed the rented car round the first bend. Beside her, McCullain glanced out of the window at the passing hedgerows. He'd been sleeping for the past hour after crossing the border at Belcoo, and now they were on the side road that would pass by Lough Gill on the way to Sligo, heading westwards and south all the time.

Now he was awake and trying to hold onto the fading details of the strange dream, and wondering why the recurrent nightmare had changed. The scene at the ford had been so familiar it felt as if he'd been there before, a long time ago. The feeling hung about him like a sense of *déja-vu*, before it started to drift away like a mist under the light of the sun. McCullain shook his head and looked out at the scenery again. Trees on a nearby hill were russeting down from dark green. Somewhere in the distance a lapwing mewed.

Liz stared straight ahead, hands still tight on the wheel as the miles rolled by.

And Sean McCullain pondered the fact that for the first time his recurrent nightmare had changed.

6

Dr James Connarty was holding court as he normally did on a Friday night, especially after a good week's work, and this particular week had been exceptional. He leaned against the mantelpiece beside the glowing fire, savouring the heavy smell of peat smoke that wafted from the fireplace and the aftertaste of his last swallow of dark red port.

'Now we've established that it's certainly a passage tomb and *almost* certainly from before three thousand BC,' he said. Around him there were a few nods as he revealed the already known.

'But I've a feeling that it's a good bit older than that, maybe a thousand years further down the line, which would certainly make it one of the oldest in this part of the country, maybe in the whole of Ireland itself.'

He paused to have another sip of his port. Siobhan Kane looked up from the notes she was writing in the log and nodded to him. 'If it's that old, then it's a very special grave. It's bigger than anything of comparable antiquity, and the style is different in several ways.'

Siobhan fanned out a few black-and-white photographs on the table and put on a pair of wide-framed glasses to study them. She looked almost stocky under the bulky Aran-knit sweater that was several sizes too large. Her hair was the thick chestnut colour that is more common in the south than the far west of Ireland. She had it rolled up in neat pleats, and this, together with the reading glasses, gave her the look of a spinster librarian. Behind the lenses, her eyes sparkled intelligence in the rosy glow of the peat fire.

'We haven't reached the burial chamber yet, but the passage is unusual. As you all know, they are normally flagged corridors that slope gradually down to the centre. This is the first I've seen with steps cut into the stones.'

'Yes, it is unusual, although there's something similar at the megalith in Cleggan. But the workmanship here is of a standard you wouldn't expect, considering the tools they had to work with. That's what's got me a wee bit excited, you know. We're only a few yards into the barrow and already we have interlocking kerbstones and a series of steps. They built this one to last, I'm thinking, and they built it for someone with some considerable status.'

'So who do you think it was for?' asked Terry Munster, sprawled on an armchair in front of the cottage fire and nursing his customary can of Guinness.

'Ah, well now, Terence,' Connarty said with the mischievous reproof that all the students and graduates had learned to expect. 'I'm never finished explaining to you that archaeology is all about painstaking research and meticulous attention to detail. We all work in a truly dedicated fashion without allowing ourselves those flights of fancy the film-makers imagine us to have. No, we're not the Indiana Joneses of Ireland. We just take what we find and piece it together.'

Dr Connarty was winding himself up and they all knew it. Terry sat back, waiting for the punchline that was certain to come. He looked the archetypal young Irishman, broad and muscular and with a shock of jet-black hair that fell over his eyes in tight curls, and he had a gentle southern brogue with a nature to match. This was his doctorate year, and he couldn't have enjoyed himself more than working with Connarty.

The older man took another sip and then beamed round at them.

'On the other hand, I'd be a rotten liar if I told you I never stayed awake thinking about finding a huge mound of gold and jewels and discovering it was the treasure King Ailel had packed as his going-away present. And when I find that, then it's goodbye to all this digging up old graves in windblown hillsides and off to study something more suited to a man of my tastes and talents.'

'And what would that be now?'

'Epidermal photochromatology in antipodean female anthropoids, of course.'

'What in the devil's name is that now, Dr Jim?' Terry knew he was setting himself up as the straight man.

Connarty's eyes twinkled in anticipation, but before he could reply, Siobhan spoke up: 'He wants to go and study women getting a suntan on a South Sea island, the old bugger.'

From the corner of the long pine table Agnes Finnegan and Theresa Laughlin, both first-year undergraduates, giggled in unison. They wouldn't have dreamed of speaking to the professor in such familiar terms.

'Don't we all,' Terry said, 'though I can't tell you the women around here are so bad, except there's maybe just not enough of them for a well-educated fellow like myself.'

'And maybe they'll be building monuments to your exploits, Terence,' Connarty said with a chuckle. 'Or on the other hand, their fathers might just leave you swinging from a tree.'

Everybody laughed at that one, and Connarty took the moment to light his pipe. He sucked in like a faulty engine and billowed blue smoke.

'But that's all in the future. Let's go back to the past. We can be sure that the tomb was built for a powerful leader.'

'So who would be the contender?'

'That's the big question. When we find the outer ring, it should give us a fair idea of the importance of the dear departed.'

'You mean we'll find out what a dirty old despot he was,' Siobhan put in dryly.

Agnes Finnegan, small and dark and the butt of Terry's gentle jokes on account of her disabling shyness, asked the obvious question.

'That's where, if things *do* follow the expected pattern, we'll find the remains of his young companions,' Connarty said. 'His, ah . . . fellow travellers, so to speak.'

Siobhan translated the professor's hyperbole. 'What he means is the four-and-twenty virgins he took with him for the ride.'

Agnes got the message and blushed mightily. Terry chuckled quietly into his Guinness.

'Yes,' the professor continued. 'It was a tradition, you know. Normally it was twenty-one for the high kings and princes, which they thought was enough to keep them amused on the way to the Lands of the Dead and after they got there as well. Apparently it was a great honour to be selected. The girls seemed to go willingly, maybe even competed for the chance. When we reach the main chamber, we should find the cremated remains of the young ladies, poor souls.'

'And do you think there's a chance that this could be the grave of one of the Connacht princes?' Siobhan asked.

The professor thought for a while before replying. When he did, it was with the conspiratorial air of someone who was taking them all into his confidence.

'I'm hoping for more than that. When I mentioned the treasure of King Ailel, I wasn't kidding, not entirely. No. It's been an ambition of mine ever since I was bitten by the history bug when I was just a slim wee fellow about the same age as Agnes here.'

'But Ailel didn't necessarily exist,' Terry interjected. 'He was pure myth, surely.'

'Well, he was a mythical figure, and part of the great mythological tradition of Ireland. But if any of you have ever listened to a word I've said over the years, especially you and Siobhan, you should know that you cannot discount myths when you think of history. On the contrary,

34

you look to the myths for clues, and we've all done that. Strip away a legend and the bare bones like as not tell you a truth. Now if I find Ailel's grave, then I think I'll find something more important than that.'

'What's that, Dr Connarty?' Agnes asked, her light accent speaking straight out of Cork.

'Well, my thinking is that the King of Connacht was outlived by his dear wife by forty years or more. The good Queen Maeve was a tough old scoundrel, but some of the old western legends say that she was buried beside her husband when it came to the last, so she could join him in Tir na n'Og. I think he went first to get away from her, but we've had precedents where widows unlocked their husbands' tombs and were laid beside them.'

'I see a flaw there,' Terry said. Theresa looked at him as if he'd spoken heresy. 'What about Queen Maeve's tomb at Knocknarea – isn't there a legend about that?'

'Well spotted, Terence. Top of the class,' said the older man. 'Sure there's a legend about Misgaun Maeve. There's a thousand of them. There's also a legend that tells you she was alive at the time of Christ, and that's patently untrue. No, I think that site's a wonderful way of bringing in the tourists, but it's only a cairn on top of the highest hill west of Sligo, and nowhere near as well built as others all over the west. If you think that the Queen of Connacht was the most powerful woman in all of Ireland, descended, so they say, from the Fir-bolgs, then they wouldn't just have tumbled a pile of boulders on her.'

The professor warmed to his theme. 'The terrifically handy thing about this part of the world is that it has stayed pure, and will probably remain so, despite the depredations of young Terry there. In the oldest legend, they drove the Fomorians off the mainland and into the sea, and the Fir-bolgs held off all comers until they bred with the Danaans. After that, they were never invaded by the Nordics, who took everywhere else and changed the names. So here, the legends have remained constant and strong. One I picked up a long time ago down at Killary harbour was about the tomb of the Faerie Queen, and it's stuck to me since then, going on thirty years now. The old women down there collect the old stories like we collect photographs, and an ancient lady told me about the grave that was built for a king and used for a black queen.

'Now here's the interesting part. She said it was raised at the end of the never-ending sands on a point of rock that faced the *cuirt-slugan*, which is a whirlpool, to the west of the Hill of Serpents.'

Siobhan had heard the story before, but Terry drawled: 'Now with clues like that, how come you've spent all these years looking for it?'

Again Theresa looked shocked at his nerve.

'Well, I have and I haven't. There's been a hundred and one things to do, including teaching you archaeology and trying to give you manners as well. If there was ever a spot that fitted the bill, here it is. We're on a point of rock at the north of Tallabaun Strand, which, if you don't know, is the longest beach in Europe, and if you don't believe me, go for a walk down it some day. Kilgallan is almost south of Clare Island, and what do we have at the turn of the tide between there and here?' He looked around like a schoolmaster surveying his class.

'A whirlpool?' ventured Agnes.

'Indeed we do. The Coortslugan, twice a day, every day of the year. The longliners avoid it because the currents are fierce. And then, to the west of us, what do you see?'

'Croagh Patrick,' Theresa said quickly.

'Exactly. And that's the hill from which the good saint is supposed to have banished all the snakes in Ireland, though how he did it four thousand years before his God was born, we'll never know. So maybe I'm wrong, and probably am, but if anything fits the legend, this place does, and as you'll know, Maeve wasn't just a queen. They say she was of the two worlds, and ruled over the faeries as well.

'If I'm wrong, then I'm wrong. And if I am, and she's not buried here, then there's still a chance of finding good old Ailel, who, they say, was buried in his war chariot, along with all the treasure he amassed in battle. If that's the case, then it's goodbye rainy old Ireland, and hello Bali.'

Siobhan chuckled. 'You talk a good story when you've had a port or two. But you'll be digging away in old Ireland until they put up a mound for you.'

'Oh, heaven forbid that should happen, woman,' the professor countered quickly. 'I don't mind poking about in old graves, but you'll never put me in one of them. Sure I've a terrible fear of being buried and then dug up by the likes of me in a thousand years' time. No. I'm going for the gas jets, my dear. Simple and quick, and I won't lie under rocks for ever.'

At the west edge of Kilgallan, a few hundred yards past the crossroads on the Westport Road, the row of houses begins to peter out. The arms of the cross on the road will take you north to the bay or south to the cluster of small farms as far as Kinnaleen. Westwards the main road goes to the vast sandy emptiness of Tallabaun Strand and demotes itself to a rough track winding itself around even smaller hamlets that have been deserted since the black days of the famine. On the east end of town, the road that comes from Westport splits just before it crosses the old two-span bridge over Roonah Water. One side of the split takes travellers over the dismal moor to the Mulweelrea Mountains and, further on, down to Galway. On the west edge, heading out towards the Point and before the lane that takes you down to the cottages, there is a small, whitewashed house with a good slate roof and shutters on the outside of the windows that give it a surprisingly Continental appearance.

The crying of the baby woke Maura Quinn from a light sleep. She had dozed off without meaning to, or even realising that it was happening, as she was knitting a pair of yellow bootees for little Jacky, sound asleep in his Moses basket.

Maura dreamily shook herself awake and eased herself to her feet, feeling the twinge on the tender spot where they had taken out the stitches only two weeks before. Once again, she felt grateful for the inflated ring that Jack had bought her at the tourist shop in Westport. It may have looked silly, but it was surely a blessed comfort.

Maura was twenty-two years old and had a pretty, round, freckled face that was quick to smile. Jack had a good job at the market in Westport ten miles away. He'd the gift of the gab, she always said, and he agreed with that. There was every chance that the gift would let him take over as auctioneer when old Paddy Mulherron gave it up in a few years' time, and then, naturally, things would be different.

Little Jacky, whose hedgehog thatch of black hair told Jack he'd never have to worry who was the father of his son, had that same clean, tanned complexion that Maura found so irresistible in her husband of ten months. She crossed to the crib, pausing only briefly to look out at the gathering clouds that hung, threatening rain, over the moorland.

Jacky was mewling in that shivery way that the newborn do, toothless mouth agape and face reddening to purple. His tiny hands had slipped from the tight wrap of the shawl and were shaking with the force of his cry.

'What's the matter, darling boy?' she crooned. 'It's that you're hungry again, is it?' She bent over the crib, smiling down at her baby, delighting in his cries that had gone from kittenish mewling to a lusty, demanding bawl.

'And you just filled to bursting at lunch-time,' she said proudly, reaching to hoist him from the tiny basket. Jacky was unaware of the attention until her hand slipped under the back of his head, and with the instinctive realisation of his mother's presence, he redoubled his efforts, screwing his eyes so tightly his black eyebrows knitted together like commas in the middle, making sure there was no denying his insistence.

Hugging his warm squirmings against herself, Maura carried her baby to the rocking chair where she'd fallen asleep, and eased herself back down onto the ring. Jacky was fighting and wriggling in his determination to be fed. She held him firmly in the crook of her arm while she unbuttoned the loose cardigan of Jack's that she wore when it got cold in the little house. There was a small damp patch on her blouse, evidence that the demands of the baby were reflected in her own body. She peeled back the light cotton and her soft breast ballooned out. Her swollen nipple, until only a few weeks ago a rosy button, was now, to her, a huge brown udder. Behind it she could feel the soft pressure like a vague pleasurable ache.

'Come on then, you little starveling,' she whispered, shifting her baby round from her hip and cradling his tiny furry head in her hand. She eased his face towards the nipple and watched with unalloyed delight as his mouth sought urgently for purchase. She let him find it himself, enjoying his panicked mouthings until his lips caught the bud and clamped themselves onto her. Maura still hadn't got used to the wonderful feeling of bonding between her baby and herself when he started to feed. It was as if she and little Jacky had become *fused* into one person, one creature. She felt the suction of his hot little mouth and the hard and furious tug against her nipple.

She sat back against the cushions of the overstuffed rocker, swathed in the *oneness* of feeding her infant. Maybe the stitches did itch and nip at the tenderness underneath, and perhaps the final contractions of labour had been rolling waves of intense pain, but this, this *singularity*, made it worth any anguish. She gave herself up to the sensations inspired by Jacky's rhythmic suckling and her mind drifted onwards. She saw her baby in a year's time, when he would be crawling about on the carpet in front of the fire, playing with the family of woolly soft animals that they'd started collecting only two months after the honeymoon down in Cork. Drifting on, she saw him, dark-eyed and handsome in his uniform, on his first day at school. She could envisage him sitting in the prow of Jack's curragh, fishing with his father across the bay at Achill, proudly watching his old man rowing against the wind. Further along the road, she knew she'd see him, tall and broad and beaming down at her as he graduated in his black gown from Dublin. A doctor? A lawyer? That's what Jack would want for him, the grandson of a land-poor mackerel fisherman.

And all that from this little scrap who pressed his tiny face against her breast, eyes screwed up with the concentrated effort of sucking her milk. Maura sighed pleasurably, replete with the mother-love that had started to grow in her from the day she felt his first tickling stirrings deep in her belly. Jacky sucked on.

The room darkened swiftly.

It was as if heavier, blacker clouds had rolled in to smother the pearl-grey overcast that had blanketed Kilgallan since the morning. The little shuttered window in the living room let in enough light for comfort, even on cloudy days, but the abrupt change sent shadows spreading from the corners.

Despite her warmth, Maura shivered in the sudden eddy of cold air. She pulled the heavy-knit cardigan round her, spreading it to cover the baby spreadeagled on her belly. Maura's thoughts were still far off. She didn't even notice the swift darkening. The peat fire snuffled in the grate, its rosy glow diminished as the shadows grew longer, swelling out and up the walls.

Maura closed her eyes and her thoughts sleepily trundled on. Her breathing evened out as sleep raced to overtake her as quickly as the shadows that were enveloping the room.

Inside the room, the air coalesced, became thicker. The peat fire's glow faded as if seen through darkened glass. The spreading darkness flowed faster until Maura was sitting in a room of deep shade. The only sounds were the snuffling of the tiny baby at her breast, and the soft, heavy breathing of the woman asleep.

Then her eyes opened.

There was a tingling between her ears, a buzzing, far-off sound, like whispers in a long corridor. The darkness and cold crowded in and the air crackled with tension. Maura looked around in the dark, unafraid, unaware that something had *changed*. Inside her head came insistent whispers that tugged at her. She closed her eyes trying to make out what they were saying, and the dark from the room poured over and through her. She opened her eyes again and the whispers changed slowly to a throbbing, like the slow beat of her blood behind her ears. All conscious thought drained away.

Maura looked down at the baby still swaddled under her cardigan, his black hair spiked up as if against the sudden chill. She smiled down at him in the darkness and crooned to him. The words were *old*, and as if something else were using her mouth, she didn't even realise she was saying them. She stared at the tiny scrap of life sucking a living from her body, as if something else used her eyes to see. Mother-love evaporated as she watched the little jaws' motion and felt the incessant rhythmic tug on her nipple. Still crooning strange words, she felt a sensation of hunger and sudden hot *anger* at this little *man* who was draining her.

And underneath that thought, in a mind that was still asleep, she dreamed a dread vision of terror where her baby was lost, stolen by the darkness, and she could not find him, no matter how frantic her search.

In the little living room with the shuttered windows, the glow of the peat fire smothered by the shadows that had sprung from nowhere, Maura took hold of her baby and prised it off her nipple. It gave a muted little squeak of frustration, and the mouth searched urgently in the dark. She held the tiny head in her hands and shifted position so that Jacky could be manoeuvred. She brought the baby close to herself and hugged it against the skin between her swollen breasts. The pillows of flesh ballooned out on either side of the little head as she forced him against herself.

Panicking for air, the baby struggled mutely, his cries cut off. She held him firmly, though it didn't take much effort. Jacky squirmed and twisted, instinctively fighting for breath, but to no avail. Gradually, his efforts lessened until the motion stopped, except for the shivering of nerves that came even when the muscles relaxed. Eventually the shivering stopped and the tiny body was still.

In the darkness Maura's eyes glittered, and a wide smile flashed across her face, a smile of savage glee. Then her eyes snapped closed. Swiftly, the shadows shrank down, fading back into the corners, behind the dresser and the other armchair. The glow of the peat fire swelled out, as if it had suddenly been fed with clean air. The room warmed quickly, and Maura, exhausted now, slept unfettered by the dream that her baby was lost.

On her belly, her baby started to grow cold.

*

It was six o'clock when Jack Quinn came back along the twisting road from Westport, eager to be fed and eager to see his wife after a long day. But what he looked forward to most was lifting his baby boy from the Moses basket to cuddle the tiny frame in his big arms.

He drove the old Ford past the crossroads after the bridge and trundled it down towards the house. The brakes squealed mightily outside the front window, as they always did, announcing his arrival. It had become a joke between him and Maura.

He turned the handle and pushed the door in ahead of him, aware that something was different. At first he couldn't figure it out; then it came to him. The smell, or the absence of it. Ever since he and Maura got married, he'd loved to come home to her. When he stepped through the doorway, he'd hear the sound of her humming to the baby and the crackle of the fire, and the tantalising smell of cooking would waft its way from the back of the house.

This evening, there was no sound except the dim crackle of one peat sod shifting in the grate, and there was no warm taste of stew on the air.

'Hello,' he called into the still house. 'I'm home again and starving to death, woman of the house.'

No reply. He unbuttoned his thick sheepskin jacket that had kept him warm on the stand all day and peeled it off. He slung it on the hook in the wall and strolled down the small lobby towards the living room.

'Big market today,' he said, as usual, starting off with an account of his day. 'Corrigan unloaded five hundred of his hill ewes. The place was like a good-going battlefield all day long.'

He turned at the doorway, still talking, and then stopped when he saw Maura, still asleep in the rocker. The baby's little head was half-hidden, except for the thick fur of black hair, under the folds of Jack's cardigan. The picture of mother and child stilled his tongue, and any minor annoyance that his meal would be delayed vanished in a moment. He stood for a minute, taking in the bonny sight of his wife and their baby, before crossing the room, slow and soft, to sit himself on the arm of the chair. His weight rocked it forward an inch or two and Maura woke with a start.

'What. . . ?'

'Hush now,' Jack said, quietly.

'What time is it?' Maura asked, her sleepy eyes wide and bewildered. She looked around the room as if confused.

'Feeding time for babes and sucklings, I can tell, while good working

41

men have to wait in the queue.' He shot her a mischievous smile. 'Unless you want to feed me some of what he's been having.'

Maura seemed to come to full wakefulness.

'Oh, be off with you and your gab,' she said through a yawn. 'I must have gone to sleep, though I don't even remember it. I haven't got a thing ready for your tea.'

Even as she said it, a voice inside her head was tugging at her, trying to tell her that something was *wrong*, but she was still too heavily mired in the afterwave of sleep to make it out.

'That's the long and slippery slope, Maura Quinn, and you not a year married. Next thing I'll be having my dinner down at Donovan's and you'll be sitting here with your baking pin for a shillelagh.'

He leaned forward, still smiling, and put his arm across her shoulder. He reached his other hand to gently stroke the baby's fine skein of hair.

'Poor wee soul's cold,' he said, and as he did so, his voice slowed, a swooping plummet in the space of four small words from jaunty right down to dread.

'What's the matter?' Maura asked, although the chittering messages inside her head were suddenly loud and screaming at her to wake up to the moment.

Something's wrong. Something is WRONG!

'What's . . . oh no.' The words came out in a shivery whisper. 'The baby . . .'

She hauled herself to her feet, almost losing her balance as the rocker swung backwards, pushing Jack away with the force of the movement. She ripped at the cardigan, peeling it away from her baby. Its little head lolled lifelessly. Both its eyes were closed. It could have been sleeping.

'Maura? Maura, what's wrong?'

She ignored him, her mind totally concentrated on the slack little bundle. Jacky didn't move. His tiny, perfect hands were splayed open. She reached to take one in her own and felt the dread cold.

'Oh, mother of God no,' she said in a hushed, *terrible* quaver.

Jack came round from behind her and reached for the baby, the dawning anguish widening his eyes.

'Let me . . .'

'No,' Maura moaned, twisting herself away.

Jack forced her round and grabbed for the baby. Again its head lolled. He took it in his hands and pulled it away from her, turning the little bundle round so he could see it. Maura stood, paralysed, her hands still in the position when she relinquished her hold.

'Jacky,' her husband shouted. 'Jacky-boy . . . Wake *up*.'

42

He held the child against his own body, *willing* warmth into it. But he too felt the cold on the back of the little head, and a greater cold that started to well up from the pit of his belly.

'Come on, boy. Wake up. Wake up now, do you hear what I'm saying? There's a good boy, come on now, won't you.'

Jack stopped, and looked at his wife. She stood there, stricken, all the colour drained out of her face so that her freckles stood out like moles. Her eyes were bottomless pits of sickening, horrific realisation. The image would be imprinted on Jack Quinn's mind for as long as he lived.

He turned again to the baby, pulling it away from his body and staring into its placid face.

'Jacky-boy. Come on, baby. For the love of Christ *breathe!*'

There was a sudden clatter. Maura collapsed to the floor as if every nerve in her body had been suddenly cut.

Jack stood there in the cluttered room where the small shuttered window let in little light. In his arms, he held his dead baby against him and rocked it in its sleep.

8

'It's old,' Dr Connarty said. 'Very old. *Ancient*, as a matter of fact.'

He was waxing enthusiastic, as he always did when he had an audience. Behind him the entrance to the tor loomed dark, a narrow passageway that arrowed straight into the side of the small hill.

'Nearly five thousand years, near as we can tell.'

'*Wow*.' Nancy returned enthusiasm in her customary way.

'Wow indeed, young lady. About twenty-five times older than your United States of America.'

'And it's a grave?' Tom asked. Nancy had seen the diggings when they had gone for a stroll along the pathway and round the hill. The tor was on the other side of a belt of trees, hidden by the thick late-autumn foliage, in the centre of a wide field. It stood like a miniature mountain, rising tall and green from the sea of grass around it.

'Well, it is a grave of sorts, that's for certain. Whose grave it is, we don't know yet, though I'm sure Siobhan there will be the very one to work it out.' He waved to the chestnut-haired woman striding towards them with a wide blue folder tucked under her arm.

'Siobhan, meet Tom and Nancy Ducain, who've come all this way to find their ancestors.'

'Then they might have come to the right place, though with a French name, perhaps they haven't,' Siobhan said with a smile.

'We spent two weeks in Paris,' Tom said, reaching forward to offer his hand. 'I might have a French name, but I can hardly speak a word of it. Anyway, Nancy's the Irish one.'

'Here on holiday, I suppose?' Siobhan asked, and Tom beamed proudly.

'Sort of. We just got married, and we're still on our honeymoon, more or less.' Nancy blushed a little and put a proprietorial arm around his waist, hooking her thumb over the top of his jeans at his hip.

'Congratulations to both of you,' Siobhan said cheerily. 'And what brings you to this godforsaken corner?'

'It was Nancy's idea. She wanted to see some of the country her people come from.'

'Well, if they came from here, I can't blame them for going over the water. It's a lovely place, but it's bleak as a witch's backside in the winter.'

44

Nancy laughed aloud, and Siobhan smiled. The girl looked cute and empty-headed, but friendly enough for all that.

'Are you one of the diggers?' Nancy asked.

'Heaven forbid,' Siobhan said with a genuine laugh. 'I've done my share of that over the years and I'm delighted we have some fine young muscle to do the heavy lifting. I just try and figure out whatever it is they've dug up.'

'What have you found, then?'

'Oh, there's a great many things, and we're not right inside yet. We only have another two weeks before we have to get back to Dublin, so we're in a race against the winter to get inside the chamber.'

'Is that where the body is?'

'If it's not, then we're going to have a fine surprise, and the professor here is going to have a hard Christmas explaining where all the money went,' Siobhan said mischievously.

'Ah, never a truer word was spoken,' Dr Connarty said. 'But the signs here give us a little confidence, and that's what archaeology is all about. It's ninety per cent perspiration and ten per cent aspiration. Or maybe it's the other way round. But the most interesting part of the whole thing so far is the carvings on the lintel and door posts. They continue on the walls right down the passageway.'

Connarty indicated the slab of stone that formed the top of the entrance to the tunnel. It was heavy and massive, cut in an oblong shape that rested on two pillars made of the same rock. There were carvings deeply etched into the surfaces, fine and detailed, as if this was the first time they'd seen the air since the day they were cut.

'What does it say?' Nancy asked.

'That's the trick question, sure enough. We don't rightly know.'

'But we have a fair idea,' Siobhan put in. 'It's most likely to be some sort of *geis*.'

'What's that?'

'Like a curse, or a taboo. They didn't like people disturbing their graves. Nobody does.'

'And aren't you worried about that?'

'I've been doing it for the past umpteen years, and so far nothing's happened. Probably they just wear out after a long time. I'll keep my fingers crossed.' She flashed Connarty another mischievous look. His eyes twinkled back at her from behind his polygon frames.

'Can you read those squiggles?'

This time Siobhan laughed gently. 'Well, yes and no. I can maybe read one word in ten, for it's an old language. It's much older than the

Ogham script that was pretty universal in Ireland two thousand years ago, and it even predates the runic style of the early settlers. That tells us that this is a very old barrow, but it's been made by craftsmen of wonderful skill, and from that, we know that it was built for an important reason.'

'Hopefully, for one of the early kings. One of the old Irish heroes perhaps,' Connarty added.

'Wow,' Nancy said again.

'As you say,' Connarty said with a smile.

'Doesn't the writing tell you who they buried?' Tom asked seriously.

'That's what I'm working on,' Siobhan said, opening the folder. 'I've taken some rubbings, though the carving is in such a good state of repair that I don't really need to. Except this is for working on during the term.'

She held out a couple of sheets of thick, translucent paper. 'Look. Those lines here. They spell out something that's very like an ancient west Ireland word, and also like the Gaelic of both the Irish and the Scots. And here again,' she indicated with a strong forefinger further along the line, 'and here too.'

'What's it say?' Nancy asked.

'I haven't got it all, mind you, but that one says *mor*, which in both languages means *great*. Here now is *righ*, which I would translate as *a shroud*. The words before and after are probably descriptive, but if you take the two together, then what we have is something great, shrouded like a corpse. That's what you tend to find in a burial chamber anyway.'

Siobhan scanned the line of rubbings, which were light against the dark charcoal marks on the paper. 'Here's the same word, with another ending. It looks like *righinn*, which is a bit of a puzzle. The ending changes the word, although that could be just style. *Righinn* in some of the dialects could be taken as a princess, or a nymph. Further north, in the old Gaelic, it would mean a serpent. Or it could mean something else entirely. The great thing is that these carvings will be like a Rosetta Stone for us. We can see how the language has changed over the years, and that will give us a terrific insight into the culture of the folk of prehistoric times. I'll have enough work here for ten years.'

Siobhan paused for another scan of the sheets. 'Here's an interesting one. Look there. *Babd*. That's most likely part of the *geis*. You pronounce it *Bav* and that's a very old name in Ireland. And here too, the word *Sidhe*.' Siobhan pronounced it *Shee*.

'They both mean a sort of fairy from the underworld. Now this is either a curse against her entering the grave and taking the spirit away,

46

as some of the fairies were supposed to do, or it's a threat to anybody disturbing the tomb. The *Babd*, or *Baibh* in medieval Gaelic, was a terrible sight in the eyes of men. So with a curse like that over the door, there would be few who would risk her wrath.'

Terry Munster had been working steadily all morning, removing the tightly packed stones and loading them into a wooden cart that he trundled back up the flagstones and upended on the ever growing pile of rubble. For all his size, Terry was a delicate worker. He was more used to sifting through fine layers of sediment with a small hand pick and a stiff-bristled brush, gingerly and methodically searching for the minute fragments of evidence that would help the team piece together the lives of those long dead. Here, in the tunnel, there was no finesse. The end had simply been stopped up by several tons of rough rock that had to be moved by brute force and shifted outside. Despite that, he enjoyed building up a sweat, and once he got up a head of steam, Terry could work tirelessly.

It was after the communal lunch round the big table in the cottage he shared with Jim Connarty that he finally came to the end of the rubble pile and found the stone wall. Terry had shifted ten barrowloads of broken stones out to the mound and went back in for another. He trundled the cart down the hard floor, feeling the rickety thump of the big wheel on the joins between the stones. Behind him the daylight dimmed and his eyes adjusted to the faint glow of the small electric bulb up ahead, set in a protective metal cage suspended from the roof. He bent his neck to avoid scraping his head on the low ceiling and trudged the twenty yards up the slight incline.

Halfway there, Terry stopped suddenly, feeling the barrow push its weight back against him as he did so. At first, he didn't know why he had halted. Then he felt it.

There was a *change* in the air.

That was the only way to describe it. And a sudden chill in the passageway, as if the air had solidified. Terry, still stooped, turned to look back to the opening, and he froze before completing the motion.

There was no daylight at all. No opening back there, where he'd come into the passageway, either. He turned again to look at the far end, faintly illuminated by the light-bulb. It looked dimmer than before, and further away than it should be.

At this point, Terry was not afraid. He simply lowered the legs of the barrow to the ground and then slowly walked up the corridor towards the outside. He went ten paces in the dim shadow and the air suddenly grew warm again. A pale rectangle of light shimmered in the air and became stronger with every step until the daylight broke through. He strode the last five yards and out onto the site. Sunlight forced its way through thin clouds. Across the way, Agnes and Theresa were on their knees working on the small side dig, and Jim Connarty and Siobhan Kane were talking to a couple of strangers. Despite the distance, Terry's roving eye could appreciate that the young woman with the dark-haired man was a stunner.

He turned back into the tunnel and looked down to the far end. The daylight only reached a few feet inside. He went back in and retraced his steps. Halfway down, the air began to crackle cold again, as if he had walked into a refrigerator. He turned to face the entrance, and again, it was gone.

'Must be dust in the air,' he told himself, although he knew there would have to be a ton of the stuff to block the light so completely. Still, there was work to be done. Whether it was dust, or some optical illusion, it didn't really matter. Time was running out, and wondering about the odd phenomenon wasn't getting the rock shifted. He hefted the barrow and shoved it down the passageway. He reached the rubble wall and eased himself past the barrow to where he'd left his pick.He worked the metal spike between two stones and swung the haft left and right, feeling the steel bite in and shuffle the stones apart. He gave an extra heave; the stone on the left popped out under the pressure and its mate rolled out easily to land with a clatter on the stone floor.

Then, without warning, the whole wall simply peeled away and came crashing down in an avalanche.

Terry's reflexes shoved him backwards. The edge of the barrow caught him behind his knees and he fell with a small, surprised yell. If he hadn't fallen, he might not have escaped without a broken leg and maybe a couple of stove-in ribs, but his momentum tipped the barrow over. It rolled on top of him, and as the wall crashed down, the upended cart formed a metal shield that protected him from the worst of it.

The pounding of the stones as they cascaded down was like a massive drumbeat, loud enough to make Terry's ears ring. He could feel the pressure on the back of his legs as the barrow was pressed into his calves by the weight, and he tried to pull them towards him, but couldn't move.

The roar subsided quickly and he lay there panting for breath as a cloud of dust swirled and tried to settle. Minute particles of stone caught in his throat and made him cough so hard he felt a pain well up under his ribs. When the spasm passed, he wriggled to get his arms free and shoved at the carapace that had shielded him. It moved an inch and then clattered back down. The weight of stones pressed it hard against the ground. Terry sank back in the dark, chest heaving with the effort.

The lip of the barrow jammed against his legs, the pressure causing a red pain across his muscles. But otherwise he was unhurt, and the team weren't far away. He called out in the dark, hearing his own voice echo metallically in the confined space. He tried it again and realised that his voice was going nowhere.

Cramped down under the barrow felt like it did as a child, when he would awake and find the sheets had wound round him as he turned in his sleep. Already, because of the awkward position, he could feel his body begin to ache with the need to *move*.

'Another fine mess you've got yourself into, Terry,' he muttered to himself.

He twisted, feeling the metal bite hard against his legs. Though it flared fiery, he ignored the pain as he inched his way round from his side to lie more or less on his back. From under the rim of the barrow there was a low light, which went some way to overcoming the feeling of claustrophobia. But not quite far enough.

Now he was lying face-up, the rim was pressing down onto his shin bones, and that was a lot worse than it had been when it was only crushing muscle. The pain soared and he jerked instinctively. His skin scraped against the edge, followed by an immediate warm trickle of blood.

'Bloody hell,' he grunted feelingly, and shoved hard against the barrow, pressing his back forcefully to the ground and pushing his arms straight with all his strength. This time the barrow *did* move. There was a rasping shriek of metal against stone and a rumble of shifting rocks. Terry could feel the veins stand out on his temples with the sheer effort, and he groaned at the strain. There was another squeal of friction; then his arms locked and the barrow flipped over, slowly, to its side. It crashed down onto the pile of stones.

The pain burned two identical tracks below his knees. The rough denim of his jeans was cold and clammy against the tender skin. Terry let out a long sigh as his pent-up lungs emptied themselves in the aftermath of effort.

Immediately they bellowed back in again, sending a quick rush of oxygen. In the dim light, little stars spangled themselves on the dark shadows before winking out as his breath began to even. Terry shook his head and forced his body into a sitting position. He felt a shard of sharp stone cut into his palm, but the pain was only slight. His feet, protected by the big ploughmen's boots that he wore on a dig, had been undamaged by the rock fall, but he had to drag them out from under the weight of the loose stones. Sitting up against the wall, he reached a hand over and rapped a rapid riff on the slanted side of the barrow. The metal rang out a quick rhythm.

'Just as well you were here,' Terry said, noting the fresh dents in the old pitted surface.

He slowly got to his feet and looked at the pile of stones. They had fallen away from in front, sliding in a wave that carried the rubble a few yards along the tunnel. In the space where they had been, a solid wall loomed, but this one was no hard-packed infill of boulders. The stones were square cut and crafted so that they fitted and locked to one another in the same fashion as the masonry that formed the tunnel and its sloping roof. Immediately, Terry realised that he had reached the end. Beyond this wall was the burial chamber that had lain untouched for centuries, for *thousands* of years.

'Bingo, old son,' he said to himself, and just as he did so, the light flickered in two swift pulses, the first orange, the second dopplering down to a dull red as if the power running through the looping cable stapled to the walls had been leeched out. One more feeble surge, and then the bulb winked out like a snuffed candle.

'Damn,' Terry said aloud into the well of pitch-black. He turned away from the wall; sure enough, no daylight at the open end of the tunnel. Like a massive door had clamped shut, leaving him in a long stone tube.

Groping with his hands, he sought the upturned barrow, planning to scramble over it and make his way to the outside. As he did so, his boot rolled a small rock and he lost balance. His left hand shot out instinctively and rapped off the wall, skinning his knuckles. Terry's breath whistled with the tight pain; his fingers clutched at the cable dangling down in a low curve. As soon as his weight pulled on it, the light flickered once and died again; then a strange blue ripple of energy snaked itself along the black insulation of the wire. It was like St Elmo's fire, silently and weirdly writhing.

The blue hazy lines squirmed along the cable in a sizzling stream until they reached his hand. Instantly Terry felt a surge leap through his body. His head snapped backwards so hard that he bit his tongue. His arm jittered, spasmodic flexing that almost wrenched it out of his shoulder socket. Then the jolt threw him against the wall with enough force to sock the breath from his chest, and he landed heavily on the rubble mound.

Dazed by the blow and disoriented in the solid dark that denied him any point of reference, Terry did not know how long he lay there. When his head began to clear, and more little stars, orbiting crazily behind his eyelids, were winking out, he groggily opened his eyes. The strange unearthly light began to stream fuzzily along the wires, arcing off and into the stone. Dimly Terry thought there must be some sort of short circuit leaking the current out of the cable and into the earth. Had he not been dazed he would have realised the absurdity of the thought. He shook his head and felt a dull pain shoot up from his neck. The muscles felt as though they'd been squeezed by a large hand.

The wall beside him seemed to shiver strangely as if shaken by an underground tremor. The motion picked up the interference patterns of the St Elmo's fire. Bolts of soft blue frizzled through the stone and suddenly the wall just faded out of existence. One moment it was there, solid and vibrating like a tuning fork, and then the light seemed to dissolve it entirely.

With that, Terry knew he must be dreaming. He *had* to be dreaming.

One dreadful moment later, he hoped to God that he *was* dreaming.

Beyond where the wall had been, he could see the inner chamber, lit up by the flickering surges. It was a large, low, circular room built of stone. Around the walls was a series of vertical niches built into the stonework, and in the centre, a massive block of basalt, polished smooth and carved with intricate hieroglyphs.

The huge stone sat squat and ponderous right in the centre, black as night in the strange light.

Tery stared at it and felt a flicker of fear. The temperature plummeted: he knew it was freezing because his breath came out in clouds, forming hoar frost in the air. There was a crackling in his ears and the thick curly hairs on the back of his neck tried to straighten themselves right out and stand to attention.

Dread oozed deep inside him, and he *knew* it was coming from the stone. The blue light faded down, sending deeper shadows spreading out from the edges of his vision; but Terry barely noticed. His eyes were riveted on the massive stone that looked so out of place in the empty chamber. As he stared, the blackness swooped in, flowing over the stone like a river of night, then expanded towards him. He could see a vague shape within the darkness, like two long arms that snaked out hands threatening to grasp him. But the shadows did not run along the floor the way they would do in normal light. The black sinewy shapes were reaching across the room through the *air*.

Terry's hand flew up in a reflex to ward off the attack, and as it did so, it smacked against something hard, bruising his already scraped knuckles. Instantly the wall flickered back into being, hard and solid, stretching from the floor to the roof of the passageway as if it had always been there, all those thousands of years.

Terry stepped back, panting heavily, his heartbeat thudding at his temples in a fast pulsing rhythm.

Through the solid wall two arms *stretched* towards him.

The fright was so great that Terry again fell, landing on his backside with a jarring thump.

'Holy mother . . .' he blurted in his panic, ignoring the leaping pain in the base of his spine. He scuttled backwards, away from the hands that shoved themselves through solid rock and reached out long bony fingers towards him. Gnarled and wrinkled, incredibly long and alien, they opened and closed, searching blindly. As if *sensing* for him, they groped around, reaching out further and further.

'Get off me,' Terry wailed in fright.

He shoved himself away with feet that slipped on the loose rock. It was like one of those dreams where, no matter how hard you try to get away from something bad, you can't make any headway. His boot finally found purchase and shoved enough to get him onto his feet. He clambered over the barrow and bolted up the tunnel without looking back. He had taken ten paces when the strange light flickered and died, leaving him in pitch-darkness. The thought of being stuck in the dark with those horrible scrabbling fingers gave him the spurt he needed to propel him up the passageway like a frightened rabbit. Five steps further on, the light-bulb flicked back to life. But Terry didn't hang around. He raced twenty yards like a sprinter, heading towards the rectangle of day that appeared as soon as the light had sprung on. He scooted out of the entrance into the flat field and came skidding to a halt some distance away. His big boots made two long grooves in the soft earth. He blinked in the light, still breathing hard, and looked around.

Nothing had followed him from down there. No long arms snaked out to grab him. There was just the dark rectangle of the tunnel mouth that he'd seen for weeks since they discovered the passageway.

'The very man,' Dr Connarty called across from the group that stood near the cottage. 'What's your hurry, Terry?'

Terry spun round, mouth agape. Then the reality, the *normality* of the scene outside the tor overwhelmed him.

Connarty was reaching a hand towards him, mild concern on his face. Theresa and Agnes were kneeling in their own bare patch of digging, looking up at him. To the right were the two young people he didn't recognise, standing beside Siobhan.

There was no alarm. There was nothing out of the ordinary. In fact it was so damned ordinary that a wave of hysterical relief bubbled up inside his chest. He strangled it. The dust of the tunnel caught in his throat and he doubled up, spluttering.

And in that paroxysm the whole weird episode was shoved from his mind.

Out in the daylight, Terry's brain told him that he couldn't *possibly* have seen what he'd thought he'd seen. When the coughing fit subsided, he straightened up, aware that everyone was looking at him, and feeling just a little foolish.

9

Sean drove up from Lisdoonvarna along the road that skirted Galway Bay. In the cathedral town he found the offices of the *Times* and in the darkroom he dealt himself in for an hour, playing cards with the picture printers while his films developed in the tank. He'd been in the office before and was as welcome a new face as any other travelling photographer. The wire room booted his pictures down the line and head office called back to say they'd got them, so he went for a beer in a students' bar while Liz tapped out her story on a borrowed typewriter in the corner of the newsroom.

The bar was as smoky and dark as the beer they poured. It was filled with students and young graduates, all huddled together in large groups that pulled in newcomers and spun off leavetakers sporadically like slowly agitated atoms. Sean sat on a stool, half-reading a newspaper and enjoying the beer and the hubbub of conversation in those fine clear Irish tones. It washed over him in a pleasant wave. The students left him alone, more or less, their eyes intent with the earnestness of their views as they argued and debated amongst themselves with the fervour of students all over the world, but which only the Irish have truly perfected.

In the corner, he watched a young fair-haired boy and his spotty companion being verbally lanced by two girls with flashing dark eyes and soft, determined west-coast accents. From somewhere he remembered a phrase:

All their fights were happy, and all their songs were sad.

It had been said, or written down sometime by somebody who was trying to describe the Celtic people. To Sean, who, if he looked back far enough would find Irish blood singing sad songs somewhere in his veins, it was probably true. They loved a good argument, and if you sat in a pub in a village way out in the bogs, you would hear mournful songs that would bring a lump to your throat and make you think of home, loves lost, chances missed.

He finished the paper and ordered another stout, watching it pour into the glass, bubbling a dirty brown before separating into pure black with a creamy white head. It was going down a treat when Liz came through the door, standing framed in the light, peering into the gloom as her eyes adjusted to the low illumination. She was wearing a pair of tight jeans and a light tan leather bomber jacket, and the light shone through the ends of her cascading fair hair, limning her in a soft gold halo.

If she stopped being such an arse, Sean thought to himself, appraising her with a photographer's eye, she could be a halfway decent woman. Having said that, on her recent showing, that might take some doing.

He raised his newspaper from the bar and held it up to signal her to the far end of the room. At first she missed the movement and came in tentatively, a hand over her eyes to cut out the light from the lamps on the wall. Then she caught his eye. She pushed her way through the crowd and got to his side. Sean heaved his pack off the stool, clearing a space for her. She eased herself onto it.

'Get it done all right?' he asked.

'Yes, but it took me ages to phone it over. The copytaker either couldn't type or she couldn't spell. I think I got it down on paper quicker than she did, and I was *writing* the damn story.'

'Why didn't you wire it?' he asked. He looked down at her with one eyebrow raised and, she was sure, a smug glint in the shadow of his eyes. Before she could answer he butted in to ask her what she wanted to drink.

'What's that?' she asked, pointing to his half-full glass.

'Guinness. The real stuff.'

'Is it any good?'

'You might have to acquire a taste.'

'Let me try some,' she said, and before he could say anything, she reached across and hefted the glass. She lifted it to her lips. He watched while she took a drink, and continued to stare when she put her head back and quaffed the lot in one long, slow pour.

'It's not bad,' she said, after licking her lips and thumping the empty glass down on the bar. It sat there with the dregs of foam slowly sliding down the inside, reflecting red in the light of the wall lamps. She looked up at him and raised an eyebrow.

'I'll have another,' she said. 'And while we're at it, just because I haven't been around as long as you have, you could put me right instead of putting me down.'

'What do you mean?' Sean asked, as he indicated to the barmaid to pour another two pints.

'I didn't know I could use their wire service. It would have saved me nearly an hour on the phone.'

'That's hardly my fault, is it? I thought you would know.'

'Well, I'll know the next time. Thanks for your help, McCullain.'

She reached for her pint and lifted it from the bar. Sean simply stared at her. He reassessed his earlier view. If she wasn't such a stuck-up, *bad-tempered* arse, she might just make it.

They left Galway in the afternoon as the clouds were piling up from the west and heading inland over the swampy bogs of Connemara. When they took the turn north the narrow road angled straight across the lowland in some of the bleakest country Sean had ever seen. Liz had kept a sullen silence ever since they left the city, which suited him fine. He didn't mind conversation, but if it was going to be a bickering argument every step of the way, he preferred silence. Overhead the dark clouds, blown by a soft west wind, trailed gauzy rain over the black tarns that spread out on either side of the road. The pools looked greasy and slick and reflected little light. All around the bog stretched for miles, broken only by dank tussocks, hummocks of rocks, and big single stones that looked as if they'd been scattered by a giant hand.

'I think we're in the wrong country,' Liz said, breaking the long silence. 'I thought this was supposed to be the Emerald Isle. I've never seen anything so desolate.'

Sean nodded. 'It's bleak enough. Makes the Rannoch Moor look like a picnic spot.'

'Where's that?'

'In Scotland, near where I was brought up. Miles and miles of bog and heather and nothing else. People get lost in it.'

'They'd get lost here, I'll bet.'

'Believe it. Look at those tarns. They'll go down fifty feet or more into the peat. Anybody falls in one of them and they're gone for ever.'

'It's kind of scary.'

Sean took his eyes off the road for a moment to look at her. He smiled at her first admission of human failing.

'Nothing to be scared of, except drowning, or hypothermia.'

'Yes, but if you were stuck out here on your own, anything could happen. It's like something out of Tolkien. Or Thomas Tryon. You can imagine all sorts of things.'

'I wouldn't have put you down for reading those kinds of books,' Sean said.

'That's because you don't know much about me,' she replied. 'You just put me down anyway.'

Here we go again, Sean thought to himself, preparing for the next onslaught; but it never came. Liz lapsed back into silence as the car rolled along the flat road through the flat country. The tarns and tussocks flashed by on either side and the gauzy rain kept falling.

It was nearly four in the afternoon when they arrived at Westport, where they were booked in, according to Liz, at the County Hotel, a picturesque red sandstone hotel on the corner of the square by the little canal that drained itself into Clew Bay.

The receptionist was stout and friendly and smiled all the time, even when she told them there was no trace of the booking in the register.

'But it was made a week ago,' Liz said, and Sean could see what was coming.

'It's not in the book now, dear,' the woman said, eyes saucer-like behind thick lenses. 'Maybe it's the Murrisk Hotel, or the Clogher further down the square.'

'No, it's this one. I wrote it down.'

'Now did you call to confirm? I know we always ask, especially at this time of year.'

The look on Liz's face told them all that she hadn't called to confirm. 'But it was a *firm* booking,' she protested, colour already rising.

'Well, that's an awful shame, my dear,' the woman said kindly, still smiling. 'And it's an even bigger shame that we just don't have any room at all in the place. It's the market, you see. The autumn fair's on all this week, and there isn't a room to be had, I don't think, in the whole of the town.'

'Can we get a coffee in here, and maybe a sandwich?' Sean asked, before Liz exploded again.

'Surely, you can,' the woman said brightly. 'If you just go through to the lounge, I'll have some sent through.'

She bustled into the room behind the desk and Liz turned to Sean.

'There's no point in staying here if we haven't got a room. Damn them. I made that booking myself.'

'Well, there's no point in worrying about it. If the place is full, we can't make them take us in.'

He took her by the arm and, surprisingly, she let him ease her into the lounge.

'Let me make a phone call and see what I can do.'

She nodded curtly and he went back to the lobby, where the glass shell of a phone booth jutted from the wall. She saw him consult a small, tattered book that he drew out of a hip pocket, then thumb coins into

57

the slot. She heard him talking to someone, obviously a friend, from the tone of it. A young girl came, carrying a tray loaded with a coffee jug, cups and a vast plate of sandwiches. Liz poured herself a large cup and spooned sugar into the dark brew before pouring the cream over her spoon and watching it float to the surface. The coffee was hot and strong and marvellous. The sandwiches were even better.

A few minutes later, Sean came strolling back into the empty lounge and shrugged off his weatherbeaten green thornproof, slinging it over the back of a nearby chair. He ran a hand through his dark hair and then down the side of his cheek. The movement made a rasping noise over his stubble. He needed a shave. She raised an eyebrow in question, but he ignored it while he poured his own coffee, took a big gulp and sighed with pleasure as it scalded his throat.

'That would put hairs on your chest,' he said approvingly, then stuffed a complete sandwich into his mouth and chewed with obvious relish.

'Well?' Liz finally asked.

'That was Paul Convery. Works with the tourist board out of Dublin.'

'I don't know him,' Liz said.

Sean shook his head. 'No, you wouldn't. He was before your time. Used to run the Irish bureau. Terrific guy.' Sean said all this in short bursts between swallows of his second sandwich.

'Anyway, he says there's nothing up at Knock at this time of the year.'

'I know, I tried there first.'

'But he's found us somewhere to stay. Says it's a great wee place called Kilgallan, just along the road. He's getting on to them just now. All we have to do is show up.'

'That's great. I don't fancy staying in a bed and breakfast on one of those farms,' Liz said, cheered by the news. She actually smiled, and it did wonders for her face. Sean reassessed his second opinion. She *could* be quite something if she smiled a bit more.

They finished all the coffee and every sandwich from the big plate, and bundled themselves back into the car. The fine tendrils of rain had become a thick drizzle, falling from clouds which seemed to scrape the treetops.

They took the road down at the harbour and headed west. About ten miles out, the massive rearing shape of Croagh Patrick hill poked up from the flat lowland. The misty clouds piled around the base so that the peak looked like an island jutting darkly out of a grey sea. Out on the right, the expanse of Clew Bay was completely hidden in soft rain.

'Does it ever stop raining here?'

'I hope to Christ it does, otherwise I'll never get a picture taken at all,' Sean replied.

The rain slackened, then ceased by the time they got to the fork of the road and came up to the bridge. Sean stopped the car and eased himself out, stretching his legs and taking in the clear, damp air.

He sauntered over to the wall and put his hands on the wet stone. There was a tang of salt on the slight wind, telling him the sea was only a few hundred yards away past the belt of willow and alders that crowded the stream. Beyond the bridge, he could see the huddle of houses that must be Kilgallan, topped by the old squat church tower bearing a plain black cross.

Liz sat in the car and watched him look around.

Sean peered over the moor on the left and then turned back to view the downstream side. He leaned over the parapet and looked down into the water, deep in thought. In the shadow, the stream flowed black and the swirls and whorls of the current threw back a red tinge of peat. The water must have travelled a long distance through the bogland before draining out into the flow, he thought.

Further downstream where the brook tumbled shallowly over rocks, there was a murmur of running water, but under the bridge it was silent, moving with the hypnotic calm that spoke of depth. Sean leaned forward, easing himself over the rough, crumbling stone wall that paralleled each side like the ridge scales on some mouldering dinosaur. He shaded the light above his eyes with one hand and stared into the depths. Down there, his reflection peered back, shimmering with the movement on the surface. It looked as if he was hanging on an underwater wall, straining for the surface. The movement wavered and danced in a slow, rhythmic motion that held Sean's eyes.

Then, of a sudden, the movement quickened. Down below, his reflection expanded, floating up towards him, rising swiftly to the surface.

Sean jerked back in surprise, the way one does when the inexplicable happens and the brain identifies the strange and out-of-place and sends the chemical surge that prepares the body for fight or flight. Then his mind overrode the surge. It must have been an optical illusion. He looked down again and sure enough, his reflection was way down there, wavering, vague. He peered at it, and the rhythmic surface lulled away the initial reaction.

'It's time you had a break,' Sean said aloud to himself.

He watched himself with eyes almost out of focus as his own image expanded and contracted slowly in the smooth flow.

Then again – another change. This time it was no movement, but a change in the image itself. Sean's heart did a little double flip that jarred against his ribs.

It was no longer his *face.*

His eyes widened as he recognised the features down below in the water. He saw the short brown hair and the eyes wide with surprise, and it was *not him.*

The head turned this way and that and he saw the mouth slowly open to say something. His mind took over and added the sound.

'What the hell . . . Let me . . .'

They were the words he had heard when the crowd had closed in around the young plain-clothes soldier, just before the wheelbrace had come down on the side of the man's head.

And there, down *there*, he saw it again. The head turned, aware of the motion, and something hit. The man's face contorted with the sudden pain of it and a wide gash flowered on the side of his temple.

The words came back with terrible clarity.

'Get the bastard. Kill the cunt!'

Old Anglo-Saxon words spoken in Irish accents. Almost matter-of-fact. Cold and hard.

Below in the water, the image writhed. Sean saw the motion and his mind heard the thud of the metal battering onto the man's head. Pieces flew outwards in a spray of red. The man's face contorted again, but this time the shift was not only in expression. The man's *features* had been altered entirely by the murderous blow. One eye was almost squeezed out of its socket; the eyebrow slumped. The cheekbone was a sunken depression. Blood poured through lips that were drawn back in a sickening rictus over gritted teeth.

Sean's hands clenched on the stone. Beyond him the water murmured and burbled over the stones, but the sounds in his ears were the hoarse cries of the angry crowd and the gasping, groaning sounds from the doomed man.

Again the image changed, became a shape floating slowly upwards from the depths of the water. The shape, small and white, turned slowly. Arms trailed wetly.

Sean saw a little boy.

His red hair trailed in the flow. His body was pale, terribly pale, with the whiteness of long submersion. It looked as if the water had leached

60

all natural colour from the skin. The small figure tumbled and somersaulted slowly. A foot broke the surface, the skin puckered and wrinkled, then slipped under again. Mesmerised, Sean saw the little body roll with the flow until the head came up again. Pale eyes, wide and almost colourless, stared up.

The mouth opened slowly and a small bubble of air wavered up. The face rocked upwards and broke free of the surface. Sean felt his body stiffen.

'Oh, my God,' he said under his breath.

Then the mouth opened further and a small stream of water dribbled out from between colourless lips. There was a cough, like that of a child who has swallowed water while swimming. A reedy voice floated upwards towards him, a little wet voice.

'Help me, mister. Please help me.'

Sean was riveted; frozen with surprise.

'Would you help me out of the water, mister? I can't swim.'

Sean was about to call out to the child. His mind hadn't quite taken in what he was seeing, but something stopped him. He stood there for a frozen second, trying to rationalise the pitiful sight of the bleached, sodden body floating in the black water under the bridge.

Then the boy's face rippled and changed. It sank below the waters, disappearing into the black depths. Suddenly it turned, started to float upwards. It was no longer a boy, pallid and dead. The face had changed into a wasted, misshapen thing that rose towards him, swimming fast to the surface. Sean's heart thumped and his fingers locked on the stone.

There was a splash as it launched out of the water, the terrible wounds red and gaping, the teeth still clenched together in the extremity of agony. The black surface exploded with a great rushing sound as the thing propelled itself up and out. Water cascaded in a murky, frothy fountain.

Sean couldn't move. The shock of the change and the sudden motion had frozen him where he stood. His breath was still locked inside his lungs, and his eyes were transfixed by the thing that hurtled, impossibly, from the water. It was as if the world had suddenly gone into slow motion. He couldn't move, but everything else was picked out in vivid detail. The droplets of churned water flew up in an expanding cone, and a heavy dark shape soared out of the maelstrom. The face was raised towards him, crumpled and deformed, and as it shot up from the water, it changed further. The lips drew back in a snarl and the arms, which had been trailing behind it, reached up into the air. The hands were long and grey and the fingers were hooked to grab. In that instant of clear detail, Sean saw that the fingers were gnarled and obscenely withered, not the fingers of a young man at all.

Only three or four feet away, the mouth opened with a quick snap. Water and blood poured out from the corners like thick saliva. The teeth were not white, but old and blackened and incredibly *long*, as if withered gums had shrunk. And the hair was no longer brown. It was long and tangled and grey-white. It seemed to pull away from the scalp with the water that poured off. The change flowed over the thing, altering it from one obscenity to another horrific, grotesque shape.

Finally Sean's lungs unlocked. His breath swooped back in with such force that the terrible image wavered in his vision as the oxygen flooded his brain. He jerked back off the wall and almost lost his footing on a small pile of fresh sheep droppings.

Far in the distance a voice called out to him. His mind still perceived everything in slow motion: the voice had deepened to a drone. He couldn't make out the words.

From below, a snarling growl vibrated through the stone, a freezing, *thunderous* sound that twisted the air itself with fury and hate and shivered in his spine. The rush of air into his lungs was enough to bring the world back into real time. The thundering growl speeded up, gaining tone until it was a high-pitched wail.

From behind the voice came again.

'Is there something wrong?'

Liz was walking towards him from the car, her short leather jacket draped across her shoulders. The slight wind caught her hair, spreading strands across her face. Her steps made rasping noises on the loose stones of the old road.

Sean noticed all these things in the strange half-level of his consciousness that stood apart, aware of the normal, the *acceptable* minor details, while the main part of his mind struggled and recoiled from the sight of the terrible thing under the bridge.

'Back!'

'What?' Liz called. She was only twenty yards away and walking towards him, arms casually folded.

Sean tried again and his throat clamped shut. There was another sound from the other side of the crumbling parapet, a scrabbling as if something had clamped onto the rough stone and was clawing its way upwards. He twisted round again, instinctively, though every impulse was to get away. The urgent messages were running up and down, trying to override the conscious rejection of what he had seen. He looked over the edge and saw the thing, and his heart stuttered again. It was decayed, hideous, *shrivelled*. He recoiled as one long, bony arm reached upwards, fingers splayed wide, and then hooked to dig into the spaces between the blocks.

'What's the matter?' Liz called from closer in.

'Get back. *Get away!*' Sean managed to shout out.

'For goodness sake, McCullain, what are you playing at?' Liz said crossly. She had seen him lean out and then haul himself back in a spastic, almost drunken lurch. It was exactly as if, like a drunk, he'd bent himself over the wall to be sick, and then stumbled backwards. Even at that distance, his face was grey and ill-looking.

He came towards her, twice looking behind him with quick jerky movements as if he expected something to come clambering up from the other side. The expression on his face was exactly the opposite of the self-assured laconic calmness that was his norm; his annoying, *exasperating* norm.

'Are you car-sick or something?' she asked with gloating sarcasm. 'Or was it something I said?'

Sean shook his head. 'Back to the car,' he said.

'Wait a minute,' Liz said when he reached her. 'What's wrong?'

'Nothing.' Sean simply did not want to believe what he had seen, far less tell Liz about it. He grasped her shoulder and tried to spin her round. She twisted against the pressure, and her jacket fell to the ground.

'Hey, what do you mean. . . ?'

'Come *on!*'

'Now just you wait a minute,' Liz protested, but Sean didn't wait. He roughly shoved her back two steps.

'Right. That's enough. That is *it*,' she snapped. She stood there on the road, her back to the wall, feet planted wide. The leather bomber jacket lay in a small heap. In Sean's ears the sound of the wailing still grated against the small bones inside his head.

'What the hell's got into you, McCullain. Have you cracked up or something?'

There was a movement behind her and Sean's eyes flicked over her shoulder. A long hand with twitching fingers scuttled like a grey crab on the top of the wall. He opened his mouth to bawl a warning, but Liz caught his look and spun round, her head coming between his line of vision and the nightmare hand.

She stood like that for a second or more, then turned back towards him. As she shifted, he saw there was no hand. The top of the wall was bare. The screeching sound cut off abruptly.

'Well? Are you going to tell me?'

'I thought I saw something,' he mumbled.

'Like what?'

'I don't know. Something in the water.'

She looked at him warily, wondering if he was going to grab her again, then scooped up her jacket and turned in one movement. Before he could even register it, she walked swiftly towards the wall and looked down to the water.

Nothing happened. No long scaly hand reached up and grabbed her. Her body did not flinch. It was not dragged over the side. She did not scream.

Liz unbent and turned back towards him. 'There's nothing there,' she said simply.

The paralysis that had glued his feet to the road gave way. He stepped over to the parapet and stood beside her, afraid to look over. She just stared at him challengingly, and he forced his body to bend.

Down there the water was black and tinged with the red residue of far-off peat. Small whorls and swirls spun slowly on the smooth surface. Two reflections, one dark and one fair, peered back up at them.

'What did you think you saw?' Liz asked.

'I don't know,' Sean lied. 'Something moving.'

'And it was that scary?' She looked him up and down. 'Come on, McCullain. You've been around. You've seen all the terrible things. What's so terrible that it's got you shaking in your shoes?'

She was laughing at him. Sean could see it in her eyes, and oddly enough, he warmed to her a little. She turned back to look into the water and he watched her.

'Maybe it was just a reflection,' he said, feeling his heart slow down.

'Yeah, probably it was,' she said, and then her body stiffened.

Sean noticed the movement immediately and followed her eyes down to the water. There was a sudden surge and a splash as a grey shape humped itself out from the surface. It turned quickly and Sean got a flash of matted hair and long teeth in a skull-like face.

Liz let out a little gasp of fright and jerked back. Sean put a hand out to grasp her arm and was just on the point of dragging her away when the thing in the water turned again and two great black arms reached out from the black pool, clawing into the air.

'Oh shit,' Sean said.

Then realisation burst through. They were not arms at all. They were twisted branches moving in the slow current. The whole thing jumped into focus.

The dead sheep that was tangled in the branches of the submerged tree-stump rolled over again in the water. The trailing branches and twigs snagged the bottom of the stream and the stone edges of the bank, giving the whole mass enough momentum to lift the decaying carcass almost clear of the surface. Its wool was matted and peeling away from a bloated hide. The bones of the skull showed through the skin and the black eye sockets stared lifelessly, filled with the peat-coloured water. Its bottom teeth jutted out from a maggot-eaten jaw, long and discoloured. In the cold light of reality, it was just a dead sheep, putrid and grotesque, but harmless.

Sean let out a long sigh of relief, and beside him he heard Liz do the same.

'Nearly gave me a heart attack,' Liz said finally in a shaky voice.

'Me too.'

'I thought it was coming out. Some kind of monster.'

Sean nodded again, still holding onto her arm.

'Was that what you saw?' she asked.

'Must have been. I didn't think.'

'That's why you wanted me to go back, isn't it?'

'Yeah.'

'Poor old McCullain. Scared of a dead sheep,' Liz said, and then started to laugh. It was a small, giggly laugh that was more the release of tension than humour.

'Yeah,' he said again. 'I'll never live it down.'

'You want to get your camera out and take a picture?'

Sean shook his head. Inside he was still feeling a bit shaky. It might have been a dead sheep in the water, but that was *not* what he had seen. And now, he wasn't so sure exactly what it was that he had seen; *or imagined*, rocketing up from the water. He felt the way he did when the visions came to him in the night, when the reels of his mind ran free and the faces of the doomed men in the crowd stared out at him with haunted eyes, and he awoke, shivering and sweating and wondering if he wasn't cracking up.

'Did you hear something?' he finally asked.

'Like what?'

'A noise, from under the bridge, when I looked over the first time.'

Liz looked at him. She was standing close to him and he could see the searching look on her face as her eyes flicked left to right, staring alternately into his.

'No. I didn't hear a thing. I thought you were being sick. What did it sound like?'

'Nothing. It doesn't matter.'

'I think we should get on.'

Sean nodded. He pointed to the town that lay just ahead. 'We're just about there anyway.'

She followed his indication and took in the huddle of houses and the small church tower. 'That's it?'

'Yes. That's it.'

'It looks like a one-horse town to me.'

They walked back to the car. Sean waited until Liz got into the passenger seat before he turned to look at the wall on the bridge. There was still nothing there. There had never *been* anything there. Of that, he was certain. He hoped.

But he was also certain that he'd better get a grip on himself. Since that day in Belfast he'd had time to stand back, and reassess, and as the dreams constantly rocked him out of sleep, shaken with the images of sudden, pointless death, he wondered if perhaps he needed some help.

10

They had found little Mickey Boyle's body the day after he'd failed to turn up for his tea. The search, more frantic as the hours dragged by, went on for most of the night and well into the morning.

Sure, they'd searched under the bridge, and more than once, but the flashlight beams had been reflected back by the swirling peaty water. Nobody even noticed the little bundle of clothes lying between the sitting stones. Throughout the night Sinead Boyle sat by the cold grate, her hands clenched, white-knuckled, around her rosary beads while the rest of the children sat quietly unable to sleep.

It wasn't until daylight that one of the farmers who had tramped the shoreline and beaten the woods along with the rest came across the pair of sandshoes, one of them upturned and showing the slick of drying algae on its sole. Then he found the mud-stained t-shirt crumpled and still damp. He leaned out over the water and raised a hand to his brow to shadow the morning light that spangled up from the flow beyond the bridge.

He saw the pale outline down there in the depths without realising what it was, but something made him probe down with his shepherd's crook. It snagged the boy's arm.

Dermid Mullen pulled the little body to the surface. It was pallid and slowly tumbling in the flow. The farmer reached down and grabbed the small hand that reached out in mute appeal and hauled the boy towards him. As the head broke the surface, the blue eyes seemed to roll blindly in their sockets and a little dark stream of water flowed from the boy's mouth. Dermid gently eased the flopped body onto the hard stone, then walked out from under the bridge into the sunlight, blinking back sudden tears. He called to the other fellows who were searching the marsh downstream. They came up to the bridge quickly and gathered round in silence, none of them knowing what to say, all of them fathers.

Somebody went off to find Danny Boyle who was down at the mudflats along with another group of searchers. He ran up from the shore and along the bank of the Roonah Burn like a man possessed. Dread was written into every panicked stride. He came barrelling under the bridge and skidded to a halt, big boots sending sparks on the stones. His eyes were wide and staring as he shoved everybody out of the way and threw himself to the ground beside his dead boy.

They turned away, ashamed to hear his anguish as he pleaded with his dead son not to be dead. They knew, but for the grace of God, they too would be kneeling under the Roonah's humpbacked bridge, demanding the impossible, feeling the full unbearable horror of the loss of a child.

The hoarse wail of a bereaved father echoed out from the bridge and into the morning. It was fully half an hour before Danny Boyle eventually emerged from the shadows under the bridge with his dead boy wrapped in an old, torn jacket. The rest of the men followed on that dreadful walk back into the village, towards the waiting mother.

It was another day before they found Rita Burke's car down on the rocks. A passing angler saw it when the tide went out and mentioned it in the Tallabaun Inn bar. Somebody mentioned it to Toomy Toner, because the romance was well-enough known, and he went off to have a look because he was supposed to have dinner with Rita and she hadn't shown up at his place. He was a shy fellow who hadn't the confidence to push himself forwards with her and didn't even realise the extent and permanence of her plans for him.

They called the Garda, old Peter O'Neill, and they had another search of the jagged coastline under the cliff where the rocks had been twisted and warped into sharp spines. The car was a mangled wreck and the incoming tide had festooned it with long trails of kelp which slithered like green tentacles over the battered bodywork.

Of Rita, there was not a sign, and she never did show up. Out in the bay there's a current, caused by the strong tides swirling between the islands, that can drag a body for miles. What she'd been doing in her car down at Tiraun Point, nobody knew, although there were those in Donovan's bar who speculated that she could have been down there meeting some fancy man, maybe one of the tourists who came for the fishing in the summer and autumn, but that was just the kind of idle chat you can expect in any pub in all small villages.

Certainly, there was never any connection made in anyone's mind between Rita's disappearance and little Mickey Boyle's drowning. Nobody had passed by on the road that went over the bridge, and even if they had, they wouldn't have seen a thing, for Rita's car had been driven off the road and into the small stand of alders at the side of the field.

No-one could understand what little Mickey had been doing swimming in the Roonah Water. Sure, his mother had wailed heart-rendingly at the wake in the crowded front room of their house, he couldn't even swim.

Garda Peter O'Neill filed his report and sent it along to the station at Westport. The doctors down there had done a post-mortem and there wasn't a mark on the little fellow. He'd drowned, and that was that.

The Boyle family got to mourning, and the whole village turned out for the funeral, just as they would soon turn out for little Jacky Quinn, too. Peter filed his other report on Rita Burke, who was listed as a missing person, though everybody on the south side of the bay knew that she was dead and gone and would be missing for ever, unless a freak current threw her on to the mudflats, and there wasn't much chance of that.

The deaths of two children in the space of a couple of months cast a pall over the village of Kilgallan. But the place had seen bad times before. The village was smaller than it had been way back in the 1840s when there were thirty wee ones dead from starvation in the one year, and another forty the year after that. Kilgallan had survived that, thought it was touch and go for a while.

It could survive the deaths of a baby and a little boy, though these were the kind of things that mothers dwelled on in the dark of the night, and fathers thought about in the odd moments during their working days.

Sometimes these things happened, and Kilgallan was just the same as anywhere else. Wasn't it?

11

There were other people staying at the cottages that week in autumn. Two days before Tom and Nancy Ducain arrived, two German couples from Hamburg had enjoyed a week in Kilgallan, and none of them had minded the price of the lager they served in Donovan's bar or in the lounge at the Tallabaun Inn, which was winding down for the season. Mike O'Hara had had a good enough summer, and, his hotel rooms vacating one by one, he was getting the dust sheets out and closing down the annexe. Only the four rooms in the hotel proper were occupied by regulars who would be leaving at the end of the week, allowing him to close everything but the bar, which did just enough passing trade to merit staying open throughout the winter.

Another English couple gave up their cottage after two weeks' birdwatching out on the mudflats, from where they'd return every evening loaded down with their big binoculars and cameras and filled with enthusiasm over their sightings of the eider duck and shelduck vectoring in from the far north in great winter wedges.

Tom and Nancy had the up-slope cottage on the side of the little incline, towards the edge of the field. It gave them a good view past the rest of the encirclement and out towards the bay.

In the third cottage along, maybe a hundred yards from the workings, a curtain twitched at one of the windows.

'What's happening?'

'Oh, just some new arrivals. The girl and boy who came last night,' the man at the window said. Brian Cooney was a thin-faced man with bushy eyebrows that half-hid his eyes. He spoke in a thick Northern Ireland accent.

The woman sitting at the table reading the newspaper lifted her eyes up from the page.

'They British?'

'No. I heard them. They're Yanks, likely. No trouble for us.'

'Good. I don't like it here. It's too exposed.'

Cooney peered through the window again and then turned away, coming across to the table. A tea-pot sat snug in its cosy and he hefted it to refill his cup. The tea came out of the spout dark brown and tar-thick.

70

Bridget Massey watched the movement. She slid her own cup over towards his and he poured until the brew swilled close to the brim.

'Nothing wrong with this place, as long as we stay quiet,' said Cooney. 'It's better here than up at the hotel, where everybody knows your movements. And on top of that, we're Irish anyway. We don't stand out amongst all these foreigners. Everybody notices what they're up to, especially in a wee place like this.'

'But it's the foreigners that worry me. They could be anybody.'

'And so could we.' Cooney took a sip of tea and screwed up his face. 'It's like hot asphalt,' he said, though the word came out *ashfelt*, 'and it's not even hot.'

He shoved the cup and saucer away with an irritated motion. 'Here, Bridie, shove on the kettle and make another pot, will you now?'

'What do you think I am at all? Your wife?'

'That's exactly what you are, sure now,' Cooney said, letting a smile crease his face. 'That's what they all think, isn't it?'

'Just as long as they think it, and you don't take any ideas to yourself,' Bridget said in a warning tone. She rose from the table, and crossed the shady room to the cooker and turned the heat on under the big aluminium kettle.

'And what sort of ideas would they be?'

'Ideas above your station,' Bridget said. 'Sure Padraigh would have both your knees off if he thought you were getting ideas like that, wouldn't he now?'

She crossed the room again, this time coming round to his side of the table. She leaned forward and put her arms round the seated man's neck. She could smell the warm man-scent from his hair.

'Well, he's not likely to think that, is he?' Cooney said.

She leaned into him, the swell of her breasts warm against the short hair on his neck.

'I hope he doesn't. Not while he's still got the franchise for Black and Decker in Belfast.'

Cooney laughed out loud and she squeezed forward against the shaking motions. Bridget was twenty-three years old and her brother Padraigh Massey was a powerful man in Ulster, with contacts in every town in the Province and the Republic.

'Do you think he'd not understand, then?'

'Oh, he might understand, but he doesn't like anybody messing about with his wee sister. He's got the notion that I'm still a convent girl who's never been kissed yet.'

'And we both know different to that,' Cooney said, and laughed

71

again, snuggling his head closer. She leaned over and kissed his brow softly.

'But we'll have to tell him sometime.'

'Aye. If you think of a way.'

'If he's that bad about it, why did he let you come down here with me? He knew we would be cooped up for long enough.'

'I told you, he thinks I'm the innocent. I was in the Legion of Mary, and girls like me don't have anything to do with the likes of you.'

'Sure you don't,' Cooney said with heavy sarcasm. 'And what have you been doing for the last five days?'

'Just passing the time, that's all I've been doing,' she said. 'Sure you never thought I'd fallen for you now, did you?'

'Never crossed my mind for a moment,' he said, reaching up with one hand to slide his fingers into her dark brown hair, cascading over his brow. He raised his face and pulled hers towards him. She nuzzled close and their lips met fleetingly at first before she pressed hard onto his mouth. She moved around the chair and slid a leg over his knee until she was straddling him.

'Cooney, you're a bastard,' she said huskily, when they finally broke away.

'Too many compliments,' he said. 'How's a man to get through the day.'

'I still don't like it here.'

'There's nothing for it, now, is there? O'Farrell will be arriving any day now, and we have to sit nice and quiet until he gets here.'

She shifted position on his knees, grinding herself into him. 'I'd hardly call this sitting quiet.'

'It's not my fault you're a noisy bitch,' he said with a smug grin, and she threw back her head and laughed out loud.

'Padraigh would kill you for that.'

'I'm not so easy to kill,' he said.

Bridget snuggled into him again, arching her back to press her breasts against him just under his throat.

'I don't know about that,' she said, forcing her mouth once more onto his. He felt her small tongue slip between his lips, writhing against his own: the warmth of her body; the pressure inside himself rising higher.

She pulled back again after a while and licked her lips hungrily.

'If that's going to kill me, you can carry on until I drop,' Cooney said, staring hotly into her dark brown eyes.

'I've got other ways,' she said.

'I'll bet you have, an' all.'

'Yes, like this.' Bridget reached down between them and her hand came up with the gun that had been jammed into the shoulder holster slung on the back of the chair. With a quick motion of her hand she pulled back the lever on the short barrel. It gave a metallic double click as a round was fed into the chamber and then a harsh clunk as she cocked it. She held it steadily and moved it up close to his face. His eyes nearly crossed as they tried to peer down the black hole of the barrel.

'Bridie, what the devil are you doing with that thing?'

'I thought you said you were a hard man to kill.' A broad grin spread over her face. She had good, white teeth and lips that were red from their hard kiss. She pressed the barrel against his forehead. It felt cold on his brow.

'You could kill anybody with that,' he said quietly. 'Now would you put that thing down.'

'Only if you say you're sorry for calling me a bitch,' she said, still smiling.

'Never,' he said, staring up at her from under the gun.

'Not even with a gun at your head?'

'Not even with a Black and Decker at my kneecaps.'

She lowered the gun. The pressure had left a red circular mark on his forehead.

'Oh, you're a hard man to be dealing with,' she said, and slid the weapon into its holster. 'But you shouldn't leave that thing lying around where anybody can get their hands on it.'

'I need it for protection.'

'Who from?'

'From noisy bitches like yourself. Now come here and see what happens to girls who play with loaded guns.' He hugged her, hard, feeling again the warmth of her body pressing into him. Still holding her tightly, he slid down to the rug on the floor and clamped his mouth onto hers. She slid her hand round behind him and started hauling his shirt from where it was tucked into his waistband. He could hear her breathing come suddenly fast and heavy. He reached his own hand up under her lambswool sweater and felt the hot smooth skin.

On the far side of the room, the kettle boiled and the whistle began to sing. As the pressure built up, the sound spiralled up and up until it was a piercing screech.

On the floor, Bridget Massey and Brian Cooney never heard it.

A few minutes later, the whistle, forced off the short spout, clattered to the floor with a tinny rattle. Clouds of steam billowed out and immediately began to condense on the windows, fogging them down.

Water vapour gently drifted onto the bare skin of the two people on the floor and mingled, unnoticed, with the perspiration that coated their bodies. Eventually the water in the kettle boiled away and the aluminium base began to glow.

Across the other side of the encirclement of cottages, another curtain moved very slowly back to its original position. The movement was so gentle that from the outside it would never have been noticed.

'Tell me,' demanded the man seated at the table.

The man at the window moved forward a step. From where he stood, the small space between the curtain and the window frame afforded him a fairly wide field of vision across the sward of green in the centre of the meadow to the cottages opposite. To the right, beyond the stand of trees, was the tor. He could see the group of figures gathering near the entrance to the tunnel.

'Nothing much. The dirty diggers are doing their stuff. The newcomers are with them.'

'The Americans?'

'Yes, both of them.'

'What do you think?'

'The Yanks?'

'Yes. What's their story?'

The stocky man at the window shrugged. He was wearing a pair of moleskin trousers and a much newer version of the battle-scarred and scratched coat that Sean McCullain wore, the accepted uniform of all outdoorsmen from photographers to gamekeepers and foresters.

Hugh Sands slipped it off and slung it over the back of a chair.

'They're just youngsters,' he said. 'No threat.'

'I expect you're right,' Edward Laird agreed. 'Couple of tourists, I should think. There's not much happening around here.'

'Not much except for them across the way.'

'That just makes it easier for us.'

Sands sat himself down at the table and looked at the electronic bits and pieces scattered on a couple of sheets of newspaper.

'I hope you can put that back together again,' he said.

'If I can't we're both up shit creek with no way to call for help.'

'What's wrong with it?'

'Nothing that should have been there before it left ordance, that's for certain. Loose connection on the aeriel, I think. Bit of solder should do it.' Laird had a trace of an east-coast Scottish accent that had been weathered down into London neutral by long immersion.

The two men were at ease, relaxed and obviously used to each other's company.

'How about our friends across the way?'

'Nothing to report,' Sands said dismissively. 'I took a hike along the back of the road and down towards the shore. They've been in all morning and it looks as if they plan to stay.'

'Lucky old them.' Laird brought the delicate tip of the soldering iron against the base of a small wire which he was holding against a contact. He touched the point lightly, using the small finger of his left hand to guide the fine wire on the join. There was a faint hiss and a greasy whiff of flux. Where the tip had touched, a small point of silver solder shot back the light of the lamp on the table.

'She's some piece of stuff. Pity about the family connection.'

'I'd rather have her than her brother, that's for sure.' Laird began to reassemble the radio parts. It looked complex, but he worked quickly, almost automatically, using a fine jeweller's screwdriver. Sands looked on approvingly.

'You reckon anything's going down? We've got nothing on either of them so far, apart from the Massey connection and the fact that they're a long way from home.'

'I don't know if it's "going down" or not,' Laird retorted. 'And since when did you become a damned Yank anyway? You'll be asking for a furlough next.'

He looked up at Sands. 'They've been tailing that Provo bastard Massey for months. He's a clever shit, but you'd expect that from one of their commanders. Everybody knows he's got something on somebody inside and turning the screw for anything he can get. We'll get him one of these days. Meanwhile we've got his sister down here with somebody her brother would normally let nowhere near her unless we're truly mistaken. So we sit, and we wait.'

'I don't trust any of these shits, even if they haven't got any form,' Sands said.

'They've *all* got form. They're Irish, aren't they? Every one of them's up to their armpits in it, but that's not the point. Cooney's just small beer, a message carrier at most. Never goes anywhere. This is his first trip, and it's hers as well. Paddy Massey normally has her wrapped in cotton wool and won't let anybody near her. So, they wonder, why the hell is she down here on the edge of the great beyond, pretending to be Mrs Cooney?'

'Could be the real thing.'

'Could be. Maybe even Massey has put the word out to have her found and hauled back. Then the bold Brian can look forward to a pair of National Health crutches.'

'Private crutches, I should think. There's nothing left of the Welfare State.'

Laird snapped the casing back onto the radio with a forceful click. He lifted his eyes and looked across the table at Sands. 'No Welfare State? Don't tell me you're going bolshie on me?'

'Who needs it, anyway. We shoot 'em and they patch 'em up. We're costing the country millions.'

'That's politics. They never taught us that. Ours is not to reason why.'

'Thank God for that.'

Laird hefted the heavy green radio and turned it to face him. He thumbed the black button on the side and a faint hiss of static sprayed out of the metal grille near the top. He put it to his ear.

'Shamrock waiting for Arthur,' he said quietly. There was another hiss, then a small burp of a connection.

'Arthur at home,' came a clipped voice, very loud in the room. Laird immediately turned the dial and the voice faded down to a whisper.

'Just a check call. Had a problem with the aerial. Seems to be fixed now.'

'Roger, Shamrock. Story to tell?'

'No, all quiet. We'll recheck at eighteen hundred.'

'Carry on, boys. Talk to you later.'

The tinny voice said over and out and Laird responded in like manner.

'Wonders of modern technology. That's nearly a thousand miles, and we're fifty from the nearest pick-up. Came in clear as a bell.'

'Pity they don't make them right in the first place,' Sands said. He shoved his chair back from the table and got to his feet, walking towards the dresser to pick up a large book.

'Fascinating stuff this,' he said. 'I never knew there were so many birds. It's not bad cover. I'm beginning to enjoy it. You know, I thought I saw an avocet down on the flats. And there was a heron. I even got a picture of it.'

'That's the stuff,' Laird said. 'As long as you can hold your own with all the other bloody birdwatchers around here, we'll fit like a glove. And if we get good at it, there's always something to look forward to when we retire. I wonder if Attenborough needs any help.'

'I don't think he'd let us near his wildlife,' Sands said. 'You know what it's like.'

Laird raised his eyebrows in question. 'What's that?'

'Well, it's all that basic training. Letting your instincts take over, and all that sort of thing.'

Laird nodded. 'What about it?'

'It's just that when I see something move, all that training comes to the fore, and my instincts make me want to . . .'

He swivelled in his seat and his hand darted behind him, whipping back up blurringly fast. In it his long-barrelled black gun reflected the light from the lamp as he swung it right up into the air.

'. . . blow its fucking Fenian head off!'

12

Agnes Finnegan and Theresa Laughlin were working on the far side of the bare ground where small pine pegs, joined by lengths of twine, marked the lines of the old workings. The turf had been peeled back, revealing red earth. Between the twine-paths, the dirt had been carefully scraped away and the underlying gravel had been meticulously sifted for the ancient scraps of refuse left by the builders that would give clues to who they were and when they had built the tomb.

When Terry Munster came stumbling out of the tunnel mouth, both of them had looked up to see what was happening. Like the others, they had heard the muffled crash of falling rocks and felt the slight tremor in the ground under their knees.

Connarty and Siobhan Kane, joined by a curious Tom and Nancy Ducain, walked across the bare patch to where Terry was standing, legs splayed, hands on his knees, bent to cough the dust out of his lungs. In the grey light of the overcast day, he felt a little bit foolish. Down in the dark of the tunnel, his eyes had seen shadows and his mind had played tricks with them. He thought he'd seen a pair of arms reach out for him, but *that* was impossible. Ridiculous.

Still, it had given him a fright. He was glad of the coughing fit, which disguised the fear and the subsequent embarrassment and obviated the need for any explanation.

'Are you all right, Terry?' Connarty asked jovially when he reached him. He put his hand out and clapped the young man heartily on the back. Terry coughed some more and then straightened up.

'Found the end,' he said in a voice that was tight from the coughing spasms. 'There's a wall.'

'Oh, good man. You hear that?' he called across to Agnes and Theresa, who were already making their way up the dug-out path towards them. 'Terry's got to the end of the infill. We're just about there.'

'There's something wrong with the lights,' Terry said, now past his coughing fit. 'They were flickering on and off, and then they failed altogether.'

'We'll have a look at the generator later,' Connarty said. 'But first I want to see that wall of yours. Come on, Terry. You've done all the hard work, you can show us all.'

The young man turned and led the way back to the passageway.

The rectangular entrance was a flat black space in the side of the hill. The gateway looked solid, shaped and crafted from pure darkness.

Connarty went in first, followed by Terry and Siobhan. The rest tagged along in single file. There was barely enough room for two people to pass, as Terry had discovered with the wheelbarrow, which had shafts almost wide enough to touch each side. He had scraped his knuckles many a time as he trundled the rubble from the far end to the outside.

'Watch your feet,' he called to Connarty, striding boldly ahead. 'There's a lot of rubble underfoot.' His voice echoed down the narrow confines, giving it an eerie, reverberating quality. Despite his fright in the tunnel earlier, there was no alarm now. Perhaps the safety of numbers did that, but Terry, solid and stolid when it came to archaeological matters, had dismissed his fear. He had worked in too many tombs and was too good at his job to be bothered for long by flights of fancy.

There was a yelp from up ahead and a muted curse which was amplified by the acoustics in the passageway. 'I just barked my damned shin on your bloody barrow,' the professor said tightly. Even in the dim light of the bulb which was now coated in dust, Connarty was just a shadow. Everyone could hear his voice grating through gritted teeth. The professor was limping and trying to rub his shin at the same time. It was an awkward little dance that made Terry and Siobhan smile to themselves. For all their affection and admiration for Dr Connarty, he could be a mite pompous, and it was at times like this that he got a certain comeuppance. He finally stopped jigging and straightened up. From his breast pocket he whipped out a handkerchief and flicked it across the light-bulb, scattering the dust. In the passage, the light immediately glowed brighter.

'Now what have we here?' he said.

Terry stepped forward and angled the light on its hook to show where the rubble had peeled away.

'There it is,' he said simply.

'And so it is,' Connarty said. 'Look here, Siobhan. Look at this workmanship.'

She crowded close to the professor, then reached forward to peer at the wall. The interlocking stones were black and smooth and looked as though they had been cut only the day before.

'I've never seen anything to match this,' Siobhan said. 'It's terrific. If this is the entrance to the chamber, then it's the most finely crafted I've

79

ever seen. You could be right, Jim. This looks good.' She studied the wall. The square-cut stones were perfectly preserved. Some of them were still coated with gravel from the infill, but higher up, above head-height, was a lintel that spanned the passageway, heavy and massive. She craned her head, squinting in the low light to peer at it. 'There's more carvings there.' She reached up to touch the stone lintel. Her outstretched fingers moved slowly towards the surface, working forward, tentatively inching their way. A fingertip brushed lightly against the smooth face.

A small shock ran through her, a thrill of vibration that sparked from the stone to her fingertip and rushed up her arm. It was as if she'd touched a live electric wire.

'Oh,' she said, in a small, startled gasp.

Immediately the light-bulb brightened and just as quickly faded. There were two pulses, and the power drained out of the filament, fading from yellow through orange to a dull red.

'What's happening?' Agnes called from the back. There was no room in the passage for her to see past the press of bodies.

Siobhan did not hear Agnes's call. She stood, rock still, with her hand still out and upstretched against the stone. The thrill was sizzling painlessly up and down her arm, shuddering through her nerves. She could feel the skin tighten and the fine fair matte of silky hairs on her forearms rise like hackles.

From somewhere nearby, a voice asked: 'Are you all right, Siobhan?' but she heard nothing. The little hot surges seemed to *weld* her hand to the stone, pulsing a strange energy into and through her in bursts of fire. The tunnel went black and Siobhan could *see* the rivulets of weird blue flashes pulse from the wall into her fingers. It was as if it flowed into her veins and lit them all up from the inside so that she could see *through* her own skin and watch the play of energy.

Then inside her head she heard a voice. No – not a voice, just a *presence*, a feeling of something *else*. It came so swiftly and so darkly that Siobhan was caught unawares, her attention focused tightly on the energy running through her and into the stone lintel.

In a split second, she was overwhelmed by an intense feeling of pure *dread*. There was no other way to describe it. It was as if she was abruptly smothered in dark, pure-black, *terrible* darkness.

'Oh,' she said again, in a little gasp.

Inside her mind the wave of darkness blotted out all other sensation. It came like a deep cloak of depression that enveloped her in folds, and in it was a terrible threat. She could *feel* it pressing down on her, a vast barren anger aimed directly into her mind. The force of it was immense.

Then, instantly, the darkness cleared and she could see again.

But she was alone.

Connarty and Terry Munster and the two Americans were *gone*. They had vanished as if they had never been there.

And *here* was not where Siobhan had stood with her hand against the wall. She was somewhere else. It was strange, yet familiar. She tried to puzzle it out, but it wouldn't come to her. She was standing in a gloomy place, although she could not feel her body. All around her was cold, deep and penetrating, and beyond that, sound. A strange noise, something she had never heard before.

A blank stone wall encircled her, and the noise was coming from behind the wall. She moved slowly towards it, though she knew her feet did not walk her there. She listened, hearing the dull beat of her own heart and the strange, gasping noises that were muted and muffled behind the stone. There was a man there. She *knew* it. She could sense his presence: she could hear the deep, desperate whoop of a man gasping for breath, a man choking slowly to death. How she knew, she did not understand. The sound grew louder and louder, filling her ears, and she could feel her own breath back up as her throat tightened.

The deathly gasping continued, loud and frantic. She could picture a chest heaving and lungs bellowing and a mouth opening and closing to snatch at air. She could sense eyes rolling wildly and a head swinging from side to side as consciousness faded. She reached out her hand to touch the stone, to find out *where* the trapped man was . . .

. . . and suddenly she was back in the tunnel again.

'Are you all right, Siobhan?' Dr Connarty's voice came out of the gloom. 'Is there something wrong?'

Reality snapped back again and Siobhan found herself standing with her hand pressed up high against the lintel. The light flickered again then blazed as brightly as before. She shook her head in a quick motion as if to clear it.

The dark feeling of oppression had simply *vanished*. There was no play of strange pulsed energy writhing in the veins of her arm. There was no rattled gasping.

'What's the matter?' Terry asked. He had seen Siobhan reach out and then freeze for no more than a few seconds.

Siobhan turned round and blinked bewildered eyes. 'What?'

'I thought there was something wrong,' he said.

She looked quickly from Terry to the professor, her mind off balance, trying to think. 'No, I'm fine. I was just feeling the stonework. You didn't see anything, did you?'

'Like what?' Connarty asked.

'Like . . .' Siobhan paused. The strangeness was gone completely and she was left with a feeling that she didn't know what to say. It was obvious from the expressions of the other two that they had seen nothing, and that meant her experience was completely subjective. Which also meant it hadn't happened.

'I thought I saw a movement.'

'It's just the shadows.'

'And the light flickered for a moment too.'

'The light? I never saw that. Did you, Terry?'

'No,' Terry said. He hadn't seen the light flicker, though when he'd been in the tunnel alone, he certainly *thought* he had seen it wane and fade out, but that was after he'd fallen over the barrow and had the breath socked from him.

'Trick of the light,' Siobhan said, putting as much normality into her voice as she could, though she was sure the shakiness was evident. Her legs felt weak and shaky too.

Connarty looked at her questioningly, but Siobhan shrugged. She reached out to touch the wall again and hesitated a fraction before her fingers connected. She didn't want to see that strange light again. Then she mentally drew herself together. *It had been a trick of the light, nothing more.*

She completed the motion. Her fingers brushed against the cold stone. It was dark and smooth and heavy with age. But it was just stone. Nothing happened. She drew her hand back again.

'Right, we'd better get this rubble cleared up and then we'll see what to do with the wall. Terry, it's going to need your expertise.'

'And my broad shoulders as well now, isn't it?'

'I rather think it does, Terry old fellow,' Connarty said, and he and the young man exchanged a laugh. Siobhan stood and watched them, but her mind wasn't with them.

Neither Sean nor Liz noticed the team working at the tor when they came down the track from the village.

At the hotel in Westport, Sean had got fair enough directions from Paul Convery and had arrived, much like the two young Americans, in the main street, not half a mile from the hump-backed bridge over the Roonah Water. It was getting into early evening when he found the turn past McGavigan's funeral parlour and nosed the estate car close to the crumbling wall of a derelict outhouse. Beyond that, an old hearse, long and black and dented, lay axle-deep in a nettle patch that was fading to the crinkly brown of autumn.

'That's their back up if they've got a big funeral,' Sean said. 'They take you out in style here.'

Liz looked at the battered old black car, with the long plate-glass window on its side starred at one end where some child had hefted a casual rock. It looked strange, sitting hunkered on bricks, a little shabby, a little forlorn, a little sinister.

'I wonder what they use now,' she said.

Sean eased the car past the nettle and brambles scraping the wheel arches. The track was pitted and slightly raised in the middle section that was unflattened by wheels.

'On these roads, probably black tractors. Nothing else will do.'

Liz smiled at the idea, though she didn't let him see it. 'Where are we going?' she asked, looking out at the narrow lane ahead. An overgrown hawthorn hedge trailed branches laden with heavy clumps of dark red berries that knocked on the slight breeze.

'Just down the way a bit,' Sean said. There was a slight lurch and a splash as the offside wheel dug into a puddle that filled one of the depressions. He changed down a gear. The engine whined as it took up the strain and hauled the car out and forward with a bump.

'I just hope it's got *en-suite*,' Liz said. 'I was up twice last night and couldn't find the bathroom.'

'Oh, it'll have everything. Paul said it's the best place to stay in the whole of the west coast.'

'What's it called?'

'What's what called?'

'The hotel. Does it have a name?'

'Probably,' Sean said vaguely. He spun the wheel manfully to steer round the bend, and a few yards further on he slowed to a halt outside the gate of a small crofthouse. Immediately two small dogs leapt up onto the low wall and started yelping in shrill voices at them. Sean got out of the car before Liz had a chance to say anything. She watched him cross to the gate. A short, dumpy woman with a weathered face and ruddy cheeks that told of hard, windy winters, came up the garden path. Liz saw the two of them speak for a few moments and then the woman went back to the house. Sean reached a hand out to pat one of the dogs, and Liz failed to suppress an involuntary laugh when the small terrier twisted its head swiftly and snapped at him. Even in the distance she could see its lips drawn back in a furious snarl. Sean just managed to snatch his hand away in time before he lost a finger, and he eyed the small dog with a thunderous expression that was every bit as threatening as the one the dog glared defiantly back.

The small woman returned, this time wearing a green, flapping coat. She pointed along the path and handed something to Sean, who nodded and came strolling back to the car.

'Are we nearly there?' Liz asked.

'Just about,' Sean said. 'It's just around the corner.'

'You'd have thought the hotel would have been in the village. What did they want to build it out here for? The town's in the middle of nowhere as it is.'

Sean shrugged and looked straight ahead as he put the car into gear and drove slowly in the direction the woman had indicated. They passed the low hedge of privet and went over a cattle grid that thrummed underneath them; and then, in front of them, they saw the cottages.

'Where the hell are we?' Liz demanded.

Sean kept driving round the semi-circular drive, until he came to the cottage that was second furthest in, close to the stand of scraggy elms.

'This is it,' he said, and hauled himself out of the car again. Liz said something, but the sound of the car door closing behind him cut her off. Immediately the passenger door opened and Liz launched herself out and faced him over the top of the car.

'What do you mean, "this is it"?'

'This is the place. Paul Convery fixed it up,' Sean said neutrally. He already had the tail-gate open and was hefting out his camera bag and the big aluminium process case.

'But where's the *hotel*?'

'There isn't one. We're staying here.'

Liz stood and stared at him, mouth agape, as he crossed from the car to the cottage and slid the key into the Yale lock. The door swung open and he bent to pick up the case, then walked inside. From where she stood, she saw a light come on, framing his silhouette, and then he disappeared.

Still speechless, she followed him. A peat fire glowed in the big hearth and a large, old-fashioned kettle was steaming gently on the range.

'Mrs Gilly says that everything is ready for us. The heating's been on for more than an hour, so there should be plenty of hot water.'

'Oh no, McCullain. I don't know what you're up to, but I'm not staying here. *No way.*'

'What's the problem?'

'Are you joking?'

He looked at her with that half-serious, half-quizzical look on his face which was so hard to read, but too easy to suspect. He simply shook his head and put his camera gear on the wide pine table.

'Nothing wrong with this place, and they'll even give you a blank receipt so you can fiddle your expenses.'

'You don't get the picture, do you, McCullain?' Liz said, eyes flashing blue anger. 'I'm not staying here. Not with you. I want a proper hotel with a decent restaurant and *separate* rooms.'

'Oh, is that what you're worried about? Well, don't be,' he said with an amiable grin. 'There's two rooms. You can have your pick.'

'You still don't understand. I don't want to be stuck out here in the middle of a field in the back of beyond with *you*. Now where's the bloody hotel?'

'There isn't one, not with any rooms, for thirty miles, and I can't be bothered with that.' He turned round to face her. 'Don't worry about it. You'll be perfectly safe.' He looked her up and down almost disdainfully. 'Perfectly safe.'

He turned away and she felt anger rising at the sheer calculated *nerve* of his measuring glance.

'All I want is to get something to eat, then something to drink, and then I want some sleep. If that's a problem, take the car and go along to the Tallabaun Inn. It's a waste of time, for they're shutting for the season and they haven't any rooms left open. Here, go on. Pick me up in the morning if you get fixed up.'

Sean reached into the pocket of his coat and brought out the keys. He slung them across to her and they looped, jingling and reflecting the peat-fire glow. She jerked out a hand, not quite quickly enough and the heavy key-ring rapped off her knuckle and the bunch spun to the floor with a clatter.

'Shit,' she said aloud. She bent down, scooped up the keys with a quick, angry movement and walked through the door. He heard the car open and then the slam of the driver's door closing. The engine turned, caught and roared throatily. Then it cut off again, and Sean smiled quietly to himself. By the time Liz appeared back in the cottage again, he had managed to wipe it off his face.

'Right, McCullain. I'm going to take your word for it,' she said harshly. She was standing, framed in the doorway, with the firelight casting a glow on her hair. Her chest was heaving with the burst of anger and her cheeks had reddened right up on either side of her eyes.

'Good old you,' Sean said, and immediately regretted it. He didn't want to challenge her. He really did want a meal and a drink – maybe three or four of them – and a good night's sleep. He hadn't had a *proper* night's sleep since before he had flown back to Belfast for the final trial. He was dead tired.

'What?' Liz demanded hotly.

'Good. I'm glad,' he backtracked. 'There's nothing wrong with this place. Better than some of the hotels. Look around.' Liz came in and went through the room to the kitchen, glancing around, inspecting the place. While she did, Sean went out and got her bags from the car, and his own big rucksack that he took everywhere.

When he came back inside, Liz was back in the wide living room.

'It's all right,' she said. 'Better than it looks from the outside.'

'That's what Paul Convery said. They were only built last year. All mod cons.'

'I'll take the bedroom to the right,' she said.

'Good. I'll have the other one.'

'And remember, McCullain, I sleep alone.'

Sean stopped in the act of dumping his rucksack onto a chair. He turned towards her. 'What was that?'

'I don't want any funny business from you. No midnight walkies.'

'Don't flatter yourself, girl,' Sean came back quickly, and his brows gathered down so hard his eyes were hidden in the thundery shadows underneath. 'You just remember that I never asked for this job, and as soon as I get Robertson, I'll be off like a ferret up a roanpipe. You wanted to come here and write your crap and I just got roped in. So don't *you* get any ideas on that score.'

He slung the bag down and thumped it onto the table. He turned and threw her such a black glare that she flinched, before he spun on his heel and went into the small passageway that led to the bedrooms. She stood there for a few moments, still hot with anger but also feeling more than a little foolish. In the past two days McCullain had impressed her as being a little strange, a shade weary and a lot cynical. He obviously knew his business and he had a huge reputation. But he never once looked at her the way a man looks at a woman. That thought struck her in an odd slant that carried more regret in it than she would have cared to admit.

The picture of his black, thunderous brows knitting together over his grey eyes stayed at the forefront of her mind. He was a big, almost craggy man, and probably tough as old boots. Not for the first time, she thought with a decent haircut and a smile on his face, he could be one good-looking guy.

She shied away from that thought. *Could be* if he wasn't such a damned supercilious *bastard*.

She leaned over the table and fumbled with the catches on her bags, feeling that she had made a bit of a fool of herself. It didn't matter where they stayed. She was a news reporter. She was a journalist. She could take care of herself.

It was just that McCullain was a pompous shit who looked down his nose at her because she was a newcomer. Angry tears of resentment sparked at the back of her eyes and she blinked them back peevishly. She rummaged in her bag and started hauling her overnight clothes out.

From down the passageway came the sound of running water. He was obviously having a shower, and that was good. It saved any awkwardness later.

A few moments later, she heard his deep voice, muffled by the closed door and the running water. He was humming or singing a tune. She couldn't make it out, but he was definitely singing something. He had obviously forgotten her outburst – and his – of a few moments before.

13

The work of prising the stone blocks aside with a three-foot steel crowbar fell naturally to Terry Munster, though everybody mucked in to help clear the rubble. It was tight and sweaty, working in the narrow passage, but even Dr Connarty got his sleeves rolled up and heaved stone with the rest of them. When it was cleared, Terry got to work with the wedge, angling the flattened point with difficulty between the fine cracks, forcing his weight against the metal this way and that until the stone started to move.

It took less time than anybody expected. There was no mortar holding the squares of stone in place, only the compression and the fact that they had been cut so expertly that they locked onto one another to keep the wall intact. When the first stone moved, it did so with a gritty groan, reluctant to shift from the position it had held for fifty centuries.

It gave up its grip a millimetre at a time, with Terry straining hard enough to bring a sweat to his brow. Dr Connarty took a hand after fifteen minutes or so when the centre stone had been squeezed out an inch or more and his exertions persuaded it to move even further. Ten minutes later there was a screech of stone on rock and the first square fell away, tumbling with a crash onto the hard floor.

'You beauty!' Terry exclaimed excitedly. His words reverberated up the passageway, bouncing off the flagstones, giving his voice an odd, phased, out-of-sync sound. In front of him a small puff of dark dust billowed out from the hole.

Dr Connarty got to his knees and pulled the flashlight from his pocket. He edged his head against the hole, and as he did so, Terry had a sudden replay of his strange experience of only a few hours before, when the shadows had seemed like hands reaching out from the wall. The image came back in such detail that he almost reached out in alarm to drag the professor back from the gaping black square.

But then Connarty flicked on the light. The beam pierced the fine cloud of dust, catching the motes and setting them twinkling in the narrow cone of light.

'Oh, yes, Terry,' Connarty said, and the excitement in his voice was plain and undisguised. 'It's the chamber all right. And it's damned *big*.'

'Can you see anything?'

'There's something in the centre, but it's dark, and the light can't carry far enough. We'll have to take the rest of the wall down.'

Connarty peered into the space. The light reflected off his polygon frames and made his eyes glint. He shifted the flashlight beam this way and that, but there was little detail to be seen. He got to his feet and handed the light to Terry.

'Here, you made the breakthrough. Take a look at something nobody has seen for five thousand years. You're part of history now, young friend.'

Terry hunkered down and edged close to the hole. He raised the torch and angled it between the stones, squeezing forward as far as he could go until his chin was resting on the masonry. Ahead of him the beam flitted ghostlike across a faraway wall. He shifted its position and followed the light. There was something there in the centre of the chamber.

The light caught the shape and moved on, almost of its own volition. Terry brought it back again and played the beam over a dark shape. It was squat and massive, squared off, though slightly flattened. He couldn't make out what it was, because when he shone the flashlight on it, the beam seemed to fade, as if it was being drawn right *into* it.

'You see anything yourself?'

'I'm not sure. There's something in the centre, but the light's not strong enough. It could be some kind of sarcophagus. It's big, anyway.'

'Just what we've been hoping for, my boy. I don't think there's any point in waiting. We should get this wall down now.'

Terry stayed hunkered in front of the small space, still playing the torch beam over the dark mass in what appeared to be the centre of the chamber. The thing still seemed to swallow the light. No matter how much he directed the beam onto it, it cast back no real reflection. It was dead, flat black, like a hole in space.

But it fascinated the young archaeologist. He couldn't draw his eyes away from it. It was like a *presence*, squatting there in the tomb. He could *feel* it sitting there, dark and somehow threatening.

Just as that thought came to him, he remembered what he had imagined when he was down in the tunnel alone and the rock infill had slid off the face and nearly crumpled him flat under the barrow. He had seen – or thought he had seen – *through* the wall itself. And he had envisioned a great, squat stone lying in the centre of an empty chamber. It was the stone that had seemed alive with shadows – shadows that reached out, sending arms of pure darkness stretching towards him and grasping for him.

In his mind's eye he replayed that scene as the torchlight tried to pinion the dark shape and merely succeeded in sliding past it and round it, making the ponderous mass more mysterious, more eerie.

Terry had never had that feeling in a tomb before, and as an archaeologist in Ireland, he had visited and worked in hundreds of them. There were hundreds more he had still to explore. But in each of the ones he had seen, he had only found a sense of history, a wonderful feeling of continuity through the ages, from prehistoric times to the present. He had seen the tombs not as places of the dead, but as centres where the living could communicate with the spirit of people of long ago.

Here there was something *different*.

As he knelt there in the cold passage, another cold sensation stole through him. Watching the beam from the torch fail to cast any light on the thing that sat there in the chamber gave him a shivering feeling of *wrongness*.

The more he stared at it, the stronger the feeling became. Inside he could feel his heart speed up and his breath quicken, though he knew his fears were groundless. This sensation of doing something terribly *wrong* came from deep down within him. It was a cold anxiety that shuttled through him inexplicably, and try as he might to force it down, it refused to go away.

The thought came to him, very suddenly, very forcefully, that he wished he hadn't moved that stone in the wall. For an instant he wanted to heave it up from the ground, jam it back in the space and shut in for ever whatever it was in the chamber that sent scaly fingers of fear trickling up his spine. It was as if he could put back the stone and close over the box that he opened. He was filled with a morbid dread that he had unlocked something *black*, and that only bad things would come of it.

Terry gave his head a little shake. It was silliness, he told himself crossly. He stood up and gave the torch to Dr Connarty. The professor did not notice the odd look on the young man's face. He was still aglow from the final discovery of the central chamber of the tomb.

'Nonsense,' Terry told himself, not realising he spoke the words aloud.

'What's that?' Connarty asked.

'Nothing,' Terry said quietly. 'Right, let's get to it,' he added, bending down to pick up the jemmy.

Finn Finnerty was a giant of a man, as his father had been before him, in contrast to his wife Miread who was built like a sparrow, a tiny, deceptively delicate-seeming woman. The difference had always caused a great deal of crude but good-humoured rustic speculation about how they managed what they obviously had done, since they were gifted with a pair of round-faced twin boys who looked set to grow to their father's size.

Finn was a simple farmer. He was big and grizzled and had a long lugubrious face that would spontaneously crease itself into a wide, humorous smile. He had hands like shovels, gnarled and calloused from digging and ploughing.

On the day that Terry Munster finally found the wall, Finn was in the north field digging up the late potato crop. It had not been a bad year so far. The swedes were high and fattening well, good feed for the sheep over the winter, and the barley had come in full and heavy after some worry about late rains that held back long enough to see the crop ripen. In the field that was bordered by a scraggy thorn hedge – the one that separated Finn's lot from the piece of land where the university folk were wasting time (*he thought*) in digging a hole in the tor, for no crop result – Finn had worked since first light, with only a short break for his midday meal.

The potatoes were coming up easily and steadily. The shaws were tall, their white flowers had just died off, and the seed heads were beginning to swell. Each plant was yielding a full harvest: big, white potatoes, eight or ten to a shaw. Baskets punctuated the ploughlines close to the hedge, and Finn had one strapped to his back. The previous months he'd got some of the youngsters in the village to howk up, but the latest crop was one he could bring in himself from the small field; enough to see him and the family over the winter and through the spring, and some left over for trade.

In the late afternoon, with shadows lengthening, Finn straightened his back and let out a sigh as the muscles unlocked and eased off. Tonight there would be a warm bath and then a couple of well-earned pints of Guinness down at the pub, after he'd read the twins their story, and with his big hands tucked them up in their bed in the attic.

Out in the west, the sun was sliding down towards the sea. Finn couldn't see it, for there were big clouds rolling in, but there was enough of a glow in the sky to shine through and give him a rough idea.

Ten baskets, filled to the brim, sat in a line close to the hedge. Finn filled the last on his back and trudged up the furrows, feeling the wet earth clog the cleats of his massive black boots, almost doubling their weight. But it felt *good*, carrying the land he worked along with him.

Up at the scraggly hedge, he unshouldered the wicker basket and set

91

it down with the rest before sitting himself down on the nearest one and pulling his rag out to wipe his brow where the dusty sweat had gathered under the brim of his hat. The crop *was* good, and the best thing about it would be the first boiling of potatoes straight out of the ground and simmered on the range to be eaten with his own butter on a heaped plate. He could feel the sides of his tongue trickle and tickle at the thought of it. With a sigh of good feeling, he pulled his cigarettes from his pocket, lit one and inhaled. Finn never smoked until most of the day's work was done, and he felt he deserved this one.

The shadows lengthened perceptibly as he sat and smoked. There was a stronger breeze blowing now, welcome and cool as it fluttered the neckerchief he wore tucked into his shirt, and the clouds were piling up darker, shading out the dying light. Finn flicked the last of his cigarette into the hedge, watching the small red fire tumble into the shadow, and heaved himself to his feet. The tractor was down at the far end, next to the gate, and he trudged towards it. It was an ancient grey and rust one, with a smoke stack that towered over the cab and then jinked at an odd angle where it had clipped the lintel of the barn door. Finn started the engine and was surprised that it coughed into life first time. It juddered once then jerked itself out of the rut, and he steered it along the edge of the field with the trailer rattling and bouncing behind.

He got to the far end and parked in the middle of the line of baskets, then got down to finish off the work. Each basket had two handles, one at the rim and the other near the base, to make the cumbersome weight easier to manage. Even for a man of Finn's stature it was heavy going, but he'd done it all of his life, and a dozen of them were nothing to worry about. He worked stolidly until there was space on the flatbed for only one more. This one was at the far end and he had to trudge the thirty yards to where it stood alone, a low shadow in the corner.

When he reached it, the big bank of clouds had built up until it was nearly dark. In at the intersection of the two hedgerows, it *was* dark. Just as he bent down to heave the last one to his shoulders, he heard a sound close by. He stopped and straightened up. There was a rustling in there at the tangled base of the hedge, the noise a blackbird makes when it scours for grubs.Finn grinned, picked up a small sod of earth in his big hand and chucked it casually into the hedge where the sound came from. He'd expected a bird to go squawking in alarm out of the other side with an indignant flurry of wings, but there was only silence. Then just as he turned for the big heave, the rustling came back, this time louder. Further along the hedgerow, there was another noise, like something scuttling among the dried bramble runners. Finn stopped again to listen.

Closer in, there was a movement. He could see the brambles and willowherb shiver as something moved them aside. Immediately he thought it might be a cat, or even a fox after the chickens which roosted in the small coop close to the croft-house. The passage of whatever it was continued, and further along, there was another movement, and then another. The rustling sound came louder, unseen things moving in the deep shadows. Finn stooped and picked up a handful of hard pieces of earth and slung them in, one after the other, aiming at different places. The clay rattled through the bracken and briars with heavy cracks. The sounds stopped, but there was no noise of animals scurrying in flight.

Quizzically the big man strode up to the hedge and tried to peer inside. He could see nothing, and he assumed that whatever had made the scuttling noise had gone.

No sooner had he turned to the last basket than the noises started up again, but now there were more of them. They came from all along the shadowed base of the hedge where the edge-plants crowded and tangled round each other.

'What the devil is it?' he muttered to himself. He turned back to the hedge and was about to peer in again, when there was a movement right in front of him. The fronds shivered and crackled with the weight of something that forced them outwards. Finn stood back.

Out of the shadows a big toad lumbered, fat and warty, onto the trampled earth. Finn took a step back, surprised but not alarmed.

He had seen plenty of toads before, but this one was *huge*. It sat there, squat and bloated. Behind it came more rustling and another one made its ponderous way through the autumn undergrowth. It was even bigger than the first, at least as big across as Finn's calloused hand. It hunched in the dying daylight, just at the edge of the shadow, fat forearms tucked down and pointing inwards against its swollen, pulsing belly. Finn moved, and the toad cocked its head in a quick jerk, fixing him with a beady yellow eye.

'My, you're a big pair of ugly creatures.' Finn eyed them warily. Toads were among the few creatures he would rather not see in his way. He wouldn't have touched one of them for anything; for sure, didn't everybody know they were poisonous buggers. But he was farmer enough to know that they ate a lot of the things that ate a lot of what he grew, and that was good enough to leave them alone. The very sight of them, though, disgusted him. There was something nasty and diseased-looking about toads that repelled even a big simple countryman like Finn, who could spend half the night with his hand up the rear end of a cow, covered in blood and shite, and think nothing of it. Toads were on a par with the maggots that would squirm out of the carcass of a sheep up on the moor, and on the same level as devil's coachmen that would twist their ugly, shiny black bodies to squirt poison at you. There was something dark and witchy about them all.

Finn took a step back, mystery solved. He didn't like to kill the toads, horrible disgusting things though they were; as everybody knew, it brought you bad luck.

There was another rustle and a third toad crawled out on fat legs, shoving its way past a clump of dry cow-parsley that crackled and split under the pressure. This toad was even larger than the other two, big as a rat and blistered with dark, soft-looking lumps that covered its back. A few yards along the hedgerow, another one lolloped out from the undergrowth, and beside it another, then another. It seemed the whole line of thornbushes was *alive* with the ugly things.

The farmer took a couple of steps backwards into the freshly dug patch, a vague feeling of unease creeping up on him. He had never seen the creatures in such numbers, not even in the spring, when they came down out from under stones and logs and gathered in the slick pools at the reed-beds alongside the Roonah to slither and clasp each other and send out their jelly-strings of eggs. At this time of year, they should be back under the logs, slowing their sluggish heartbeats for the winter hibernation. What brought them out into the open, so big and fat and poisonous-looking, was a mystery.

They came crawling and scuttling and hobbling over the boulder-sized lumps of clay, seemingly unafraid. Finn felt a shiver of disgust at the sight of them. He turned and bent to pick up the last basket of potatoes. When he grabbed at the base handle, his big fingers clenched on something soft and cold and yielding. He completed the grasping movement before he was even aware of what had happened, and the motion of heaving the basket upwards pressed the big amphibian hard against the wooden handle. The pressure of Finn's exertion squashed the thing's stomach flat. It bulged out on either side and suddenly burst with a pulpy popping sound. Finn's hand jerked back in a reflex, and the toad's intestines, mashed between his hand and the wooden loop, splattered all over his fingers, dripping in a slimy trail to the ground.

'*Jeesus!*' he exclaimed feelingly. His hand was covered in a slick, greasy mess. He held it up and felt an oily wave of disgust wash through him. The broken, squashed body of the toad lay on the ground, deflated. Its back legs were moving slowly as if it was *still* trying to crawl away, as if there were some dark life driving it onwards. Finn flicked his hand violently, and specks of the toad's insides flew off. He wiped the palm on a fallen potato shaw and then went back to the basket. This time he checked first. There was no toad under the handle. He braced his feet and hefted the weight up onto his back and strode off towards the tractor. Behind him, around him, in the shadows he could hear the soft scuttlings of fat amphibians still coming out of the hedge.

He reached the trailer and slung the last basket aboard, then walked round the side towards the tractor. Only a few feet away, his big ploughman's boot came down and squashed another toad into the ground. Again there was a squelching sound as it burst asunder.

'Shite,' he said, automatically turning to kick his boot against the big treads of the rear wheel to shake off the mess. Shaking his head, he climbed up onto the driver's seat and started the engine. He wheeled the old tractor in a circle and brought it trundling back towards the gate. Just at the edge of the hedge, he looked back to check that the baskets were still fixed in place on the flatbed. Sometimes one of them would roll over and give him ten minutes' extra work, but they were all standing tightly wedged together. He turned back, and then something jarred at his consciousness. He did a double-take that almost cricked his neck. There, on the nearest basket, a huge warty toad sat right on top of the new-dug potatoes. He jammed his foot on the brake and swivelled round in his seat. It wasn't just one toad. There were two of them, sitting there, hunkered on the top of the overfilled basket, just staring at him. There was a movement, and a third clambered up on top of another pile.

The vague unease that had crept through Finn Finnerty expanded into a strange feeling that was close to fear. Toads were poisonous night things. He didn't want them clambering all over his crop, infecting them with whatever they carried in the soft lumps on their skins. He put the gear into neutral, leaving the engine chugging, leapt out of the saddle-seat, strode quickly back to the trailer and hauled himself aboard. There were dozens of the things, humping and crawling over and between the baskets. Finn hated to touch the creatures, but there was nothing for it. He reached out quickly and grabbed the nearest one. Its skin was clammy and cold, and as his fingers clenched on it, he could feel the bobbly lumps on its back give way. He felt a slimy wetness oozing on the skin of his hand. Even as he lifted the bloated thing, it twisted in his hand. Its mouth opened in a wide toothless gape and came down with a snap on his knuckle. It wasn't that painful, but the actual fact of it, a toad biting him, was enough to make him pull his arm back in alarm. His fingers jerked open and the toad went flying into the shadows.

Finn reached for another one, his hand shooting out and hooking it off the potatoes in a snakelike motion, so as to actually *hold* the thing for as little time as possible. The toad went spinning off towards the hedge. He turned to the next, and then his heart did a terrible little *flip* inside him. The horrible thing, this one much bigger than a rat, was oozing slime from its skin onto his crop. He felt his stomach lurch at the thought of it, and with a strangled gasp he shot his hand out to flick the toad right off. As he did so, the creature moved a fraction and Finn's fingers went into the pile of potatoes. But instead of rapping hard against the tough tubers, the fingers just *sank* into them.

Now scared and very puzzled, his interest was diverted from the toads. He peered down at the hand that was sunk up to the wrist in the potato pile. Right in front of his eyes, the smooth white surfaces of his late crop were shrivelling, turning brown and pulpy. He drew his hand out, and it came away with a sucking sensation, as if it had been submerged in a turbid liquid.

The potatoes were rotting away even as he watched. He could see them *deflate* as they withered. Then his nostrils caught the pungent, powerful smell of rot as it came wafting up from the basket.

'Holy mother of Christ, what's happening here?' he said, now panicked. He spun round, almost overbalancing, and looked quickly at the other basket. The potatoes there seemed to be settling into one another, slowly sinking down from a heaped pile into a soupy, putrid mess. The one next to it was worse. The basket was actually *dripping* pus-like slime through the tight weave of the wickerwork. Around him the big toads crawled wetly.

Now very badly afraid, Finn turned back, about to leap from the trailer. Night had fallen swiftly and he just wanted to get out of there, away from this shadowed corner of the field. His mind reeled in disbelief and disgust and horror, and reeled with the fear that whatever poison was coming off those terrible creatures and blighting his potatoes might just do the same to him. As his weight shifted, the trailer tilted. Whatever happened next, Finn was never to find out. The tractor engine suddenly roared and, though he had pulled the handbreak on, the big machine jerked forward. Finn's arms pin-wheeled for balance as the weight of the baskets shifted. The trailer shuddered and the ball-catch at the front slipped out of the socket. The centre of gravity moved; everything tilted. The trailer's rear sank down in a swift swoop and the front end came up all at once. The big farmer was spilled out, along with the baskets and the mess they carried inside them. The trailer's momentum carried it round in a swift arc and it slammed down on top of everything. The edge came down with a crashing thud that smacked the front of Finn's skull and drove his head into the soft earth.

Freed of the pulling weight, the tractor rumbled along the rutted track, turning slowly. A few moments later, it completed the circle. Engine chugging, the great wheels at the back rolled it over the fallen shaws, digging into the newly turned earth. When it reached the trailer, its front wheels clambered up the sloping ramp, pressing the weight even further onto the unconscious farmer who lay underneath. A few seconds later, the push was too great and the engine chugged to a halt. The tractor rocked for a moment and then was still.

Miread Finnerty found the tractor angled up on the trailer more than an hour later when she came out to call her husband in for his supper. All she saw was the big machine canted at an angle. There was no sign of Finn at first.

A half-hour after that, half a dozen men from the village, led by Peter O'Neill the village Garda, got the trailer back upright, and they found Finn squashed into the ground under a mound of freshly dug white potatoes. Nobody figured out how he had got there, and he was in no position to tell them.

Donovan lent them his van to take Finn off to the hospital in Westport, where the doctors took one look at him, hooked him on a drip and sent him down to Galway. There neurosurgeons spent more than fifteen hours just keeping him alive. It was to be three weeks later that big Finn came out of the coma. He had a terrible scar and a dent on his forehead that made him look as if he'd been hit with a balpeen hammer. It took another six months of intensive therapy before he was allowed back home again, and by then it was all over in Kilgallan. Finn was brain-damaged, so the head doctors decided, and so he was. His left arm wouldn't move properly and he mixed up a lot of words. He had a concentration span of about three minutes.

Strangely, he could talk for hours to anybody that would listen about toads. He was obsessive about them. He wouldn't go to bed at night unless he checked under the bed and in the cupboards to make sure there were no toads. Nobody had a clue what he was talking about, but, they said, brain damage can have all sorts of effects.

About the night of the accident, nobody could get any sense from Finn Finnerty. The friends and neighbours who hauled him from under the tip-loader saw nothing except the big man lying terribly injured under his pile of new-dug potatoes. Of the toads, there was no sign.

14

Once the keystone was removed, it was only the work of an hour or so to prise the rest of them out and cart them to the open. Siobhan and Agnes took it in turns to photograph the progress. The two younger women had marked each stone before it was removed and put the corresponding identification on a grid for the archaeological report. When the wall was finally breached, everybody wanted to have a look inside the chamber that had lain locked since the dawn of time in Ireland, and Connarty couldn't deny their enthusiasm. He could hardly contain his own.

Siobhan went through first, bearing the light in its metal basket and trailing the insulated cable behind her.

'It's big, all right,' she called back to them. Her voice reverberated in a jangling series of echoes. Agnes and Theresa followed, with Dr Connarty and Terry bringing up the rear. Once they were all inside, Siobhan panned the light all around, letting them see the dimensions of the central tomb, if tomb it was.

It was a cavernous, circular stone room. The walls were dusty and dry, and although the light wasn't strong enough for detail, it was clear that the room was perfectly spherical, the circle only broken by five tall indentations in the walls.

In the centre of the chamber, alone, a massive single block of stone rose from the rock floor as if it was *part* of it, not put there, but *carved* from the living rock. It squatted almost five feet high and more than that along its sides. It was stygian black, cut smooth and then etched across its entire surface in a mass of shapes and lines.

When Siobhan flicked the light across it, both she and Terry simultaneously drew a sharp breath, though no-one heard them among the echoes. Terry even took a step backwards when he saw the stone. It was exactly as he had seen it *before* he had breached the wall.

Siobhan recognised the shape too, from what she'd thought she'd seen when the lights had flickered out and the strange rivulets of power had sparked from the wall and run up inside her skin.

Unaware of each other's experience, each was unwilling to voice whatever it was they thought they had seen.

In any case, it was Agnes who got the fright. Connarty and the two

99

others were inspecting the stone. The professor was muttering to himself in his usual manner, giving an on-the-spot spontaneous commentary of the stone and its carvings. Theresa and Agnes had made their way cautiously in the shadows to the wall on the far side. Agnes tentatively reached out both hands to feel the dry stone. She trailed her fingers across it until she reached one of the tall, rectangular indentations.

'What do you think this is for?' she asked.

'No idea,' Theresa said. 'I thought there would be more in here. But it looks empty.'

'Maybe somebody got here before us.'

'Well, the professor will be disappointed,' Theresa said, watching as Agnes probed at the wall. Her friend drew back.

'I think this might be hollow,' she said, reaching into the pocket of her jeans and drawing out the little digging tool that she'd been using on the gravel of the dig. 'It doesn't look like the rest of the stone.'

Agnes touched the tool on the stone, and there was a small ringing sound that quickly disappeared among the other echoes. She dug between two pieces of masonry.

'I think maybe you shouldn't be doing that,' Theresa said. 'The professor will want pictures first.'

'I'm just checking,' Agnes told her, 'to see if there's —'

Before Agnes finished her sentence there was a small scraping sound from the wall, as if something had moved.

'Don't you think you should leave it alone? It might not be safe.'

'I think it *is* hollow,' Agnes said, ignoring her. She stepped forward and put the digger back into the small space, and suddenly the small shifting sound was a *big* shifting sound as the whole section of the wall shattered and all the stones just slid to the floor with a rumble that filled the whole chamber with noise.

'What in the name of the saints are you doing there, girl?' Connarty bellowed with uncharacteristic loudness across the tomb. He came striding past the big stone to where Agnes and Theresa stood, wide-eyed and trembling with the fright of the sudden noise and movement.

He was about to bellow some more, but then there was a rustling sound from within the darkness of the niche which had been exposed when the thin wall collapsed.

'I was trying to —' Agnes started to say in a small, shaky voice. A sudden movement in the shadows was picked up by the light at the other side of the chamber. Agnes caught the movement at the corner of her eye and spun round. Something came out of the dark niche and threw itself upon her.

'Holy mother!' Connarty gasped.

Agnes shrieked, a ringing scream pitched high and loud in the enclosed space. The scream bounced backwards and forwards off the dry, smooth walls in ricochets so loud they hurt the ears. Beside her, Theresa let out a wail of pure fright.

Agnes's wide eyes saw the face right next to hers: brown and terribly wrinkled. There were great black eyes and huge teeth that lunged at her neck. Her scream rose higher, and even Connarty jerked back in alarm. Then the thing rolled clumsily and fell to the ground. There was a rustle and a crumpling rattling sound, and the noise of something metal hitting the floor. Theresa had backed up against the wall and Agnes fell against her, not even realising that her hands, reaching out in panic, had hooked right into the skin of Theresa's shoulders.

'Get it off me. *Get it off!*' As soon as her screaming stopped and she was able to draw in enough breath to get the words out, she bawled in blind panic. Her heart was tripping away madly somewhere in her throat and she could feel her knees give under the strain. Little lights danced in front of her eyes and she was sure she was going to faint.

From the other side of the stone, Siobhan flashed the light round and pinioned them all in the glare.

Something lay crumpled on the floor.

'Hold up there now,' Connarty barked, and everybody froze.

'Keep the light on, Siobhan,' he said, this time less urgently. 'It's all right. I can see it now.' His voice sounded a little shaky, but he still managed to put some authority into it.

He walked forward and bent down cautiously. A few yards away, Agnes was still trembling with fear, her whole body shivering with the force of it, and Theresa, close to hysterics, was numbly aware of her friend's fingers clenched on her skin. Connarty reached out a hand, slowly, as if the thing on the floor might bite him.

'Heavens above,' he exclaimed. 'It's a man.'

Agnes and Theresa both broke into muffled sobs.

Terry strode across the wide chamber and joined the professor. 'So it is,' he said. 'And he's been here a long time, by the looks of it.' He called out to Siobhan, 'Can we get a little bit more light over here. I think we've found a mummy.'

'Indeed, that's just the very thing we've found,' Connarty said, excitement coming back into his voice. 'Now would you look at that?' He slowly turned the thing over. There was a dry rustle and a shrivelled head swung into the beam of the light.

It was old. It was incredibly old. Dry as paper, and with parchment

101

skin drawn tight over cheekbones. There were two hollows where eyes had been, sunk deep into the head, the eyelids grotesquely caved in. The movement caused the head to loll on a spindly neck that was so thin Connarty could make out the individual vertebrae. The mouth was drawn back in a rictus that exposed long, yellowed teeth sprouting from gums that had shrivelled back to the bone. It was a hideous sight, but lying there on the cold stone, the decayed, dried-out husk of a man was no longer threatening.

Theresa managed to prise Agnes's fingers from her shoulders and the two of them tentatively shuffled over from the wall to have a closer look. Agnes was sobbing, the fright still controlling her reactions. Siobhan positioned the light on the stone, which was as far as the black cable would allow, and joined them at the body.

'Amazing, just amazing,' the professor was muttering. 'Look at that. The preservation's perfect, even better than the Bronze Age fellow they found in the Alps. It's the dry that does it. Look,' he said, pointing to the round dome of the head. There was still some black hair attached in scraggly tufts to the yellow skin. On the forehead, as plain as anything, were dark lines drawn in circular shapes.

'He's had a tattoo. The design's still intact,' the professor said, unable to keep the wonder out of his voice. He shifted position and rolled the body right over. A thin, gangly arm that looked longer than it should flopped to the ground with a bony rattle. Just above the wrist was a plain, heavy gold band, and there was a similar, more ornate one around what had been the biceps. It rolled about on the papery skin that was stretched over bone.

'He was a wealthy young fellow, by the looks of it,' the professor said.

'How do you know it's a *he*?' Agnes asked in a shaky voice.

'There's a big clue that many a medical man would have missed.'

'What's that?' Theresa said, almost as shakily as Agnes.

'There,' Connarty said, pointing to the end of the arm. They all looked. The arm stretched out into the shadows. They could just make out long, emaciated fingers that were clenched tightly round something. They leaned forwards to see.

In the dead man's hand was an axe, heavy and bladed with smooth stone. It was dull, though there was gold wire on the shaft that picked up the light.

'That's a warrior's battleaxe,' Connarty said with some satisfaction. 'They buried him with his weapon, standing up.'

He stood up himself and looked around the vault. 'And I'm sure there's more of them here too.'

'I thought it was a blocked-up passageway,' Agnes said, her voice still holding enough hesitation to show that she hadn't completely got over her fright.

'Well, that would have been my thought too,' Connarty said. 'That's what you'd expect. But if the others are the same as this one,' he said, gesturing around at the four other niches, 'then it's interesting.'

Even in the low light, they could see his brows furrow behind his glasses.

'How do you mean?' Terry asked.

'I mean that if this is all there is, just a block of stone and some dead men, it doesn't help us understand why this thing was constructed in the first place – unless there's something underneath the stone.'

'A tomb for warriors?' Siobhan asked. Her mind was reeling with the force of the memory. She'd touched the wall and the strange *power* had rippled into her and she had *heard* the man gasping for breath, dying from lack of air. And now she was looking down at a warrior who'd been walled up in a niche in the chamber *thousands* of years ago. A strange unbalancing feeling crept through her, as if reality had flipped inside-out for a moment, leaving her on the edge of something she couldn't understand.

'I rather think not,' the professor said. 'You wouldn't get the craftsmanship like here.' He raised his face to look up at the arching roof. 'Not for fighters. No. You might have found their remains in a beaker maybe, or even cremated, but not standing up in a hole in the wall. This is something different, and I rather think you'll find the answer for us there,' he said, jerking a thumb at the stone.

Siobhan walked slowly away from where the group stood around the dead man. Agnes looked down at him. When the face had turned and she'd caught a glimpse of the parched and wrinkled face and those long, snarling teeth, she'd thought her heart was just going to stop dead. Now the ancient corpse looked quite pitiful, a small, emaciated thing with stick-like arms and legs and vertebrae showing through skin stretched taut.

'It's covered in runes,' Siobhan called over. 'It's too dark to make them out, but there's months of study here alone.'

'And a few years' work on this poor soul and his friends, if they're there,' Connarty said. 'I've never seen such a perfect state of preservation in all my days.'

'Doesn't look too perfect to me,' Terry said with an attempt at levity. 'Looks as if he could use a good drink.'

Beside him Theresa giggled nervously.

'That's what makes me think this wasn't built for just a few warriors,' Connarty said. 'It took a year, maybe two, to craft a place like this with the tools they had. You can prepare a tomb for kings and even queens, but they never made that effort for their fighting men. And if this fellow had died in battle, there would have been nothing left of him by the time they got the roof on the place.' He paused and looked around at the three who stood closest to him.

'It's too early to say for certain, and remember I'm no forensic man myself, but it looks as if he died after the tomb was constructed.'

Siobhan felt a sinking feeling in her stomach.

'And that would only mean one thing, I think,' the professor went on.

'What's that?' Siobhan asked from the far side, never taking her eyes off the indentations on the smooth block of stone that looked as though they'd only been carved the day before.

'Well, remember I was telling you about the companions the kings would take with them to the underworld?'

The girls nodded in unison, still standing close to each other, as if for protection from the shadows.

'It could mean that these are the companions.'

'You mean, he was just an ould *bugger*?' Terry asked, chuckling as he did.

'Not at all. I mean that this could be the tomb that was built for the old queen. Apparently she had a fair old appetite for young men.'

Connarty pointed to the squat stone. 'I think the words will give us a clue, but I've a suspicion that there might well be another passage under that thing.'

'Do you mean they killed this man and walled him up here just because the queen was dead?' Theresa asked.

'If it is indeed the queen's tomb, that's exactly what would have happened. And there's another thing,' he said, pausing and letting the echoes die away for effect.

'Go on,' Terry said impatiently.

'Look at the fellow. Dried out like an old stick. But there in his hand you see his battleaxe. As far as we can see in this light – and we'll know better later on, of course – there isn't a mark on him. So it's my thinking that he wasn't killed at all.'

'What does that mean?' Agnes asked.

'They probably bricked him up here alive,' Connarty said flatly. Again the echoes of his voice died away, leaving a long silence.

'You mean they buried him alive?'

'I'm sure that's exactly what they did, for there's no binding or strapping, and it's not all that easy to make a corpse stand up in a hole in a wall. And if that's what happened, then he went willingly and all.'

'Committed suicide?' This in a hushed tone from Theresa.

'Surely. He'd have stood there and watched them build the wall, and he'd die of thirst down in the dark.'

'But why?'

'That's the way they did things. If they made a promise, they kept it, and remember, Queen Maeve was a terrible powerful woman.'

'If it *is* Queen Maeve,' Siobhan said. In her mind she could still hear the ragged, frantic gasps for breath.

'What a terrible thing,' Agnes said softly. In the dim light Siobhan saw her make the sign of the cross very quickly, almost furtively, as if warding off evil.

'They would have considered it an honour to die with their swords in their hands and guard a queen on her way to Tir na n'Og,' Connarty said.

'That's women's lib for you,' Siobhan said. 'I wonder if they made it to the other side.'

'This one stayed back in the interests of historical knowledge,' the professor said, 'and, with some luck, we'll have a few others to examine.'

He stepped back from the corpse. 'Right, the real work begins now,' he said, rubbing his hands together enthusiastically. They made a dry, rustling sound in the cavern. 'But, Agnes, no more digging without my say-so. I don't want any more accidents, either to us or the artefacts, understand?'

Agnes nodded, embarrassed.

Connarty turned to Terry and asked him if he could fix up some lights for the place, and told Agnes to fetch some plastic sheeting.

'We have to keep this very dry,' he said, 'for the fresh air will rot him quicker than a flash. Is there anything you need, Siobhan?'

'Just as many pictures of these carvings as I can get. Then I can study them at leisure.'

'And then we'll see what's under this rock,' Connarty said, patting the hard stone.

As he did so, he felt the tingle of cold radiate into his fingers, as if the heat of his body was being drawn right out of his hand and into the stone. He drew his hand back quickly, with a little gasp of surprise, for in the first touch, the deep cold had felt like a *burning* sensation.

'What's wrong?' Siobhan asked.

'Nothing. Just cold,' he said vaguely.

He put out his hand and touched the flat stone again, this time prepared. The cold seemed to leap up and into his skin. His hand started to go numb almost immediately.

The professor stared at his outspread fingers, puzzled by the quite *shocking* coldness that stole through his palm and seemed to drive itself into his bones.

There was a strange *twist* in the atmosphere, an alteration in the *feel* of things, and he imagined himself standing there alone in the dim light. The small sounds that Siobhan had been making as she crouched to scan the carved lines on the rock had gone from his consciousness. It was as if there was just him and the stone block and the fierce coldness that welded his hand to the smooth stone.

He looked down and saw a dark shadow creeping out of the monolith and stealing into the tips of his fingers like a liquid. For some reason, it looked as if the shadow was flowing upwards and *through* his skin. The movement was so slow and smooth that he kept his hand there, feeling it grow colder until there was no sensation in it, just a draining numbness. The darkness rippled up his fingers and over his knuckles in an ominous stream.

Connarty was not afraid; more bemused and interested. This was a strange phenomenon.

He looked over his shoulder, and Siobhan was gone. So was the light in its basket.

But there was another light in the tomb, a strange half-light with no apparent source. His eyes had adjusted to the shade and he could see quite clearly.

On his outstretched hand the dark flow was creeping up his wrist, little fingers of shade probing at his forearm. He tried to draw away from it, but he couldn't. It was as if his hand was stuck to the stone, *melted* into it.

'What's this then?' he heard himself say, and there was no echo. Maybe the words had been spoken inside his head.

He swivelled his eyes and looked at his hand. The fingers were *sinking* into the hard surface. He could feel them passing through the rock, becoming part of it. His skin tingled with the sensation as though muscle and bone were being pulled down into some deep blackness, and the cold of it burned like searing frost. It was as if the stone had suddenly become transparent. One minute it was solid and black, and then the paleness of his hand was pushing, quite impossibly, into its surface. He could see *into* the rock. Below the surface was a deeper dark, and the dark *writhed*. It had no shape or form, but it was like something that roiled inside the monolith, drawing his hand down towards it. The cold became even more intense and he could feel his nerve-endings recoil.

He felt his shoulder twitch as he pulled his weight back, and inside the stone the darkness roiled more quickly, as if a turbulence had surged through it. With a fleet, striking movement, like a black snake, it reached for his hand, trying to grab it, to bite on it, to trap it inside the stone.

The image of being caught by the rolling shadow flitted across Connarty's mind. He saw himself being dragged bodily through a membrane and down into infinite darkness by something that was formed of shadows; hard, twisting shadows.

In that instant, he felt a force of terrible *hunger* reaching for him, drawing him towards it. Fear jolted right through him from the back of his neck to the taut tendons bracing his heels. There was a sucking, *gripping* sensation on his hand, then a little rubbery *snap* as his arm suddenly came free. He brought his hand up to his face, peering at it. There was a blackness across the palm, like a stain under the skin.

He gave a small gasp of disgust, and the blackness, a shadow *inside*, just seemed to drain out of him. He felt the unwelcome tingling in his fingers as the control of his nerves came back to him. The black shadowy stream trickled out into the air and dissipated.

Connarty tried to flex his fingers. They were numbed down to the bone, stiff with paralysis. He tried harder, and his little finger twitched, and then his thumb moved.

His breath came out in a little sigh of relief, and Connarty took another two steps backwards. His foot caught the insulated cable that looped in from the opening to the chamber, and he lost his balance. His leg buckled under him and he staggered to the left, almost crushing Siobhan with his weight as his arms pinwheeled for balance.

'Oh,' he grunted, just managing to prevent himself from falling. Siobhan turned from where she was kneeling at the side of the stone and put up a hand to grasp his elbow, helping him regain equilibrium.

'Are you all right now, Jim?' she asked.

'Just about,' he said. 'Tripped over the wire.'

'I thought you'd taken a fit, for a minute.'

'Me too,' he said quietly, and Siobhan laughed. Obviously she'd been unaware of what he'd experienced.

Later on, he told himself, if she hadn't seen it, then it hadn't happened. It was just a trick of the light, of the dark. Of the *mind*.

15

The awakening came with such sudden speed that the shock was a hot fire of pain that sleeted through her dark consciousness, a single cataclysmic explosion of identity.

She was suddenly alive. The *Shee* was suddenly *alive*.

And in the moment of that baneful conception, the memories and the knowledge and the hunger and the anger came together in a shocking mental *crash* that was like a physical force.

The darkness was still infinite, *here* where she was still imprisoned, held immobile by bonds of stone, by words which had not lost their power for countless generations.

Countless generations!

The knowledge of the passage of time came instantly to a mind that had lain dormant for thousands of years, riving like a knife to the core of being.

They had trapped her *for ever!*

Bound like an animal here in the infinite black, with no escape. They had cursed her as she had cursed them, but their song had been so strong. It had burned like fire and stolen her power.

Oh, but she had cursed *them* in that moment. She had tried to turn them, to break their minds, but they had been protected by the song and had covered their eyes and blocked their ears and burned the smoke in their noses so they couldn't even smell her.

Her newly awakened sense of self froze when that vision came back to her, and with it came the hot black fury. She was trapped, bound here in this cursed never-ending dark, but now all of her was together and *awake*, and while there was no sensation of touch, or sight, or taste or hearing, there was memory, and hunger. And the boiling, bubbling *anger*.

She had rested, sated, in her special place where none but the brave and foolhardy and the doomed dared to venture. She had slept, glutted with all the good things these living creatures contained. She had been dreaming a cold dream and she was sluggish. The day had dawned and the sun was rising in the east, pushing itself out over the mist that surrounded the bottom of the mountain. The peak rose above the *harr* into the light of day. Close to the peak there was an overhang of jagged rock that led to a hollow, which in turn led to a deep cleft. There in the dark of the cave, she slept, a shadow within shadows.

How could they have taken her? How could she not have *known*?

That was a mystery that even her knowledge could not penetrate. But they had come in the dawn, the old men with their eyes bound by leather masks. There had been a singing, but she couldn't make out the words, and there had been the terrible smell of burning that had oozed into her sleep and kept her there. And into the dark of the cave they had brought a searing *light*, an unfaceable brilliance that chased the shadows out of the cleft and left her pinioned on bolts of white. The smell crippled her. She could not even *change*. She tried, screaming at them, forcing herself away from the light and failing, trying to alter her shape to that of any earth creature that could withstand the day, but she was locked into her own form, and that could not tolerate the light.

'Leave me!' she thundered, bellowing frustrated rage, but they did not quail. '*Get out of my place!*' she shrieked.

Still they came, blocking her path until she was surrounded with the light that burned and sizzled. There was a strange ululating sound that weakened her even further, bound her with rings of noise, and the smoke that billowed from the stone cups they held on the ends of their long sticks clogged her throat.

The light came closer, burning out from things they held in their hands, lines of white that looped and sparkled like ropes and coiled around her without touching. The pain of the light was *exquisite*, a shrieking thing that burned over her skin. She could feel herself *melt*, her eyes *shrivel* under its white force. She tried to bellow her pain and anguish and terrible anger but the noise was only a gurgle in her throat.

The circle of old men backed away and the light went with them. She thought it would free her, but no, she was trapped within it. It coiled around her in a net of woven beams that did not touch, yet pulled her with its force. All the time, the sound was in her ears, and the old men, sure-footed though they were, blinded by the leather skins over their eyes, dragged her outside, rasping her fury until the walls were shivering with the pitch of her hate.

There she felt all her strength draw from her, for she could not change herself into a raven that would soar for the cover of the trees, or a wolf that would snap at her captors and race across the moorland. Whatever song they sang, they bound her within it and she was powerless against it.

They took her down from the mountain and along the track that led close to the end of the land where it met the sea. There was something built there, something man-made, of stone. She could see it, through the hateful bars of light, and she quailed. She did not understand it, but she saw *trap*, pure and simple.

The group of old men, blindfolded, surrounded by young ones who kept their eyes averted, dragged her inside and down a narrow tunnel. She twisted and turned. Hope grew. It was dark down there, the dark that she needed. Maybe she could work some of her magic away from the daylight. If she could get them to take away the light, then she'd *have* them, and then they would see *who* was the trapped.

But the insidious foreknowledge pressed in on her like a weight. There was a room like a cavern, and light from torches flickered on the walls. They brought her from the passage into it, and the blinding cage that trapped her sent golden streams running over the rock.

The sound got higher and higher, clearer and clearer. It rang in her mind: *a chant*. Strange words of power reverberated on the stone walls, echoing and mixing, building up and doubling in strength with every passing moment, until the whole stone cavern seemed to shake with the intensity of the power.

She twisted and turned again, trying to find a way out, but there was none. She felt herself change from the inside, her body stretching out then withering down until she was a hag, pleading in an old woman's whine to be allowed to go free. She saw one of the young men start in surprise and she seized the moment, altering her appearance in a smooth flowing movement, growing taller within the light, filling out, until she was a woman of terrible beauty. The young man at the edge of her vision turned towards her and looked directly into her eyes. She saw his own eyes gape widely in surprise. His mouth fell slackly open, and she *commanded*.

She saw his body shake in a spasm, and his hand went to his belt. She shoved her command into him, and he pulled a knife from a furry sheath and with one swift movement plunged it into the back of one of the old men. The ancient fell soundlessly and the cup on the stick clattered to the stone floor. The light guttered and went out. Immediately she felt a lessening of her bonds. Her voice returned and she *stretched* out, battering at the edges of the light-cage. The sounds of the chant came louder now, the hard voices of men singing into their own echoes. There was a swift movement at the edge of vision, and the young man who had killed the elder went down in a heap.

She pushed at the net, but it failed to give, and she screamed in frustration. One of the other men picked up the cup and thrust it at the light. Immediately the bowl blazed with white fire and the cage tightened.

They dragged her onto the smooth stone squatting at the centre, and surrounded it. She felt herself hauled onto the dark surface. She probed at the stone with her mind and sensed nothingness, a vast eternal depth *within* the stone, and her prescience told her again: *trap!*

One of the old men made a signal, and the younger men guided them to their positions, walking in time to the echoes of the chant. The sound was a ravening pain in her ears.

The most ancient of the shamans started to speak, his voice a strange, high-pitched sing-song.

'Begone from this place for ever, serpent, death shroud. Be banished in the flame of the Lord of Light,' he sang.

The smoke from the burning sticks billowed up from the cups. It reeked foul in her nostrils that were flaring and snuffling like those of a trapped animal.

'Be caught for ever in the clouds of confusion from the mountain ash and the witch hazel,' he sang.

'That's what they burn,' she thought, realising the true power of it.

The old man raised his hand. Five young men came forward, their heads high, their eyes tightly closed. She sent out to one of them, but his mind was filled with a song of glory and the thought slid off and away.

'The five near-kings give themselves to guard you in this place for all time, *babag-baibh*, filthy goblin. Theirs is the glory.'

'What glory is that, you fools!' she ranted, hearing her own voice scrape along the walls like claws. The old man acted as though he had not heard.

'Be for ever here, in the darkness within that lives for ever and travels beyond this place to the unending depths,' the ancient chanted.

Around the walls, she saw the five young men, swords and axes in hand, knives at their hips, stand themselves within the niches on the walls. Their eyes were closed and their faces were smiling with the sweetness of the song they heard inside them. Immediately others started to mount stone upon stone.

'Puny *men*-folk to stand guard!' she raved. 'I will eat their *souls*, just as I ate the soul of the fool you sent to me.'

As if he had heard her, the old man sang in his thin, wavering voice: 'Avenged be the innocent we sent to fill you, for his is the final sacrifice you exact from this land. His glory will be sung as long as men live in this place.'

Then she realised the plan within the plan. They had sent a young warrior to her, to his death, thinking himself to be the hero. But he was a callow youth who had not known he was only the poisoned bait, the meal that would make her sleep while they came for her.

The song rang in her ears. *Where did they get the power?*

The sound rose, stronger, vibrating the walls. The bindings of light tightened, and she felt herself pushed down onto the stone. The song changed and she felt the stone open up, like black water, and she was pushed down *into* the surface.

'Curse you, frightened little mortals. Curse your audacity,' she screeched.

The force shoved at her and she felt herself sink helplessly, realising the hopelessness of her situation. They meant to do it. They meant to trap her in this place, and she saw, with certainty, that it would happen.

'I put a curse on you and this land,' she screamed. 'When I am gone, you will have only death and disease and famine. Your sons will kill your brothers, your fathers will kill your daughters. You will be betrayed forever by those who will steal your kingdoms and ravage your lands. Your children will die wasted from hunger and your people will flee my curse in your thousands. This will be a *dead land*.'

She roared out a blast of frustration and hatred. She screamed and writhed against the power that held her, cursing them so that the walls shook, but the old, blindfolded men had forced her downwards into the stone.

She felt the cold of it through her as the oldest of them sung his song. The words had shivered her with the enormity of power.

'The Sword of the Son of Light bars your path to the Land of the Young and keeps you between the worlds. You are broken, your strength and your evil is as dust. We rend you and send you to the blackness from which you sprang.'

An immense force dragged her down and into the stone. Its substance merged with her own and she felt herself fragment and dissipate. She could sense the *infinity* encapsulated within the mass of rock and a terror of that unending space shuddered through her.

She screeched and she wailed, ever sinking into the depths. The last thing she saw was the face of the old man, now triumphant behind his mask, and then there was pure darkness. Immediately, all sound was cut off and the dread cold swamped her. All thought flickered, guttered and died.

She was gone.

16

Liz Cannon was still angry with Sean McCullain. He'd fixed up this place knowing that it wasn't a hotel, and that they'd be sharing a cottage. He had brought her here under false pretences, she decided, and that rankled. What rankled even more was his open disdain when she had suggested that there might be some other underhanded motive in this. What right did he have to look at her like *that*? Who did he think he *was*.

Liz fumed. It didn't help that despite herself she had fallen in love with the cottage on first sight. It was perfect in its Irish homeliness. The peat fire glowed warmly in the big slate hearth, and the old-fashioned range set beside it looked as if it could cook a banquet. The smell of peat smoke was heady and dry, a tantalising flavour in the air, and the living room was at once snug yet expansive. If she had wanted a cottage, it would be *exactly* like this one. However, she thought, if she desired just such a place, she would choose who she would share it with. It would not be that pig-headed, smug *button-pusher*.

When Sean had gone into his own room, still humming tunelessly to himself as if he'd forgotten, or didn't care, about the words that had passed between them, Liz slipped into the bathroom for her own shower. Surprisingly – *for a man* – he'd picked up the towel and slung it into the wash basket. The floor was unexpectedly dry. He was obviously more fastidious than his rather rumpled *lived-in* appearance would suggest. That was a point in his favour, she thought, then shied away from the idea. She didn't like him enough for that. Didn't *want* to like him enough, she assured herself.

Twenty minutes later she emerged from her own room, with her leather jacket over her shoulder. She'd put two clasps in her hair, which held it up away from her face, and she'd put some make-up on, artfully light, enhancing rather than disguising. He was sitting in one of the big armchairs by the side of the fire and she could see the flickering red glow on his face. He was relaxed, leaning back with his eyes closed, and she had a glimpse of his profile. He had a strong nose that had taken a knock or two in its time, and a small scar on his forehead that dug a white line into the heavy black brows. He'd shaved off the stubble of the day and his chin, quite a *manly* chin, she thought, was angled to the side, the

113

way his head was leaning against the curved back. She stood for a few moments, wondering whether to say something or just cough, when his eyes opened and flicked towards her. The darkness of them caught the firelight and for a second they looked as though they were flaming at her.

Then, strangely, he smiled. It was quite a soft, surprised smile as if he'd noticed her for the first time.

'You're looking okay,' he said.

She looked straight back at him. 'Okay? Thanks a million for that, McCullain.'

'Oh, don't get on your high horse,' he said, though there was no real irritation in his voice. 'I mean you're looking fine. *Good*.'

'Well, that's a rare compliment. I see you've changed your shirt . . .'

'And I've put on fresh jeans and, if you want to check, my underwear and socks are in pretty good nick.'

'No thanks,' she said, but at least he had made an effort since they were going out for dinner. Some photographers looked like saddle tramps. It seemed to go with the job.

'Why don't I take your picture?' he asked casually.

She shot him a glance, immediately suspicious. 'What kind of picture?'

'Oh, tits and bum, french knickers, that sort of thing,' he said lightly.

Liz opened her mouth ready to unleash an indignant string of *I told you so's* to be followed with a complete demolition of his character, when he laughed out loud, a big mirthful bellow.

'Come on, I'm only kidding. Just a head-and-shoulders for your byline file. You suit your hair like that.'

Her mouth closed shut in surprise. When she managed to get it open again, all she could retort was: 'Is this some sort of come-on, McCullain?' though the tone was not as harsh as the words could have conveyed.

'If it is, I'm sure you'll have plenty to say about it,' he replied calmly, not even looking at her. He walked over to the table and snapped open his camera case, bringing out the black Nikon and hefting it expertly in his hands.

'Here. Sit on the arm there, beside the fire,' he said, still looking down at the camera, fingering the focusing ring, not looking at her at all.

'Are you serious?'

This time he did turn and look at her. She thought she could detect a glint of humour in his eyes.

114

'Sure I am. This'll only take a minute.'

'I've heard that before, and it's often the case,' she said before she realised what she was saying. If she could have bitten the words back she would have, for she didn't want to give McCullain *any* ideas.

She needn't have worried. The big man threw his head back and laughed heartily. When he finished, he still couldn't keep the smile from his face, and his shoulders were doing a little jiggle as he tried to suppress another convulsion.

'I'm sure it has,' he said finally, and giggled again boyishly. 'Right, put your backside on the arm. There.' She sat.

'Now turn towards the fire a little. That's fine. And raise your chin a little. I don't want a shadow under there.' McCullain had gone into his photographer's mode. She watched as he fiddled with the aperture control, and then swung the camera around, peering through the viewfinder, moving his body this way and that.

'Right. I want to get a natural colour here. The fire gives a nice glow. Good for skin tone,' he said, moving in closer. The camera clicked as he released the shutter and the motor drive whined as it wound the film on.

'Is that it?' she asked.

'Just one. Hold it,' he said, and she instinctively froze. He shot another frame, then another.

'Turn towards me.' She turned.

'Tilt back. No, further.' She tilted further, enjoying the attention.

'Have you got enough?'

'Just a couple more. This time with flash.' He fixed on the unit with a snap and plugged in the lead. There was a juicy, high-pitched hum as the power surged up. In a few moments he got her to sit forward, head cupped in her hands. The camera flashed, but the flash was pointed backwards to bounce off the wall behind him so there was no sudden brilliance to stab her eyes. He made her sit up straight, and took a three-quarter and then a full profile.

'I charge modelling rates,' she said.

'And I charge photographer's rates. I score,' he said absently, footering with the controls of the camera, making an adjustment here and there.

'Right. Now I want a couple of different expressions,' he said. She sat motionless, face straight.

'Did you fart?' he asked, and her expression immediately changed: brows drawn down in a frown, mouth set.

Flash, the camera caught it, and then she realised what he'd done. It was as simple as that. A casual barb in a question that triggered off the response he'd wanted, and she'd handed it to him on a plate.

Then she realised he was giggling. His shoulders were going up and down again, though she couldn't see his face. In the background, the flash whined, and then she laughed, spontaneously, a big, full-throated laugh through opened teeth.

The camera flashed three times, catching the evolution of her laugh. Through the lens, McCullain could see her eyes crinkle up with the mirth of it and her parted lips curving up from white teeth. Her hair, in motion, caught the light on either side of her face and he froze the movement, capturing the laugh on film.

'That's the one I wanted,' he said, and it was with a sudden thrill that she saw he'd double-bluffed her. He'd given her the line that would make her frown, in order to catch the upside when she realised she'd been taken. It was a smooth move. She would give him that, at least.

'Okay, that's it for now,' he said, turning away to dismantle the camera. She watched him, his broad shoulders hunched over the metal case, putting away his gear with the methodical precision of long practice.

When he had snapped the case lid and slung the whole lot under the table, he turned to her, a vague smile playing on his face. 'The camera loves you when you laugh,' he said matter-of-factly. 'You should do it more often. It suits you.'

'Rare to find things to laugh about. It's a tough old world.'

'Tougher than you know, kid,' he said, and she flicked him a glance to see if he was being smug, but he had turned away from her, so she couldn't see his expression.

'And I suppose you *do* know?' she asked, feeling the irritation creep back into her voice. She didn't like him patronising her. Didn't like being called *kid*.

'Indeed I do, sure enough. But that's only because I've been around a whole lot longer. Everybody gets to see it eventually.'

'I'd say it was experience and not age.'

'That's true enough, but the longer you go on, the more chance you've got of getting the experience. It's as simple as that. I've got a good ten years on you. I've had more chance.'

'How old are you, McCullain?' she asked and then wished she hadn't been so gauche.

'Ten more than your twenty-five,' he said, turning towards her, grinning.

'How did you know that?' she asked, surprised.

116

'We're both journalists,' he said, still smiling. 'If I'm going to work with somebody, I find out about them. I checked your files.'

She stopped and stared at him, open-mouthed.

'I suppose you did the same for me,' he said. She caught the glint in his eye when her expression gave her away. She hadn't, and he knew it. She'd known for days before he did that they would be working on the Irish features, but all she knew about McCullain was his reputation for being one of the best in the business. She'd never considered that a photographer would do what any reporter would be expected to do: check up on people.

She turned away, professionally embarrassed and once again feeling a little foolish.

He caught her discomfiture, and came up beside her.

'Don't worry about it. I'm just careful, that's all. It helps in the job. It comes with the extra ten years,' he said, and lightly tapped her on the shoulder. As soon as his fingers touched her she felt her arm jerk as if a little warm shock had sparked between them.

'Come on, let's eat. I'm starved,' he threw in cajolingly, picking up his own leather jerkin from the back of a chair and slinging it over his shoulder.

She followed him out, and when they got to the car he stopped and looked at her across the roof. An eddy of wind blew her hair to one side, exposing her jawline to the light from the cottage window.

'I meant what I said,' he called over.

'What's that?'

'The camera loves you when you laugh. You should try it more often.' He ducked down into the car and she got in the passenger side.

'But it's crazy about you when you're angry,' he said, and laughed to himself. She couldn't help but smile. She could still feel where his fingers had touched.

The harbour at Westport is a sheltered haven in a narrow inlet of the bay where fishing smacks in their hundreds used to gather at the turn of the century, laden with herring and haddock. The tide that surges across the flat expanse of the bight is channelled ever tighter so that in the harbour there's a difference of fourteen feet or more between the rip and ebb. Even at low tide there's still a deep channel that allows sizeable boats to berth comfortably. Nowadays, there are only a few craft sitting on the ends of their ropes alongside the seawall. There are still a dozen or so black capstans that make good seats for the small boys who come to this part to fish for flounders and eels, and the main road takes a twist

117

to the left then right so that it snakes between the row of wharf houses and the water.

Those houses, old and brown and weathered from the west wind, are no longer the homes of the longshoremen and traders. Some of them have been converted from store-barns into bay houses for those with a few pounds to spare and a yen for the salt air. There's a chandler's shop where once there were half a dozen. The rest of the ground-floor fronts have been taken over by the kind of businesses you see in out-of-the-way seafront towns. There's a craft shop and a place that sells sheepskins which are pricey but mostly useless in the damp drizzle that blows in on grey curtains from far out in the bay. There's a shop that sells fishing tackle, and next to it, on the end of a close-huddled terrace, in an old building that once stored hemp ropes and oak spars, there's a surprising little restaurant, run by an English fellow and his Irish wife.

This was where Sean McCullain brought Liz Cannon on their first night, after he'd taken her photograph by the red fire in the cottage at Kilgallan. Liz didn't mind him driving as he steered the car fast over the hump-backed bridge and along the black winding road that stuck to the shoreline. Dusk was beginning to set, and to their left, looking north and west, the sky was reddening down to purple. Out on the bay the tide was low, showing a flat expanse of tidal flats. In the distance, low grey pancakes of islands seemed to drift on the night-mist that was beginning to rise. A few miles onward, to their right, the towering mass of Croagh Patrick, that tall, conical hill, reared up more than two thousand feet from the flatland. On top, on its pinnacle, where the dying sun's rays caught the last forty feet or so, Liz could make out a building.

'It's a church,' Sean explained, never taking his eyes from the road. 'Paul Convery said it's worth a look. They say that's where Saint Patrick banged his drum to drive all the snakes from Ireland.'

'Is that true?' Liz asked.

'What, the legend?'

'No, about there being no snakes in Ireland.'

'Yes, but there never were any, as far as I remember. I saw it in a nature programme once. They figured out that Ireland had separated from the rest of Britain before snakes evolved.'

'The legend sounds better,' Liz said.

'They always do.'

At the edge of Westport, Sean swung the car in a tight loop and jammed the brakes on a few feet from the edge before they plunged into the muddy-looking water of the harbour. It was a calm night, and the deep, unstirred water swelled and shrank in the tide-pulses coming in from the bay. Here and there, a clump of bladderwrack blistered black fingers along the surface.

Sean got out of the car and stood at the edge, breathing in the salt air, before turning back and heading towards the row of buildings.

The restaurant was called, simply, The Quay. On the outside there was a glass-paned box in which the regular menu, written in a tight hand in black ink, displayed the fare: Clew Bay oysters. Atlantic prawns. Smoked salmon.

'Seafood,' Sean said. 'Couldn't be better.'

'Do they do a steak?' Liz asked, still scanning the menu.

'Most likely,' Sean said, swinging the door ahead of him. Liz followed and he held it open casually for her, not making a big thing about it. It seemed an automatic move. 'And our lords and masters are going to pay dearly for tonight.'

Inside, the jovial, red-faced, Irish-looking fellow who had a cultured South of England accent bid them an incongruous thousand welcomes. Sean asked for a table for two.

'You're in luck, just,' the restaurateur said finally, eyes alighting on a white-covered round table next to a mullioned window. 'It's for four, but it's all we've got.'

Sean followed him forward. They sat down at opposite sides, and the fellow brought them a small basket filled with thick discs of fresh bread. The wheaty, hot smell drifted tantalisingly upwards and Sean felt the under-edges of his tongue tighten in anticipation. There was a bowl with pats of butter moulded into shells and whorls.

The wife brought over the menu and asked, in a soft southern accent, if they'd like a drink. Sean looked up at her and she twinkled a pair of merry dark eyes at him.

'Scottish, is it?'

'Yes,' Sean replied.

'Well, many welcomes to you both,' the woman said lightly, 'and I hope you like your dinner here.'

The owner came back to take their orders. Sean asked for mussels and a seafood platter that included marinated herrings, with locally caught smoked salmon. Liz ordered prawns and a fillet steak.

Just as they started to eat, the door to the restaurant opened and a young couple came in. Sean watched as the owner bustled towards them, neatly swinging past the chairs that impeded his path. Liz turned and the two of them saw the pantomime of them asking for a table. The owner regretfully shook his head and raised his hands, palms upwards.

There was a disappointment immediately apparent on the faces of the young couple. The man looked down apologetically to her and raised his eyebrows in that universal declaration of helpless resignation.

'That's a shame,' Liz said. 'All the other places will be busy.'

Sean got to his feet and crossed the intervening distance. The young couple, he slim and neat, she tall and lean with a mane of blonde hair, were turning towards the door.

'Just a minute,' Sean said. The owner turned towards him and the girl stopped just as the man's hand reached for the door handle.

'Listen, there's not much chance of getting a table anywhere tonight,' Sean said.

'That's true enough. The town's full for the market,' the owner said.

'Why don't you share with us. There's room.'

The girl looked up at her partner, asking the question. He seemed to think for a second, then nodded.

'That's real good of you, sir,' he said in an educated American accent. 'I really appreciate it. Both of us.'

'Oh, good,' the owner said. 'Saves a disappointment.'

'It sure does,' the girl said. 'We've come right through Westport. This was the last place. Everywhere else was overflowing.'

She looked at the young man, then back to Sean, and flashed him a dazzling smile that lit up her face. She reached out a hand towards him and he shook it. Her grip was dry and warm and surprisingly strong.

'I'm Nancy Keenan,' she said, then immediately cupped her hand to her mouth, in a natural, girlish motion. 'I mean . . . Nancy *Ducain*.'

'We just got married,' the man explained, grinning. 'She hasn't got used to it yet.' He shook hands with Sean. 'Tom Ducain.'

'Sean McCullain. Come on. We're over there.' He led the way.

Liz was half-turned round in her seat and Sean made the introductions with the two strangers.

'We couldn't find a table anywhere. I thought we'd *starve* tonight,' Nancy said, and smiled at Liz. She had the most perfect teeth Sean had ever seen, and a pair of bright blue eyes under dark golden brows. Her hair was a cascade of honey waves, lighter than Liz's own. The girl was limber and athletic-looking and obviously relieved to find somewhere to eat.

'That's the one thing I can't understand about this place,' Tom said. 'Great place to visit, but hardly anywhere to eat.' He looked up quickly at Sean. 'No offence, though. I'm not knocking your country.'

Sean laughed. 'Not my country. I'm from Scotland.'

'You are? Hey, I'd never have guessed. You sound just like the folks here,' Tom said ingenuously. 'We're from Vermont.'

They fell into easy conversation while the food arrived. It was truly marvellous, each dish laid out on delicate porcelain platters. The mussels were dripping in a sauce that defined sea-tang and the smoked salmon was exquisite. They traded questions and answers as well as tasty morsels from their plates until coffee.

'How about you two,' Nancy asked. 'You married or what?'

'Heavens, no!' Liz said quickly, almost choking on a piece of apple pie. 'We just work together. I'm a journalist. Sean's a photographer.'

'What she means is that we're both journalists. I take pictures,' Sean corrected mildly. Liz shot him a look that Nancy caught.

'I thought you really *were* a couple,' Nancy said.

'Well, we do live together,' Sean said, eyes smiling over the top of his coffee cup.

'Just for tonight,' Liz added.

'We've got a wee cottage along the road a bit,' Sean said, as if she hadn't spoken. 'In Kilgallan. It's a bit past that big hill.'

'Croagh Patrick,' Nancy interjected. 'Where the snakes were driven out. That's amazing.'

'What is?' Liz asked. She wasn't now sure she was keen on the young American, though she could see that McCullain undoubtedly was. He hadn't taken his eyes off her all night, but Tom didn't seem to have noticed. The realisation came to her with a little green tickle of resentment, which she suppressed quickly. *What the hell do I care?* she thought.

'That's where *we're* staying,' Tom put in. 'For the next week. We're exploring the whole west coast.'

'Yes. It's wonderful, isn't it?' Nancy enthused. 'I've always wanted to come here. I think it's so *romantic*. And the *history* . . . Have you seen the place they've been digging?'

Sean shook his head, eyebrows raised in question.

'Just next to the cottages. Some kind of old burial place. They showed us it today. It's terrific. I mean, *thousands* of years old.'

'Must have a look at it tomorrow,' Sean said.

'We won't have time,' Liz said back, and not for the first time, Nancy thought there was something *odd* about the two of them. Not *weird*, or worrying. It was just that at first she'd been *sure* they'd been a pair. They had looked so *right* with each other. Nancy might have looked like the cheerleader she'd never been in high school, but behind those blue eyes, she had a sharp intellect and even sharper instincts. She taught physics on campus at the old-money university and had the kind of inquisitive mind that had sailed her through her own examinations with near enough straight As. She had noticed the body language that passed from Liz to Sean and it had puzzled her. Liz's dry, almost petulant manner belied the way she *was* with McCullain. It was as if there was some kind of need there that the woman shoved away from herself, denying its existence. Already Nancy liked Sean McCullain, and she could see why Liz was attracted to him, even if she pretended, to herself and everybody else, that she wasn't. He was tall and wide-shouldered and had a lived-in face that might not have been altogether handsome, but was intelligent and attractive in a craggy sort of way. But it was his dark grey eyes under the heavy brows that told the real story. There were crinkles at the corners that spoke of the natural laugh which he'd shown during the meal. There was also something else about them, some hint of a shadow that could have been wariness, or maybe even sadness.

'We won't have time,' Liz was saying. 'We have to get down south and then up to Knock.'

'Might as well use the cottage as a base for both,' Sean said, helping himself to another coffee, then offering the silver jug around. He poured out the thick cream over the back of his spoon: the white pooled out onto the black surface.

'That reminds me. I must have a few more pints of Guinness while I'm in the ould country.'

'I tried that,' Nancy said. 'Isn't it *awful?*'

'You get used to it,' he said.

'We don't have a year,' Nancy said, and they all laughed.

Later, when they'd finished, Tom wanted to pay the bill to thank them for letting them eat with them, but eventually, after a to-and-fro argument, they split it down the middle. Tom bought brandies all round, and late on, feeling mellow and warm, they all headed for the door. Behind them the owner and his wife wished them a good night and a safe journey.

Out on the quayside it was dark and a pale moon had risen south of the bay, silvering the still waters. There was no wind and the night was not yet cold.

'Thanks a million,' Tom said again. 'That was the best night I've had in days.'

Nancy nudged him mischievously. 'I hope not,' she said with a laugh.

'Not if you're just married,' Sean joined in.

'Well, one of the best. If it hadn't been for you we'd have had tea bags and cookies.'

Sean turned to go across the road to where he'd parked the car. When he reached it he called back: 'If we don't see you again, have a good holiday.' Tom waved back from beside his rented car.

Nancy took Liz by the hand and thanked her too.

'You saved our lives tonight. If you're ever in Vermont . . .'

'If I ever get the chance,' Liz answered the unfinished question.

'Oh, and . . .' Nancy said. She paused, as if unsure about what to say. 'He's a good man,' Nancy said, nodding over to where Sean was opening the car door. 'If I wasn't married I'd have a go for him myself.'

She smiled, to show she was only joking. Then on a quick impulse, she leaned over and gave Liz a quick, womanly hug. As she did so, she whispered: 'I'd hold on to him if I were you.'

She moved back and Liz looked at her. Nancy winked and smiled that perfect smile that lit up her face. She turned to Tom, who had his hands in his pockets, and put her arm through his.

'Come on, big boy. There's a peat fire waiting for us.'

Tom laughed and they moved off. Liz crossed to the car. She had a little puzzled expression on her face.

Sean started the engine, reversed tightly and then angled the car onto the road, heading westwards again.

'Nice people,' he said agreeably. 'She's an absolute stunner.'

'I noticed you noticed,' Liz said, her eyes straight ahead.

'Great face to photograph. Good lines.'

'A bit empty-headed, I'd say.'

'No. I think she just gives him priority. She's bright enough. And that meal,' he said, changing tack. 'That was truly superb.'

He speeded up and switched the headlamps on. The last of the light was gone and the twin cones angled straight ahead in a reverse perspective. Croagh Patrick was a dark hump against the sky, solid and set. The car snaked round the corners, and eventually the last of the outlying cottages was behind them. Here and there a clump of trees, willows and alders, would blur by on either side. They got to the fork of the road, taking the right, and beyond that there was a belt of elms that drooped shady branches like long fingers.

Sean had been humming absently to himself, his voice a low, soft rumble that sounded as if it was coming from his chest. Liz was full and sleepy. She sat curled in the passenger seat, legs drawn up, head on her shoulder, eyes shut.

Near the end of the trees, something moved in the light of the full beams. Sean peered ahead, maintaining speed, and then the vision struck him with full force.

It came swooping down from the overhanging branches, something black and fluttering, like a bunch of old rags which tumbled quickly then darted straight at the car windscreen.

'Wha —'

The question stuck in his throat and Sean put a hand up instinctively to ward off the thing that came bulleting in blackly right at him. He got a glimpse of long dark arms reaching forward, skeletal fingers curving into claws.

There was a juicy, high-pitched whine in his ears, like the sound of his flashgun charging itself, exactly the kind of sound that he *always* heard inside his head when he was going to have *that dream* again. It was the tickly, taut violin string resonance that presaged the sudden lurch into the real and unreal world of the dream. He felt the weight of his body change, lightening itself as it did in his sleep, feeling the numbness spread through his limbs as if his mind had decided that he was going to *have* the dream, like it or not, while there was nothing his body could do about it. All this happened in the fraction of a second between his eye catching the fluttering shape and the face leaping into focus, the horrible, wizened, *distorted* face that swooped in front of his own. In that instant everything slowed down. Time stretched out. Sean heard his voice shout '*what*' and the long syllable dopplered down, elongating, like a tape that had been slowed beyond comprehension.

In the expanded time-frame he heard his heart give a hard, strong beat that pounded like the distant double boom of a big drum. It faded away with a soughing sound behind his ears. He saw, out of the corner of his eye, a leaf caught tumbling from a tree, curled in flight, moving as through syrup. The noise of the engine, too low to be heard, had faded out. It was as if he was alone within an encapsulated bubble of real time while the rest of the world, the rest of everything, had slowed to a snail's crawl.

Right in front of the windscreen, the vision soared at him, hands outstretched. The face, leprous and scabbed, horribly wrinkled, terribly *ancient*, came looming in. The eyes were like pits, and the mouth was open in an eternal scream of fury. Rotted teeth, sharp and twisted, poked out from peeling gums. Matted hair flapped like moulded ropes on either side. From the dead sockets under ridged brows, there was a gleam of feral red.

It was the face he'd seen leaping from the water of the bridge, defying gravity to soar upwards in a black fountain towards him.

But that wasn't a face. *That was a dead sheep . . .*

The apparition screamed at him soundlessly, but inside his head, he could *hear* the reverberation of it, a foul shrieking that drilled through him. The claw-hands reached and scrabbled at the toughened glass. Sharp nails bit into the clear screen. He could see them, long and black and pointed, piercing *through* the laminated pane, coming straight at his throat.

He jerked himself back, pressing himself into the seat. His left foot rammed hard, reflexively stamping down on the brake pedal. It moved agonisingly slowly. His knee had come up and then his foot had gone down, as if he was treading through warm tar. It touched on the brake and continued its motion.

In front of his eyes, only a foot or so away, dreadful claws were knifing their way through the glass. Behind them the hideous face opened its mouth, and a tongue that was black and pointed and covered with pustules like a toad's skin unrolled and darted forward, a snake's palpating fork except for its arrowed tip, barbed and venomous and obscenely long. Things crawled in the matted hair, moving with that lurching motion of hard-backed carapaced scuttering insects. The nose was long and hooked and the nostrils flared on either side, held wide by double-folds of wrinkled skin. All over the narrow cheeks, between the fissures of wrinkles, there were poisonous-looking lumps that sprouted thick, stiff hairs.

In his head he heard the scream ringing so high he could feel his eyes water with the intensity of the vibration it set up inside his skull. His foot came down and he felt the brake catch. The nose of the car began to swerve to the right. The claws came on through the glass, black daggers set in grey skin, edging their way towards him. Inside him, he felt the familiar *twist*, his body snapping into some new frame of reference. A spasm racked his shoulders as if muscles under his skin had humped and swelled: there was a creaking sound in his neck, like bones stretching, and the sides of his temples throbbed with something that was not a heartbeat. It was too damned *fast* to be a heartbeat.

Behind his ears, the mosquito whine returned, contracting itself up from the low, sub-audible buzz, swiftly soaring up through a fluting note into the juicy tickle. His heartbeat then returned, BOOM, slow and sonorous, *boom boom* faster. Something big and black hit off the windscreen with a wet thud and tumbled over the roof, clattering as it hit again.

'What the fuck?' Sean finished his shout. The words came welling upwards as if somebody had turned on the fast button on the recorder, speeding him up. Around him the capsule ruptured like a bubble and he was back in *normal* sequential time. The car slewed suddenly to the right, out into the middle of the road, as his foot pressed the brake pedal so hard his heel thumped down on the carpet. He could feel the back wheels slide with that strange dizzying lurch of forward motion given a sideways drift. Automatically his hands spun the wheel left again, into the drift, trying to take the pressure out of the spin. For a second it caught, then the wheels skidded on wet autumn leaves or some road-surface slick, and the wheel turned uselessly in his hands.

Beside him, Liz let out a scream of fright as she tumbled off her seat and onto the floor in a tangled heap.

'Stay down,' Sean bawled over the screeching of the tyres and the juddering of the suspension. He felt the car tilt, the motion of a slow roll, then the nearside wheel miraculously caught something rough, enough to turn the nose, to slam the raised wheels back onto the road. The car slithered and skewered its way and then spun in a complete compass-needle swing until it was facing backwards. The motion continued and Liz yelled again, this time in real fright. Branches whipped against the side panels and there was a huge *spang* as a branch snapped under a wheel arch, and then the car just slid off the road into a tangle of bracken and alder with an almighty thump. Sean was thrown sideways and his head painfully hit the window, just above his ear.

The engine coughed several times and then died.

Sean let his breath out in one long sigh.

From down in the dark, in the passenger's floorwell, Liz's voice came up: 'What the hell are you playing at, McCullain? You nearly killed both of us.'

'Something on the road.' he said, voice shaky.

'What?'

'I don't know what. Something came out and hit the windscreen,' he said.

'I didn't see anything. You must have fallen asleep,' she said, equally shaky, but anger rising in her voice. 'Bloody hell, you could have killed us.'

'Shut up a second,' he snapped, heart still racing. He could feel the nerves judder and shiver along his arms, and the looping roll in his stomach that spoke of the adrenaline hit.

'Don't you tell me —'

'Oh for Christ's sake shut the fuck up,' Sean bellowed back at her. 'Something came out of the trees and hit the fucking window and if I'd been fucking sleeping we'd have gone into the trees a hundred yards back, but we didn't and we're alive and in one fucking piece,' he roared.

'No need to shout,' Liz came back in a small voice, as if suddenly scared, not just of what happened, but of McCullain's anger.

'Right. Just let me get my breath,' he said. She heard him take a deep fill of his lungs, and let it back out again, once, twice, a third time, deliberately trying to bring himself down from a high.

'Something came out of the trees. I don't know what in Christ's name it was. It came straight for the car. Just a shadow. I never got a good look at it,' he lied. 'I tried to stop and we went into a skid. But I think the car's all right. And I'm sorry I swore, okay?'

Even Liz could hear the shaky quality of his voice. He must have got a real fright.

Sean opened the car door, shoving it against the brambles until it was wide enough for him to squeeze out. Liz came out on the other side. Both of them looked along the road. There was just a dim passage under the overhanging trees, but enough peripheral light from the headlamps, beaming their way into the grove, to see the road surface. It was empty. Nothing there.

'What was it?'

'I dunno,' he said. He certainly didn't want to describe it to her, because there was one thing of which he was sure. He had seen something, but what he had seen was not what he had been shown in the strange, stretched-out time of the *vision*. No sir, no way. That was just part of the run of dreams he'd been having ever since Belfast. Different, but similar.

Not for the first time, Sean thought that he might be having a little problem; a little *mental* problem. Somewhere inside his head, some of the axons and dendrites had been sizzled numb by what had happened when he saw that crowd and the two men with death in their eyes.

McCullain had been around. He'd seen death and destruction in many of its forms, but the one in Belfast had been different. It had *got* to him, in the way that nothing else had before. It had got under his skin and into his head and he was paying for it now.

The thought that there might be something wrong inside his head scared the living daylights out of him. He had always known his own *self*. Lived with the balance, rolled with the punches. But now. *Now*. On this night, beside the car angled into the hedgerow, after seeing the grotesque obscenity that had swooped down, an abomination that couldn't exist except in the shadowed pathways of a sick imagination, McCullain suddenly thought that it was high time he had a rest, just to clear his mind; to try to scatter those dreams, those things that swung into vision in front of his eyes.

127

Standing at the side of the car, looking down a gloomy, eerie roadside where nothing lay, no tattered crow that might have fluttered into the beams of his headlights and been converted by a tired, *bruised* mind into something unthinkable, McCullain made a decision. He did not tell Liz Cannon what his decision was. She'd find out soon enough.

He slowly squeezed himself back into the car and started the engine. The lights dimmed a little as it caught, then he eased the clutch into second, feeling the wheels skid on the slick surface. Then one of them caught enough on a branch underneath the mud, and the car lurched out of the hedge and onto the road. Sean made a three-point turn and they went on their way. Half a mile on, they came to the hump-backed bridge. McCullain gunned the car up and over in one swift stomach-sinking glide and drove for the cut-off track to the cottages.

17

Donovan's bar stands at the corner of the main street through Kilgallan where it is bisected by the little road that goes, on the west, down past the tor towards the ring of cottages, and on the other side, the moor road that connects a string of outlying farms before it disappears out beyond the peat bogs. The main street is the first leg of the Killadoon Road that trails its way past the deserted hamlets that have been crumbling since the potato famine, and snakes down the edge of the immense Tallabaun Strand, where the flat tidal sands stretch out as far as the eye can see.

Sean McCullain put his hands on the edge of the bar and cast his eyes over the gantry. There were rows of bottles filled with smoky whiskies, both Scotch and Irish. Some of the labels were old and unfamiliar. The bar, warm and dimly lit, had a fine wooden counter, dry and pitted and shiny from years of elbows rubbing its hard grain to a fine polish. On the far wall was the inevitable massive slate fireplace in which a fire glowed. Even from twenty feet away, Sean could feel the rosy warmth.

A fine smirr of rain had been falling like a mist as he and Liz came along the track. They'd parked the car at the cottage and Sean had stacked a few more bricks of dry peat on the dying fire, then told her he needed a drink. That was no exaggeration. He *needed* a drink. The image of the thing he'd seen – *thought he'd seen* – on the road in from Westport kept flitting in front of his mind like a recurring ache. He was still shaken from the sudden lurch he'd felt inside when the car went into its spin on the wet road. It was fair to say that Liz too had a fright, although she'd seen nothing. The abruptness of the skid into the hedge had been tempered by the fact that she was half asleep and by her instantly flaring annoyance at McCullain for slewing them off the road.

When he'd told her he was going for a drink, she'd considered whether to let him go on alone while she stayed in the cottage. But the night was not yet late and she had nothing to read, so she told him she'd come along. She tried pitching her voice to the tone that said she was only going in a bid to beat boredom, but failed.

In the close warmth, Liz took off her jacket and gave it a shake to let the moisture flick off, then sat down on one of the heavy stools jammed up against the brass footrail. Behind the bar a huge barrel-chested man with a grizzled russet beard matched Sean's stance. He had wide, strong fingers with ginger hair on the knuckles. Arms thick from rolling barrels were covered in freckles.

'Well, big fella,' he boomed. 'What'll be your pleasure?' The big man had a surprisingly mild voice, softened even further by his Mayo accent. Sean drew his gaze away from the gantry and met the landlord eye to eye. He was the same height, but the bearded man looked twice Sean's girth.

'And something for the lady and all,' he added.

Sean ordered a pint of Guinness and a Talisker malt whisky, which had been one of his grandfather's cure-alls. The old man was born on Skye, where they made the dark, peaty malt, and had passed on the taste for it down the generations. Liz said she'd have a brandy, and the man set up the spirits first then let the Guinness separate out into a black body and a creamy white head before placing it on the bar. Sean passed over the notes and slid onto the stool beside Liz.

'The price of it would make your eyes water,' a voice said at his side, and he turned to face a small, stocky man with rimless polygon glasses.

'True enough,' Sean said agreeably. 'But the flesh is weak and the spirits warm the heart.'

'That they do indeed. But in a country where a few pennies on the price of a pint can topple a government, you'd think they'd make sure a man could have a decent drink without facing ruin.'

Sean nodded and the man stuck out his hand.

'James Connarty,' he said, and then half-turned to introduce the two others. Sean shook hands with the young man with the shock of black Irish hair and leaned past to do the same with the woman. She had rich auburn hair, neat in its pleats, and a heart-shaped, intelligent face.

'We're the dirty diggers,' Terry said. His handshake was firm and Liz felt callouses on his palm that told of heavy manual labour.

'You're farmers?' she asked.

'Wish we were, for there's more money in it,' Terry said back. 'No. We're working on the tor. Archaeological dig.'

'I heard about that tonight,' Sean said. 'We met a couple of Americans who said something about an old tomb.'

'Ancient tomb, young fellow. Positively archaic,' Connarty said. 'Nearly five thousand years old. It's a major find.'

'He'd say that anyway, just to keep the grants coming,' Terry said, winking at Liz. Just then, the door behind the bar opened and a young girl came out, and Terry's eyes swept away from Liz.

'Well, good evening to you, Miss Donovan,' he called across. At the far end of the bar, the big man, who was pouring a pint of beer, turned his head.

'Hello, Terry,' she said with a gentle lilt. 'Professor. Siobhan.' She nodded to each. 'It's a fine soft night, isn't it?'

The girl was slightly built and had a mass of black hair that tumbled onto her shoulders. She looked as delicate as the big man was brawny. Her skin had a translucent quality that was heightened by the smattering of tiny freckles on the bridge of a sculpted, pert nose and spreading delicately on high cheekbones. Her eyes were so dark they looked as black as her hair, and stood out lustrous against the pale skin.

Terry sighed and Sean caught Siobhan smiling to herself.

'Oh, I'm in *love* with that girl,' Terry said theatrically.

'No. You're in lust, as ever, Terence. That's why all the mothers lock up their daughters at night. You're nothing more than a pillager and a ravisher, if truth be told.'

'That's all in the past. It's Maeve I'm head over heels besotted with. Strike me down if I tell a lie.' He hefted his pint and sank half of it in a massive swallow. 'No wonder a man turns to drink.'

'If Declan Donovan thought you had designs on his daughter, he'd turn you inside out,' Connarty said, laughing.

He turned to Sean. 'And what brings you to this edge of the great beyond?'

'We're working on a couple of stories,' Liz interjected. 'I'm a reporter. We're just passing through.'

'What do you do?' Siobhan asked Sean. He told her he was a photographer, and she immediately answered that she could have used his expertise.

'I'm working with Polaroids at the moment, and they're not really up to the job. The flash isn't strong enough.'

'How big is the place inside?'

'About fifteen yards in diameter. It's pretty big.'

'You need more flash than you've got, that's for sure,' Sean said. He took another sip of his whisky, feeling the trickle of heat spread in his chest. 'Maybe I could have a look, if you don't mind.'

'Surely. You're very welcome,' Siobhan said, with a smile. 'It would be a great help.'

'We have to go down to Cleggan tomorrow. I'm doing a feature on the power station there,' Liz said.

'That'll be the peat-fired station?' Siobhan asked. Liz told her it was.

'I've read all about it. It's been in all the papers,' Siobhan said

131

innocently, and Sean almost choked on his drink. Liz shot him a dismayed look.

Further down the bar were three men who were the merrier for the several pints of dark beer that had come out of the hand pumps. They were speaking in loud, jovial voices and every now and again there would be an explosion of laughter from the group.

Sean raised an eyebrow in question.

'Fishermen,' Siobhan said. 'Come up from the oil rigs for a couple of weeks. They're out every day in the bay and in here every night telling tall tales about the ones that got away. They'll drink the bar dry in two weeks, that's for sure.'

'Sounds like my kind of people,' Sean said. 'I haven't been fishing in the past year.'

He swivelled round in his seat to face her. She was a capable-looking woman, maybe in her late twenties. The white Aran sweater looked as if it was knitted for someone two sizes larger, but couldn't disguise an ample, strong-looking figure.

She caught Sean's quick appraisal and matched it with her own look. Her eyes sparkled with intelligence.

'How long are you here for?' Sean asked.

'Just another week. I've been here on and off since the spring, but we all have to be back in Dublin for the start of term, so we're against the clock, you might say. I'm the professor's number two. I'm the paleolinguist.'

'What's that?' Liz asked.

'Ancient languages,' Sean said, and Siobhan gave him an approving nod.

'Yes. I studied the old Gaelic and Celtic languages, and this dig looks as if it's given me enough work for the next ten years. We've found carvings all over the place which are very unusual. Not the kind of pictograms you'd expect, but something much more like the runes that predate Ogham script. I've taken a few rubbings and more Polaroids, but there's a lot more to be done. I've started a bit on the translation, but it's not easy going. We don't really have anything that goes back as far as that.'

'Whose tomb is it?' Liz asked.

'That we don't know,' Siobhan said. 'But we did find something interesting. You see there's a —'

'There's a lot of things we have to think about before we discuss it here,' Dr Connarty interjected quietly. He and Terry had been talking together and he had heard what Siobhan was about to say.

'Ah, yes,' she said. She dropped her voice. 'Some of the local folk aren't so keen on what we're doing. But we *have* made a significant find. It's going to make a very good story, if you're interested.'

'I think we might be,' Sean said. Liz said nothing.

The three anglers were vying for the attentions of both Declan Donovan and his daughter. The bar-owner didn't mind the overt passes the oilmen incessantly made at Maeve. They had done the same thing when they had come to Kilgallan at the tail end of the winter to fish for the big cod out beyond Clare Island. They were typical roughnecks on leave. They fished hard and they drank hard and they were laid back enough to chat up any woman who walked into the bar, without causing offence. A blind man could have seen through them. Maeve, however, blushed furiously every time, but there was no harm in it. Donovan was sure that if she gave any of them the nod, they'd run a mile. He ran the best pub in the whole of Mayo, and that carried a lot of clout. Nobody on this side of the bay would do anything that would get them barred from his place.

Frank Wysocki was the only man in the bar who was even bigger than Declan Donovan. There were a couple of locals down at the other end, where the room widened out around the fire, who were maybe as tall as he was, but Frank was built like a bull. His shoulders would have made Sean McCullain look slight by comparison and he had a short greying beard that seemed to sprout up from the hairs on his chest, bristling their way out of the opened collar of his chambray shirt. He had hands like shovels, and when they hefted his pint of beer the whole tumbler seemed to disappear into it. His loud, booming Santa-Claus laugh could have been overpowering, but was so natural it was infectious.

'You tell your daddy you're having a day off tomorrow and I'll take you out on the boat,' he was saying to Maeve. The girl dropped her eyes, embarrassed again.

'That would be like running away with a Polack grizzly bear,' Pete Coia said. He was whip-thin, with Italian dark hair, and spoke in the same Canadian accent as his big sidekick.

'Better that than a greasy Spic on a starvation diet,' Frank said, and boomed out again, his sizeable belly jiggling up and down with his laughter.

'Don't listen to him, kid. When we run out of bait we just stick Pete on the end of a hook and let him wriggle.' Beside them Doug Petersen cawed laughter.

'Don't know what you're laughing about,' Pete said. 'It's like Crocodile Dundee meets Sasquatch. I could write the movie.'

'No worries, mate,' Doug said in a good imitation of Paul Hogan that didn't take too much of an effort. He was a rangy fair-haired man with a ruddy complexion and crinkles at the corners of his eyes that bore witness to a lifetime under the sun.

'How long have you got now?' Declan called over to them after he finished pouring the pints.

'Another eight days. We're out on the bay tomorrow and then maybe we'll have a couple of days up at Beltra Lough for the salmon. Mike O'Hara across at the Tallabaun Inn says he'll take anything we catch.'

'Just make sure you get the money first.'

'Oh, Mike's okay,' Frank Wysocki said. 'I told him he could arm-wrestle for the price and he said he'd rather pay straight cash.'

Everybody laughed at that one. Big Frank Wysocki, whose family had been loggers for five generations, looked as if he could tear a man's arm from its socket.

In the cottage nearest the straggle of trees, and closest to the one that Sean and Liz had taken, Brian Cooney looked up from the paper he was reading.

'I'm going to go up and phone in a minute. Want to come?'

'Not tonight,' Bridget Massey said. She was sitting in the opposite armchair with her feet drawn up under her, nose buried in a paperback novel.

'It has to be tomorrow, or the day after that,' Cooney said. 'We'd best be prepared for them coming with the stuff.'

'Don't worry. My brother will have everything fixed.'

'What about the newcomers?'

'Mrs Gilly says they're only staying for a night or so. Says they're reporters. The man's Scottish and she's English.'

'Don't like the sound of that. It could be a cover.'

'Don't be paranoid,' Bridget said, looking up from the book. 'They're just passing through.'

'There's a lot of Scots in the UDR *and* in Special Branch.'

'I know that, but the old woman says they got fixed up by the tourist board only this morning. There's not much we can do about it, so we'd best not worry about it.'

'And how about those two over there?' he said, indicating a general direction with a nod of his head. 'The birdwatchers.'

'I think they're a couple of pansies,' Bridget said with a grin.

'There's something funny about them.'

'That's what I said.'

'No. More than that.'

'Well, they haven't bothered us so far. And we can keep an eye on them. If there's anything wrong, then we can move. My Padraigh can fix it up, no problem.'

Brian Cooney seemed mollified. He put the paper down and got up and unhooked his jacket from the peg near the door.

'Sure you don't want a quick one?'

'Maybe later,' she said, eyes still on the page. He picked up his hat and crammed it on his head, pulling the peak down over his eyes.

'Maybe not such a quick one,' he said.

'Oh, boasting again, are we, Cooney?'

'Sure it's no boast. Don't you bring out the best in me, Bridget?'

'If that's your best, you'll have to try harder.'

'Away with you, girl,' he said. He bent down to give her a quick kiss and she raised her head to meet his mouth with hers, opening her lips and easing her tongue on his. A moment later, he pulled away.

'Any more of that and I'll never get to the phone.'

'Hurry back now,' she said, flashing him a hungry look.

'One of them's just gone out,' Hugh Sands said. He was standing in semi-darkness at the edge of the window-frame, peering through the slit-gap between the curtain and the wall.

'Which one?' Laird asked.

'Hard to tell. Cooney, I think. Gone down the track.'

'On his own?'

'Looks like it. Think I should check?'

'Yes. He's probably gone up to the pub. Keep an eye on him and I'll make sure she's still in there.'

'You get all the easy jobs,' Sands said, grinning.

'That's because I've got more stripes,' Laird said easily.

Sands shrugged himself into his dark gamekeeper's waterproof jacket and zipped it up to the neck, then pulled the catch down again to leave a space. He dug his hand in deep, right down under his armpit, and brought out his gun, checked it quickly in a practised motion, then slammed the magazine hard into the butt and slipped the weapon back into the holster.

On the day they'd arrived, only hours after Cooney and Massey had turned up, Laird and Sands had reconnoitred the whole area with skilful precision. Laird, the senior man, had a habit of going by the book, as if he was reading from the manual of the counter-terrorist service.

Always find every route in and out of the location. It will give you the advantage over the enemy because it cuts down thinking time.

They had quartered the place, found every vantage point, every nook and cranny where a man could hide and stay hidden. They had found the places where they could see every cottage and the approaches, even down to the small jetty beyond the tor. Since they arrived, nothing had happened, but Laird always insisted it was better to be *sure*, all the time.

This was just a routine surveillance operation of peripheral suspects, suspects by *association* rather than any knowledge of activity. But pressure was building in the northern province. Politicians were wielding muscle, and the security forces had poured enormous numbers into the latest counterstroke in a bid to get results that would look good in the tabloids. With an election almost certain within the year, it was *definite* that heads would roll if a vote-catching coup did not materialise. Laird and Sands were only one unit of many that had been sent hither and yon on what would, in the vast majority of cases, prove to be wild-goose chases. Special Branch had spread itself wide, and spread itself thin; but the sister of a known commander of the Provisional IRA was worth watching.

The younger man let himself out of the back door, which was only twenty yards away from the straggling line of trees and saplings that bordered the main road into the village. There was only one road into the field where the cottages stood, one road that a car could use. But there was also a track down to the jetty and another one that would take walkers down to the shoreline where the Roonah Water spilled sluggishly into the bay. The vehicle access twisted to the right then left again past Mrs Gilly's little house and up to the village. Through the trees there were a number of tracks made by rabbits and enlarged by small boys hunting chestnuts. A drainage ditch there had a couple of pine logs angled over it for a makeshift bridge, and by using that track, it was a walk of less than a minute to Donovan's bar.

Sands took a chance and went across the road and in through the double doors that had old-fashioned etchings on the glass panes. A blast of heat and laughter assailed him, and Declan Donovan nodded to him. Sands opened his coat, checking first to ensure that his holster was right out of sight, sitting over his kidney, and ordered a pint.

Two minutes later, Brian Cooney came in, slipping quietly through the door and straight to the bar. Young Maeve served him a porter and Cooney asked her for some change for the machine.

'Cigarettes or phone?'

'Both of them,' Cooney told her. She went to the till and slipped the note under the tray and scooped out a handful of silver.

'There you are now,' she said, counting them out into his hand.

Sands eyed the position. Ideally he wanted to be round at the far end, near where the phone was screwed onto a wall in the corner. Even then he would have difficulty in getting close enough to hear a word without making it obvious. And anyway, men in pubs don't move around unless they know everyone else, or unless they're policemen or Salvation Army collectors.

Sands hunched over the bar and sipped his beer. Cooney took his drink across and stuck it up on the shelf between the phone and the old dartboard that was shedding pieces of cork onto the hard floor. Sands saw him dial, and then start to talk. There was an obvious couple of questions, from the way the man was standing, then a long hiatus as he listened. Finally he said something into the receiver, nodded quickly as if the person on the other end could see him, and then hung up. He retrieved his drink and came back to the bar a few yards away from Sands.

Beside him, the three oilmen had got to the expansive, roistering stage and their laughter filled the bar. Next to them were the newcomers, the big dark-haired fellow and the blonde, good-looking girl, in conversation with the archaeologists who were digging a hole in the hill. Down at the far end there was a crowd of local folk, mostly lanky, long-faced farmers taking up most of the hard benches set on the walls, talking amongst themselves in their soft brogues. At their feet were a couple of collies stretched out, half-asleep in front of the fire.

Outside, the moon was just a vague luminescence behind thick clouds that continued to let out their fine drizzle like a curtain of mist.

Edward Laird moved quickly and quietly in the dark behind the cottage, close to the belt of trees. The wet grass muffled his footsteps and the fine rain damped the sound down even further.

There was a light on in the kitchen of the cottage where Cooney and Massey were staying. Laird had already checked the front of the house from his own window and noticed the slit of light where the curtains hadn't been completely closed. At the back the light beamed out, sending a long rectangle of illumination onto the grass. He ducked down below it and moved into the shadow, edging up to the window, but not close enough to let the light reflect on his face. It was one of the first lessons he'd learned in night surveillance. From the inside, when there's a light on, most of it is reflected back on the glass, making it

137

impossible to see out. Conversely, if the light is switched off, a watcher can look out without fear of being seen. At this particular time, it mattered little. There was no-one in the kitchen and the door was closed. Laird moved off round the side of the building. He crept up to the front window, making sure there was no-one watching from the darkened bedroom – no, the curtains were tight shut – and silently eased himself in front of the pane.

He had to stand on tip-toe to get his eye to the chink in the curtain. It afforded him a narrow-angle view of the room.

Bridget Massey was sitting in the armchair, reading a book. There was no-one else there, so that meant that Cooney had left. Laird hoped that Sands had picked him up and stuck with him. He eased himself down from the window and turned to the right, past the small flowerbed that fronted the cottage wall. He got to the corner and a light came on in the window of the adjacent cottage, framing him in sudden brilliance.

'Shit!' he mouthed and ducked back against the wall out of sight, feeling the stone wall rasping against the tough material of his jacket. He waited there for a few moments, deciding what to do. He didn't fancy walking out into the light, for there he could be seen from any of the cottages, and anyone prowling at night is under suspicion.

Instead, he slowly made his way round to the back again. He turned the corner and was halfway along the wall when he realised that the kitchen light had gone out. He stopped, frozen for a second. Either Massey had moved, or there had been someone else in the house all along.

Laird decided the best thing would be to make for the trees, which would at least give him cover. He walked six steps and suddenly the back door of the cottage slammed open and Bridget Massey came out. The light from inside the house speared Laird in mid-step, but the woman didn't even look in his direction. She was carrying a paper bag filled with something and bent to lift the rubber lid of the dustbin.

It is likely that Laird would have gone unnoticed, standing still on the grass, but for the fact that his radio coughed a short burst of static. Instinctively he jammed his hand in his pocket and switched the damned thing off, but it was too late.

Bridget Massey gave a small cry of alarm and whirled around, holding the dustbin lid up like a shield.

'What the hell are you doing here?' she called out in a shaky voice when she'd got her breath back.

'Oh, my heart,' Laird said, putting his hand up to his chest, trying to seize the initiative. 'You gave me one hell of a shock.'

'Gave you a shock? What the devil are you doing, sneaking around out here?'

Laird coughed loudly, twice, trying to imitate the sound his radio had made, all the time thinking: *Damn them. What a time to call!*

'There's a nightjar in the trees. I thought I'd try to spot it, though it's not easy in this light. Did you hear it?'

'No I never did,' she said, still holding the lid up against her.

Just then a bird hooted from deep in the shadow of the stand of trees.

'There it is again. But it's too dark in there. I wish I'd brought a torch. Did you hear it just then?'

She nodded.

'Ah well. Pity to have heard it and not added it to the collection. They're not too common around here, or anywhere, for that matter.'

He started moving away, making his movements as casual as possible, almost sauntering. 'I think I'll have to go and have a stiff drink. My heart feels as if it's going to give out. Goodnight.'

Bridget Massey said nothing. She watched him warily until he got past the corner and was out of vision. Then she let out her breath in a long, shaky sigh. Her hands were trembling and it took her two attempts to get the dustbin lid fitted back in place. She stood there for several moments, making sure the man had gone, and then went back into the house, closing the door quickly and slamming the snib down to lock it. In the living room, she turned the light down low and went to the window. Across the way she could see the man walk up the path and into his cottage. The door threw out some brief light then cut it off again, and he was gone.

Bridget crossed to the cabinet and brought out a bottle of whiskey. She poured a large measure and threw half of it down her throat.

'Silly bastard,' she said aloud. 'Scared the shite out of me.'

She swallowed the rest of the measure, feeling the burn, then poured another one, this time a smaller measure. She carried it across to the fire and sat herself back down in the armchair. The shakes were easing off, thanks to the whiskey, and her heartbeat was slowing down. She picked up her book again, but she was still too agitated to read. The man had said he was looking for some kind of bird. A nighthawk or something. No, a *nightjar*. Bridget couldn't tell a thrush from a blackbird, but she had heard something hooting out there in the dark trees, true enough. But there was something else that was stuck in her memory. She couldn't quite put her finger on it, but there was something she'd heard that was odd. She chased the memory around but it wouldn't come out. She took another sip, beginning to enjoy the glow, and the nagging in

her mind faded down. She picked up the book absently and began to
read.

18

On the night that Edward Laird scared the daylights out of the woman whose trail he had followed down through Ireland from south of Belfast, a light wind began to ruffle the tops of the trees that lined the track down from the village, and the smirr of rain started to slant across the field in a succession of waves. It was dark down there at the tor, hidden as it was from the lights of the village by the screen of old elms and limes. The moon was three-quarters full but the cloud was too thick to let even a glimmer of it shine through. Way out at the far side of the bay, ten miles across the water, beyond the notorious Coortslugan hole where the tides met, the light on Achillbeg rock winked weakly, and most of the time its beam couldn't push its way through the thick veils of misty rain.

There was no-one at the tor. Dr James Connarty was on his fourth whiskey and was waxing more than enthusiastic about the history of old Ireland. Even the three oilmen who were spending two weeks of their month's leave fishing in the salt and fresh waters had joined an expanding crowd which included Sean McCullain and Liz Cannon. The locals tended to stick to their own side of the bar. Hugh Sands took the opportunity to make himself known to the other newcomers, telling them that he and his friend were birdwatchers, a cover that let them wander about quite openly with high-powered binoculars. Brian Cooney had two pints and left, and Sands extricated himself to make sure he went straight home. He did.

Agnes Finnegan and Theresa Laughlin had gone down to the cinema at Westport to see Michael Douglas being stalked by Glenn Close, then came home early and went to bed. Agnes said her prayers, kneeling down by the edge of her bed, while Theresa, not quite so conscientious, read a romantic novel.

The village of Kilgallan started to batten itself down for the night as the wind rose.

And down at the tor, it was dark.

If anyone had been there to see, they would have noticed the dark entrance to the tunnel that led down to the chamber, gaping like a mouth on the side of the hillock. If they had looked closer, they would have noticed the shadows lengthen and darken, coiling thickly upon each other, as if a deeper dark had overtaken the night.

But there was no-one there to see.

And down in that deep and solid blackness, the thing that had awoken from an eternity of sleep ranted and chafed against the bonds that held it, the *geis* that were being unlocked one by one.

Hunger twisted inside, a hunger for revenge. All of its scattered parts had drawn together from the furthest reaches, gathering and coalescing, pulled by the gravity of its awakened *self*, and now that it was awake there was a raging fire inside.

It cast around a black thought, feeling for what it sought.

There was life. *Hot life*.

It could sense it, out there beyond the bonds of the stone against which it clawed and scrabbled uselessly.

If anyone had been inside the central chamber of the tor and had shone a light into that stone, they might have seen the shape of something foul and loathsome floating within, something so appalling, so profane that it would harrow the eyes to look at, would sear the retinas with a coiling, *changing* obscene shadow that radiated a deadly cold and a burning hatred.

The thing cast out tendrils of its mind like black snakes, and where those powerful coiling thoughts moved, shadows deepened. Small animals shivered in their burrows as a creeping terror froze their muscles, impaling them on the black headlights of approaching horror. Owls whooped and fled through darkness to get away from the deeper black that spread out from the tor. In the undergrowth, creeping things took on life. Spiders awoke and felt the fire of hunger and went stalking. Toads lumbered from under rotten logs, spurred into motion by something that drove them out from the damp holes and sent them hunting. At the edge of the bay, in the mats of bladderwrack and kelp that swirled in an odd tide, shelled things went crawling out from shelter and slithering things uncoiled and nosed into the shallows.

The shadows moved on, deepening the night dark.

Along the Killadoon road, close to Finn Finnerty's farm, old Maureen Doyle hauled herself out of her easy chair to put another peat on the fire. Maureen was seventy-nine years old and had lived alone since her husband died ten years before. Her hair was white and sparse, and pink, freckled scalp showed through. Her shoulders were bent with the weight of the years and there was the saw-edged bite of arthritis in her hips. Old Maureen moved slowly and bent over the rush basket that held the turf bricks. She was done, she knew. Old and worn and done. Above the sagging roof, a gust of wind blew in a swirl and sent a breath down the chimney to stir the ashes in the grate. The old woman breathed heavily with the effort of loading the fire.

There was a rapping at the window as the climbing rose, moved by the wind, dragged its scaly thorns across the glass. Around the house the wind rose higher, its turbulence again blowing down the low chimney stack to send a billow of thick smoke from the fire out of the grate and into the room. The old woman coughed as the smoke clogged her throat and brought tears smarting in her rheumy eyes.

She stood up, blinking them away, and caught sight of herself in the old mirror that hung over the fireplace. She froze in the act of turning.

The face of a girl stared out at her from the burnished smoky depths of the mirror. It was the face of the girl she had been, so long ago the memory of it was just a vague, tenuous recollection of summer days, of speed and of laughter.

But there *she* was: dark-haired and blue-eyed, with a round face and dimples on either side of her lips. Old Maureen opened her mouth and the pretty girl in the mirror did the same.

'Holy mother of God,' she whispered on an indrawn breath, and her reflection mouthed the words exactly.

The bonny girl looked surprised and shocked; bewildered.

The old woman felt her heart flutter in her skinny chest, beating like a bird's, sending the blood pounding fast, too fast, in her temples. The girl in the mirror blushed, as if her heart too was beating furiously. Maureen felt her breath back up; she gasped with the need for air, and as she did so, the girl in the mirror hitched her own full breasts, as if she too was trying to catch her breath.

Maureen stared and her young, *impossibly young*, reflection stared back. The girl lifted a hand to her forehead, a smooth hand, unlined with the cracks and wrinkles of the years, rubbing it against a pale, unfurrowed brow that was framed by raven curls. Maureen found herself doing the same thing, imitating the movement, unaware that she had actually done it.

'Holy mother, I'm losing my mind sure enough,' she said in a voice that was more of a moan.

The dark blue doe eyes gazed back at her, soft and moist and bright with promise, a-glisten with *life*. The old woman stared into them, and as she did, she recalled days of summer with the smell of pollen musky on a warm wind. It was so *long* ago, but suddenly it was like *yesterday*. Years peeled away in her mind like layers of an onion; body memories, long forgotten in the deadly ache of age, came unravelling through her.

143

She felt again the hard pain of the birth in the candlelit room and Katy Fogarty the old midwife telling her to push *now*. Push and push and push. The ripping sound of new life clawing into the world, the startled bleating cry of her baby boy, red and slimed from the womb. The boy who had grown to the fine young man, the image of his daddy, and had gone off and got himself killed by a bomb in somebody else's war in somebody else's hot little country.

It came back in a rush, the pain and the love and the heartbreak. And before that, the feeling of *life* sprinting through new veins; young, *vital* veins.

Maureen stared at the young girl in the mirror, knowing the pretty lass was a figment of her imagination, a picture conjured up by an old, tired head, the way they said the old folk did, clawing their way back to their childhood in a final last stand against approaching oblivion.

She didn't mind. Not now that she realised. She was old and tired and her body was crumbling and slack. The young girl in the mirror smiled at her, showing teeth that were perfect and white, teeth long gone in the old hard days when the dentist was a travelling man who set up his chair in the back room of the Kilgallan bar and pulled out teeth with the aid of a pair of pliers and a bottle of whiskey.

The echoes came back now. She could feel them stirring in her body. Those doe eyes sparkled with shy, girlish laughter, and Maureen felt the resonance of it vibrate inside her, the way a guitar string will sing the note of its twin.

'Ah yes, those days were *good*,' she murmured, nodding to the colleen as if she were actually there. The girl nodded back, beaming her lovely smile.

Behind the reflection the smoky shadows shifted and rolled. There was a movement within, a slow movement of someone approaching through the dim reflection of the old, darkwood door.

It came as a whisper, so soft her mind heard it before her ears did. *Maureen, Maureen, won't you come away with me to the hayfield now?*
Her breath caught again in a small gasp that stopped midway.
Maureen, dear of my heart. Come away now to the hayfield.

Those were the words he'd used. The whisper came back to her, fresh and hot over those more than sixty years. She'd been working here, in this room, helping his mother, who'd been upstairs in her bed, laid low with the consumption that weakened her more every year, even in the summer time. She'd been burnishing the old mirror, *this* old mirror, old and smoky then, and she'd been about to stack up the peats, when he'd come in behind her and laid his hands on her hips. He'd whispered to her and she could smell the straw on him and the green sap on the hands that slowly slipped about her waist. She'd looked up then, seeing him in the mirror, dark eyes and black curls that came over his ears. He'd whispered and she'd felt the tickle in her ears and the surge in her breast and the warmth that stole over her whole body like a tempting sin.

The corn's in, and my da's gone up to slake his thirst. Come on now to the hayfield while the sun's still warm.

He said it again, and this time she could hear it, reverberating through her down those decades. And in the mirror, behind the girl's reflection, the shape came out of the shadows and put strong hands on the curves of her hips.

He leaned forward, nuzzling her curls with his cheek, want in his eyes, *need* in his hold. And Maureen *felt* it. She felt those hands again at her waist, and smelled the fields on him.

'Holy mother, it's my Daniel,' she breathed.

The touch of him was like a little fire on either side. The old woman felt the small daggers of arthritis on her hip, a constant nag now in the damp autumn, blunt themselves down and fade. Where they had been, just below those hands, was now a warm tingle.

'Oh, what am I thinking after all these years,' she said aloud, a high tremolo, shaken with unwanted emotion.

'All gone, my Daniel, and my Danny boy, and now I'm old and I'm done,' she told the girl in the mirror. Behind the girl, Daniel looked at her with concern in his eyes.

'Never done, Maura sweetheart. Sure, you're the heart of my life and the sin of my heart. Come to the hayfield, won't you now?'

On the side of her head, she felt the warm pressure and instinctively leaned against it as the memory of the moment swooped in on her.

'All gone, and now just my old head playing cruel tricks on me.'

'No, darling. No trick. What are you saying to me, girl?'

'Too old and tired,' she quavered. 'Oh but those were sunny days.'

'Not old, girl, not you. Not ever,' Daniel whispered in her ear. She could feel the rough of the stubble against her cheek, and she almost wept at the deception of her mind.

The hands on her hips wandered upwards. She could feel them warm now against her old ribs, and her skin tingled with the touch. Slowly they moved round and up, cupping her breasts in either hand.

'No. No.' It was almost a sob. Even if it was just her old mind showing her pictures from the past, she didn't want even his memory to feel those shrivelled paps that hung down like sad dried pouches.

But even as the thought came to her, the warmth of his touch set a surge inside her. She felt her breasts swell, pressing against the gentle roughness. His fingers found a nipple and it shuddered and puckered, straining out from her skin, pulsing a hot ache through her.

'Oh Daniel, I loved you so much I could have died,' she sighed. 'And now there's nothing left for me.'

'No, girl,' the voice whispered in her ear. 'I'll always be here for you. And what's all this silliness? You'll never be old, not to me.'

'Old and done,' she said, and her whiny voice cracked with the effort.

'No, silly girl. You've been dreaming, for sure. Would you look at yourself, Maura? You're but a slip of a girl.'

The hand squeezed and tickled and hot rivers spurted upwards from the pit of her stomach to the tips of her nipple. Down below, there was a clenching, dragging sensation that was almost a pain. She felt her hips slowly move, trying to catch the sensation, to press against it, to surge with it.

She opened her eyes, which she'd closed when she felt him against her, and saw him clearly, staring from underneath those black brows, right into her.

She looked down and saw her blouse string had unloosened at the neck, showing the curve of her white, smooth breasts.

'What. . . ?' she started to say, and the voice told her to hush. The other hand slipped down from her waist and pressed against the valley between her thigh and her flank, sending the surge racing in a tide of need. She felt her heavy skirt being rucked up at the side and then the hand was on the skin of her leg. It edged around, the callouses rough against the smoothness, and then the fingers were teasing down *there* at the centre of her.

'No, *no!*' She whimpered as the old feelings came back so hard they shuddered through her.

'Just a dream, heart of my heart,' came the voice, and it was Daniel talking to her, though there was something about his voice, some echo that was *different*, some other sound *underneath* his words. 'Look at yourself. You're *my* girl. My young colleen.'

The fingers moved slow and rhythmic, and she could feel herself tighten as the hot pressure inside her built. Unable to bear it any longer, she turned round, away from the mirror and into *him*. As she did so, the questing fingers were instantly *there* and her hips bucked hard against them.

'Just a dream?' The thought hit her like a blow.

A dream of being old and sore and tired. A dream of being alone and on the point of welcoming the long sleep?

'A dream, darlin',' he said to her, and pressed himself against her, all the manliness and strong maleness of him.

And she *felt* it. She felt the softness of herself. He bent down his head, nuzzling her with his lips, and she craned up to him, still riding the wave that his fingers stirred in her seas. She felt the touch against her lips, and her mischievous tongue poked out past her teeth – *her teeth* – to lick at him.

Oh, to feel the heat of youth. To wake up from the dream of age and find him again! Inside her chest, her heart pounded hard and she felt her breasts press against his hard chest, tingling with the friction of her flaxen blouse.

He pulled her to him and pressed a hand on her shoulder, bearing her downwards. Her knees sagged and he gently eased her to the old rug that was warm from the heat of the fire. Slowly, gazing into her eyes, he unlaced the bodice until her breasts spilled out. She could see the dark pink of her nipples standing out.

A dream. A terrible nightmare, she thought.

He unhooked the string of her plaid and let the heavy cloth fall to the side, exposing her to the air. Down there a fire was burning and she could feel the pressure, the need, to quench herself with him. He knelt up and peeled off his own rough shirt, showing his broad, muscled shoulders, before starting on his own buckle. She turned her eyes away, wanting to look, but not wanting him to see her do it.

Oh, he was beautiful, and if she didn't have him now, she would *burst* with the want of it.

'Come now, Daniel, be quick. *Be quick!*'

He leaned over her and put his weight upon her, squashing her breasts in a way that sent tingles all over her. Down there she felt the hardness of him, pressing on the soft outside, almost teasing. It nuzzled like a blind animal, then found its way in. There was no hesitation. She opened and he drove into her and she moaned, high and girlish with the wonderful *filling* of it.

She raised her hands and grasped his shoulders, pulling him further into her, pressing herself upwards from the rug, trying to get it *all*. She gasped and then opened her eyes.

And she saw him *change*.

Inside her, everything froze. It was as if she was speared on a stalactite of pure ice.

In front of her face, Daniel's features seemed simply to *melt*. The skin puckered and shrivelled and the eyes shrunk into their sockets, as if they had been seared by a blast of heat and sizzled to nothing. The nose

147

shrank away, crumpling down into a hole of its own. The mouth, grimacing from the effort, widened even further, and the lips peeled back over teeth that stuck out from blackened gums. The smell of him changed, whisking away the summer scents of corn and green shaws and dry earth. In its place came a foulness like rotting meat and mouldered corruption. Pieces of hair fell away from the head, and the skin there went taut then started to crack, exposing the whiteness of bone.

And inside her – *inside her* – she could feel something *dreadful* worm its way in her depths, something cold and jagged, ripping at her in sudden ferocious stabs. The ice that had frozen her shattered and she tried to pull away. She felt a scream build up inside her chest, an *awesome* scream of pain and fear winding up like a heavy spring.

Inches from her face, the loathsome apparition mouthed at her, slobbering liplessly: '*Maureed. Darlid. Just a dreab.*'

The scream came then, high and so piercing she could feel her own skull resonate with it. Above her the mirror cracked in a sizzling lightning pattern and then slipped from the wall, crashing against the slate sill of the fireplace and shattering into a thousand slivers.

'*Lub you, Maureed,*' the apparition grunted at her from a mouth that was rotting and dripping onto her.

She felt her hips buck again in the panic of trying to draw away, to draw the thing *out* of her, and behind the burning pain in her core, where she was being clawed and ripped by sharp spikes, came the other pain, the saw teeth of arthritis whining against the joints of her hips.

'Holy mother, get *out* of me,' she managed to wail.

And the thing laughed. She heard it through that ruin of a mouth and smelled the stink of corruption that washed over her.

Inside, behind her ribs, her heart was pounding out of control. She could feel that too, hammering so hard it hurt, but that pain was nothing compared to the soreness inside her and the black terrified anguish that gripped her entire being.

She felt the scream build up again. The pressure in her lungs was hot, unbearable. She opened her mouth, and a piece of the face dripped off between her lips, sliming over her gums; her breath locked. Her heart hammered in three heavy pulses and then the pain took her. It ripped out from her chest and surged down her arms and soared up into her head. The face above her, that obscene ruin of a dead man, immediately started to fade away from her, as if drawing back. It seemed as if she too was racing away from it down a long tunnel. There was another hard pain, but by then she was far away from it, flying further and further and further, and then there was oblivion. *Nothing*.

Molly Kelly, who came in every morning to do the washing and look after old Maureen, found her at breakfast time, lying in front of the dead fire and covered with slivers of glass. She called Dr O'Brien, who came bustling along in his little Mini and pronounced her dead. It wasn't entirely unexpected, because old Maureen had been poorly these past few years and he had privately considered she wouldn't last another winter. What did surprise him was the cause of death. It was plain to see; Molly Kelly had wisely left everything as she'd found it. Perhaps not wisely. Molly had dropped her loaf of fresh bread and half a dozen eggs right onto the floor and gone running out of the house in a panicked sprint.

Old Maureen was lying on the floor, almost naked. Her blouse and cardigan were opened wide, exposing the shrivelled little breasts that dangled on each side of her skinny chest. Her skirt was opened out and her legs were splayed. Between them there was a pool of blood. Immediately Dr O'Brien thought some pervert had broken in and raped the old woman, and he felt a wave of disgust shudder through him. But then he made a brief examination and discovered the secondary cause of death. The old woman's womb had prolapsed so that it almost protruded at the top of her skinny grey shanks. And it had haemorrhaged so badly she must have spilled nigh on four pints of blood. It was an unusual thing to have happened, but not impossible and not improbable. Just to make sure, he had her body sent down to Westport for a post-mortem, and the pathologist there found she'd died of a cataclysmic heart attack, a rupture of her left ventricle that had spilled the rest of her blood into her chest cavity. Death had been quick. And old Maureen wouldn't have to suffer her arthritis for another winter, which was a blessing. The post-mortem also revealed a series of strange lacerations to the prolapsed womb, which didn't readily offer any explanation. But by the time the report was made out, it didn't matter too much. What was going to happen in Kilgallan had already begun, and there was no stopping it.

An hour after Maureen Doyle's heart burst in her chest, an hour after she'd seen the apparition of her husband and had seen him rot above her on the floor, Miread Finnerty, whose husband was still down in Galway with a caved-in head, was bathing her twin boys.

Miread was a practical woman, as small and slim as her husband was tall and broad. She didn't know what she was going to do with Finn down at the hospital, and no word yet whether he was going to live or die. Despite the worry, she got on with it. The cows needed milking and the chickens needed feeding and while there were plenty of offers of help, Miread knew it was better that she just kept herself busy rather than sitting around and worrying. Worrying came in the dark hours of the night when she'd wake up weeping tears of fear at what would become of the boys and herself. Now that the crops were in, the work wasn't too hard, and she could plough with the tractor if it came right down to it in the winter. But there was no way she could run the small farm on her own and bring up Paul and Dominic as well.

She tried to thrust the thoughts out of her mind, though it wasn't easy. She'd had the boiler on for the past hour, had run the big bath on the top landing and called the boys upstairs. They weren't much older than toddlers, identical in their ginger-haired freckled fairness that proclaimed the genetic inheritance they'd had from their father. They were robust youngsters, happy and mischievous in the way that boys tend to be, and she hid her fears from them as best she could.

She tested the water with her elbow and then hefted both of them into the bath, one at each end. They didn't like their hair being washed, but submitted to her scrubbings with resignation, spluttering as she dunked them with cupfuls of water to rinse the bubbles.

After the main cleaning, she lobbed a few plastic toys into the water for them to play with as they soaked, and went back downstairs for the towels.

In the kitchen the smells of supper lingered and the heat of the old range cooker wafted upwards towards the dark rough-backed beams that spanned the low ceiling. Miread could hear the gurgling in the pipes as the water tank filled, expanding and pinging behind the plaster of the walls the way it had always done since she'd come to the farm as Finn's bride. It was an old house, one of the oldest in the village, but one of the best too. Finn was good with his hands and could tackle any job in his slow, painstaking, thoughtful way. He'd built the kitchen units himself, laying out the room in the way that she'd wanted, making it her domain. But still he liked to sit there at the end of the table, comfortable in the heavy wooden chair, with his big gnarled hand around a man-sized mug of tea and his nose deep in the newspaper, a silent, warm presence while she bustled, birdlike, at her cooking.

The kitchen was empty of him. She could feel it like an ache. She knew he was down there in Galway, barely conscious, and that she wanted to be there with him, but she also knew that he would want her to be with the boys, for while there were many in the village who had offered to look after them, she couldn't leave them.

She bit her lip, walked over to his chair and set herself down on it. It was bigger than the rest, more massive, and higher than the others that were tucked under the broad deal table. The wooden seat was worn smooth and shiny from his hours of sitting there, and her feet hardly touched the ground. Her elbows on the table, she stared down at the dry surface she'd scrubbed so often that the grain stood out in grooves. *His seat*. Where he should be now. Miread felt a tear prick at the corner of her eye and tried to blink it back, failed, and felt the droplet tremble, fuzzing her vision, before slipping out to trace her cheek and drop to the table.

Without warning, a sombre wave of despondency blanketed her. It was as if the light had gone from the room, smothering her in a trough of dejection. Tears simply spilled from her eyes and dripped, unwiped, onto the table.

She didn't know what to do. She didn't know what to think. She felt completely helpless, adrift in a sea of gloom. The depression was so sudden and deep that all of Miread's feelings were swamped. There was no other sensation but intense *futility*.

Then she had the premonition. She saw her husband down there in hospital with that huge bandage wrapped mummy-fashion on the top of his head, and the horrible *crumpled* look of his face, as if it sagged inwards from his browline. The one eye she could see was tight closed, just the glisten of a tear in the crease. No movement there – only a desperate cold stillness. She saw the doctors pulling up the sheet until it covered him over, leaving just a big man-shape. The doctor was shaking his head and looking regretful. She saw Patsy McGavigan's long, lugubrious face, grey in the early daylight, with his professional look that he wore at every funeral. He was standing at the door with his black hat in his hand, shaking his head like the doctor had done. The familiarity those people had with death, the constructed looks, the time-served mechanisms of their posture: they were all there, and Miread *knew* this was the truth, that her Finn was dead. She saw the coffin arriving in McGavigan's good hearse and the six big men, farmers all of them, ease it onto their shoulders for the second-last journey. In her mind's eye, the men walked slowly, as if wading through thick liquid, up the path to the house. The coffin was awkward at the door and a chip of brown paint came off as the edge of it caught. There was a *smell* about the thing, a chemical smell that seemed to waft upwards and outwards from the box they'd packed him in. She could sense the ministrations of the undertaker and felt a shudder ripple through her. They had opened him up and cleaned him out and put stuff into his veins. He'd be in his Sunday-best suit, the one he would never wear again, the one she'd sewn a button on only a week before so he'd be smart down at the chapel.

In deadly slow motion, the solemn-faced, grizzled farmers laid the box down on the three chairs. There was a soft *clunk* and a scrape. There were murmurs in the background, sympathetic noises and the weeping of women. She saw old Father Cullen looking mildly bewildered, his deafness isolating him from the ordinary sounds.

Then she was walking towards the coffin, slowly. Her legs wre unsteady, as if she might fall, but there was a hand on each elbow. Someone was supporting her at either side, guiding her towards the box. A hand reached out with a brass key in it that looked just like the tool Finn used to turn the water-cock in the garden. There was a slight squeal of metal.

The lid was moving upwards, opening the coffin for the wake.

She felt her heart stop dead. It was as if a hand had reached inside her and *clenched* the beat to frozen stillness. The lid creaked up and lifted away.

The sounds drifted off. The shuffling and snuffling and uneasy coughing faded out, leaving her in the centre of a silence so thick she could have woven it. She was suddenly alone at the wake. All her senses were focused on the open box and the shape that lay within. She felt herself drift forwards, closer. She tried not to look, but there was an irresistible force that turned her head, bent her neck. The magnet drew her eyes unwillingly down. There was a black cloth spread over a shape there. Her hand moved of its own volition, reaching out – though she tried to pull it back – grasping a fold of the material and drawing it away.

The sight of Finn was so appalling that her heart kick-started back to pounding life, thrashing madly and uncontrollably.

He lay in the coffin, hands folded over his chest. There was no suit. He was naked, his big frame somehow shrunken. His skin was grey and damp-looking.

But his face. *Oh his face*! She heard the thought like a scream. It was a crumpled *ruin* of a face. The left eye was tight closed, but the other one was open and had rolled round in a terrible, inhuman squint. There was a jagged gash in his skull where the hair had been shaved away, leaving one half of his head covered in his thick ginger hair and the other grey and puckered, and a dent the size of an orange from his temple right across his brow. A mess of criss-cross cuts and cross-hatched stitches tangled within the depression, and the wounds were peeling back like old linoleum and dripping a thick pinkish fluid.

Oh, it's his brains, it's his brains, her mind yammered.

The eyebrow bone was crumpled and sagged downwards into the socket, *shoving* the eye round and forcing it out into that monstrous squint. She could see stitches, coarse black threads, badly knotted and binding his lips together in a grotesque pursed clamp. And there were more of them, a great mass of them on a gash that went from his neck right down to his pubic bone. Her eyes flicked down the length of the appalling wound, her glance alighting then darting away from the tangle of red hair and the shrivelled grey limpness below. They were drawn back to the huge wound. It was as if he'd been slashed from throat to groin. But more than that – his ribs seemed to have been crushed downwards, or taken away entirely, for his broad chest now sagged in the middle, held together by the mess of stringy stitches that strained at the pallid skin so tightly she could see where the needle-holes were ripped by the pressure.

Inside her own chest she could feel an enormous pressure build up, a dreadful eruption straining to explode.

Then his closed eye opened. It happened so quickly, so crazy and *normal* that it didn't register in Miread's mind. As if a sleeper had simply awoken, the eye swivelled towards her, blue and watery, unfocused. In the other, crumpled socket, the bulging eye there jittered with movement, but failed to turn outwards from its abysmal squint.

A sound like a shallow breath. She saw his chest move up and down slowly. Finn's battered head turned towards her, making a small scraping sound against the black cloth in the coffin. She couldn't move. The horror of that movement was so great she was simply petrified, turned to stone, while inside her the pressure swelled.

He strained, shiveringly, heaving himself upwards. The tough threads that held the wound's edges together made ripping sounds as the skin tried to pull apart. She could see the dark line on his abdomen split wider as the stitches failed to hold it, and from the ragged edges of the huge cut dribbled a red watery stuff that trickled down into his hair. The grotesque thing that was her dead husband put a hand on the edge of the coffin and his crumpled head turned to face her directly.

Mmmph.

The noise came from somewhere in the face. Muscles strained and the pallid eye rolled.

Miread stared, her own eyes bulging out in shock.

Finn's dreadful cadaver made the little noise again, then the jaw moved. The threads that bound the lips stretched, pulling on the skin, and then pulled right *through*, ripping along like a zipper, tearing the skin into ragged strips.

'*Wiwaeg. Wi-wayyyg,*' it said through flapping strands of flesh, and she dimly realised it was calling her name.

It raised a hand towards her and she couldn't move as the pale, fleshy *damp*-looking fingers clutched at her. They fell on her shoulder with a meaty thump and Miread's mind went blank for a second, trying to negate the whole thing.

And just then the scream came blasting from the lungs that had been locked tight, paralysed with fright. It screeched through her throat, so high and piercing that the bones behind her ears vibrated with it. The skin on her shoulder, where he had touched her, felt alive and crawling, shrivelling away from the hand.

And then he was gone. The scene winked out. There was no movement, no inrush of air; nothing. He was not there, lying in the coffin on the three chairs. He was not reaching for her. She was not standing there, but sitting in his chair in the kitchen, slumped over the table, where the tears were drying in damp splodges on the smooth wood. And she was *screaming*.

The scream seemed to go on and on and on until it ran out of steam and faded away as if lost in the distance. She gave a sob and the tears spurted from her eyes, not singly, but in a sudden flow that blurred her vision into wavy smears.

She was alone in the kitchen. The boys were upstairs in their cots. She'd come down for something, but couldn't remember what it was for a moment.

The vision had seemed so *real*, so intense. She had seen him and smelt him and felt him. She had been *there*. And it had scared her to death. She recalled the monstrous depression that had settled on her, binding her down under its dark weight. The scream had scattered it, and it was as if a light had been switched on in her mind.

She had imagined it, she knew. But there was something *else*.

Miread chased the thought, though she was still shivering from the fright and terror of what she had imagined. There was something else *behind* the imagining. Why she thought that, then, at that moment, she never discovered. But all of a sudden she had the feeling of something else *wanting* her to see her husband, dead and crumpled and obscenely alive in his coffin.

And just as that thought came to her, she realised that she shouldn't be down here, in the kitchen.

This time the fright was *real*. It was real and natural. It was *mother fright*.

Upstairs the boys were not in their beds. They were in the big bath, no more than babies, and she had left them up there to come downstairs for . . . towels. That was it. That's what she had been trying to remember. And while they were up there, on their own, she had been sitting here frozen by that vision.

For how long?

The question buzzed into her head and her eyes shot to the clock, even while she was moving out of the seat and heading for the door. She didn't *know* how long she'd been sitting there. She flew out of the kitchen, feet pattering on the hallway floor, heart hammering again, and took the stairs two at a time.

'Paul. Dominic!' she called out. There was a silence upstairs that clashed jarringly with the thump of her feet on the risers. Riven with panic, she pounded up to the top and shot across the landing and almost took the door off its hinges with the frenzy of her entry.

The boys were not there. The bathwater was hidden under a froth of bubbles. The surface was still.

'Oh my God!' she screeched into the empty room. Her eyes darted left and right and she was about to sprint into their room, knowing they wouldn't be there, when the miracle happened.

A small hand poked upwards from the mass of pink-tinted bubbles. It seemed to reach up out of them, as if trying to grab.

Miread flung herself forward and almost plunged into the bathwater. She dived her hands underneath, felt the slick little body of her son and scooped him right out in one motion, dumping him unceremoniously onto the carpet. Then she spun again and hauled Paul out, almost wrenching her back with the speed of the movement, and slung him down hard onto the floor beside his brother.

Both of the toddlers were blue. Their eyes were open and as pale and watery, as eerie, as those of the grotesque thing in the coffin that she'd seen in her mind's eye.

Miread's panic was wild and uncontrollable. Without thinking, she slapped her hand as hard as she could on Dominic's round little chest and screamed at him: *'Dominic!'*

The boy made a little twitch and then he gasped wetly. A small gout of water burped from his mouth in a cough, and a couple of little bubbles floated out, tossed in the wind of his breath. Miread turned to

Paul, still lying there, his pink body turning blue, and smacked him even harder on the chest twice. She yelled his name so loud that Dominic jerked back. Paul coughed and gasped and simply burst into frightened tears. Miread hauled the two of them to her, both little boys panting and sobbing, and she matching them with tears of fright and relief. She scooped them up and took them down to the kitchen and wrapped them in the big bath towels from the airing cupboard, rubbing and hugging them while their own sobs dissipated.

An hour or so later, they were both in their cots, asleep side by side and none the worse for what had happened.

Miread did not know what it was that had made both of them slip under the water in the bath. That had never happened before. And it had happened while her attention was diverted; while *something* had shown her nightmare pictures, blanketed her with a dread fear, frozen her into the kind of immobility that made her forget her children.

Maybe there was something of the old people about Miread Finnerty, and it is true that her own family, the Cleggans, had lived on that stretch of the west coast for as far back as the gravestones were legible.

She suddenly had the sensation of *wrongness* about the place. There was no pricking of her thumbs, only a sudden sureness that there was something *bad* she had to get herself and her two sons away from.

That night Miread Finnerty did not sleep. She was packing the three suitcases that sat on top of the wardrobe, and when she had done that, she spent the rest of the night with the boys in her arms in the big bed in her room. When morning came, she took the two of them over to Donovan's bar, which was closed, and asked young Maeve to let her use the telephone. As a result of the call, Tommy Connolly, who ran the farmstead out towards Foremoyle, fixed up for her to travel with John Shields and Mick Casey, who were running a load of tups down to a farm on the outskirts of Galway. There was plenty of room for them all in the big cab as it pulled away from the farmhouse. Tommy Connolly promised to get one of his hands to tend to the cows and the chickens, and there wasn't much else to be done.

As the sheep-truck headed out of town, Miread felt the sense of *badness* wane only when they'd crossed the hump-backed bridge over the Roonah Water. She did not look back for fear of what she might see.

Miread and her sons and Mick Casey and John Shields got out of Kilgallan. They were the last ones to get out before it all really began to happen, though nobody knew then that it had been going on since they started the dig at the tor and old keys began to turn in ancient locks.

On the way out, they passed Dr O'Brien's car as it came along the way towards old Maureen Doyle's house. Nobody gave it a thought.

All Miread could think of was getting away, as far as she could get, from whatever it was that had planted the visions in her head. She now wanted to get down to the hospital where, she'd discovered on the telephone, her husband was still very much alive and making improvement.

John and Mick, taking turns behind the big black wheel, sensed nothing. It would be two weeks before they were back in Kilgallan, and a lot of things were going to happen in that time.

But the five of them did get out, which was a wonder. If they had stayed just one more day, it would have been, for them, a different story.

Down at the tor, as the dawn brightened in the east sky, the fine sea-mist that shrouded the flat land swirled under a breath of early-morning wind. The hump of the hillock stood out above the white gauze of the harr, a dark island that seemed to float in a pale sea. Tendrils of mist crept round the pegs and lines where the archaeologists had worked, leaving droplets of condensation on the odd patch of grass and on the handles of the barrow which Terry Munster had left lying on its side in the dirt.

The morning was silent. Out in the bay, no seabirds mewed, no oyster-catchers piped, which was unusual, though nobody noticed then. The dawn was the time when the wedges of duck would come whirring down from the high peat bogs to feed on the tidal flats, but on this morning their fast wings had taken them elsewhere. Under the spreading sea-mist, the bay was flat calm, a pale mirror that reflected only the billowing whiteness above it.

A wandering breeze parted the harr around the base of the tor, and the dark entrance gaped into view. The mouth was a black hole.

Down at the end of the tunnel, the mist could not penetrate the depths at the chamber, but corresponding blackness swirled with strange life. The massive stone squatted in the centre, and within the stone, in the *infinite* confines of that carven rock, the thing that had awoken from a dead sleep had gone back to slumber, bloated with the taste of her mind-feed. She had reached out her thoughts and felt the life nearby, old and weak maybe, but, by comparison, *young*. She had squeezed within and plucked at memories, shivering the synapses and bringing those memories to life. She had revelled in the bewildered panic of the old woman, savouring her fear, scenting her hope. She had

157

stirred the need and deceived the old woman, letting her feel the years slough off like old skin, letting her become young again, vibrant and hot again. And then, when the emotion was right, tight and stretched, she had struck.

Oh, the pain of it, like a fine drink. She had wallowed in it; *bathed* in it. Through the old woman's eyes she had conjured up the man and then felt the surge of despair wrestle with the sudden *demand*. And then she'd used that imperative, as she had used it so long ago it felt like *forever*, to heighten the texture, to stretch the emotion like the string of a harp. When the moment was right, she'd changed him into the horror and had feasted on the terror. It had been hot and good. The old woman's abject fear and the sudden pain inside her came in an eruption of luscious delectability and she gorged upon it.

Still trapped, still bound by the *geis*, the thing that had awoken was still able to reach out and savour. And when she was free, *truly free*, she would have a banquet that would repay her for the generations of oblivion. She would have her revenge, and it was already beginning.

After the old woman, she had flitted on, drawn by something familiar, yet unknown. She had felt the other woman's fear and disquiet, and she had dimly sensed the male children, two of them, but twinned, which made them hard to pinpoint. But it was through the woman, through *women* while she was still trapped, that she could work best. There was something familiar here, something a part of her had sensed before, although the memory of it was so vague as to be intangible. It didn't matter. The memory of toads came fleeting in to her and then scattered.

She had taken the woman's thoughts and *twisted* a nightmare, feeling again the fear build up. She knew she could use the woman's menfolk against her and then take the anguish when it exploded.

The panic escalated, the dread expanded. And then, there was something *else*. The woman had *sensed* the invasion and had shucked herself away from it, throwing it out.

The thing that had awoken in the tor snarled silently in fury as the woman slipped out of the nightmare and, driven by mother-love, scooped her babies from the water into which, made drowsy, they'd slipped, and brought them back from the edge.

But she had already mind-fed, so the loss was nothing. She would have another chance, for these people had *forgotten*, and in that forgetting they were like cattle, ripe for the eating.

And when she was free – *she could sense that freedom approaching on a fast wind* – then there would be a feasting that would make her old rampaging a blessing by comparison.

Down underneath the tor, the surface of the stone coalesced and the shadows drew back into it, leaving the squat, carved rock sitting silent and massive in the darkness. Inside it, between this world and the lands of Tir na n'Og, the thing that had awoken went back to a replete slumber and dreamed of release.

Gradually, on the outside, the mist began to evaporate under the autumn sun that arose in the east, and the bay was like a silver mirror on the slow ebb tide.

Yet still no seabirds called out over the water. The dunlin and the redshank had moved to other mud-shores. No terns dived for sprats.

All was quiet.

19

The dream catapulted Sean McCullain out of sleep, and for a moment he did not know where he was. He had awoken, sitting bolt upright and with both hands out in front of him, warding off an imagined blow, or delivering one. His chest and belly were slick with sweat and his eyes were staring into the darkness of the room.

It had happened again. He had been *there* watching when the iron had gone up and then come crashing down and the blood had sprayed and he had seen the eyes staring at him, eyes that were filled with the knowledge of ending. And as he watched, the face changed. Suddenly, it was not the face of the young man, but his own. There was a gash on the side of his forehead that was dripping red and his own eyes were wide and staring. The iron went up again and came hammering down on the top of his head, and there was an instant of numbing pain and his vision took on a pink hue.

It was a strange, terrifying *inside-out* experience, watching this happen to himself from a distance yet also feeling it as it happened.

Then, as before, the feeling of weightless numbness sleeted through him, and he could feel the *change* coming again. There was a weird *flip*, a twisting sensation, and he was there, not watching, but feeling it, living it. Hands reached for him and an iron arced down. Yet this time it was no iron. It was a club with a black stone at its head. He felt his body writhe with sudden power and his own hand went up to snatch at it. He felt the shock of impact, a fleeting pain, and then nothing save the singing of the blood in his veins. Words came from his mouth, words that he had never heard, never spoken before, a sing-song guttural chant that meant *everything* though he did not even know what he was saying. His right hand came up, hard and swift, and there was a sword in it. He swung it against a distorted face and saw flesh fly. There was a scream, and a goblin-like thing tumbled away from him. A hand scrabbled at his shoulder, and he merely turned his head and bit at it. Teeth crunched on bone and a foul, slimy taste filled his mouth. He spat out what he had bitten off and spun to his right, swivelling his hips, and the bright blade scythed through another of the *wights*. The head spun off, tumbling in the air, and landed with a thump. There were screams and snarls and his body contorted inside and he felt himself move with the *speed* rushing through him. It sang inside him, sizzling in his head, and he hacked joyfully at the grotesque things that leapt and scuttered from the rocks. And then it was over. Around him the goblin-like grey things lay broken and ripped. Inside him, he could feel the *change* dissipate, his muscles and his bones righting themselves.

And the scene changed again, back to the car in the graveyard, where the face loomed at him from the tangle of wrestling bodies and the tyre iron went up and his voice screamed: '*Yes. Kill the bastard!*'

As soon as the words were out of his mouth the horror of what he had said, spurred by the battle-fury of the *before*, hit him like a blow.

He saw, in slow motion, the tyre iron descend towards the helpless head. He held his hand out to try to draw it back, and realised it was *himself* who was wielding the killing iron, sweeping it down for a death blow.

'*Oh, for Christ's sake no. . . !*'

And he woke up in horror.

It took a few moments for him to reorient himself and to allow the heaving of his chest to subside. The sweat started to cool on his skin, bringing him out in goose flesh that had as much to do with the dream as the cold. The dream began to fade from the forefront of his mind, breaking up and fragmenting, but leaving him still with a terrible feeling of *wrongness*.

He reached over in the dim light to the bedside cabinet and found his cigarettes. He drew one out and flicked his lighter, eyes narrowing at the brightness of the flame, and drew in deep. He blew out the smoke in a long, shuddery sigh.

'That's it,' he said into the shadows. 'I've had enough of this.' He lay back on the pillow, drawing the duvet up to his chin, gathering his body warmth, and lay thinking.

Now the dreams were changing, making him a central part of them, and they were savage. In them *he* was savage.

Sean drew smoke in again, remembering. The first change had been just after he and Liz had crossed the border, heading into old Connacht. He recalled the strangeness, the feeling of *déjà-vu* as they had passed the swaybacked, dilapidated cottages and mean farms. The image of the dead cow came back, stark against the grass and reeds, splayed like a sacrifice on a stone. That image was clear and somehow familiar.

They had driven on, and the feeling of gloom, a ponderous weight of depression, had pressed in on him as they headed west into unfamiliar –yet to him, strangely familiar – territory. Even the very air had smelled

161

oppressive, but the scent of it was not new. It was like some memory long-ago forgotten that came tantalisingly close to the surface, almost close enough to grab and hold onto, before dancing away. And then the dream had changed into that unreal yet achingly familiar battle, where he had sensed himself *alive* as never before, charged with weird power. In the dream he *knew* who he was, and why he must fight, and he revelled in the ferocious *right* of it all.

They had travelled down through the old kingdom, past hills and lochans that were like landmarks in McCullain's sight: things seen before. It was as if he was coming home after many, many years, though he knew he had never seen any of it in his life.

And the dreams had continued, asleep or awake. He'd *become* the man in the centre of the crowd, a victim of the anger and the hate. He'd *become* the warrior, bearing the weight of Ireland's battles in his sword arm. And twice now, he had seen the image of something so monstrous that his mind had instinctively rejected it. Yet even in that image was something already seen, and that, he knew, was *impossible*. He knew there had never *been* such a thing as he had seen under the bridge, or hurtling through the night air towards him. That was something from a fever dream, the product of a mind that badly needed a rest.

The night before, he'd made a decision, and this latest dream now catalysed it. He knew what he was going to do. Liz Cannon might not like it, but she'd have to go along with it. Sean McCullain decided he needed a break, and he needed it right away. They had one job set up for that day, and he'd go along with it, and then he was going to have some time off. Time to take some pictures and time to maybe get some fishing in with the two Canadians and the Australian he'd met the night before. But mostly he needed a couple of days to let the fresh wind blow away some of the cobwebs that were gathering in his head and scatter the dark thoughts that were sending him these recurring nightmares.

Sean McCullain was a straightforward man. He was a practical fellow, honest and professional in his work, generally considerate to those he worked with. But he knew that if he didn't do something to get rid of the dreams that came to him in the dark, he'd crack up completely, and that scared him more than anything in his life.

He finished his cigarette and lay in the dim light, watching the curtain over the window get lighter as morning approached. Eventually, he hauled himself out of bed and put on his clothes. In the next room, he could hear Liz Cannon snoring lightly as she slept on. It was nearly nine o'clock, but there was no rush. He let her sleep and quietly slipped out of the cottage into the autumn morning.

Outside, the air was fresh and still. There was a slight mist creeping lazily over the dew-spangled grass, giving the circle of cottages a fairytale appearance, like an Irish *Brigadoon*. From where he stood, Sean could see the bay between the dips of the line of hillocks that barred the way to the shore on the north. The water, mist-covered, was still as glass. It was quiet. No birds sang.

Sean made his way up the path at a leisurely pace towards the village. He'd picked up a short branch that lay beside the gate and lopped off the heads of thistles as he walked, feet crunching on the gravel.

There was a small shop on the corner, next to McGavigan's undertakers' parlour, that sold just about everything. He bought a couple of newspapers and some provisions, including a bottle of whisky and a half-dozen cans of beer. The woman behind the counter chattered away to him as she put everything into plastic bags, and wished him a pleasant day as he left.

Down the path again, Sean came across Dr Connarty and the rest of the team he'd met the night before, along with two younger girls who hadn't been in Donovan's bar.

'Morning to you, Mr McCullain,' the archaeologist called across, beckoning him over.

Sean nodded hello to them all and Siobhan treated him to a warm smile.

'Just as well I got you so early,' Connarty said. 'You were saying last night about the photographs, and I was wondering if you had a moment?'

'Sure,' Sean said. 'Let's take a look.'

Connarty beamed at him and led the way to the entrance of the dig. 'Mind your head, big fellow,' the professor warned. 'Sure, young Terry's fetched himself a right sore smack more than once.'

He walked into the mouth and Siobhan moved in next, with Sean and Terry behind. The two girls stayed outside.

'Mind your feet now,' Connarty added unnecessarily. Most of the rubble had been hauled out and the tunnel was well cobbled. A set of lights newly strung along the cable brightened the passageway considerably. At the far end, there was a second entrance, beyond which more lights had been set up, though in there it was still quite dim.

'Here we are. It's altogether fascinating,' the older man said.

Sean squeezed past Siobhan in the narrow doorway, brushing hips with her as he did so. She put a hand on the small of his back, guiding him through with a gentle touch. He turned to her briefly and she gave him another warm smile.

'Thanks,' he said.

'Any time,' she said back, and a little message flicked back and forth between them that neither Terry nor Dr Connarty noticed.

'This is the place,' the professor said, gesturing round the cavernous chamber. 'Sure, we need more lights, and I've already got some coming in from Dublin in the next few days. But it's still blacker than all hell.' He turned round to Sean. 'Do you think you can do anything with this?'

Sean looked around. The chamber was round and there was a squat stone, like a tombstone, right in the middle. He gauged the distances, working out the strength of flash he would need. Then he nodded to Connarty.

'I've got a twenty-millimetre that'll get the width. Lighting would be a problem, but the slave units should be enough for that.'

'What's slave units?' Terry asked.

'Remote flashes. I can set them anywhere and they'll expand the light round the walls. No problem.'

Sean walked around the stone, measuring it up. It was solid and set. He leaned forward to look at the carvings. They were intricately cut lines of tight squiggles and crossed bars that resembled hieroglyphics. There was something familiar about them, though he knew there shouldn't have been. It was as if he'd seen them before somewhere, but he couldn't remember where, or when.

There was something about the stone too that drew him, and that was odd. It was just a chunk of stone that had been carved long ago and found only a few days before, but still and all, a chunk of stone.

Yet there was something more. Sean bent forward and touched it tentatively, as if unsure that there would be no reaction. Under his fingers the stone was cold, much colder than the morning air that penetrated through to the chamber. For an instant he got a flash of the dream, of himself holding a sword that caught the light of the sun, and then it vanished. There was a small tremor at his fingertips, as if the stone had *shifted*, and then it was gone.

He walked around the ponderous block, eyes still fixed upon it, when his foot caught on a sheet of black plastic that was lying on the flagstones. He almost lost his balance, and put his hand out to right himself – and again felt the cold shiver on the top of the block. He twisted his body, and there was a slithering sound as the plastic that had caught around the toe of his shoe was dragged to the left. Something caught Sean's eyes – he did a swift double-take and the thing on the floor flicked into focus.

'Oh shit,' he said loudly as the image imprinted itself in his mind.

The dried-out corpse grinned widely at him, staring upwards through hollowed sockets. Sean felt everything below his navel contract with sudden fright.

'What's up?' Terry said, then he followed Sean's line of sight. 'Don't worry about old Bryan Boru.' He laughed. 'He scared the bejasus out of me when I caught a sight of him, but he's harmless.'

'What in God's name is *that*?' Sean asked when he got his breath back.

'Probably the archaeological find of the century,' Connarty said quietly from across the chamber. Siobhan had moved closer and had put a hand on Sean's arm.

'I've got a transport coming all the way from Dublin for him this morning, along with a special sealed container to keep him dry.'

'But what *is* it?'

'One of the old people,' Siobhan answered. 'We don't know if he was a sacrifice or whether this is his tomb. But he's certainly the best-preserved cadaver that's been found so far, even better than the peat-bog men.'

'It's godawful-looking,' Sean said. He crouched down to have a look at the long-dead warrior. The face was shrivelled, shrunken and tight across the bones. It looked as if it would crumble if it was touched. He pulled back the sheet and saw the arch of the breastbone under a cracked and peeling leather jerkin and, stretching down, a long wizened arm on which the flesh had withered down to the bone so that the joints stood out like growths. The slender, fleshless fingers were curled around the pommel of a heavy stone axe with a blade that was nicked and notched along its edge.

The axe, more than anything else, made Sean take another look. The haft was smooth and polished and carved with snake-like circles. A leather thong attached to it was looped around the slender wrist. The stone was whipped on with fine braided twine that was set in something that could have been resin.

It was just the kind of axe he'd seen in his dreams. The kind that he ducked and parried when he wielded his sword with wondrous boiling glee.

Connarty nodded at the other niches in the walls.

'There could be more too,' he said. 'This could be bigger than we all know. Just think, we can probably find out what this fellow had for his breakfast.'

'You can tell that, from this?' Sean asked.

'Sure we can. All that's missing from this old warrior is moisture.

165

The cells are dried out, but once they are wet again, they'll be in such a perfect state of preservation we'll be able to find out his blood group and take his fingerprints and all. It's amazing what we'll discover. Why, with the techniques they have today, they could probably clone this fellow.'

'I wouldn't go as far as that,' Siobhan said, 'though it's a nice thought.'

"'Tis indeed, my dear. Just think of that. If we could resurrect one of the old heroes, that *would* be a miracle.'

'I don't know about heroes,' Sean said. 'I thought they were all dead.'

'And so they are, and here's the living proof,' Connarty answered, then he realised what he'd said and chuckled. Sean, his small scare fading away, joined him.

'Well, what do you think? Can you help us with the pictures?'

'Yes. I'll get it fixed up later, if you like.' He turned to Connarty. 'I'll bring my gear along in the afternoon. But now I need my breakfast.'

He took a last look at the thing on the floor before Connarty and Terry covered it over with the plastic sheet, carefully tucking in the edges underneath the cadaver, then turned to the door. Siobhan walked up the passageway with him.

'You know, there's a story here,' he said thoughtfully. 'You say there's never been anything like this found before?'

'Not as far as I know, and I *should* know. There's hundreds of megalithic tombs all over Ireland, most of them out in the west. Sure they've found ossuaries . . .'

Sean raised his eyebrows in question.

'Urns for bones. They were a very ceremonious people, you know. Went in a lot for cremation, which is very frustrating for us, for that doesn't give us much to work on. Some of the tombs, you'd get twenty or thirty urns stacked up. Mostly young women, as far as we can tell, and we know that some of the kings and princes liked to take their women along with them to make the afterlife more pleasant.'

'Sounds like a good idea to me,' Sean said, grinning at the thought.

'Only if you're a prince and if you believe in the afterlife.'

Sean chuckled.

'But this is the first time we've found a complete cadaver, and it's amazing that this one is so well-preserved. We've not broken into the other niches yet, and we're not likely to until we get the sealed containers we need. If there are more bodies in there, we're as well to leave them until conditions are right.'

Sean walked alongside her to the edge of the dig, where he'd left the carrier bags, and explained what he would set up in the afternoon.

'I'll see you then,' said Siobhan. 'Now I've got to go and work on the carvings. It's not easy.'

'Found anything interesting?'

'Plenty. I'll tell you later if you buy me a drink tonight.'

'I'll buy you a drink anyway,' Sean replied.

'And I'll look forward to that,' Siobhan said, and sent him another tentative smile that carried more than one message.

Sean smiled back at her, acknowledging both messages, and turned and went along the path, whistling tunelessly as he went.

At the cottage, Liz was up and about. She'd obviously had a shower, for her hair was still damp-looking and had coiled itself into ringlets, making her look even younger.

'You were up and out early,' she said, as soon as Sean banged open the door.

'Couldn't sleep,' he said, backing into the room, shoving the door shut with his hip.

'I couldn't even have a cup of tea. There's not a drop of milk in the fridge.'

'Not to worry. I brought breakfast,' he said, turning round so that she could see the big plastic bag.

'What's that?'

'Oh, bacon, eggs, mushrooms, sausage, that sort of thing.'

'McCullain, I take back everything I said about you.'

'I'd wait until I tasted the cooking,' he said, crossing to the kitchen.

He dumped the stuff on the surface and started stacking the fridge, then slid a handful of rashers onto the grill and set it warming. In minutes the smell of smoked bacon started wafting out.

Liz had the table set for two when he finally emerged from the kitchen with a tray stacked with the biggest fried breakfast Liz had seen in years. She felt a trickle at the sides of her tongue at the very sight of it. Beside the two heaped plates, there was a stack of toast and a pot of coffee that was trickling steam from the spout.

'That looks absolutely marvellous,' she said with genuine enthusiasm. 'I didn't know you could cook.'

'Anybody can do this,' he said agreeably. 'And there's plenty more. I got enough to last the week.'

'Almost a shame we won't be here that long,' Liz said from behind a mouthful of soft-fried egg. 'This could almost be worth staying for.'

'That's what I want to tell you about,' Sean said, cutting a rasher of bacon. 'I'm taking some time off.'

'Lucky you. When?'

'Ah . . . today?'

'Nice one, McCullain,' she said, not even looking at him. She raised the coffee cup to her lips and took a drink, and then licked her lips.

'No. I mean it. It's all fixed.'

'What's all fixed?' She put the cup down and raised her face towards him across the table. 'What are you talking about?'

'I phoned the office and told Dave Robertson I was taking time owed, starting today after the power-station job. I was due a break before I was in Belfast and it's time I had one. I want to get some down-time.'

'Don't be silly,' she said flatly. 'We've got work to do.'

'No we haven't. The power-station piece is for next week, and we can do Knock any time. It's been done to death anyway, so a week won't make a scrap of difference.'

'Very good, McCullain. But I've been wound up by experts. Pull the other one.' She bent to her breakfast again, dismissing him.

'I'm serious. Robertson's okayed it. Nothing else he could do anyway, but he would never have sent me here in the first place, and McIntyre will get his arse kicked for assigning me here right after Belfast.'

She looked up at him and stared into his eyes. 'You really are serious, aren't you?'

'Sure I am. As of this afternoon, I'm on holiday.'

'But what about me? What am I supposed to do?'

'You get a free holiday if you like, and then you can do Knock next week.'

'If you think I'm going to stay here for a week with you, then you've another thought coming,' she said, her voice rising sharply and colour flooding into her cheeks.

'That's up to you.'

'You'd better believe it. I'm getting right on to the features desk to get them to change it.'

Sean shrugged. 'Please yourself. I bet a tenner they don't wear it.'

'We'll see about that,' she said, now angry. She shoved her chair back from the table and it made a scraping squeal on the tile floor. She stood up and put her hands on her hips, bending towards him aggressively.

'Oh, sit down and finish your breakfast. You can phone from the village when we're heading down to Connemara.'

She looked as if she was about to say something else, then stopped herself. She sat down again heavily and put an elbow on the table.

'Fair enough. At least we'll get today's job done before you can think up any further methods of dereliction of duty.'

168

Sean laughed, loud and hard.

'Listen, Liz,' he said, when his laughter subsided. 'Dereliction is one thing, and taking a much needed break is another.' He stopped and looked at her directly, and she could see the quick anger under his brows. Then it backed down, held tightly under control.

'Let me explain. I *need* a break. That was my sixth time in Belfast giving evidence at that court. Every time, I have to go through all that again, and quite frankly, I'm done in. If I don't get some time out, I'm going to crack up.'

'Oh, don't be silly. Everybody's got pressure,' she said angrily and glared at him. But there was something in his eyes, not anger, only a weariness, that made her wish she could have bitten the words back.

'Sure we have. You, me and everybody else. Pressure goes with the job, it comes with the territory.' He stopped, as if searching for the words, then went on: 'And sometimes, you have to shuck it off, like I have to now. Every night I dream about it. You weren't there, so you don't know. Every night I dream the same thing, every bloody night in life. And if I put the lights out in the darkroom I see it again, and again, and again. This morning I was awake at six because I had the dream again and it's driving me nuts. So all I need is to get a couple of days off. I just want to sit and *not think* for a while. Maybe take a few decent pictures for a change. Have a few beers. Maybe even go fishing. Robertson understands, and he won't change his mind. He'll back me, because he knows I don't quit unless I've got a good reason.'

He stared at her from across the table. 'Phone them if you like. I don't think they'll send somebody else across, and believe me, I need the time. So instead of acting like Attila the Hen, you might as well go along with it. I'll get the power-station piece done today and Knock next week, and if you like I'll throw in another story that's better than any of them.'

Liz, about to say something, seemed to change her mind. She opened her mouth, paused, and then surprised McCullain.

'What was it like?'

'What was what like?'

'Belfast. I mean, you've been around. You were in Panama and I saw your stuff from Ethiopia. What was so bad about Belfast?'

Sean looked down at the table, and then back up at Liz.

'I don't know. It just got to me, that's all. People die all the time, but this one got under my skin. I couldn't work it out. It was something to do with the fact that they're all the same people. It was just madness, and for some reason, I was a part of it. I told you that after that, I started

169

reading up about Ireland, trying to find out all I could, something that would tell me *why*.'

'And did you find the answer?'

'No. I found a lot of things I didn't know before, so I understand better, instead of just being an outsider looking in. And I think I understand the Irish *people* better. They've got a tremendous history and a wonderful heritage of culture. It's just that it seemed to get screwed up along the way somehow, and that's why things like Belfast happen.'

There was a silence. Finally Liz said: 'I'm still going to phone the desk.'

'Sure you are. You wouldn't be half the reporter you could be if you didn't.'

For some reason, Liz flashed him a glance, perhaps to see if he was bullshitting, then relaxed when she saw the straight look in his eyes.

'How good a reporter do you think I could be?' she asked girlishly.

'From the feature they've used today, I'd say not bad at all.'

'What do you. . . ? Have you seen. . . ?' she blurted, half-rising from her chair.

'Of course. I brought one down with me.'

Liz whirled and strode across the room to the table by the window where Sean had dumped several newspapers. She pulled out the thick tabloid from under the broadsheets and started flicking the pages over, halting finally near the centre.

'Oh, they've given it a good show.'

'That's because it's a good read,' Sean said, his attention now back on the plate.

'Pictures came out well. That one of the old men looks terrific.'

'That's what I'm paid for,' Sean said agreeably.

Liz came back to the table, still reading her own story. '*The sadness behind the festival*,' she read out. 'That's the caption.'

She sat down, still reading and then, several minutes later, during which Sean had time enough to scour his plate clean with a piece of buttered bread and pour himself a second coffee, she looked up from the newspaper.

'You were right,' she said quietly. 'And thanks.'

Sean didn't push it. He knew she was talking about his input into the *real* story behind Lisdoonvarna.

'Any time,' he said.

'But I'm still going to make the call,' she added, though not angry now.

'Sure.'

She waited, wondering if he'd say anything else, but he didn't. 'By the way, what's this other story you were talking about?'

'It's a good picture piece, and a first.'

She sat up in the chair, both elbows on the table, interested. 'Go on.'

'They've found a body.'

'Big deal.'

'Yes, but this one's pretty damn old, from way back in the Iron Age or the Bronze Age or the Stone Age, for all I know. And there's never been anything found like it anywhere. Not ever.'

'Sounds good. Where is it?'

'And I'll be taking the pictures this afternoon. Interested?'

'You bet.'

'Okay. Make your phone call and then let's get this power-station crap done and I'll fix you up with a *real* exclusive.'

Liz stopped in her tracks and twisted round to glare at him, then saw the crinkles at the corners of his eyes tighten as he tried to suppress a laugh.

'Very funny,' she said, but the fight had gone out of her voice.

Sean stacked his gear together and loaded it into the estate while Liz waited for him in the driver's seat. He got in and she drove off, out past the tor and through the village, stopping only to make a phone call from Donovan's bar. When she came out she got back in the car and drove along the street and across the hump-backed bridge before they took the road on the right that led across the moors to Connemara in the south.

Half an hour down the road, coming down to the steep fjord at Killary, Liz turned to him and said: 'I've been told to stay.'

'Fine,' Sean said, showing nothing.

'But there's one thing I want to tell you.'

'Go on.'

'If you ever call me Attila the Hen again, I'll kill you.'

'Fine.'

Further down the road, she sneaked a look at him. The corners of his eyes were still crinkled with suppressed laughter. Unable to stop herself, Liz started to giggle.

Nancy Ducain felt the exhilaration race through her. She was breathing heavily, but evenly, as she went up the steep path towards the summit. The blood was pounding in her veins and the long muscles in her thighs were hot from the exertion. The sweat-band round her forehead was

171

damp with perspiration, but she was feeling *good*. Above her the summit of the hill loomed, craggy and tumbled with broken rocks. Here and there, tussocks of tough grasses and coiled roots of heather clung to the hollows. Far off to the west, a buzzard keened plaintively, rising on the still air. Nancy pounded on and up, heading for the top.

There was a small ridge on the mountain that edged out like a narrow shoulder, and without breaking stride she angled to the right and sprang on the rocks towards the edge. Below her the ground fell away sharply, a steep slope that went down in a swoop for several hundred feet then levelled itself out smoothly to a flat plateau of brown heathers and buff grasses.

Tom was just a speck down there. She could see him sprawled beside the table cloth they'd spread out with the picnic, and she could just make out the square of the tourist map beside him.

'Race you to the top,' she had said, and he'd looked at her as if she was crazy.

'No way. It'd kill me,' he'd said, after looking up at the crag.

'Oh, come on. The exercise is good for you.'

'Exercise? You've exercised me enough to keep me fit for a year,' he said with a low-level lascivious grin. He put his arm around her neat waist and pulled her towards him.

'No you don't,' she said. 'Not out here in the open air. And I'm sure it's against the law in Ireland.'

She turned her back and his hands slid over her belly. It was tight and concave. The muscles were feminine, but hard. She wriggled her shoulders against his chest and he could smell her hair, clean yet musky.

'I want to go up there,' she said.

'Why bother? It's just another hill. The place is full of them.'

'I bet there's a great view from the top.'

'Yeah, you can probably see New York from there.'

He tightened his arms around her, snuggling her closer, nuzzling behind her ear. 'You can do all the running you want back home. Why not just relax and enjoy the peace?'

'No challenge,' she said, easing herself out from his clasp. 'I want to go look. Coming?'

He shook his head. 'Nah. You'll just put me to shame again. I can't keep up with you. Just don't be long.'

'Sure you don't want to come?'

'No way,' he said. She could sense he didn't want her to go. 'I'll be back down before you know it,' she said, and turned lightly, limber on

172

her toes, and started up the path. He watched her from the back, admiring the grace of her movement. She was wearing a tight pair of jeans and white running trainers that flashed as she raised them high over the clumps of heather that edged onto the track.

The hill steepened, but Nancy kept up her pace, spreading her breathing to match her stride and feeling the heat build up. From below, the track had looked steep, but halfway up, it really started to climb, forcing her occasionally to bend forward and use her hands on the rocks for purchase. But it felt *good*. The sensation of effort and the flood of oxygen through her muscles gave her such a feeling of well-being that it had spurred her onwards and she had pushed herself hard.

On the ridge, she stood in the clear autumn air, looking out over the broad russet sweep of the plateau and the valley below it. There, the silver line of the Roonah Water looped, snake-like and meandering along the floor of the vale, flowing north towards Kilgallan. To the west, stretching beyond the rolling low hills and hummocks, was the great bogland where more water glistened in tarns and sinks. Scars on the surface showed where generations of families had staked their claim to the peat-cutting. Further west, she could catch a glimpse of the sandy sweep of Tallabaun Strand, fuzzed out by the haze of distance and merging silver with the sea. Way out in the Atlantic, there were few clouds hovering over the ocean.

Up here, near the crest of the hill, the air was cool, and Nancy bent, hands on knees, drawing it deeply into her lungs. After a moment or two, she stood erect and put two hands up to her mouth and gave a remarkably boyish whistle that shrieked down from the height. She waited a few moments, letting the sound carry, then saw Tom turn and look upwards. The small white patch of his face swivelled this way and that, trying to get a glimpse of where she stood, then he jumped up and waved. She returned it, wishing he had joined her, but knowing that the fast climb would have tired him out and probably bored him.

Waving again, she turned, like a chamois on the rock, and headed up the last hundred feet or so. When she reached the top, there was a pile of stones in a pyramid shape, a cairn set down by countless summer climbers marking their defeat of the steep slope. She picked up a loose rock and added her own to the pile, then clambered right up on the mound, surveying the scene again.

Down on the road, a large green livestock lorry passed, its engine just a faint buzz in the distance. She traced the line of the curving road that for a while paralleled the stream, and found Kilgallan in the distance, nestling in the slight hollow close to the bay.

The town was dark, which was strange, for there was little cloud.

She raised her hand against the bright sparkle from the distant sea and peered across at the village. It was as if a cloud had blown between it and the sun. The fields around it were dark against the lighter colours on the other side of the bridge over the Roonah. As she watched, the shadow seemed to spread outwards, taking in the south of the village past the Tallabaun Inn and the cute little farmhouse beyond that. A little wind blew up, cooling the perspiration at her neck and making her shiver just a little. Way down there, the shadow seemed to be spreading, racing out from the town in a dark flow, turning the buff-coloured rough grasses at the edge of the valley to brown.

Nancy got down from the mound and started along the path. Now, above the village, a small cloud began to form, building up from the warmer air coming off the sea and darkening the land below it even further. She could just make out the hump of the tor next to the delightful little cottage where they were staying for the week. It looked like a black blot in the field.

Behind her there was a sudden whooping sound and then a very startling rough barking noise, loud in the quiet air.

Nancy stopped and whirled round, almost losing her footing on the dry scree, and saw the bird sitting on the cairn. It was a hooded crow, black and grey, with a shiny black beak and little beady eyes. It lowered its head and cawed again raucously.

The noise echoed down the valley. Nancy stopped for a moment and stared at the ugly carrion-eater. It stared back, as if challenging her to try again for the peak on the top of the hill. Then it bent and started pecking at something that was lying under its splayed claw on the flat top-stone. It looked like a small animal, though Nancy couldn't make it out. The crow tugged hard at whatever it was, and its head rose up with a jerk. Something dangled wetly from the beak. The crow's mandibles clicked together in a series of gulps and the morsel went down its throat.

Nancy shuddered, turned on her toes and started to jog down the track.

Way down the valley, the shadow seemed to be spreading further out from the village, sweeping its darkness down towards the strand at the edge of the sea.

Nancy stopped once more at the shoulder ridge and watched the spreading umbra. For some reason, it gave her as much of a shivery feeling inside as the disgusting sight of the crow on the rock.

But then she built up speed until she was racing on the track as it levelled near the base. The joy of the exertion scattered the shivery feeling, and the clear air bellowed in her lungs and made her feel wonderful.

Back at the cottage nearest the tor, Siobhan was busy, engrossed in her work. The broad table was strewn with pages of rubbings and notes, and at the edge, jostling for space with the big coffee mug, there were two old textbooks that were bible-thick and had worn leather bindings.

She didn't even notice when the professor came in through the unlatched door and sat down at the chair opposite.

'They'll be here later with a vacuum box,' he said. 'The department has fixed up storage for as long as we need, but already they're twitching to get their hands on him. Flannery is arranging X-rays first of all, and they want to get cracking on carbon-dating. There's great excitement.'

'I can believe that,' she said.

'He wanted to get the summer team together and clean the place out, but the last thing we need at this stage is to have dozens of people clambering about. I told him so.'

'Good for you. Oh, by the way, Sean McCullain will be coming across this afternoon to take a series of photographs for us. He can do prints, but only in black and white. He says we can have as many transparencies as we like, compliments of the newspaper.'

'Well, that's grand. Seems like a nice enough fellow.'

'I think he is,' Siobhan said, and her eyes grew thoughtful, speculative. Then they focused again.

'There's another thing. He wants to do a story on what we've found.'

Connarty looked at her. 'D'you think that's wise? It's a bit early days yet.'

'I can't see how it can harm us, and he's on the spot. We can't make any great claims at the moment, but I think the evidence shows that what we're doing is worthwhile. And some advance publicity might help when it comes to the other places. Most of the tors all over Ireland have been flattened by farmers who don't like bloody great humps in their fields. The more people know about this, then the more chance there is of saving the few that are left.'

'Fair point, Siobhan, more than fair.' Connarty nodded thoughtfully. 'In fact, it might be a very good idea indeed. It might help give our work a wider audience, not to mention a little more funding, eh?'

'Maybe a lot more funding.'

'Yes, that is a possibility. D'you think they'll do it?'

'I hope so. It'll make a nice change to see archaeology in a newspaper. If we were saving the whales or saving the rainforests, we'd get all the coverage we could want and all the sponsorship we need. But when we're trying to save a bit of old Ireland for the sake of posterity, we've got to go round with cap in hand.'

'Just so, Siobhan,' Connarty said, with a faraway look in his eye. She knew he was thinking of fame beyond the college walls, and maybe even a *Telefas* chat with Gay Byrne, broadcast nationwide. 'And, of course, his camera could help you in your work.'

'I'd prefer to work from decent photographs than rubbings and notes. And the Polaroids just don't get enough of the carvings.'

Connarty eased himself up from the seat and went across to the stove to fix himself up with a cup of instant coffee.

'How's your end of it going?' he called over his shoulder.

'Parson's egg, I'm afraid. There's a lot here that I can get and there must be a lot I'm missing.'

'Tell me about it,' he demanded, pulling the chair round so its back was butted against the edge of the table.

Siobhan ruffled through the pile of papers and found her spiral notebook. Its pages were filled with the neat, even handwriting of a scholar used to taking copious notes.

'First,' she said, 'you have to realise that some of the forms are very similar to the old Ogham and the early languages; there are some differences. The cadence of language hasn't changed much at all, and that helps. You get the balance, if not the entire meaning.'

'Yes, Siobhan, that's the tourist guide over,' he said mischievously, 'but what does the damned thing actually say, girl?'

She flashed him a smile and bent to her book. 'Most prominent is the phrase *Shee*. That's what it translates into Ogham as, and it crops up regularly all over, even on the lintels and the corridor walls.'

'The *Morrigan*,' Connarty said enthusiastically.

'They refer to her also as the *Babd* and the *Shee-doom*.'

'And so she is. The *Babd* is central to the Celtic cultures. Death figure.'

'Yes,' Siobhan said, poring over her notes. 'There's something here about the sea and the land. And the warriors to guard.'

'That'll be one of them in the box on its way to Dublin, I shouldn't doubt for a moment,' Connarty interjected gleefully. 'Just think, we might have the oldest recorded burial, the most ancient cadaver, and on top of it all, his own epitaph.' He looked as if he was mentally rubbing his hands together.

'Early to say,' Siobhan cautioned. 'There's something here about the curse of the *Sidhe*.'

'The *Shee*, eh? Well, you'd expect that, wouldn't you,' he said. 'Nothing like an old curse to keep out the grave-robbers. Mention the *Shee* anywhere and it would give desecrators the shivers, that's for sure.'

'I can tell that most of it is written in some kind of metre, which wouldn't be unusual, though the gist of it eludes me. But I'll get there.'

'Of course you will,' he said encouragingly. 'You're doing a grand job already.'

Siobhan's brows knitted as she went over her notes, and then drew one of the sketches down towards her.

'I really do think there's something of a warning in this lot. There's so many mentions of the *Babd* and the *Sidhe*' – she properly pronounced them *Bav* and *Shee* – 'that I've a feeling there's more to it than meets the eye. The warriors to guard gives a clue . . .'

'It does indeed,' the professor interjected. 'It could be that I was right after all. This might be a *queen's* grave. And if we can show that it really is Maeve's tomb then it's a find in a million.'

'That's not what I meant,' Siobhan said, running a hand abstractedly through her hair. 'It's more complex than that. I recognise something about the Lord of Light.'

'That would be Lugh.' In his accent it sounded like Luke.

'Yes, I suppose,' she said nodding. Her lips were moving as she slowly read a smattering of sense from the squiggles.

'Listen to this,' she said, and her voice took on almost a sing-song quality:

> *The sons of kings, to guard the sleep*
> *Five brave, to watch and promise keep*
> *Between the lands of men and youth*
> *Forever stand their watch.*

'Now that's wonderful, isn't it,' Connarty said, but Siobhan didn't seem to hear him.

> Something something *Shee*
> *Forever barred in light*
> Something *curse*,
> *Wakening is worse.*

'What does that mean, d'you think?'

'Haven't a clue yet. I'll puzzle it out, that's for sure, even if it takes the next five years,' Siobhan said determinedly. 'But it is odd. Maybe I'm getting some of it wrong, but it doesn't sound like a grave inscription to me. There's something *powerful* about it.'

'What do you mean?'

'There's an awful feeling of *warning* here.' She leaned over the scatter of papers. 'Look, there.' She pointed a finger down at a carefully drawn copy of a section of the carving.

A neverending geis *be upon this place, where light has prevailed. A price on he who enters here, the serpent's lair. On him be the price of this land and the price is death.*

'Strong stuff right enough, but that's what you'd expect. That convinces me that this is an important tomb. They didn't want anybody getting in, so they scared the living daylights out of them.'

Siobhan looked up from the drawings and sketches. 'I'd like to agree with you, but there's more to it than that. The words are too strong. There's warnings and curses, and the threat of the *Shee*, but there's nothing to suggest who the place was built for.'

'I've a feeling it's under the stone. We can't shift it now, but I'll bet there's another passage there. Stands to reason, don't you think?' The professor's enthusiasm was evident on his face. This was certain to be the culmination of his life's work, his crowning glory. His aspirations were almost making him perspire.

'You could be right. I hope so, Jim,' Siobhan said, and gave him a small smile. 'But we won't know until I've got the gist of this, so run along and let me get on.'

Connarty grinned puckishly. 'Surrounded by nagging women I am. I can't wait to get back to Dublin and some crack with real men for a change.'

'Get off with you, old misogynist that you are,' she said with mock anger. He left, and when he had gone, she bent to her notes.

She *would* puzzle this out. The carvings were so extensive that they could prove to be a Rosetta Stone for her, enabling her to work out the roots of the old languages which, evolved over thousands of years, had in some ways remained the same.

She looked again at the close-packed lines and squiggles. There was something there, she *knew* it. But *what?*

Something in the strange rhyme, the odd cadence of the words, gave her the strangest feeling of unease. The words conjured up the *Sidhe*, the *Shee* of the old world, the ancient goddess of death and destruction who, the legends said, had flitted wantonly throughout the land, gorging herself on the souls of her victims.

The *Shee*. She was the epitome of *wrongness*, of complete *evil*. And she came in female form, the shape-changer who could be all things to all men, but who had the powers of madness within her. There was too much of her about the place, and the tenor of the words indicated that they were written with great care, as if there was a powerful motivation behind them.

Here on the stone, so far as she had read, there were no words of epitaph to the dead, no praise to the deeds of a great king or queen.

There was only the grim feeling of *warning*.

Siobhan read over the last piece she had uttered: *A price on he who enters here, the serpent's lair.*

'Now if that's not a warning, I don't know whatever a warning is,' she muttered to herself. She read the words aloud into the quiet of the room, and for a moment, a shiver of cold wind seemed to eddy round her, making the banked-down fire glow a little brighter. She felt the shiver inside her, and then it was gone before it even registered.

Yes, she thought, *there's something about this*. Something in the words that tickled away, came close and then drew back elusively. She hadn't worked it out yet. But it was just a matter of time.

20

As Sean had known it would be, the visit to the power station down at the south end of Connemara was, in journalistic terms, a pure bummer. Even he was embarrassed for Liz's discomfiture when she finally drove out through the chain-link gates at the end of two hours of boredom. He refrained from saying he had told her so, but her tight posture, even sitting behind the wheel, said that she expected him to say it. Despite that, she knew she would have no reply.

The building was modern and blocky and the peat fuel was delivered in lorries and stacked in great hoppers. It went in one end and burned, and turbines whined and high voltage came out the other end, just like any other fossil-fuel generating plant. That was it. There was virtually nothing of interest to photograph and little to say about the place except that it burned peat instead of coal, and wasn't that just wonderful in a place like Ireland, where everybody did just the same.

Sean said nothing for the first mile or so. The manager of the plant had been hale and hearty and could have talked the hind legs off the proverbial donkey. His enthusiasm for his plant was irrepressible, but that didn't alter the fact that there was no story. He had given them tea and biscuits and a glossy brochure before the tour, and Sean had accepted a Scotch at the end, having run off four full rolls in colour of plant and machinery which turned out to be mainly in shades of grey.

Past the turn on the trunk road north, Liz overtook a tractor dragging a trailer loaded with a pyramid of purple swedes and travelling at walking pace. Irritably she gunned the accelerator and raced the car up the slope. At the crest, she slowed down a bit, and finally spoke.

'All right. I agree.'

'With what?' Sean asked, calmly.

'You were right. There was nothing in it. We shouldn't have bothered. I'm going to get a red face when I phone the desk.'

'So don't phone them.'

'That's all right for you. I pulled out all the stops to get across here.'

'Don't worry about it. Wait till tomorrow and then we should have some good stuff from the professor. You can play that for points against this one. They'll go for it.'

Liz drove on. She was drumming a forefinger on the wheel, agitated and annoyed with herself.

'Don't worry about pictures. I'll take a break from my holiday and run them off for you, and you can Red Star them over,' he offered.

'Would you really?' she asked, surprised.

'Aye, no problem, Attila,' he said, teasing, but she didn't react. 'Anyway, I want to do it. It's a bit of fun. And then I want to go down to the Point and get some real pictures done. It's a long time since I've done a landscape.'

'Thanks,' she said, and he could hear the relief in her voice.

They drove on in silence for several minutes, then Liz said: 'You like taking pictures, don't you?'

'Sure, it's my job.'

'But it's more than that. I can tell.'

'Yeah, I suppose you're right. You could say it's my hobby. I'm just lucky I do it for a living, though half the time, to tell you the truth, it can bore the pants off me.'

He thought about it for a moment, then continued. 'They say the camera doesn't lie, but that's not true. I can make it lie in its teeth, and you'd never know the difference. But it *can* tell the truth. Not every picture is worth a thousand words, but now and again there's a photograph that doesn't need words to tell the story.'

'Like the old men at Lisdoonvarna?' she asked.

'Only to a certain extent. They were just old men in a bar. It needed your words to tell what they were all about.'

'It was a good picture.'

'They were *good* words.'

'Thanks again, McCullain.'

'All right,' he acknowledged. 'I like working with light. That's what photography is all about, using light to paint a picture.'

'That's a nice way of putting it.'

'I suppose so, but it's true enough. There's light and there's dark, and I have to use the light to make a picture. I took my first one when I was six, and I've had a camera in my hand ever since. It's difficult to explain, but the light fascinates me. It is always pure, but there are different ways of seeing it and using it. Also, it affects everything it touches.'

Liz listened as he talked, again thinking of the difference between the professional and the man. She was also aware of the fact that his very professionalism had intimidated her to such an extent that her first reaction had been to fight him. Even then, she knew she had been wrong and he had been right, and while that still rankled, her anger had

181

gone. What she really wanted was to show him she was as good a reporter as any, better than some. Perhaps they *had* got off to a bad start. She had misjudged him, while he had had her measure, as clearly as if he'd taken a picture. She sneaked another glance at him and felt an inexplicable *squeeze* down in her belly.

'It's been part of most religions,' Sean was saying. 'People thought light had the power to cast out evil. Probably goes back to the Stone Age. Rembrandt, he painted light. I just try to use it.'

'So you're an artist, then?' she asked, and he could hear a light-hearted challenge in the question.

'Con or piss?' he threw back, equally lightly.

'Probably a touch of both,' she said, laughing.

'Takes one to know one,' he added, smiling along with it.

After the pass beyond Killary, Sean asked Liz to take a turning to the left, where a narrow road that was tight enough to allow only one-way traffic, except at the passing places, veered across the moorland.

'Where does this take us?' she asked.

'Nowhere at all,' he said. 'It comes back onto the main road about eight miles along. I saw it on the map. I just want to see what's there.'

She shrugged and steered the car left at the junction. There was a slight incline, up which the road took a serpentine route, and then a long straight slope down onto the plain below.

It was barren.

There was no other way to describe it. There was a huge flat expanse of bogland stretching out on either side, and black tarns filled the gullies and depressions out into the distance. Even Sean McCullain, who had spent much of his childhood on bleak Rannoch Moor in Scotland, could see how desolate the bog was.

'A godforsaken place,' he said, almost to himself, after they had gone a couple of miles along the tortuous road.

'Damned scary,' Liz agreed.

On either side, tumbled, moss-covered boulders slick with lichens poked out of the sparse grasses like rotten teeth – or gravestones – a moraine of grey and black rocks that had been weathered by bleak winds and hard winters into eroded stumps. They seemed to shove themselves out of the barren black soil as if escaping from the depths.

And yet the bog was magnificent in its empty eeriness. Above them, the sky was filling with clouds that built up from the west, overshadowing the whole gaunt expanse.

Sean asked Liz to stop the car. On the nearside was a hillock studded with worn rocks.

182

'I want to go up there and get a shot of this,' he said.

'It won't make a postcard scene,' Liz said, slowing the car to a halt. 'This is like the backside of the moon.'

He nodded. 'That's why it's worth a picture.'

He opened the tail-gate and she could hear the click and rattle as he hauled out the gear he needed. She rolled the window down on her side and sat with an arm curled over the back of the passenger's seat, watching him climb the hill. There was a wind blowing across the flatland, moaning low and ruffling the patches of heather. On the other side of the road, there was a pool of water crowded with algae and bordered by sphagnum moss. In the centre the water was black and looked as if it went down to the centre of the earth. It looked cold and slimy and threatening. Way out in the distance a curlew wheeled a few lonely notes that were carried away on the wind.

Up on the hill, Sean sat himself down on a rock, back turned to the wind while he loaded his camera and snapped a short wide-angle lens onto the heavy black body. From his vantage point on the hill, he could command a view right across the bogs to the far-off hills that swept up from the flat depression.

The plain was the bleakest piece of wasteland he had ever seen. Below him stretched the miles of brown bracken and heathers, dotted with the strange boulders that humped out of the ground like dead markers on an ancient battleground, and between them, in the cracks and depressions, were the scummy flat stanks of brackish water.

He checked the light then took a picture, visualising how it would print out. The desolation in the viewfinder was indeed breathtaking. Bleak and lonely, it seemed to go on forever. He could imagine himself here, at the centre of it, the only man left in the world. He was reminded of the dread marsh in *The Lord of the Rings*, where the strange Gollum creature, warped and misshapen by the evil forces, had followed the heroes, beset by the flickering lights of the souls of dead men. This was such a marsh. Sean knew, from experience, that an unwary traveller could walk out from the meandering lonely road and into the bog and sink in a tarn, or into the soft, floating peat, and be lost for ever.

He shot off several more frames, taking different angles, and then did the same again with a long lens that brought the distant moraine rocks into sharp focus. He narrowed the aperture right down, adjusting the shutter speed to cope, so that the focal length expanded, making the jagged, weatherbeaten stones crowd in on one another, like an incredibly ancient ring of standing stones.

Satisfied with the series of pictures, he started packing his equipment into the backpack, wrapping each piece in a chamois leather, when there was a sudden blare from the bottom of the hill.

Down in the car, Liz had watched Sean ascend the hill. She had watched as he bent to sort out his camera and then wandered off past the low crest until he was out of sight, leaving her alone in this strange wasteland.

He'd been right, of course. The bleakness here *was* magnificent.

But it was eerie too. All around was nothing but treacherous-looking wet bogland that seemed to shiver under the moaning wind. The jutting stones reminded her of a story she had read of ancient rites and old, isolated communities. An eddy of wind blew across the plain and swirled around the car, causing her to shiver. She thought that if Sean hadn't been there, she would have been scared to be alone in this place.

Sean? Liz realised she'd thought of him by his first name, rather than the McCullain she'd called him since they'd met up in Belfast. She would have thought some more about that little change, but her train of thought was interrupted by a light scuffling sound close by her elbow.

Startled, she swivelled round in her seat just as a face loomed right up at her from the side of the car. She gave an involuntary cry, and another face joined the first. Then, on the other side of the car, a hand planted itself palm-down on the window and she jerked her head at the sound.

They were men. Five or six of them, clustered round the car.

Vacuous eyes stared at her silently. One of the men had a huge wart at the side of his nose and a slick of dribble at the corner of his mouth. Beside him, a gnarled thing with a repulsive squint leered in at her. His lips drew back, showing an expanse of gum in which a solitary blackened tooth was set at an odd slant. He cackled gleefully right next to her face.

Suddenly petrified, Liz threw herself back from the open window, grabbed the handle and wound it as hard as she could. A hand groped at the rising glass, and the winder caught for an instant, sending her fear soaring. Then the winder jerked free, and with a small screech the glass rose. The fingers withdrew just at the last second and the bevelled edge of the window clunked home into its slot. She rammed down the lock button and stretched quickly across the seat to get the one on the passenger's side. It snapped down with a relieving little click.

The strange, cracked laughter was cut off, but the odd-shaped face pressed itself up against the window, so close the bulbous nose was squashed flat, and grey lips smeared a grease of saliva across the pane. Dismayed, Liz pulled herself away from it, eyes wide.

The men crowded round the car, saying nothing, though the faint sound of idiotic laughter reverberated through the window.

It was as if she'd been accosted by inmates from some asylum for the insane. They were *odd*-looking men. Their faces were queerly twisted and slack. One of them, much taller than the rest, was stick-like and elongated, and his head had a strange slant to it as if it had been squeezed while still soft. Beside him, a shorter man, with blubbery lips and a flat cap that was two sizes too large for him, twitched piggy eyes spasmodically. He reached out a fleshy hand and drew it down the window in a weirdly lecherous pawing movement.

Still riven by fear, Liz could feel her breath coming in short gasps as the group of misshapen, moronic strangers milled around outside, pushing and shoving the car so that it began to rock on its springs.

She swung her eyes round, past the press of bodies, trying to find an avenue of escape. At first she thought of shoving the door open and taking to her heels along the narrow road, but there were six of them, and they would catch her easily, especially the crane-like one with the long, stretched limbs. Beyond the road, the moor widened out, dark and threatening, and surely dangerous to anyone who missed a step on the sheep-tracks. Sean was out of sight beyond the top of the hill, and the thought suddenly came to her that if she ventured out of the car at all, they could catch her and *do things* to her.

In her mind's eye, she saw them grab her; felt those fleshy hands on her body. She imagined herself screaming while those misshapen faces pressed up against hers, trailing saliva across her mouth, while they cackled with manic, *mindless* laughter. Horrorstruck, she squirmed against the thought of their hands on her legs and breasts, on her thighs, *inside her*.

I could die here. The thought suddenly lanced through her.

One of the men clambered up onto the bonnet and leaned in over the windscreen, his face slack with dull lechery.

'*Get off!*' Liz yelled, and for a moment, the malformed man's expression looked bewildered, then it went back to being vacuously threatening.

Liz banged her hand down on the centre of the steering wheel and the horn suddenly blared.

The half-wit on the bonnet got such a start that he slipped and rolled off. The car rocked alarmingly with the shift of weight, and Liz felt a surge of triumph.

Without a thought, she rammed her hand down on the pad and the horn blared again, loud and flatly raucous, across the moor. Beside her head, hands thumped at the window, but she closed her eyes tightly, not wishing to see any more, and thumped the horn in a staccato series of blasts, knowing that this, if anything, should attract McCullain's attention. She gritted her teeth, fighting down the sick panic, as the hands banged at the window, that he would not get here before they got into the car. The agonising thought came to her that he might be far out on the other side of the hill and that the sound of the horn wouldn't carry against the moaning wind. Around her the car started to rock in a violent rhythm as the strange men shoved it this way and that, pushing it up on its springs and then crashing it back down again.

'Come on, Sean,' she shouted aloud. 'Get down here, for God's sake!'

No sooner were the words out of her mouth than there was an immediate flash of daylight beside her as the man nearest her shifted away from the window, and suddenly Sean McCullain was there, tall and broad, towering over the group of men. She could see his brows knitted right down and the hard flash of fury underneath them. At that moment, he was the best sight she'd seen in a long time. He looked as if he was ready to kill, and the fleeting notion struck her, so quickly and passing so fast that it hardly registered in her mind, that he looked magnificent.

Hearing the horn blare up from the road, Sean's first thought was that the sudden harsh sound would scare the wildlife for miles around, assuming there was any to be seen beyond the one or two sheep that had strayed onto the bog. When he was taking pictures, he'd heard the lonely call of the curlew off in the distance, and the only sight of life had been a big hooded crow that had flashed blackly into the viewfinder of the long lens and settled to a crouch on one of the jagged stones. It had cawed once, and he'd taken a picture of its opened beak, the camera catching the glint in its black eye that had speared right into the lens. Apart from that, the expanse of bogland on the plateau that stretched away towards Kilgallan, hidden from view in the distance, was empty, devoid of life.

He had stood from his crouched position, hefting the backpack on his shoulder and walking up the incline to the top of the hill. When he got there, he looked down the few hundred yards of slope towards the car and for a moment stood confused. There was movement around the white car, and at first he thought the black and brown shapes were a herd of cows, before the movement separated into individual bodies. There was a crowd of men milling around the car, pushing at it hard enough for him to see it sway back and forth. The horn blared in short, sharp bursts out from the mêlée.

Sean bit off a curse and started down the hill, walking quickly then breaking into a run. The camera gear bounced against his back, but he ignored it. As he thundered down the hillside, he could see the group of men more clearly: dressed in flat caps and old jackets and big, clod-hopper boots, there was something oddly disjointed about them. When he got closer he was reminded of a Jack Nicholson film filled with mental patients. They looked like an escape committee from a psychiatric ward, or a home for the retarded.

Yet seeing them clustered around the car, pawing and shoving it, instantly brought back to him that *other* crowd round a car. Twisted, hate-filled faces came suddenly back to mind: the scrabbling at the door; the yanking of the handle; the dragging out from within. That memory came at him like a blow in the pit of his stomach, overwhelming him with a sinking, prescient dread.

His feet had hit the road, sending up a small spray of loose gravel, and he had run the last few yards towards the car, angling his direction towards the driver's door, where two of the men were pressing themselves up against the glass. Without a thought he had grabbed at a collar and hauled back, pulling a strange little burly man aside so hard the fellow had spun round and fallen on his backside with a thump that shut his toothless mouth with a dull gulping sound.

'Hey you!' Sean bellowed now at the other man. 'Get the fuck out of here!'

He grabbed at a shoulder, met with some resistance, and swivelled his hip to jerk the man away.

The man turned and raised a hand; whether in self-defence or in aggression, Sean never found out. Instinctively he shot out his right and snapped his knuckles into the man's ribs. There was a short thud. The stranger's breath whooshed out and immediately he doubled up, gasping.

All motion stopped for an instant.

On the other side of the car, three of the men, all with oddly *squashed* faces and slack mouths, stood staring at him, eyes empty. They looked mentally retarded, all of them, imbecilic and malformed.

'Just what the hell are you playing at,' Sean bawled, and the three of them flinched childishly. None of them said a word. The two on the ground next to him slowly got to their feet and sneaked round to join another at the back of the car, and then the group merged on the far side, standing in a huddle, all staring at him.

One of them turned and picked up a long wooden implement, like an oar, with a flat blade at one end. The others followed suit and stood, like

187

a raggle-taggle army of goblin guards at the side of the road. Still they said nothing, just eyed Sean as he stood there staring back angrily. He looked at the men and then at the spades they carried and wondered if they were going to make a move. He considered it quickly, estimating that if they did, he'd have to get one of those things off one of them and fight back, maybe for his life. For a swift, angry second, he felt the boil inside him that would welcome that, relish the *battle* of it.

But there was no movement, except for the shuffling of their feet on the loose stones beside the road. They seemed undecided, possibly even *unable* to decide, what to do next.

As they stared at him, with empty eyes and sly witless faces, Sean felt a small chill work its way into the heat of his anger. They looked so devoid of any reason, any intelligence.

He rapped a knuckle on the window and pointed to the lock. Liz reached up and flicked the button up and Sean opened the car door.

'Shove across,' he ordered brusquely. She could hear the anger in his voice. She hoisted herself up and over the gear lever, awkwardly shifting her weight, and manoeuvred into the other seat. Sean got in and sat down heavily, unslinging his backpack in the same motion. He swung it past the wheel and across to her side.

'Here, hold this,' he said. She grabbed it, felt the sudden weight, and let the bag settle uncomfortably on her knees. He slammed the door shut and turned the key. The engine roared to high revs as his foot pressed the pedal, and then they were moving forwards, the wheels spinning for a second on the loose road surface.

Beside him Liz was pale and tense with fright. 'I thought they were going to kill me,' she said in a voice that was tight and trembling.

'Bloody nutters,' Sean said through his teeth.

'They just came from nowhere,' she said. 'They started banging on the car, trying to break the windows.' Her voice caught, and Sean thought she was about to burst into tears. He was right. He reached a hand over and patted her gently on the shoulder. He could feel her sudden heaving. He glanced in the mirror, looking at the road behind them, but there was nothing to be seen. The strange, threatening group of men had melted away into the bogland.

Liz made a coughing sound and started to say something, and then stopped. He could feel it building up and he stretched his hand out further, still keeping his eye on the narrow road ahead, and curled his fingers round the curve of her neck, then drew her gently and insistently towards him.

She resisted for only a moment, before allowing herself to be pulled over, then turned to face him. She leaned into his chest, burying her face against his shoulder while he wrapped his arm around her, and started to cry. Under his arm he could feel the sobs.

'There, there,' he said stupidly. 'It's all right. They're gone.' He rubbed her arm vigorously, the way one does to comfort a distressed child. 'It's all over now.'

'They could have . . .' she said, and stopped suddenly. Her words were almost incoherent through the tears. She raised her head up from his shoulder. There were two wet tracks running down her cheeks.

'But they didn't,' he said, squeezing her back down to him. 'So don't worry about it.'

'If you hadn't got there . . .' she began again, talking into his jacket. Her voice sounded wet and snuffly.

'You'd have just started up and got off your mark, leaving me with the cast of *One Flew Over the Cuckoo's Nest* in the middle of a bog miles from nowhere,' he said, striving for levity. 'I get the picture. I understand.'

In at his shoulder, the movement stopped. She sniffed.

'But then at least my shirt would still be dry instead of covered with slavvers and snot,' he said. 'So that would probably be the better option, now that I think of it.'

In at his chest, the heaving motion started up again and Sean clenched her tightly to him. They were a couple of miles along the road, nearing the point where it meandered and looped towards the main trunk. He slowed the car and pulled over to the verge, close to a drainage ditch where brackish water trickled.

'Come on now, Liz. They've gone. You're all right now.'

She raised her head from where it was buried against him, and he looked down at her. The tracks of her tears were still there, but the heaving motions were not sobbing. Her eyes were glistening, but Liz was now gripped in a helpless paroxysm of laughter. She raised her other hand, letting the camera bag slip between her legs to the floor, and gripped the front of his shirt, holding on tightly while she convulsed in the laughter that was rippling through her.

At first Sean thought she was having hysterics, but then she subsided a little and almost choked trying to speak.

'You bastard, McCullain,' she managed to get out, before fresh gales of laughter swept through her.

He looked down at her, surprised at first, and then the infection of her laughter started working on him. He could feel her jiggling against him, soft and warm, and he started to chuckle with laughter that was tinged with a certain relief.

After a moment or two of helpless giggling, she began to calm down again.

'Slavvers and snot. McCullain, you're *crazy*.'

'None crazier,' he said with forced flatness, trying to keep a straight face.

She pulled against him and put her head back on his ribs. 'But seriously,' she said. 'If you hadn't come for me, I don't know what would have happened. They looked so awful I was scared to death.'

'They weren't going for bonny baby prizes, that's for certain. They reminded me of a newsdesk morning conference.'

At this Liz collapsed into shrieks of laughter.

'Though probably you'd get more sense out of that lot back there.'

Liz held on tight until she subsided. He could still feel her curled up small against his protective body, and he unexpectedly realised how *appealing* she felt. The notion took him by surprise.

Moments later, Liz pulled herself up and brought her head away. She knuckled her eyes, wiping the tears. She looked up at him, eyes glistening and quite startlingly blue.

'Thanks, Sean,' she said.

'Ah, don't mention it, kid,' he said quickly, looking away and giving her another brief companionable, comforting squeeze.

'No, I mean it. I really was scared, and then you came in like a tornado. I thought you were going to kill them.'

'Me? *Kill them?* I was shitting myself,' he said, though his sheepish grin belied it.

'Like hell. I saw you.'

'I was just worried about my cameras,' he said, slightly abashed. 'They're delicate.'

She was still looking at him, holding onto the front of his shirt, waiting for him to turn towards her. He felt the pressure of it and faced her. Quite simply, she let go of his shirt and brought her hand up to the side of his face, cupping it gently first, then sliding it towards her. He looked straight into her eyes, still bright and blue and *grateful*, felt her lean into him. She slowly closed her eyes and raised her face. He could smell the sweetness of her breath, then felt the soft touch of her lips.

Sean hesitated at first, but Liz pulled him closer, pressing herself hard against him. He felt her lips part, the warm moistness, and then her hand sneaked right round the back of his neck and her arm dragged him closer.

In the middle of the kiss, Sean pictured her again, sitting on the edge of the chair in the glow of the peat fire in the cottage with the sudden anger in her eyes and the abrupt change to laughter that radiated from her and transformed her into a stunning woman. Inside him, his stomach did a little flip and he brought his right hand down, underneath her upraised arm and slowly, gently, rubbed it down the side of her ribs, feeling the softness. As he did, her tongue slid across his and she seemed to melt and flow against him.

Some time later, they broke apart. She drew away from him and stayed for a moment, eyes closed, teeth clenched lightly on her bottom lip as if she was judging, savouring, then she smiled and opened her eyes.

'Oh, McCullain,' she said softly.

He just looked at her, strangely unsure.

'That was . . .' She searched for the word.

'It was okay,' he said, smiling back at her, letting her know he was kidding.

'It was better than okay,' she said finally. 'I do mean it.'

'Okay is fine,' he put in quickly, mistaking her meaning.

'No. I mean thanks for what you did.'

'Oh, that. Anybody would have done that.'

'But it wasn't anybody. It was *you*, and I've been such a pig.'

'No you haven't,' he said, although he knew he wasn't being entirely truthful. But what the hell. They'd kissed and made up. He gave her another companionable squeeze.

'Yes I have. You really pissed me off, but you were right.'

'How do you mean?'

'I was just *scared* of you, I think.'

Sean threw back his head and laughed loudly at the notion. She felt the chuckles shaking against her.

'That's the daftest thing I ever heard.'

'No it isn't. Hear me out. I knew all about you, what an operator you were, and when you looked so annoyed about working with me, I just reacted, that's all. But you were right. I was just trying to show off, and you were right again about Lisdoonvarna. It made me feel bloody inadequate. An absolute beginner.'

'No. You're not inadequate. And not a beginner either. That piece today was damned *good*.'

'But if it wasn't for you, I would have written some sugary stuff about the festival that would have meant absolutely nothing.'

'Well, you didn't, and you've learned something. We've both learned something.'

'What's that?' she asked.

'You're not such an *arse* after all,' he said, and started to laugh again.

She flashed him a look, and then a grin spread across her face, showing her white teeth. 'And neither are you, big idiot.'

She looked at him steadily, drew herself forward and kissed him gently on the lips, then pulled back and settled herself in her seat. A moment later, he started the car again and drove on towards the junction.

It was just before noon when they arrived back at Kilgallan. The cloud over the village was heavy and threatening, though the wind was only a whisper that shivered the tops of the trees. This time Liz made a lunch of French toast, assuring Sean that she could do much better than that, but he just covered his with pepper and wolfed half a loaf with enthusiasm, washing the lot down with a series of large mugs of tea.

On the way in, he'd told her he wanted to see the Tallabaun Strand, which, he explained to Liz, he'd been told was the longest beach in Europe.

'Might make a picture postcard,' he'd suggested mischievously. Liz seemed to have accepted the fact that he was having a break, and since he'd offered her a potentially good picture story right on their doorstep, she was keen to have a look at the diggings.

'We can do that in the afternoon,' he said. 'I'll have to set up remotes. It's pretty dark in there.'

After they'd eaten, Sean washed the plates, thoroughly scoured the pan and neatly stacked everything away, which surprised her. Neither of them had said much after their kiss at the junction. Each had been lost in private thoughts, but certainly the atmosphere had changed between them.

Strangely, Sean McCullain was particularly startled, almost wrong-footed, by what had happened. Now, everything was different. She'd been straight. She'd been scared *shitless* but she'd kept her head. And it had taken guts for her to tell him that she was overawed by his reputation. She'd *apologised* to him and then she'd kissed him, and if truth be told – in Sean's silent thoughts, truth was being told – the kiss had not been too bad at all.

But in the hour since then, he had been unsure of how to act. He'd been out of town on jobs with women reporters before. Some of them were good, and some of them were bitches, and most of the time, as long as they did the job professionally and didn't mess him around, it didn't matter much to him. But he'd never got involved with any of them. He'd always maintained his distance, and that was one of the reasons why he'd been angry when Liz had warned him not to go wandering in the night, not to get *ideas*. Now there was a difference. One kiss, just one kiss, but that put a new slant on things.

He could understand the relief after the fright she'd got, and the fact that he'd put his arm around her. But the kiss was more than just a thank-you. That much was obvious.

While he was washing the dishes, he took a look at her, appreciating her neat body in the tight jeans, then turning away quickly when she glanced over at him.

What had happened in the car had sparked something between them. He could sense it arcing from her to him and back again like an electrical charge.

Still he was wary. She had taken on a new perspective, a new stature in his mind, but he didn't want to push it. Sean was basically a gentleman, and the last thing he wanted *anyone* to think was that he would take advantage of a situation. No, he decided, he would do nothing unless invited, and even then, he would have to think about it.

While he leaned over the sink, Liz sneaked glances at him, averting her eyes every time he turned to her.

She had kissed him, and it *had* been good. Her memory lingered on the gentleness of it, and then the hard urgency of it. She could recall feeling the roughness of his cheek, the hardness of his chest, the dark sparkle in his eyes. Then she remembered the look on his face when he had come to her rescue and challenged those strange grotesque men out on the moor, and her stomach did a slow loop. He *had* looked magnificent, tall and craggy and almost frighteningly *angry*. And after it, he had offered his comfort, snaking his strong arm around her, making her feel small and childlike and protected. He hadn't taken advantage of her then, when she was vulnerable. He'd patted her back and rubbed her arm, when some men would have taken the opportunity for a quick grope.

Then *she* had kissed *him*. He'd returned it gently, warmly, not forcing it at all, just responding to her demand. She didn't know *why* she'd done it. It just seemed to happen, seemed the right thing at that moment.

And now, what did she do about it? He'd won on the issue of taking a break, though he hadn't mentioned it, hadn't crowed or even looked smug about it. Strangely, it didn't seem to matter that much. But now she would be with him for almost a week, the two of them sharing this cottage on the end of a road that led to nowhere.

A little thrill of apprehension mixed with anticipation ran through her. She didn't know what she wanted to do, and that confused her. What also confused her was that Sean seemed to have forgotten about it, dismissed it from his mind. She sneaked another look at him, tall and broad, arms covered in lather up to the elbows, and considered his profile. He *was* a good-looking man in a sort of lived in, *normal* way. If he made a move, she didn't know how she'd react, but there was a possibility, she admitted to herself, that she would be tempted to go along with it, maybe even go the full distance with it, and that thought scared her a little.

And so the two of them danced around each other, not yet attuned, attracted yet unable to join.

But one thing was certain. They'd hauled away from the difficult stage of abrasive friction. They were becoming friends, and that *was* good.

The top end of Tallabaun Strand was only ten minutes away along a fairly good but narrow road that snaked round the headland and hugged the high shore, giving a truly impressive panorama down the immense length of the great sands. Under the greying sky the flat beige-white expanse soared out for more than two miles to where the tide rolled, and spread right down the coast beyond where the eye could see.

Sean had stopped the car on the high Point and the two of them sat there, taking in the magnificent view.

'That's beautiful,' Liz said at last. 'I've never seen anything like it in my life. It looks as if it goes on for ever.'

'About fourteen miles,' Sean said. 'It's vast.'

'And there's nobody on it at all. If this was anywhere else, it would be crammed with beach umbrellas and Germans.'

Sean started the car and drove down the incline, and followed the road along the craggy bluff that overlooked the sands. The smell of salt and seaweed blew in through the window, and way off a seagull mewed plaintively. A few miles further on, the road rose up again, and over the crest there was a deserted village. Old, crumbling cottages sagged and slumped against each other, and on the hillside beside them, a patchwork of tiny fields, each walled by a drystane dyke, huddled forlornly.

It was a strangely desolate scene. The village had been a poor one, hunched on the side of a hill on the edge of the great sand flats, buffeted by the constant west wind that blew in from the Atlantic. The tiny houses were crumbling, and none of them had a roof. Inside the shells, they could see the scales of roof shingles that had given way to the gravity of years and the worms in the timbers, and fallen in.

'Look at the size of the fields,' Liz said. 'They're all tiny.'

'That's what nearly destroyed this country,' Sean said almost angrily.

'How do you mean?'

'Every one of them was rented out to a family. They'll be no bigger than twenty yards on a side. That was their allotment. And when a father died, his sons divided up the land until they had hardly enough to feed themselves. Then, when the landlords discovered the potato would grow on this poor ground, they decided the peasants needed even less land for that than they would for corn.' He stopped, and she turned round to him. His eyes were distant, thoughtful.

'When the blight came and the potatoes rotted, they had nothing else to eat. So they died. At least a million of them.'

'But there's plenty of land,' Liz said. She pointed up at the slope of the hill beyond the huddle of garden-sized allotments. The green hill spread out behind them for miles.

'Of course there was plenty of land. But sheep and grouse-shooting were worth more than humans, that was for sure.'

'That's terrible,' she said.

'Yes. It is. And that's part of the history of this crazy country. I never even knew a thing about it until after Belfast, but it took place all right, and worse besides, and that's part of why it's happening now. There's been old wrongs and fresh wrongs and those wrongs are still going on. The only thing is, nobody knows right from wrong any more,' he said with sudden vehemence.

He got out of the car and she heard the familiar metallic rattle as he pulled out his camera. He came round to the front of the car and sat on the bonnet, feet planted onto the gritty road surface. He raised the camera to his eyes and started taking pictures. Liz watched him for a moment and then came out to join him. He snapped the shutter several times and then turned to her.

'Go and sit over there on the wall, just to give me scale,' he said. She nodded and sauntered over.

'Right. Just there,' he called. She sat down on the rough stone, on the edgewall of the patchwork of dykes, and looked out over the sands.

Through the lens, he could see the strong lines of her face and the tilt of her chin. She looked, dare he say it, quite stunning. At her neck a white silk handkerchief fluttered and the breeze caught her hair, tumbling it, adding to the picture. She raised a hand to brush away a blown hair and he froze the motion.

He stood up from the car and walked towards her a few yards, then stopped. 'If you give me a smile I won't tell anybody you kissed me.'

Her eyes widened in surprise and then immediately crinkled, and he caught the instant flash of humour.

Back at the car, Liz stood and looked out over the swathe of endless sands to where the sea, far out, foamed white waves against the smooth edge. Beyond that, out over the dark ocean, clouds were piling up high and grey into the sky and the wind pushed them in, tumbling and threatening, towards the land.

'Does this place have a name?' she asked as Sean busied himself storing his backpack.

'Tallabaun Strand. I want to walk along it.'

'No, this place,' she said, gesturing at the handful of decaying cottages.

He looked up and caught her drift. 'Don't think so. It's not on the map.'

'That's terrible. Just think: people lived here. Families grew up and died, and now it's just rotting away. When it all crumbles, nobody will ever know there was a village here.'

'It's not the only one. The whole of the west coast is filled with places like this. The famine wiped out hundreds of villages.'

'But why did they let it happen? Why didn't they share the land out?'

'That's the big question. It was greed, mainly. Love of money and land. Life was cheap.' He paused and looked at her, his face impassive. 'It still is. This is still going on. That's what I've found out. That's maybe why I've still got Belfast on the brain. The old sores have never healed. I don't know if they ever will. It's as if this place is under some sort of a cloud. It's gone on and on for so long that maybe, at the end of the day, there is no answer. I hope not, for it's one hell of a country. It's beautiful.'

'Yes, it is,' she said thoughtfully. 'Beautiful and terrible at the same time.'

She looked one more time out to the distant waves. 'I never realised it would be like this. I didn't know there was more to it. All I wanted was to see *Ryan's Daughter* country. That's why I fixed up the stories here.'

'I thought it was something like that,' he said, not looking at her, but his tone of voice showed no smugness. 'It's a romantic notion, I suppose, and despite all of it, all of this—' he indicated the crumbling cottages '—there is romance in the history. The old Celts, and that includes you and me, if we go back far enough, were full of it. You know what they say about them?'

'No, what?'

'All their fights were happy, and all their songs were sad.'

196

21

She was aware of life close by.

The sensations were dim, but they impinged on the ghastly consciousness that slumbered torpidly in the depths of the stone prison *between* the worlds.

Instinctively, the sensing part of her uncoiled and quested out, moving like an invisible shadow, a mere *twist* in the air, into the outside, beyond the dark confines.

She brushed past the strange warm pin-pricks, marking them for later attention. They were unfamiliar, almost *foreign*. The questing part slid past the strangeness of them, and out. Beyond, there was more life. The sense of it was hot. There, beyond the shadows of trees, there was a huddle of it, and some of it *was* familiar. The smell of the *other* people, watered down and diluted through the generations, but still the *same* as she had known. The incomers who had repulsed her own creatures, the Fomorian hordes, and driven them to the sea – the smell of them was in this huddle.

The pre-conscious thought slipped through and within, scenting and snuffling, like a hunting animal feeling for weakness. Around there was the buzz of mindless *small* life that succumbed easily, blankly, to the questing part. The eyes of the small life looked now with new intensity, feeding the sensations back to the *twist* of being that spread out, hazy and unseen, from the tor.

A spider hunched itself in a crack of bark, legs drawn up beside its palps. Sensations came to its six strange eyes, blurred and then quickly focusing, and something behind those eyes took what it had seen. The spider's small fangs eased forwards and down to press on the rotten wood, and the minute dribbles of poison ran from their tips.

Beyond, under a fallen log, a fat toad twitched and one eye opened. A movement nearby sprang into sharp relief on the retina, and with the speed of instinct that required no intelligence, the wide mouth opened and closed with a snap. A pygmy shrew, nosing and snuffling through the leaf litter, saw the sudden gape. Its tiny black eyes sparkled with foreknowledge and then the darkness overtook it.

The curling tendril of almost-*awareness* saw through the eyes of the eater and the eaten, simultaneously.

Moving out, it found more small life, further and further and further. Down at the shore, an eel slithered beyond the wrack that swirled at the edge of the bay. It rolled slowly and its head broke the surface, marking the shadow of the small child picking mussels from the rocks. Out on the moor, a hooded crow scanned the brown, wet bogland. It caught a movement, swung down on its wings against the wind and landed on a jagged, worn stone. It cawed, and its black eyes pinpointed the movement at the top of the small hill, sending its knowledge back to where the torpid dreams absorbed it.

And out on the bog, weak, deformed minds, dull and slow-witted, childlike minds with fault lines deep down at the core where the thoughts were generated, picked up the influence, like open-banded receivers, and began to react.

Across the moor, down at the edges, where the bog was scarred and runnelled with peat diggings, the influence tightened. Tendrils of old, twisted thought sneaked in behind the fault lines and settled in the dimness. Here was something she could use. Here were things the *Shee* could use as her own.

The dread sleep of the day went on and the black dreams of revenge and feasting went on and on and on.

'I don't like it,' Bridget Massey said. 'He gave me the fright of my life, standing out there in the dark.'

She was sitting on the arm of the chair, nestled against Brian Cooney, who was absently stroking her side with his thumb.

'Don't worry about it,' he said reassuringly, though he himself was uneasy, tense. 'There's only a day to go, and then we'll be out of here. Nobody except your brother knows we're here.'

'He said he was looking for a bird. A nighthawk or something,' Bridget went on, as if she hadn't heard. 'But he could have been up to anything. He could have even been looking in the windows.'

'And who could blame him?' Brian asked her, despite the buzz of jealousy that twisted inside him. 'I'd do the same if I were him and all. But I don't think he'll be wanting to have a look at you, so I don't.'

'Why ever not?'

'More like he'd be eyeing me up. Couple of benders, that's what I think. Two men sharing the cottage for birdwatching? Come *on* now Bridget.'

'Do you really think so?'

'What else? You think they might be Special Branch, sent down all the way to look after us? No chance of that. We're not important. We've

198

no form. And nobody knew we were coming here, apart from your Padraigh, and he's not likely to be mouthing his gob off.'

Bridget sat silent for a minute, then nodded. 'I expect you're right.'

Brian grinned and gave her a hug that was as much friendly as encouraging. ' 'Course I am, girl. And once we get this over with, we'll have to think what we're going to tell Paddy.'

'Let me do the talking. He's never refused me yet.'

'Of course I got away with it, but that's not the point,' Edward Laird said irritably. 'What I want to know is who Cooney made his call to.'

'Well, I could hardly go up and take the phone away from him, could I? He was probably phoning his bookie, or his mother. It didn't look that important. He sat about and had a couple of pints. Didn't seem as if he was in any rush. I think we're on a wild-goose chase.'

'That may well be, but if they're up to anything, and we blow it, we'll be back in uniforms as quick as you can think, and I don't relish that prospect.'

Laird bent to the table. The heavy green radio-phone was opened out into two half-shells and, inside, the capacitors and silver solder gleamed. 'Bloody phone,' he said through gritted teeth. 'Damned thing spat when I was standing out there. She nearly shit herself, and so did I, that's for sure.'

'What's wrong with it?'

'Damned if I know. Probably picked up a stray signal. I had to cough my guts out to cover the noise. I think she was fooled but it was too close for comfort. Now I can't get a cheep out of the thing.'

He stuck a small screwdriver into the innards and thumbed the switch. There was a faint crackle and then silence.

'Ordnance. These things are supposed to survive a drop from Mount Everest. Somebody's been ripping supplies off.'

'What'll we do about it?'

'Nothing we can do. I'll have to go up to the village and phone out. They'll laugh their silly heads off. And then we'll get our balls chewed when I tell them we're incommunicado.'

'Can we get another one?'

'Fat chance. This is low-key, low-level. And anyway, there's less chance of being caught on watch if this thing isn't crackling under my armpit.'

Laird tried with the screwdriver again, but the radio gave out nothing. He started to put the two halves together.

'So much for communications training,' he muttered, and Hugh Sands gave a small laugh.

'You go up to the hide and make sure you don't miss a trick. I'll go and phone home. I think I'll tell them you dropped the thing into the sea.'

'Thanks, boss,' Sands said. 'I'll do you a turn if I get the chance.' He hefted the big binoculars in the case and slung it over his shoulder. 'Sir Peter Scott reporting for duty,' he said, pausing at the door.

'Go off and birdwatch,' Laird said.

Liz was impressed with the size of the ancient chamber under the tor, though when Terry Munster drew back the wrapping from the mummified body of the ancient Celt, taking great delight as he did so, she gasped out loud and shuddered with revulsion. Automatically, she jerked herself back from the hideous, shrivelled corpse, and Terry bellowed with laughter.

'It's all right, Liz, he can't lay a finger on you,' he said, chuckling.

'What *is* that,' she said when she got her breath back.

'I call him Bryan Boru. He's one of the old warriors, as you can see by the axe in his skinny hand.'

'Is this his grave?'

'It is now, but the professor's arranging something a little more comfortable.'

'It's disgusting,' she said, and another shiver ran through her. When Terry had pulled the plastic sheet back, she'd caught a sudden glimpse of the sunket sockets and the long teeth poking in a wide grin from shrunken, dried gums. It had looked as if a monster was grimacing at her. In that instant, she felt a sudden *compressing* weight of claustrophobia squeeze in at her. Her vision spun, and the walls of the chamber seemed to shrink in towards her.

'But very important. This will get our names in the history books.'

'What do you mean? It's just a body.'

'Ah yes, and we all have that fine prospect ahead of us,' Terry said theatrically. 'But this old chap, he was walking and talking three thousand years before the good Lord. He's as old as the pharaohs, and better preserved too. He might not be able to talk, but he's going to tell us more than anybody has ever known about the old people. The professor is already calling it the most important archaeological find *ever*. And I agree with him on that.'

Liz nodded, though her stomach was still making small clenching movements that looped within her nauseously.

On the far side of the chamber, Sean was talking to Siobhan while setting up the slave units, little black boxes, at vantage points around the walls. She was outlining the carvings in the stone, standing close to Sean and occasionally touching his arm lightly, making contact, as she spoke.

Finally he was ready. He called to Liz and Terry, beckoning them away.

'Right,' he said, going straight into his photographer's mode. 'I'll take a few general ones from about ten points round the walls with the wide-angle, so stay behind me.'

He set up the tripod, peered through the lens, and then, using a cable switch, he tripped the shutter. The flash blared, and instantaneously the remote slave units, primed to respond to the flashgun beam, were set off, bathing the whole chamber in white light.

And in the depths of the black void, something that slumbered, sated and bloated, reacted with a sudden, instinctive shrinking *from the blast of pure light, fleeing into the far off utter darkness that went on forever. A mental scream blasted out from it as it shrank back at impossible speed.*

As soon as Sean triggered the flash, a shiver ran through him, like the startle of a sudden noise.

'What was that?'

'Did you hear something?' Siobhan asked.

'I thought I did,' Sean said. He listened, straining, and then shook his head. The flashgun whined, insectile. Its red light flickered like a small glow-worm in the gloom.

A moment later, he tripped the flash again and the light flared, illuminating the whole expanse of the chamber. This time there was no shiver. The light bounced off the finely masoned stones, speared the surface of the black monolith at the centre and streamed back into the lens to imprint the scene on the high-definition film.

Terry and Liz went back up the tunnel, leaving Sean and Siobhan together. The passageway was narrow, allowing little more than enough room for one person, but to Liz, it seemed even narrower, as if her shoulders brushed the walls on either side. Suddenly she had the strangest feeling that the walls had expanded, were *leaning* in on her. The thought sped her breath again and she could feel her throat constrict to a dry, tight knot. Her feet moved faster, stout walking shoes thudding on the cobbled flagstones. Ahead, the rectangle of light seemed an impossible distance away, an unreachable goal, and the jolt of panic that thought gave her almost caused her to trip over her feet. Behind her, Terry Munster moved along at his normal, lumbering pace. Liz heard his footsteps echo, heavier than hers, and her mind gave a little *flip* and instead of Terry, the big amiable Irishman, she imagined the thing that had glared, sightless and shrivelled, from under the sheet, following her up the passageway. That sent a cold shiver up her spine and she felt the fine hairs on the back of her neck stiffen, raising themselves up from her collar, and she *couldn't* turn to look. The sudden image came so strongly that she practically bolted for the light, seeing the rectangle shimmer and dance at the end of the corridor, seeming to *recede* from her faster than she could walk . . .

. . . And then, miraculously, she was *out*. On the *outside*. Her tight throat immediately loosened and she hauled in a cool breath of air, expanding her lungs so much that her breasts jutted from the fine lambswool jumper.

Terry, coming up beside her, eyed her shape appreciatively, though he had the grace to look embarrassed when she turned to look at him. He smiled sheepishly, like a small boy caught with his hand in the biscuit barrel.

She let her breath out. 'God, that's a scary place down there.'

'You get used to it. I've been in and out of that tunnel every day since the spring. Nearly killed myself under a rockfall only the other day.'

The thought of *that*, of being trapped under a rockfall down in the depths at the end of the passage, sent another shudder through Liz.

'I hate places like that. Too dark and enclosed.'

'I wondered why you raced out of there,' Terry said, grinning. 'Sure, there's nothing in the world to worry about. Old Bryan Boru, he's been dead and gone for thousands of years. He couldn't harm a fly.'

He put a hand on Liz's shoulder in a friendly sort of way, even though she'd caught his look. 'Come on over to the professor's place and you can have a coffee with us.'

Down in the chamber, Sean worked steadily, keeping up a running conversation with Siobhan while he took his pictures. He did a complete set of the whole chamber, and took close-ups and long shots of the old dead warrior, stripping back the plastic to show his full, stringy length. Then he'd got to work on the stone itself, painstakingly angling the camera to take a long series of shots of the carvings so that when they were printed, they would all overlap, like a sectional map, giving the best detail.

Finally, he took some shots of Siobhan, kneeling beside the stone, leaning on it, crouched beside the cadaver. She had a good, heart-shaped face that would come across as intelligent and warm, not drily academic.

As he had with Liz, he waited until she was leaning across the stone, looking thoughtful, then he said: 'Now take all your clothes off for page three.'

Without hesitation, Siobhan moved to lift the front of her Aran jumper, and Sean held up a hand to forestall her.

'Only kidding,' he called out, and Siobhan laughed aloud, girlishly gleeful.

'And didn't I know it, mister newspaperman,' she said. 'You thought you had me there, but I had you, sure enough.'

Sean chuckled. 'Aye, you got me.'

Siobhan let the front of her jumper fall. 'Now if you were to ask me another time, without the camera, I might just think about it,' she said, still smiling.

'I'll bear that in mind,' Sean said.

'Now come on back to the professor's place, and we'll give your friend the stuff she needs. It'll be a good story, and that could help us, you know. But not, I think, on page three,' she added with a chuckle.

She waited until Sean had unshipped his gear and collected the remote flashes, then led the way up the tunnel. Outside, Professor Connarty was walking towards the entrance with two men who carried between them a grey, metallic-looking box that had spring catches holding a lid down.

'Got all the pictures, eh?'

'All you'll need, I think,' Sean told him.

'Fine, wonderful. Now we can make sure we save what we've got. Undertaking service courtesy of the Department of Archaeology. We'll have the wake tonight up at Donovan's fine establishment.'

He gave them a cheery wave and bustled on ahead of the two men who had the box, solid and heavy, a high-tech coffin, slung between them.

Siobhan slipped her arm into Sean's and walked with him towards the cottage.

Tom and Nancy Ducain had taken the same road down by the strand that Sean and Liz had followed a few hours earlier. She'd come down from the hill, breathing hard and slightly flushed with the exhilaration of exercise.

'You should have come up with me, lazybones. The view is miraculous. You can see for miles.'

Tom yawned lazily. 'All you can see is bogs and more bogs. Anyway, I'm an old married man now, and getting up this far is enough for me.'

'I'll remember that when we go skiing this winter. I'll tell everybody I've married a sugar daddy.'

'You'll have worn me out by then,' he said. 'At least I hope so.'

'Dirty old devil, and me just a young Irish girl from the hills.' She hunkered down and gave him a big, wet, exaggerated kiss on the mouth, then drew back and settled beside him. He could smell the sweetness of her perspiration.

'You can see the sea from up there. I'd like to go down and have a look.'

He nodded. 'Sure, we can go after lunch.'

She stretched out, and Tom slowly eyed her limber length. He thought he'd done well. His dental practice was making plenty, enough to give them the kind of lifestyle that included a three-country European honeymoon. Nancy didn't seem to care much about the money. She was almost childishly hyperactive, and she had a childlike wonder in everything she encountered. He knew she took her teaching job seriously. She put the same zest into her fitness programme. Every morning she was out running, and twice a week she helped run a Shotokan school for women, which, even in an upmarket place like Vermont, as in everywhere across the US of A, was becoming more and more of a necessity.

They had a steak pie for lunch, then took the car down past the headland, stopping, at first, near where Sean and Liz had parked the car, by the patchwork of small fields.

'Looks old,' Nancy said. 'What is it?'

'Some corrals for sheep or something. That's all they grow here, it looks like.'

'You think anybody lives here now?'

'If they do, they should move,' Tom said, and laughed. 'None of them has a roof. This looks like the town that just rolled up the sidewalks and moved to California.'

They drove on, and the road swept down the slope, close to the level of the beach. There was a stream that tumbled down the mountainside in a white spray, crossed over the rutted track and went down onto the sandy shore, where it cut a groove that seemed to stretch out for a mile or more towards the sea. Nancy got out of the car and strode lightly across the way to where the stream fell between a small cleft of rocks. She bent, placing her hands on either side, and lowered her head to drink.

She came up again, gasping, after a long swallow. 'Oh, that's terrific. It's pure crystal.'

'And probably full of bugs too. There could be shit and dead sheep in it up there on the hill. You could die from that stuff,' Tom said, screwing his face up.

'Just the same as there is anywhere else. But it tastes like real water.'

'I like mine out of a bottle, preferably chilled,' Tom said.

'Ain't you a regular Jeremiah Johnson?' she asked with heavy sarcasm.

'I just like to stay alive, that's all,' he said seriously.

She got up, laughing, and took his hand, almost dragging him down onto the wide beach. The sand was clean and crisp, and the wind was blowing up little snatches of the fine stuff at the high-water mark. Further out, the sand was compacted. They followed the line of the stream until it spread out, then moved away, staying on the hard-pack, walking out hand in hand towards the water.

'Magnificent, isn't it?'

'It's like Nevada, except for the water,' Tom replied.

'And the sun. Death Valley it isn't.'

It took them more than half an hour to get right out to where the breakers crashed in on the edge of the sand. Behind them, on the rough road, the car was just a faint blue shape against the grey-green of the hill. Further up the slope, the deserted village looked gaunt. They were the only people on the strand. The wind blew in their faces, and on either side the sands spread, up coast and down coast, for further than the eye could see.

'You could imagine that we were the only people in the world.'

'There goes the practice,' Tom said drily.

'Oh, Tom, where's the romantic in you? Just think, if we were the only people, we'd be starting a new civilisation.'

'Assuming I don't fire blanks, it would be off to a good start,' he said, eyeing her up and down again.

'Yeah, at least they'd have one good set of genes,' she countered.

'As long as they're blue and as long as they're tight, that'll be fine by me,' he said, moving closer and running his hands over the taut denim on her backside.

He kissed her gently on the lips and then pulled away. 'And who said romance is dead?'

They wandered, arms clasped around each other's waists, back along the sands, the wind behind them tossing Nancy's mane of hair this way and that. Up the track, Nancy said she wanted to explore the maze of drystane dykes which had withstood the years and the winds better than the old houses. Tom followed her over a sturdy wall into a little field which was overgrown with thistles and nettles. Each was connected to its neighbour by a gate-space that allowed them to wander around the twenty or so plots. In some, sheep had huddled from the winds, leaving grey, webby strands of wool snagged on the edges of the stones and blurring in the breeze. In the corner of one, a bare ram's skull lay angled on impressive horns, white and stony and sightless.

Halfway up the jumble of potato plots, Nancy let Tom go first through one of the gateways, and then ducked to the side, crouching low, into its neighbour. Stifling a chuckle, she tiptoed along to the next junction and hid behind the wall.

Tom was talking about how intricately the dry stones were inter-locked without mortar or cement, and still standing while the cottages were falling down. Nancy didn't answer, and he turned to where he expected her to be behind him. She wasn't there, and he walked back to the entrance, casting his eyes left and right.

A small twist of anxiety poked at him when he didn't see her, then it vanished when he heard a high-pitched smothered giggle off to the right.

'Nancy?' he called out, and his voice bounced off between the walls, giving it a ricochet, echo effect.

The chuckle came again, but because of the patchwork of walls and gateways, it was hard to pinpoint it.

'Hey, where are you?' he called out, a little louder. 'Quit fooling around.'

'Try and find me,' she called back, laughter breaking her voice.

'Shit,' he muttered. 'Hide-and-seek already.'

He stood against the wall, craning upwards, seeing all around him the rough, flat edges of the wall tops. 'Come on, Nancy. You could break a leg here,' he shouted, but there was no irritation in it. Already he was crouched down, thinking he had worked out the direction, hoping to surprise her.

He crept through a gateway and into the other plot, quietly making his way through a patch of nettles and, still crouched, Indian-fashion, he hunched beside the next space, raising himself up until his eyes were just at the level of the wall.

'Tom? Oh, To-om,' she called, sing-song, teasing. Her voice seemed to come from up ahead, though the way it bounced off the walls, he couldn't be sure.

He stayed quiet, knowing she wouldn't be able to resist having a look.

'Ha. I can see you,' she shouted, this time definitely from behind him. He whirled, and just caught the flash of her blonde hair as she ducked her head. Tom raced for the entrance, spun round into the adjacent block and ran pell-mell for the next gate. He came through and into the bare patch, feet skidding on the short grass, and crossed to the next one.

She wasn't there.

Nancy had spotted the back of his head and ducked when she'd seen him turn, knowing that he'd make for where she'd been. She crouched, running, towards where she had seen him, stifling her laughter as she went, staying low so that she wouldn't show. When she passed where he'd been crouching, she went two fields further on and found a small empty square where the grass had been nibbled by sheep. She crept into the dry corner, well out of the wind, and hunkered down against the stone, listening for his progress.

Eventually he called out. 'Nancy?'

She didn't answer.

'Nancy girl. Where the hell did you get to?' His voice sounded further away. Obviously he'd thought she would move back, instead of doubling round.

She risked a look over the top of the wall, leaning her weight against the stones that came up to chest height, and peered across the maze.

He was almost at the far end, head swivelling this way and that.

'Okay. I give up. You win,' he bawled.

Nancy sank to her haunches again, enjoying this. She could hide here all day, and he'd never find her. It was like being a kid again. She huddled into the corner of the wall, content to let her mischievous game go on for a while longer. He'd start to get irritated, the way men do when they get fed up of games they think of as childish – though they could spend hours watching ballgames and playing squash and basketball without a moment's thought – then she'd let him find her.

Out of the wind, the little corner was quite warm and snug. Some ferns had sprouted in the lee and turned to brown with the approach of winter. They were dry and crackly, almost nest-like. She eased herself down comfortably into the bracken to wait. Out there, Tom searched for her, occasionally calling her name fruitlessly, and then he fell silent, as though realising that if she could pinpoint his voice, she would take evasive action. He'd decided on the stealthy approach.

In the snug ferns, Nancy felt herself relax, smiling, waiting for him to pass, so she could jump out at him. It would take several minutes for Tom to work his way down to where she lay in the corner, so she closed her eyes, leaning against the dry stone, rough and lichen-covered but comfortable. It seemed to fit her shape. Her breathing slowed down.

Then hands gently touched her sides and slipped round to cup her breasts.

Nancy grinned. 'That's how to surprise a girl,' she said, laughingly, feeling a sudden surge of pleasure at the thought of making love with Tom in this quiet nest in the corner of the maze. She turned slowly, feeling the hands squeeze against her, and she opened her eyes.

A face stared at her, an odd, flattened *squashed* face, goggle-eyed, and Nancy gasped in fright. 'Oh . . .' was all she managed to get out before a meaty hand clamped over her mouth.

Her eyes stared, bulging in fear, taking in the apparition that was only inches from her. A man. An *odd*-shaped man with a slack mouth, and a strange *deformed* slant to his head as if it had been squashed on one side. The grizzled hair stood out awry, and there was a look of feral, almost *mindless* hunger in the watery eyes. It looked as if there was no real *intelligence* behind them, the way that mentally retarded unfortunates appeared.

She tried to yell, but all that came out from behind the clammy hand was a *glmph* sound.

The hand on her breast squeezed, and she felt a sharp nipping pain. Her staring eyes caught another movement as someone else loomed to the side behind her attacker. It was another raggedy man, this one thinner and dirty-looking. The stubble of several days' growth stood out on sunken cheeks. There was a slackness to his mouth, and in the clarity of the moment, she saw a slight flicker of froth at the edges. He looked vacantly *mad*.

On her thigh a hand gripped, palpating the long muscle, and then moved upwards, fingers suddenly, *terrifyingly*, digging into her crotch. She felt the hard seam of her jeans being forced inwards towards the bone, rasping against tender flesh, and she squirmed, trying to get away from it. The man behind the first one giggled, a watery, high-pitched, animal sound that froze her muscles, chilled her nerves. Her terror suddenly swooped higher while the pit of her stomach sank like a stone.

'Tom! *Tom!*' her mind called out, but she couldn't force the words past her lips, clamped tight by the unrelenting hand. A small bubble formed at her nose and burst wetly: her lungs clenched, heaving to draw in, making her snuffle frantically.

The hand at her breast moved and she was shoved roughly to the ground. Weight pinned her down, and the hand pulled her jumper upwards, fingers hooking round the bra. There was a sharp tugging as the strap dug into her shoulder, then an elastic *ping* as it snapped. The cold hand clamped on her hot skin and she felt goose bumps crawl as the surface tried to shrink away. Her nipple was gripped between fingers, and pain sang out.

Down there at her waist, she could feel hands scrabble at her jeans, popping the stud, and then there was a coldness as the waistband was pulled down roughly. She squirmed and twisted, but the weight was too much, and her limbs didn't seem to be working properly; it felt as if they were frozen to numbness. Her panic exploded. Her arm moved at last and she reached down to grasp the front of her jeans, just as fingers poked hard at her panties in a horrendous invasion. She touched something warm and hard pushing in at her.

'Oh. *Oh God no!*' her mind screamed in a great mental blast as she realised what it was, what it *meant*.

Suddenly the knowledge galvanised her: electricity bucked through her nerves, freeing her from the numbing stasis. Rationality swooped in, and hot on its heels, swift and absolute *fury*. Without even thinking about it, her training simply took over. She opened her mouth as wide as she could and bit down *hard* on the fingers that slipped between her teeth. There was a wailing grunt and the fingers withdrew instantly.

At the same time her freed lungs bellowed: 'Tom. *Oh my God, TOM!* COME QUICK!'

One part of her consciousness heard him call back, anxiety and fear tight in the tone of his voice: 'Nancy! Nancy, where are you?'

And in the same moment, her hand jerked down, beyond the hot, stiff hardness, underneath it, ignoring the revulsion of the touch. There was a softness there and her fingers automatically clutched at it and gripped with savage intensity.

This time there was no grunt. An animal wail soared into the air. It was a wild inhuman screech that ripped up and out from the corner, and despite her fear, Nancy felt a wave of exultation sweep her up.

The man who had been pinning her down rolled as her knee jerked up and caught him between his legs. He made much the same sound as she had made when she'd tried to call out under the pressure of his hand. He sprawled to the side, flabby, ungainly.

She twisted quickly, pivoting herself against the wall, and lashed out with her foot. Her heel caught the strange misshapen face with a satisfying squelchy thud, and spittle and blood flew upwards from squashed lips. The man's head snapped backwards and he crashed onto the dry bracken.

Adrenaline surged, bringing everything into sharp, high-colour focus. On the other side of the field she saw the odd, uncoordinated movements of the other man as he sloped away through the gateway. She felt the wind ruffle her hair and heard her heart beating fast, rabbit-fast, behind her ears, and beyond that she heard Tom's urgent progress towards her, vaulting over the low walls.

She fled from the field, jinking to the right and then to the left, putting as much distance behind her as she could, straining to get to Tom. Five fields away she crashed into his arms, and the tide inside her broke. She burst into tears, sobbing hard into his neck.

'Jesus, Nancy, what's going on?'

For several minutes she couldn't speak. The dam of fear simply poured through the breach and he held her tight against him, feeling the convulsions racking her. He asked her the question over and over, patting her hair and her back and rubbing her neck. Finally she pulled away from him, and the tears were still streaming down her cheeks.

'Men,' she said, gulping for breath. 'Two of them. They . . . they . . . tried to . . .' She faltered and broke into tears again.

'What did they do, Nancy?' Tom shouted, his face a mask of concern and fear and anger. *'What the fuck did they do?'*

'They *touched* me!' she wailed. 'They were going to *rape* me.'

'Where? Where are they?' he almost screamed, and she pointed back over her shoulder.

'Two of them.'

'Two of them, huh?' Tom said, pulling back from her. 'I don't give a shit if there's ten of them.'

He stepped quickly to the wall and hauled off one of the top stones. He hefted it, grey and solid in his hand.

'Right. Let's see those bastards,' he rasped. He grabbed her by the hand, hurtling through the gate in the direction she had indicated. They got to the dry field where she'd crouched. The bracken was flattened and crumpled, but there was no sign of the men, except for an old, torn cloth cap that had snagged on the dry ferns. Tom stormed through to the other side, looked quickly left and right and, seeing no movement, clambered up on top of the wall to give himself a vantage over the whole patchwork of little fields.

No sign of anyone. Up on the hill, a crow rasped a harsh call and the wind moaned in from down the slope towards the beach. There was nothing there.

He climbed down from the wall and threw the stone with a hard, frustrated twist of his body. It crashed against the wall and splintered into shrapnel. He came across to where Nancy was standing shaking with the aftershock of the fear and the burst of adrenaline, and put his arms around her.

'There now. It's all right. They've gone, whoever they were.'

'God, Tom, I thought they were going to . . .'

'But they didn't.'

'I kicked him in the balls,' she said. 'He squealed like a pig.'

'I heard. I thought it was you,' he said.

For a moment she was silent, and then a weird, crazily funny thought struck her. 'Oh, thanks a bunch. Like a pig.'

'No, I didn't mean . . .' he started to say, and she began laughing, a little shrill, a little hysterical, but laughing nonetheless. He held her until she had finished. His hands were still shaking from fear and his anger.

'Oh Tom, you can be so dumb sometimes,' she said, and started to laugh again, this time nearer to normal laughter. It amazed him that she could do it at all, after the terrible fright she'd got from whoever – *or whatever* – had mauled her.

But relief flooded through him. She'd been badly scared, but she hadn't been harmed, not seriously, not *physically*, and she had fought back, enough to repel the attack, enough to *hurt*. A buzz of pride in her thrilled through him and he hugged her tighter, kissing her on the lips, on her closed eyes, tasting the salt of her tears, taking her weight against him.

Some time later, they walked slowly back to the car.

Down at the Tallabaun Inn, something was happening to Mike O'Hara.

He was a small, sparrow-like man with thick glasses that made his eyes look huge and bewildered, and thinning brown hair brushed back on his head, long enough to curl at his neck. He always wore a jacket and a neat little bow tie, whether he was behind the bar or in the small restaurant that catered for guests who stayed in the five neat little rooms in the annexe of his hotel.

The last of the farmers had checked out that morning, and that meant the final guests of the season were gone. The bar would stay open for passing trade, though it did little enough business through the cold, wet and windy winters. Donovan's was the place where most people drank. It was a Catch-22 for Mike O'Hara, who had bought the hotel for what had seemed a song two years before with his redundancy money. He'd had a job as manager of a small engineering company that had merged with a conglomerate and made him surplus to requirements. Mike's

211

wife, Angela, had died of cervical cancer two years before that, and the insurance money, coupled with the need to get away from Limerick and out on his own, had helped spur the move. The Tallabaun Inn had seemed like just the right place. Tourists were beginning to come over to the west coast, and there seemed to be the chance of boom times ahead, seeing as the Northern Irish tourist industry up in Ulster was having troubles with the Troubles.

Then, just as he had signed the papers that committed his entire worldly wealth to his new business, he discovered that the plans were already laid for the seven cottages behind the town on the edge of the bay. He couldn't believe it at first. Surely someone should have *told* him, he'd thought. But no, they hadn't. The county had made the grant, along with the tourist board, and the cottages, seven of them, had gone up in the field just around the corner, in direct competition with his own place.

What was worse, the fishermen and the visitors from all over seemed to prefer staying there, looking after themselves, doing their own cooking, while, all during the summer, with the exception of the market weekends, one or two of his rooms would be lying empty. There would be vacant tables in the restaurant.

Mike sat in the small den off the corridor. The roll-top desk was crammed with papers and bills and invoices. A bottle of brandy, half-empty, sat on the corner of the worn tooled leather. Beside it, a glass, half-full, reflected amber in the overhead light. Mike was more than half-drunk.

It wasn't that the business was down the drain. He hadn't thought that a couple of days before. All right, he wasn't making an out-and-out fortune, but things had ticked over.

Today, however, he had been strangely *anxious*.

Before the farmers checked out, complaining, as usual, over their bills, he had come awake with an unusual feeling of oppression. His head ached just above his eyes, and as he sat up, groping for his glasses, the blurred room spun dizzyingly for an instant.

The depression hung about him all day. Nothing seemed to be right. Everything was shades of grey, and as the day progressed, getting more dismal all the time. As the clouds rolled in from the ocean and began to build up over the headland, he felt the weight of it pressing in on him.

In the late afternoon, the bar was empty, apart from one customer who was just passing through and had stopped long enough to have a beer and a toasted ham sandwich. He finished quickly and went on his way. Mike went into his office to do the accounts, taking with him, unusually, the brandy bottle and a balloon glass.

At first he started organising his receipts and invoices, fingers stabbing at the buttons on the calculator, but the gloomy feeling inside had dulled him down, making him fumble with the keys. Twice he added up columns of figures and found he'd forgotten to put in the decimal point for pence in several places, giving him totals for money owed that were so high they were scary when he poked at the bottom line.

For some reason, he got to thinking more and more about the cottages down in the field, the ones that always seemed to be filled with foreigners, including those bookish folk from the university who were digging into the hill.

He poured himself another brandy, letting the liquid splash heavily into the glass, and took a large swallow. It was so unfair, he thought bleakly. *He* hadn't got a grant to take this place on. He looked over the pile of bills and the blanket of depression seemed a little heavier. All his money sunk in here, and him left with empty rooms for the winter.

'*Damned unfair*,' he said aloud.

The drink fuzzed his mind and intensified the resentment. He sat, slumped, in the high-backed swivel seat, feeling sudden tears of anger and frustration prick his eyes. He reached for the glass and swallowed off the rest of the brandy, and immediately poured himself another manly measure.

'It's all right for them,' he muttered, maudlin. 'They've not got all the bills to pay and wages and taxes.'

The resentment bubbled up in a hot boil. He'd like the cottages to disappear, taking with them their unfair competition and giving him a free hand to run the inn the way it should be run.

His fuddled thoughts lurched along with him as he sat and moped and drank, and eventually he fell into a snuffling, drunken doze.

It was after eight o'clock when he suddenly awoke, snapping to wakefulness instantly. Something had *changed*.

The depression had vanished completely. His mind was buzzing, hot and fiery. He wasn't drunk, but oddly *alive*, strangely *intense*. Inside him, the boil of resentment had altered. It still bubbled down there in the depths, but the maudlin, helpless feeling had gone. There was something positive and purposeful about the way he felt, an urgent alertness coiled like a spring. All the colours, the wood hues of the small, dim room, stood out, sharp and crisp. He could sense the grain of the leather on the desk, the fine grain of the smooth old wood. He could

213

smell the dregs of brandy in the glass and the faint dry odour of the dust up in the corner.

He got himself up from the desk and shoved the chair backwards. The movement was so quick and direct that the seat tumbled off balance. His hand reached out automatically and righted it. Mike left the room and went down the corridor, descending the steps to the kitchen. Voices, low in conversation, came from behind the door. He opened it and went straight in.

Fidelma Brogan, the elderly cook, was stacking copper pots on the shelf, her work done for the day. Marie Lally, the young chambermaid, was sitting at the end of the long wooden table, a cup of tea in her hand. Both women looked up as he entered.

'Just finishing up now, Mr O'Hara. I'm off to my sister's and I'll be back in the morning first thing.'

'Fine, you do that,' Mike said. His mind was clear and alive with energy. Inside, behind the eyes, it seemed to spark and sizzle.

Fidelma got her coat from the hook on the wall and wrestled herself into it. She was a stout little woman with heavy jowls and a ruddy complexion that spoke of her long association with cooking sherry. She patted a little blue hat on her head, speared a hatpin through it and into her thick grey hair, and hefted a mammoth handbag that could have smuggled a side of beef out of the freezer.

'Right. I'll be off now,' she said and bustled out.

Mike sat down at the end of the table. Marie sipped her tea absently, engrossed in a woman's magazine. She was only sixteen, a little girl who hadn't lost her puppy fat. Her hair was a mousy tangle and she had a shy, timorous manner, always avoiding direct eye contact, as she quietly went about the hotel, cleaning and making the beds and helping Fidelma in the kitchen.

Her mother had brought her up from Cashel, where the family had a couple of bleak acres in the wildlands down in Connemara, only too pleased to get another of her six daughters off her hands. Marie and Fidelma shared the tiny extension, and when Mrs Lally had ascertained that her daughter was in the hands of a capable older woman, she had been happy enough to leave her and take the bus down the coast road and home.

Mike sat at the table, thoughts still sizzling strangely. He felt a nervousness about him, an imperative jangling inside. He stared at the young girl sitting opposite. She had a soft, round face and slow, innocent eyes.

'Make me a cup of tea, Marie, there's a good girl,' he said finally.

214

The girl looked up abruptly as if she hadn't even noticed he was there. 'What was that, Mr O'Hara?'

'Just a pot o' tea. My throat's dry as a hearth full of ashes. Be a dear and put the kettle on.'

Marie nodded and shoved her chair back, turning to cross to the big cooker. The large boiler sat on a slow heat and she held the pot under it and flipped the spigot, letting the water pour out in a steamy stream.

'Can I be fixing you something to eat, sir?' she asked in that slow rustic way.

'Eat?' Mike looked over at her. His eyes had followed her as she walked across to the boiler. He stared at her as if away in a dream. Behind the thick glasses, his eyes looked huge.

'There's still an ashet of pie left, if you'd like,' she said helpfully.

Mike shook his head, seeming to come to. 'Oh no, just the tea. That'll be fine, darlin'. Just the tea.'

She stirred the pot with a spoon and clanked the lid back on before bringing it on a tray to the table, with a cup sitting on a saucer. She poured a spot of milk and then the tea itself, and went back to her chair and bent over the magazine. Mike sipped at the hot brew, his eyes fixed on the top of the girl's head. Thoughts whirled about, strange *urgent* thoughts which had as yet no form. They jumped and jittered behind the eyes.

There was a silence. The girl kept her head down shyly for a few moments, then seemed to become aware of his stare. Slowly, timorously, she raised her head.

'You like working here, don't you girl?'

She looked surprised at the question. 'Yes, sir. It's all right.'

'And it's not too hard work?'

'No, sir. And anyway, I'm used to the work, so I am.'

'And your room at the back, that's to your liking?'

'Oh it is, sir,' she replied with some enthusiasm. 'It's the first room I've ever had to myself, and that's the truth.'

'Good, good. Maybe we can get a bit of wallpaper and a lick of paint up before the season starts. Maybe you want to pick the colours?'

Marie beamed. 'Oh, thank you, sir, that would be lovely.'

'Yes. Yes,' he said absently. 'It would be grand.' He looked at his watch. It was barely nine o'clock. 'I think you should be turning in for the night.'

She glanced up at the clock. 'I've still got some of this place to do,' she said.

'Och, don't worry about it. Off you go and get to your bed early, and remember to say your prayers, won't you now?'

215

'Yes, sir,' Marie said meekly. She took her cup to the sink and washed it out before drying it and stacking it neatly with the rest of the crockery. At the door, she turned, eyes down, and said: 'Goodnight, sir.'

Mike O'Hara nodded and she went out. His eyes stayed fixed on the door, which had swung almost shut behind her. He remained there, frozen, for some time, while the old brown clock on the wall slowly ticked off the seconds. His head felt *hot*, as if there was a pressure inside. His thoughts, strange vague thoughts, danced around, and there was a high buzzing sound vibrating in the bones behind his ears.

Some time later, Mike O'Hara got himself up out of his chair and went to the door. The place was silent. He closed the door behind him with a soft *snick* and went up the stairs like a shadow. He was tingling with a peculiar energy, aware of *everything* around him, as if every nerve-ending in his skin was sensitive to the space between him and the walls. The jumbled thoughts in his head had quietened down. His body was wildly alive, but now there was a cool, shaded numbness in his mind. He went along with it.

At the end of the narrow corridor that led to the outbuilding, he stopped at the door, standing dead still. He could hear his own breath, soft and fast, *excited*, and a little pulse on his temple beating rhythmically. His hand reached out; he opened the door softly and went in on silent feet.

At first Marie didn't see him. She was sitting up on the cot bed, half-turned away from him to catch the light from the lamp on the small table. The blankets were up to her waist and she was slumped on an elbow. The flannelette nightdress with the little tie-laces at the top was loose and rumpled. Idly, absently, she lifted her hand and scratched just under her right breast. It jiggled a little and he could see the small peak of her nipple just pressing against the fabric.

The numbness swept through him in a wash that was like a dark river, submerging his own thoughts in the flow. His body was still alive and rippling with strange energy. Every detail was fixed on his mind's eye that was somehow not exactly *his* mind's eye. He stood dead still, jittering with the pressing dark *need*.

Suddenly she sensed him and her head swung quickly towards him. He heard the sudden sharp intake of breath and felt a satisfying *taste* of her startled alarm.

The darkness swooped in and rolled over him.

'Mr O'Hara,' Marie said, automatically clawing the blanket up towards her neck.

'Ah, there now, girl,' he said in a queer, quiet voice that sounded almost regretful. 'I just wanted to make sure you were all right.' He slowly came away from the door towards her.

'You are all right now, aren't you, girl, with Fidelma away for the night?'

She drew back, wary, holding the blankets against her chest. 'Sure I am, Mr O'Hara. I was just about to go to sleep.'

'Ah,' he said, as if considering this. 'Yes. Sleep. That's good. That's very good.'

He stopped at the edge of the bed, looking down on her, looking right *into her* but somehow unaware of her all at the same time.

'There's a good girl,' he whispered, and saw her shudder . . . 'You lie down now and I'll tuck you in tight. Yes. That's the thing. Tight.'

'I'll be all right, Mr O'Hara. Honest. I'll be fine.' Her hand was shaking, clenched on the edge of the blanket. The magazine slipped to the floor.

He bent over and took hold of the material. His hot, fevered hand brushed against hers. She shrank back further. He half-sat on the bedside and raised his other hand to her shoulder, insistently shoving her down. She wormed her way under the sheets until she was lying flat, head on the pillow.

'Goodnight then, Mr O'Hara. I'll sleep now.'

'Of course you will, girl. Yes.'

He gave the rolled-down edge of the blanket a little pull, and she froze. Gently but firmly, he pulled it away from her fingers, drawing it slowly down from her chin. Now she was shivering with fright, too young, too innocent, to know what to do. Her eyes were wide and her mouth was open and rounded, as if she was about to say *Oh*. Her hands trembled.

He stripped the blankets right down, dragging them off her in a long, lingering, savouring way. Then he raised his hand and ran it up her leg, on the skin, continuing the motion slowly, deliberately, pushing the nightdress up over her pale sturdy legs.

She stiffened and he heard her gasp.

On the edge of the bedpost, her dressing gown was hanging by its tab. O'Hara reached out with his free hand, drew out the silky cord at the waist, and brought it onto the bed. He took her hand, feeling the tremor as she resisted, and firmly brought it up behind her head. He lifted his other hand, which had been hungrily sliding on her thigh, and took her nerveless fingers in his. Crossed both her hands up behind her head. She was in a state of frozen immobility. He could hear her breath, fast

217

and shallow, panicked. Her eyes darted to his and away, and then back again, pleading mutely.

He tied her hands to the bedpost.

Then he got up and stood at the end of the bed, fumbling with his trouser belt. She lay stiff, eyes now tight closed, scared to look at him, to see what he was doing.

He slipped the belt through the loops and grabbed her ankle. There was no resistance when he pulled her leg downwards. It remained motionless when he slackened his grip and reached for the other ankle and drew that leg down beside the first. Quickly, yet carefully, he looped the belt through the buckle and slipped it over both trembling feet, cinching it tight, before winding the rest of the strap round the brass railing at the bottom of the bed, pulling it and finally tying a slip knot. The leather and the cord cut into the girl's wrists and ankles, but she was too terrified to cry out, too shocked to move.

O'Hara got on the bed beside her and slid up her nightdress.

Something in the darkness, in a shallow fault line in O'Hara's mind, a fault line that had started as a crack when his wife died, had widened when he lost his job, looked out gleefully and savoured the pain. The terror came off the girl in waves. Hungrily it sucked up the emotions.

The girl's face was a mask of misery and fear as she watched him ogle her body. Any second now, he knew, she expected him to do something, something nameless and terrible, but O'Hara seemed content for the moment just to stare at her captive form. Then, quite casually, he leaned forward, grasped the trailing cord that hung from the bedhead and brought it forward. She gave a small start and he ignored it. He stopped and looked at her again, then suddenly looped the cord around her neck and pushed his weight backwards, hauling on the braided silk.

The girl gave a little squawk before her air supply was cut off. Her eyes bulged instantly and her tongue stuck out between her lips.

Straddled across her knees, O'Hara pulled back hard and felt the cord bite into her neck. For an instant her body contorted in a violent, shivery spasm, almost throwing him off. He moved in a series of frantic jerks as the girl bucked underneath him. The blood swelled her face, ballooning the skin to purple, and the pain shrieked out from her throat.

The dark spectator behind O'Hara's eyes feasted on it all.

She tried to drag her hands down while her body still writhed frenziedly, struggling to get out from under him, away. The skin tore on her wrists. Her twisting went on. Her tongue stuck out, dark red turning to black. Then the last of the oxygen in her blood was used up with the terrible effort of dying. Her body spasmed once more and then went completely slack.

Out in the dark, beyond the hotel, over by the trees at the edge of the field, the tor stood like a black hump in the surrounding gloom. Inside, still trapped, still bound, and now dreadfully *alive*, the thing that had woken glutted itself on the banquet of the girl's terror.

Eventually Mike O'Hara hauled himself off the girl and stood at the edge of the bed, staring down at her with dull eyes. She was sprawled there, twisted and ungainly, blood at her wrists where the cord had cut into her in the terrible spasm. He turned, moving very slowly, and went out of the room. He didn't even bother to shut the hotel. Instead, he went to his bed.

22

Donovan's bar was a warm hubbub on a cold night. The far end of the spacious room was filled with local men, big farmers and crofters, and a few lads from the fishing boats that put into Westport and the little harbours and jetties around the bay. In the grate the fire billowed out peaty warmth. The smell of beer and whiskey mixed with the peat reek, the clouds of cigarette smoke and the heady aroma of thick-plug tobacco that the old men, sitting at the bench tables, cut up in their gnarled palms and shoved into the bowls of their heavy pipes.

Nancy had met Sean and Liz as they left Siobhan's cottage and invited them up to the bar for a drink with her and Tom. When they got there, after eight o'clock, Professor Connarty was already holding court, sitting himself up on a tall wooden bar-stool like a leprechaun, surrounded by his team. Behind the bar, Declan Donovan was pulling pint after pint, and his daughter Maeve was busy either washing empty glasses or bustling around the tables, collecting them.

'Would you look at that, now,' the professor said. Beside him, Frank Wysocki had opened a plastic sheet on the floor. The smell of fish drifted up to compete with the rest of the odours.

'That's the biggest halibut I've ever seen,' Connarty declared.

'Me too,' the brawny oilman said, grinning. 'Fifty-six pounds, and on twenty-pound-strain monofilament. It's a wonder he didn't break me.'

'What have you there in the bag that smells like dead fish?' Donovan asked, leaning his bulk over the bar.

'It's a monster,' Connarty told him. 'Look at the size of the bugger.'

'That's a big one, sure enough,' Declan said. 'Where did it come up from?'

'Over the other side, beyond Clare Island,' Pete Coia told him.

'Say, that's one helluva tide rip you got out there. We had the engine at full blast and we were still going backwards.'

'You want to stay away from that Coortslugan,' one of the men called across. He came over from the far side and looked in the plastic sheet. 'It's a biggie, sure enough. But I wouldn't fish there when the tide's belting in. Yon whirlpool would suck a trawler down and you'd never see sight of it again. There's many a skiff that's got swamped in that piece o' dirty water.'

'Nearly happened to us,' Doug Petersen said. His big red face was even redder after a day out in the wind. 'I thought we'd have to swim for it.'

'Nobody swims there and gets to shore, that's the truth of it.'

'Well, tomorrow we're staying close to the beach.'

'You'd better do that,' the fisherman advised. 'Sure the forecast says there's going to be a blow. None of the skippers are setting out on the tide.'

'Ah well, Declan,' Doug said, winking at the bar owner. 'We'll just have to stay here and keep our throats wet.'

Donovan grinned back behind his bushy beard. 'Always plenty for you gentlemen,' he said. He came round the bar. 'Now are you going to leave this lying here, or will I put it in the freezer for you?'

The oilmen agreed that Declan should store it for them, despite less than subtle hints from Connarty on his fondness for the taste of halibut.

Sean promised them he'd take a picture of their catch the next day, and the roughnecks insisted on buying a drink for everyone at the bar.

By this time, Terry Munster had moved round to the corner where Maeve Donovan was cleaning glasses. Sean leant against the polished counter, foot up on the rail, enjoying the crack and the warm stout beer.

'Last few days here,' the professor was telling the company. 'And it's been a good one this time.'

'I hear you found a body,' Declan called over, and a few of the heads sitting on the benches by the fire turned.

'That's the trouble with wee towns the likes of this,' Connarty said. 'You can't keep a thing secret. But we won't be calling the Garda about this one. He died quite some time ago.'

'Can't understand why you'd want to spend your time digging around in cemeteries,' Wysocki said. 'I thought they had laws against that.'

'Oh, sure we do. But this is no Burke and Hare operation. This is for posterity.'

'Yon place should be left alone.' The voice came from the far end of the bar. 'There's no good to come from digging down there.'

'And no harm, neither,' Connarty replied lightly. In all the digs he'd worked on throughout Ireland, there was always a voice raised in protest. Mostly it was religion, sometimes superstition, occasionally just bloody-minded antagonism from small-town rural folk who were suspicious of incomers.

'That tor's stood there for as long as Kilgallan itself,' the old man at the far end called back. He picked up his pint of dark beer and came round. He was small and skinny with big jug ears and a three-day bristle of white whiskers on his long jaw.

'Sure it has,' Connarty said. He didn't recognise the old fellow, which was surprising, for he'd been sure he'd met all the villagers at some time or another since the spring. Most of them were polite and courteous in the west-coast way. 'And it will still be standing when we're long gone, believe me. We're only taking a wee look inside, and then we'll be gone.'

This was only partly true. The chamber they'd found would be worked on for years to come, and at the end of it, no doubt it would be taken over by the heritage division and made into an attraction.

'You ought to be staying away from Bavcroo Hill,' the old fellow said. 'Sure, even the wee 'uns know that. It's a black place. Always has been. There's never been a crop grown in that field since before I was born, and there never will be now.'

'Now, that'll do from you, Niall,' Declan Donovan said quietly. 'These folk are just in for a quiet drink and a bit of crack. Just you go and join the old fellows by the fire.'

The old man gave him a filthy look and stalked away, walking with an odd list. The big scuffed boot on his right foot dragged scrapily over the wooden floor.

'Should have stayed down at his daughter's place,' Donovan said. 'He took a stroke last New Year and his right side went numb. Old fool's dead set and determined on coming back to work the croft.'

'That's a shame,' Frank Wysocki said. 'Don't they give people welfare or something around here?'

'Aye, they do that. But they can't change what's in people's heads. Old Niall's worked on his furlong for seventy years and more. There's no law says he's got to stop, and even if there was, it wouldn't make no difference at all to a stubborn old bugger like himself.'

Donovan went back to serving beers and Sean ordered a round of drinks for the company building up around Connarty.

Liz, Nancy and Tom were deep in conversation. When the motley collection of drinks arrived, Sean passed them around and went back to his position at the bar.

'Scared the living shit out of me,' Nancy said. 'It was like they were *deformed*.' She said the word with a shudder.

'That's *exactly* what they were like,' Liz agreed.

'I only heard Nancy yelling fit to bust,' said Tom, 'and *that* scared the crap out of me. If I'd caught them, I'd have killed them.'

'I thought Sean was going to,' Liz said. 'You should have seen the look on his face.'

Connarty turned on his stool. He'd only caught the last couple of words. 'What was that you were saying?'

'Nancy and I,' Liz said. 'We both had a scare today. There were some men out on the moor.'

'And down at that old ruined place at the beach. They were *weird*. You know, like . . .' Nancy put her finger to the side of her head in the universal gesture. 'Like retarded or something.'

'Like John Mills in *Ryan's Daughter*,' Liz volunteered. 'As if there was something wrong with them.'

'What would they be now, Declan?' Connarty asked the big bar-owner. Donovan continued pouring his beer, with a thoughtful look on his face.

'Some sort of local secret, is that what it would be?' Connarty prodded.

'No secret,' Donovan finally answered. 'They'll be the peat cutters. Just a few poor souls with strong backs and empty heads.'

'What's wrong with them?' Nancy asked. 'They didn't look like poor souls to me. They tried to *rape* me.'

Donovan's bushy eyebrows went up to his hairline, corrugating his brow with surprise. 'Oh, I don't think they'd do anything like that. They wouldn't maybe even know what they were doing.'

'They knew all right,' Nancy said hotly.

Donovan leaned forward on the bar, beckoning them forward with his head, and at the same time looking sideways to ensure that none of the local fellows could hear him. Connarty and the rest leaned in.

'The poor folk have always cut the peats around here. Sure there's nothing else for it. We make no secret of it, but there's always one or two folk born on the hill farms that are a wee bit touched.' He used the same temple-tapping gesture as Nancy. 'Families getting too close, if you know what I mean. The children aren't right.'

'I see,' Connarty said.

'They get looked after, sure enough. There's a few bothies for them in the summer, and in the autumn, one of the farmers takes a tractor up and brings them in. They're well out of harm's way, and there's no hurt in them at all. Sure they've the minds of babies and all.'

Donovan went back to pouring pints. Nancy turned to Liz, her face a picture of incredulity.

'Babies? Is he kidding? They tried to *rape* me.'

'Just a typical male reaction,' Liz said, nodding in Donovan's direction. 'Have you gone to the police?'

'I wanted to,' Nancy said. 'These animals should be put away for life.

But Tom said since I wasn't hurt, maybe it isn't worth it. We could get called back for a trial.'

'That would be worth it,' Liz retorted hotly. 'It's *your* body, isn't it?'

Nancy shrugged her shoulders and looked down at her drink. She seemed, to Liz, embarrassed by her decision to go along with Tom and let the issue lie.

'What the hell, it might be more trouble than it's worth,' she said. Liz stared at her in exasperation.

She was about to say more when the door opened with a clatter.

A few young fellows came in, hair and coats wet with the rain which was picking up on the rising wind outside, and started setting up a small band in the far corner beyond the hot hearth. They had an acoustic guitar, along with a big accordion. A small, fair-haired lad brought out an old fiddle from a battered case and plucked the strings gently before drawing the bow across the gut. Conversation in the bar simply died.

From the far corner a pure note sang as if pulled out tight from the heart of the old violin, and then the boy began to play a slow, haunting melody. His eyes were tightly shut and his body swayed with the slow rhythm, as if *willing* the sound into life. Very gently the accordion and guitar came from behind and nurtured a tune that sounded old as the town, old as the land. It lilted around the rafters, cut through the smoke, and Sean McCullain again thought of the phrase they used for the Irish: *All their fights were happy, and all their songs were sad*.

When the strain came to an end, there was a hushed silence as if everyone were trying to catch an echo of it, and then a spontaneous burst of applause from local folk and strangers alike. The band bowed and smiled in a brief pause, then the boy's fingers fluttered on the neck of the fiddle. A rollicking jig came rattling out, frenetic and frantic and excitingly lusty. Donovan's bar shook with the beat of it and the stamp of boots on the hard wooden floor, from feet that couldn't help but keep time.

The big oilmen were mesmerised by the music, and Frank Wysocki, for once, was silent. Even Terry Munster was distracted enough from the object of his intentions to turn round, lean his elbows on the bar and watch the band play.

The tune crashed to a stop and almost instantly the fiddle changed key and launched into an even faster jig. The boy opened his eyes and they swept the fireside, finally lighting on one of the oldsters leaning against the stone wall, swaddled in a heavy winter overcoat. A flat cap was askew on his head and his face was ruddy from the heat and the whiskey.

'There y'are, Seumas. Join us in a tune.'

The old fellow's companions nudged him until he pulled a penny whistle from the inside of the great baggy coat. He stuck it between his lips, and his fingers started dancing, fast as the boy's. Without a break he was *in* the music, piercing right to the heart of it and dancing a reel around the strings. Across on the other side, one of the younger men stepped up on his chair and lifted what looked like a shield from the wall. From the back he drew out a curved grey stick, which turned out to be a roe deer's shin-bone.

'And the *lambeg* too,' Connarty yelled delightedly. 'I've died and gone straight to heaven.'

The man swivelled his wrist a couple of times in practice and then the lambeg drum marched into the middle of the music, playing single to their double at first and then picking up the rhythm, faster and faster until the drum thrummed its powerful body-beat. All around, tackety boots were stamping on the hard floor, giving the lambeg a counterbeat to dance with.

Spontaneously big Frank Wysocki went into a strange little jig that looked like the kind of thing hillbillies do, standing with his knuckles on his hips and his chin in the air, his feet hop-tapping and heel-kicking below.

The music reeled on as if devils were after it and the women started clapping their hands and rocking to it on the heavy barstools.

Connarty turned away for a moment, and that was just to motion with his finger to Declan Donovan to fill up the glasses. Then he was back enjoying himself, his pixie eyes glistening behind the lenses.

The fiddle and the pipe and the lambeg drum riddled on until the room shook with the noise and every heart in the bar beat a little faster with the excitement of it. After half an hour of reels and jigs and fighting man's music, the fiddler set down his old instrument beside his stool. Sweat glistened on the boy's brow and his face was flushed pink with the exertion or the emotion of it. When the music died there was a sharp silence. The boy winked at the old fellow with the tin whistle and held up his thumb in approval, and then the bar erupted in another wave of tumultuous applause. When it started to die down, Declan Donovan boomed across to the musicians.

'Beer on the bar now, if you've a thirst.'

The guitar boomed tunelessly as its player dumped it on the floor and the musicians walked straight out of the corner towards the waiting pints.

'That was marvellous,' Connarty said. 'Just sublime.'

'Beautiful,' Nancy agreed. 'I've never heard anything like that before.'

'That's because you've never been in Ireland before, miss,' Donovan said. 'These tunes have been handed down in families since Saint Paddy was a boy.'

'It's powerful stuff,' Tom ventured.

'Oh aye,' Donovan agreed. 'There's always been power in that music.'

Siobhan eased herself off the stool, went across to the fireside and started talking to one of the old fellows, while Connarty started up where he'd left off before the music interrupted his seemingly incessant flow of anecdotes.

And so the night wore on and the drinks were drunk and the music played, and outside the wind off the Atlantic rose to a gale that crashed waves to white along the headland, boomed the water through the fumaroles on the rocks like the father of all lambeg drums. The rain was thrown in horizontal rods to lash against the walls and windows. Inside the pub there was fire in the hearth and the whiskey and the music. Outside the storm was stoking up.

And the shadows grew thick and dark around Kilgallan.

Down in the depths of the tor, the black mind gathered strength. The *geis* that had trapped her were breaking down. There was only one more barrier to freedom and then would come the great revenge, the slaughter.

She hunched in the dark, drawing herself in to a tight core, and then sent out the tendrils of her mind, feeling for the *leys*, the old patterns of power in the land, travelling their pathways. Oh, there had been changes; she could *sense* the difference between then and now, in the ground and the stones and in the very sea itself. So much had changed, and so much power had been drained from the land. Yet still she reached out, further and further, searching for a weakness. She reached out a vast distance into the deep black beyond.

And then she found something. A flaw. At the limit of her reach, in a place that had been much closer when the land was young, there was a crack. She flowed into the fault and her mind *pulled* with all of her strength, using the earthpower as her lever.

Way out, in the middle of the black ocean, something moved.

Out there, almost halfway to the other side, the pressure had been building up since the spring in the North Atlantic Ridge. Down in the depths, where the sperm whales hunt the giant squid, there is an underwater range of mountains that tower up from the floor of the world, nearly as tall as Everest and still submerged. As the continents drift ever further apart, the lava from the bowels of the earth wells up to fold and form new mountains where, in some distant future, a new continent may seed and grow. Here, in this black deep, the tension had been mounting as the irresistible force of inner heat battled against the immovable object of the underwater range.

And on the day when Nancy Ducain had fought off the strange, misshapen men in the maze of the old fields, when Mike O'Hara's mind went blank and he tied a young girl to a bed, the power made something move. The pressure gave out north of the Azores. Rock folded and strained, and then in one pulse of energy, it *split*.

The captain of the Royal Navy nuclear submarine *Resolution* out of Faslane on the Clyde Estuary recorded the boom from a thousand miles away when the shock wave, travelling at almost a mile a second, rang like a bell through the steel plates of his hull. Seismic stations in Buenos Aires, Guatemala and Spain recorded the aftershock as it rippled around the world, and they pinpointed the epicentre.

Above the ridge where the tensed rocks settled back and the lava spewed out like white toffee, the sea *bulged*. By seismic standards, it was an average blow. In the west, a low-pressure anti-cyclone that was sending seventy-mile-an-hour winds over the surface flattened the bulge sufficiently to reduce its force by the time the wave hit the Caribbean and the eastern seaboard of America. There was little damage.

But the same circular storm, aided and abetted by a ridge of high pressure to the south and another low pressure trough to the north, channelled the bulge on the ocean that was spreading out from the blast centre, backing the pulse-wave into a tight path that followed the rough track of the Gulf Stream. High winds that had been stoked up three weeks before on Continental West Africa and had spun across the ocean to leap north and east, picked up the bow-wave and swelled it into a wall of water that roared its way towards the westernmost point of Europe. Towards Eire.

It was almost an hour past midnight when the fishing smack rounded the headland where the fumaroles boomed like cannon on the rocks and where explosions of spray shot up a hundred feet into the black night air. It had taken skipper Desmond Lynch an hour to cover the past two miles in the teeth of the wind that was roaring towards the shore. Now, with the gale at his back, his little trawler was racing into the bay, pitching and wallowing in the violence of the storm. His mate, Derry Conlin, was braced against the hold-bars at the back of the fo'c's'le while Lynch wrestled with the wheel. Far off to the left, the light of Achillbeg Rock was only a sporadic wink whenever the boat heaved out of a trough and onto the crest of one of the big waves piling into the bay. Ahead, not more than a mile away, was the little jetty at Kilgallan that would offer a brief shelter from the storm, too brief to be a real haven.

Right at the back of the cabin, two other men were hunkered on a pile of old nets and floats, and sounded as if they were dying. Both of them, in the light of the swinging lantern, looked as if they *wanted* to die but Desmond Lynch never had the time, opportunity or inclination to snatch a look at them. At that moment he couldn't have cared less if they were washed overboard. He didn't even notice when one of the men, the younger of the two, heaved himself to his knees and was sick all over the skipper's seaboots, before being rolled by the ship's motion to lie, moaning, in the corner.

'How far, reckon?' he shouted over the crashing of the waves that thundered over the bow and engulfed the forward deck.

'Mile and half. Hard goin'.'

'I'll start cuttin' starboard.'

'Aye,' Conlin yelled.

The skipper heaved again on the wheel, forcing his weight against it to make the clockwise turn. The boat's prow came around a little, facing at right angles the march of the big waves. Lynch held it steady to take advantage of the tail wind. 'Bloody madness,' he bawled. 'Absolute madness. Should have stayed ashore.'

'Aye, skip. That's what I said an' all.'

'But they said it had to be tonight. Damn fools. And us more fools for doing it.'

'Aye, skip, that's what I said,' Conlin bawled back against the thundering sea.

'Well, I'm not putting out to sea again. Westport will have to do for the night. Once we dump these eejits, I'm running with this blow into the harbour.'

'Should be safe enough till the morn. So long as nobody sees us.'

'I don't give a monkey's shite if the whole town turns out with a pipe band, Derry boy. If it comes to staying afloat and reaching harbour I'll call the Garda myself.'

'Aye, and we'll make a couple of right good fishermen with no knees, Dezzie,' Conlin shouted back.

The wind bore them in a straight line past the thundering rocks.

They dipped dizzily and soared sickly towards the jetty. The lights of Kilgallan itself were shrouded in the driving rain and mostly hidden behind the trees that bordered the village. But further to the left, against the pitch-dark of the low hills that banked up behind the shore, there was a single light that speared out in a succession of winking flashes, guiding the fishing smack towards the jetty.

'There they are now, and thank Jesus for that,' Lynch said loudly. He angled the boat past the sea wall, counting the flashes, three short and a long, before he twisted the wheel with a wrench. The smack seemed to be squirted out of the storm and into the lee of the small stone harbour. The waves here were still high, but by comparison, it felt a flat calm. Derry slammed open the door and the rain came blasting in. He was out on the forward deck, nimbly overstepping the creels and baskets, to get the forward rope. The skipper watched him through the water-spattered pane as he twisted and slung it out into the darkness. It looped away and then pulled taut. Derry scrambled to the back and did the same thing, and then the boat started to edge slowly against the wall until the old tyres that were lashed to the side hit with a jarring thud. Lynch cut the engines and turned to the two men still curled on the nets.

'Right. There y'are now. Dry land. At least, as dry as it's going to get on a mucky night like this.'

The older of the two, a lanky fellow wrapped tight in an anorak with fur round the hood, nodded sickly. He kicked his companion, who moaned loudly enough to be heard over the whining wind, and helped the fellow shakily to his feet.

'Come on now, Seamus, this is where we get off.'

For a moment, the younger man didn't seem to know where he was. His eyes held that vacant look of the terminally seasick, as if his whole attention was fixed on the roilings of his stomach. Then he nodded weakly. There was a small trickle of vomit at the edge of his mouth, and the colour of his skin, deathly pale in the orange glow of the overhead light, said that if he didn't get soon to land that wasn't moving, there would be a lot more to come. The other man got his arm under his oxter and helped him out of the cabin and onto the deck.

Bridget Massey and Brian Cooney were on the harbour wall, swaddled in waterproofs and huddled against the driving rain. Derry Conlin, on the afterdeck, unlashed a tarpaulin that whipped about in the wind. He pulled the heavy canvas away, revealing four long boxes pinned by another series of ropes to the deck.

'Right now,' he called to the two dark figures on the quay. 'I'm not paid for the heavy lifting. If you want these, get your arses over here and take them.'

'Bastard,' O'Farrell mouthed. 'It's all right for—' He stopped in mid-sentence, choking off the words, and promptly heaved over the side between the boat and the wall.

'You watch yourself there, lad,' Conlin shouted. 'This boat's shifting enough to take your head off.'

Seamus O'Farrell hauled himself to his feet and wiped a rope of saliva from his chin.

'Okay, let's get down to it,' he said in a shaky voice. He lurched across to the boxes and waited until the mate had unhitched the knots. He and John Boyle, who had come round the Point after a five-hour trip up from the Shannon, hefted one of the metal boxes. They were heavy and awkward on the heaving deck. O'Farrell backed to the edge and gingerly got his feet onto the wall, from where he could steady the box. Brian Cooney and Bridget Massey came forward to help. Within ten minutes they had all the boxes ashore.

'I'd get these out of sight, whatever they are,' Derry Conlin bawled from the deck.

'Sure we will,' Boyle shouted back. 'What about yourselves? You're not putting back out in this, surely?'

'Not out in the ocean, man, but we're sure as you're born not hanging around here.'

'You'll kill yourselves for sure,' O'Farrell called out, his voice stronger now that he had his land legs again.

'Better than ending up in the Maze, I'll tell you,' Conlin retorted, grinning. He waited until Boyle and O'Farrell unhitched the ropes, then gathered them up and stowed them and went back behind the cabin. Already the engines had started to roar and the boat moved away. The four of them stood for a minute or so watching as it bucked when it met the heavy water beyond the lee and then, no more than forty yards out, the rain and wind and waves seemed to swallow the little boat completely.

Moving quickly, the four of them loaded the boxes into the back of the van that was parked up the road from the harbour in a space between the trees, and then hauled themselves inside. Brian Cooney, his waterproofs slick with rainwater and salt spray, turned the key and the engine chugged to life. Slowly he drove up the narrow rutted track towards the village.

Up at the cottages, he parked as close to the trees as possible, keeping the van in the black shadows. They piled out again and reversed the operation. The wind howling in the elms and the thunder of the sea booming on the far rocks gave them cover. The lashing rain ensured that no-one saw them. Finally, the boxes stored up in the rafters of the cottage, Cooney closed the van door with a thump and went back inside.

'Well, boys, welcome to the Hilton,' he said.

'Would you like a cup of tea?' Bridget asked. 'And you'd better get out of those wet things. They're soaked right through.'

'Maybe something a little more welcoming on a night like this, Bridie,' Boyle said. 'Sure, and what sort of welcome would you give your big cousin after the day I've had?' He held out his arms and Bridget went in to get a big wet hug.

'All right, Johnny. There's whiskey in the cupboard. Wait till I get some glasses,' she said. 'And you, Seamus O'Farrell, take those things off or you'll catch your death of cold.'

The younger man started unzipping his parka. Underneath, his shirt was dripping wet. Brian Cooney handed him a large shot of whiskey and he held the glass up almost reverently, watching the light streak through the amber.

'Thank the Saints,' he said, and threw the drink over his throat.

Across the way there was a light on in the window of another cottage, though through the rain it was nothing more than a dim glow.

'What was that?' Hugh Sands said, jerking out of a doze on the chair beside the fire.

'What was what?' Edward Laird said absently. He was tinkering with the innards of the radio phone yet again.

'I thought I heard something.'

'I heard you snoring,' Laird replied sarcastically. He was exasperated with his attempts to repair the equipment. 'The only other noise is that storm outside.'

'I thought I heard a door close.'

'Never heard a thing,' Laird said. 'You might as well get back to sleep. You've got the early shift.'

'You think I should take a look around?'

'If you like. There was nothing moving a couple of hours ago, and if there's anybody out there now, they're out of their minds.'

Sands shoved himself out of the deep seat. 'Might as well. Better safe than sorry.'

'Better you than me.' He dropped a small watchmaker's screwdriver onto the table, where it tinkled among even smaller components. 'This thing's got me beat. I've told the office we'll have to use the phone. They're a bit pissed off that the damned thing's bust, but other than that, they're not too bothered. They just told me to carry a lot of change.'

'They've always been a bunch of skinflint bastards,' Sands said. 'And when they count the cost of your electronics classes, they'll take it out of your pay.' He pulled on his waterproof overcoat.

'Listen, stay away from the back of the house,' Laird cautioned. 'Twice would be more than coincidence.'

'I'm a lot nimbler than you are. You stay here where it's warm and cosy. Rest your old bones.'

'Piss off,' Laird muttered, and went back to his tinkering. There was a blast of cold wet air as Sands went out the back way, and the wind howled through the cottage, carrying the sounds of the storm inside. The door closed again and silence fell.

Sands clung to the shadows, using the corners of the buildings as cover, walking slowly, almost nonchalantly. On a night like this, he knew visibility would be almost zero, especially from inside one of the cottages, through steaming panes. If there was anyone about – unlikely enough at this hour, and even more unlikely in the torrential rain – they would have their heads down against the wind, eyes slitted against the inblown downpour, ears deaf to anything but the sound of the storm. The sounds would muffle any noise he made walking on the grass and the rain would blur his outline with the rest of the shadows.

There was a light behind the curtain in the cottage where the Scots photographer and the girl reporter were staying. Another one dimly outlined the window in one of the archaeologists' cottages. That was about it. The back room of the Irish couple was in darkness, but as he skirted the corner, he could see they too were still awake. He eased himself closer to the window, but the curtains were tightly drawn. At least they were staying home tonight.

Moving slowly, sticking to the shadows, he went to where their van was parked. It stood away from the building, at an odd angle. He thought back to earlier in the night when he'd checked, and seemed to recall that the van had been further away from the corner, and parked parallel to the end wall. Now it was slanted in, with the rear doors closer to the back door of the cottage.

There were tyre tracks, but in the rain he couldn't tell whether they were fresh or not.

He stood wondering for a few minutes, while the rain beat against his waterproof hood, then shrugged. It didn't matter. They were still here, still under surveillance. They had done nothing since they got here. All was well.

Rather than going straight back to the cottage, Sands took the long route, past the stand of old elms that bracketed the field. He came to the gateway that led onto the track and went through, gingerly placing his feet on the spars of the cattle grid. Beyond that, a small lane led to the tor. Sands found himself wandering along the lane, with the wind coming at him from the side. Way out in the west, lightning flickered in stuttering streaks that outlined heavy black clouds and threw the tor into a humped silhouette. Beyond it the sea was a tumult of sound through which boomed the cannon shot of the tide surge in the kettle holes on the headland rocks.

The tor cut off much of the wind this close in and Sands walked up the marked path where the turf had been dug away, exposing the flat stones that had been laid jigsaw fashion. On either side little pegs sticking from the ground were connected with taut twine, further delineating the track.

He followed the circular path until he came to the other side, and stopped at the entrance.

Behind him, the lightning flickered rapid fire, throwing light right into the passageway. For a brief second, Sands saw his own shadow thrown out ahead of him in sharp relief on the passage floor, elongated grotesquely so that his shadowed legs were stretched long and thin, like arms reaching out from the tunnel to his feet.

The lightning flashed again and beamed down into the passage that ran straight and true into the side of the hill. For a second, he thought he saw a movement down at the far end, and then the light flickered off again, leaving his eyes dancing with a purple afterimage. He stood stock still, waiting for another flash while his eyes readjusted to the darkness.

All around him was rain and wind and noise. Behind him, the trees moaned and sighed. He turned round and the gravel under his feet rasped loudly. The sound echoed from the chamber in a growl. Instantly he froze, suddenly unnerved, before he realised where the noise had come from. And then the thought suddenly came to him: *Why am I here?*

He had come out of the cottage to check on a sound he'd thought he'd heard. It wasn't that he was wildly interested in the couple they were surveying, for as far as he was concerned, they were a waste of time. His conscientious decision was based on the thought of what his superiors would think if he reported in that the targets had done a moonlight flit from under their noses. Laird might be senior man, but the shit would fly and the shit would stick. He'd come out to check, but then without even thinking about it, he'd wandered off, out of the ring of cottages, in the worst storm he could remember and now he was standing at the gaping black entrance of a hole in the side of the hill.

The noise that had echoed down the tunnel had startled him out of a kind of vagueness, bringing his thoughts back to focus, like jumping out of a daydream. He thought back over the past few minutes and realised he couldn't remember *deciding* to come here. In fact, he couldn't even remember *getting* here.

The thought didn't surprise him unduly. He'd had it before. It came with the kind of mild surprise that you get when you've driven over a piece of familiar road and can't recall any of the trip, because the familiarity makes concentration redundant.

He stood at the entrance, aware that he'd got there on automatic, his mind obviously on something else, though he couldn't think what. The wind was at his back and shoving him just a little. The tunnel entrance yawned. Inside, there was shelter, dark shelter, out of the wind and the rain.

He took a step forward and then another, until he was only a yard or two from the entrance.

He *wanted* to go in.

It beckoned him darkly, and suddenly he was aware of the pull of it. He took a step backwards, or tried to, but when he made the motion, his foot moved *forward*. Then his other foot took a step, going in the wrong direction.

The dark rectangle drew him. Lightning flashed again and his long shadow streaked up the length of the passageway to a deep darkness at the far end. He tried to turn and found his body refuse to obey him. His foot took another forward step and instantly a buzz of alarm ran through him.

The hairs on the back of his neck twisted and rippled and a tight shiver went down the length of his spine.

I'm not going in there.

The thought came bright and hard. His foot moved another step, bringing him right up to the opening. There was a smell in the air, a musty smell that overrode the salt spray. He could sense it, cloying and heavy. His mind spun with jangled half-thoughts. He tried to collect them, gather them in tightly and line them up so that he could *make* himself walk away, but the strange, jaggedy fragments of thought danced around inside him and a trickle of fear rolled in his belly.

Just then there was a mighty blast of wind that came swooping between the low hillocks and blew hard onto the tor. From where he was standing he felt the wind pummel him from behind, almost tumbling him into the dark. And when the blast of cold air crossed the mouth of the passageway, there was a deep, vibrating hum, as if some giant had blown through an enormous pipe. The sound swelled, shivering through his bones, loud enough to *feel*, and that was enough to startle him out of the strange paralysis that had frozen him, the fearful pull of the entrance that had made his feet move in the wrong direction.

Suddenly released from the compulsion, he staggered against the wind. Down his back he could feel his shirt damp with sweat and his breath was a series of short gasps.

With the release came the need to get away. He took five backward steps, keeping his eyes fixed on the opening. Lightning flickered again and the long shadow reached out to grab him by the feet. Immediately he turned and ran heavily across the dug-up area. A few yards further on, his eyes still dancing purple and orange from the flash, he felt something grab his foot and he sprawled headlong, landing heavily on the muddy gravel. His breath was punched out of him and for a second he lay winded, his lungs refusing to haul air in. When they finally did work, he gasped in so much that little stars whirled momentarily. Without a pause, he scrambled to his feet, panicked by the thought of the long black shadow reaching out to snatch his foot, and then realised that he'd simply tripped over one of the taut lengths of twine. Bespattered with mud and gasping for breath, he quickly moved onto the track and ran down the road. All the time, the hairs on the back of his neck were standing on end as some primitive part of him waited in expectation of something at his back. Nothing happened. He reached the cattle grid and skittered across it, not caring a whit about the noise his boots made, and walked quickly to the cottage.

He got to the back door and waited outside until his breath calmed down, before opening it quietly and stepping inside.

Laird glanced up from the chair where he sat with a glass in his hand. He looked the younger man up and down.

'What the hell happened to you?' he asked, eyebrows raised. 'Been in a fight?'

'Slipped and fell,' Sands said.

'Looks as if you've been rolling in shit,' Laird remarked unsympathetically. 'I suppose all is quiet?'

'Yeah,' Sands said. He told Laird nothing about the tor. He didn't want him to think he was losing his edge. For himself, thinking back on it, he knew it was just the storm and the shadows. He was just getting jumpy, that was all. *That was all.*

During the night the band had played again that wonderful music, alternating the plaintive laments of the landless with the ribald, rugged, riotous songs that shouted joy of life and devil-take-the-hindmost bravado. A couple of times Connarty had been in tears, simply letting them spill down his cheeks, nostalgia washing over him. Siobhan had even noticed Frank Wysocki, the giant Canadian, brush a sparkle from the corner of his eye when the boy with the fiddle wove a sweet sad tune around the high lonely notes of the pipes. The lad with the accordion had sung in Gaelic, and although none of the outsiders knew the words, the music itself carried its own picture of lonely moorland hillsides, of seabirds calling across water, of solitude and loss.

It had been a memorable night. Outside, the wind had been whooping and swirling and rattling the wooden door, while in the pub it had been warm and welcoming. The musicians had played a storm against the storm until the walls shook with the vibration of tapping feet.

Over by the fire, two of the oldsters got up from their bench seats and did a queer little jig together, clamping their big ploughmen's boots down hard on the dry boards, alternating heel for toe, going with the rhythm and the steady beat of their cronies' hands clapping. Beyond them, in a darker corner, there were some young folk who seemed to be friends of the band. They came away from the table, three pairs of them, and joined the old-timers in a sort of square dance, skipping to the fast music in movements that looked as if they had been danced here forever.

Pete Coia exuberantly grabbed Theresa by the arm, almost toppling her from the high stool, and demanded a dance. The girl coloured to the roots of her hair in an instant flush which made her freckles stand out against her skin, and before she could reply, the wiry little fellow hauled her off into the middle of things.

When the band had stopped for a break, Siobhan crossed to the fire, taking with her a pint of beer which she put down in front of the old man who sat at the ingle where the heat was warmest. She squeezed in alongside him, and his eyes, pale and faded, looked up at her briefly.

'I brought you a beer,' she said.

'That's uncommon gracious of you, miss,' he replied in measured tones. There was a slight hesitation in his voice, as if his mind was searching for the words, or possibly even translating them from the

Gaelic. She noticed a slight tremor in his hand as he reached for the beer, and the old fellow brought his other hand up to steady the glass. He took a large swallow and his big Adam's apple, unshaven among the wattles under his chin, bobbed up and down. He put the tumbler down and smacked his lips, and then, very boyishly, he winked at her.

'And what would a slip of a girl like you be buying beer for an old cripple like me for?' It came out *owl crippel*.

'I was interested in what you were saying earlier on,' Siobhan confessed. 'I'm working at the dig.'

'I thought maybe ye was after my body,' he said, with a mischievous leer.

'No . . . I . . .' Siobhan flustered.

The old fellow sniggered. 'Oh no, that wouldn't be it at all. You're after bodies much older than my own, isn't it?'

She realised she'd been filleted and laughed outright. 'Something like that. I'm Siobhan.' She held out her hand.

'Pleased to meet you, Sha-vaun,' he said, pronouncing it the old way. She could feel the odd tremor in his grip. 'I'm Niall Tully.'

'You live in Kilgallan, Niall?'

'I do now. Been away these past couple of seasons trying to get my arm and leg to learn to do their share again. Now I come back and find you buggers have been over and under the place like moles in a pasture.'

'It's only history we're after.'

'Aye, and more besides, more as like,' he said. He reached and took a manful draught of his beer.

'Tell me,' Siobhan said plainly.

'What for?'

'Because I'm interested. I've been interested in Ireland and Irish history since I was no height at all.'

'Well, if you were that interested, you'd stay away from Bavcroo Field.'

'That's one of the things I wanted to ask you. *Bavcroo*. Where does that come from?'

'It's always been there.'

Siobhan looked at him, trying to work out if this was a joke, then she caught his drift. 'No, the *name*, I mean. I haven't heard it before. It's not on any of the survey maps, even the old ones.'

'Haven't heard the name in years myself, but that's what we called it when I was a lad. That's what my old grandmother called it, and her grandmother before her, for that's what she told me, and that's what I'm telling you now.'

'What does it mean?' Siobhan asked, though she already knew.

'Oh, in the English?'

She nodded.

'It's the *Witchstone*.'

'Why's it called that?'

'Well, me old granny, and she got it from hers, used to say that's where they buried the witch.'

'What witch would that be?'

'*The* witch. The *Bav*. The *Shee*.' The old man's voice rose a bit higher when he said that, and a couple of heads at the bar looked round momentarily.

'They cursed her and she cursed them, and those that dig her up and let her out will bring the curse down like the crack of doom.'

'The professor thinks it's the tomb of one of the Connacht kings.'

'Aye, well, I'm only just after telling ye what my old grandmother told to me, and *she* knew all there was to know about your history around here. No king lies under that hill. That's where they buried the *Shee*, sure enough. And if you dig her up, then it'll be worse luck on you.'

'Do you believe that?'

'Doesn't matter if I believe it or not, though my old granny was never wrong, right enough. But it wouldn't be the first time, would it now?'

'What do you mean?'

'I'm not as daft as I maybe look to a young city girl like yourself. I've read books,' the old man declared. 'Them that dug up that Egyptian fella, yon Tutankamen. Carter, wasn't it? Sure, and didn't they find themselves all cursed over the head of it?'

Siobhan laughed lightly. 'You think that will happen to us?'

He shrugged. 'All I'm saying is you wouldn't catch me digging in that place for all the Guinness in Donovan's cellar.'

He beckoned her with his hand, leaning forward conspiratorially. 'These young fellows,' he said, indicating the rest of the bar, maybe even the rest of the village, with a quick movement of his head. 'They know nothing. But I'll tell you something you didn't know yourself.'

'And what's that?'

'Yon Croagh Patrick, the big hill you pass before the hump-backed bridge. That's where the saint is supposed to have stood and drummed the snakes out of Ireland.'

'Yes, I know that,' Siobhan said.

'Well, I'll tell you. I've read books. There never was a snake in Ireland. There never were *any* snakes in the whole world when Ireland was made an island, but we still have the story.'

238

'Go on,' Siobhan prompted.

'It wasn't Saint Patrick, and it wasn't snakes neither, sure as you're born. It was *the* snake. That's where they caught the *shee-serpent* and brought her down from the heights to put her under the ground.'

The old man finished his beer and looked expectantly at his glass. Siobhan took the hint and went up to the bar and came back a few minutes later with a replacement. The old fellow took another huge swig.

'And they say that when they put her in there' – another nod of the head indicated the general direction of the tor – 'she called down a curse on them all. She told them there would be no peace in Ireland *for ever*. She said there would be hunger and famine and disease and death, and she said that brothers would fight brothers for ever more.'

He had looked at her over the rim of the glass, pale eyes watery in the light.

'And if you do know any of your history, city girl, you're bound to agree that she wasn't far wrong.'

Down at the Tallabaun Inn, Mike O'Hara was very drunk. His mind was fuzzy and dark and the walls seemed to keep shifting. His vision was oddly blurred, as if he was looking through tinted glass that gave everything a reddish hue. He had sat for two hours, demolishing a bottle of inexpensive brandy with dedicated steadiness, but rather than feeling the numbness that drink normally brought, his whole body seemed to be twitching and jerking, fired up. His skin felt tight and hot and shivery. Along in the room at the far end of the narrow corridor, young Marie Lally was still tied spreadeagled and stretched out, stiffening up on the bed.

The memory had come to him, out of a fogged mind. Her terrified eyes had rolled up until he could only see the whites when he'd whipped the cord around her throat, and the red in his vision shifted down to a near-purple. He could now recall seeing her, as if for the first time. The image was distorted, as if his eyes had changed, or as if his conscious mind was looking through other eyes that were used to a different light. His actions were jerky and his breathing rasped in an odd panting. All he had felt was the compulsion to *hurt*, and to savour the hurt. He didn't remember clambering off the bed, had no recollection of coming back to the small room and opening the bottle of brandy. Everything seemed woolly and fuzzy and the darkness swirled around inside Mike O'Hara's brain in a confusing maelstrom. He was too far removed from himself to feel guilt.

*

The thing that had trickled out a finger of *self* into the dark space in Mike O'Hara's brain had withdrawn, distracted for the moment, but it would return. The other dark tendrils of thought that had sought out the strange and the weak, were beginning to shrink back towards the centre, leaving dull, tainted confusion where they had wormed their way in, leaving the doors open for certain return. Up in a bothy at the far end of the moor, the peat cutters, huddled under the corrugated iron roof that was their only protection against the battering rain, slept fitfully. Their faces were slack and empty and misshapen. If anyone had seen them now, they would have thought they'd stumbled on a den of goblins.

Down in the darkness under the tor at Kilgallan, inside the strange carved stone that was an eternity between worlds, the thing sensed freedom approaching. She sizzled with the hot fire of it. And there was something *else*. Here, in this place, the people were the same. She could smell it, the traces in their genes. They were the sons of the sons of the old people who had caught her like a rabid dog and hauled her screaming to this place at the junction of eternity. She could sense their weakness, savour their fluttering hearts. She would feast on them as she had never ravaged before. The feeling of *happening* was strong, a fiery prescience that brought her probing tendrils back like stretched-out bands snapping swiftly into place. It was coming, and it was coming *soon*.

And beyond that, there was the *other* sense, the taste of something *new*. A different kind of people, still weak, still powerless, but not of this place. Yet, mingled with that was the scent of something that was old and familiar, and *that* scent brought with it a black emotion that was mixed with hate and desire, flavoured with the hunger for revenge and a wanton lust for a final coupling. Across the aeons, bridging the ages, came the powerful sensory buzz that riddled through her. She was old, terribly old, this thing that twisted in the dark. She still had the power, though it had been long dormant. She needed to feed again, but there was more than that.

She was female. And more powerfully than the drive of any human was the need of her own baleful self.

The *Shee* needed to breed.

23

Siobhan had come back from Donovan's bar, leaning arm in arm with Sean McCullain and Liz Cannon against the heavy rain that had sprung up. Dr Connarty hung on to Sean's other arm, for otherwise he would have ended up in the ditch. The whiskey and the music had gone to his head, and as he unsteadily wended his way down the path, he would occasionally give the contented chuckle of a man who's foolish in drink and wise enough just to enjoy it. He'd had a fine night. Terry Munster had remained at the bar.

It was late, but Siobhan couldn't sleep. She sat hunched over the broad table with papers and photographs scattered all over the surface, an untidy profusion. Outside, behind the curtains, beyond the window pane, the wind was rising fast, throwing rain in hard riffs against the glass, gusting strong enough to force its way down the chimney and make the glow of the peat fire flare red in the grate.

On the dresser, the coffee machine bubbled lazily. Siobhan had a big cup of thick black Blue Mountain set on the only available free space on the table. It steamed moodily.

The old man in the pub had sparked off an idea that fairly sizzled inside her long after she had gone back to join the others at the end of the bar. Troubled and silent, she sat down next to the professor, at first only half-listening to his conversation with Sean McCullain.

'You'll be one of us, with a name like your own,' said Connarty.

'I don't think so. I'm Scottish. Born and raised on Clydeside.'

'Oh, I don't doubt that at all, but we're all Scots if we go back far enough. And believe it or not, *we* were Scots first.'

Sean's dark eyebrows lifted in question and Connarty swept right on.

'Sure we were. The Irish were known as the Scots and we brought the name with us when we took over your part of the world. We're all the same people, us Celtic folk. Later on, we became the Hibernii, but you lot kept the old name. But anybody from your neck of the woods with a name that starts with *Mac* has got some of the old blood in them, and right proud they should be of it an' all.'

He reached out for his whiskey glass and held it up to the light, peering at its amber translucence.

'And we invented this stuff too,' he said, before swallowing the lot off in a gulp. He twitched his hand to show it was empty and Sean grinned at him. He called over to Maeve, who detached herself from Terry's shadow and took another order for them all.

'Now you'll be from Skye back a couple of generations,' Connarty went on.

'That's right,' Sean said, surprised. 'My grandfather was from the Isle of Skye. Born and raised there. How did you know that?'

'Your name, lad. McCullain. I've been on the island many a time. Did my first dig there, as a matter of fact.'

'My grandfather said we were named after the mountains. The Cuillins.'

'I don't doubt you were. But did you know where the mountains got their name?'

Sean shook his head, took a drink of his beer, and let the professor wade in.

'This'll show you how Irish you really are. The Cuillins were named after the greatest Celtic hero of them all. Cuchullain.'

'Ca-who?'

'Cuchullain, that's who,' Connarty said. 'You say it like Co-hoolin, but the spelling is Gaelic. He was the champion of Ulster and the greatest warrior this island ever had.'

'I thought that was Bryan Boru,' Sean said. 'I read that he was the first king of the Irish.'

'First in *modern* times. But there were plenty in the days when they built that tor out there. Cuchullain went to Skye to train with the Skatha – that's how the island got its name. It was Skatha's Isle.'

'And who was he?'

'*She*,' Connarty corrected him. 'She was the great female warrior. The hero went to study fighting under her, but the story tells it that he learned more than the arts of war. She was some woman, by all accounts. Maybe that's how you really got your name, eh?' Connarty's eyes twinkled mischievously. 'Maybe you're a descendent of the famous warped warrior.'

'Maybe he's warped enough as it is,' Liz said from close by, but there was no malice in it.

'Just a little bit twisted,' Sean added drily. 'What does that mean, *warped warrior*?'

'Cuchullain himself was one of them. They said that when he went into a battle frenzy, his whole body would twist out of shape and his hair would stand on end.'

'Sounds like me with a hangover.'

242

'And he was invincible like that. Partly due to the fact that he was only half-mortal, of course. His father was Lugh, the Sun God.'

Connarty pronounced it *Luke*, and when he did so, Sean looked at him quickly, his expression puzzled. 'I've heard that before somewhere.'

'Anyway, Cuchullain came back from your Skye a warrior, and he spent his days fighting the good fights in Ireland. Great man for the ladies too, though the great tales tell how he was pursued by the *Morrigan.*'

'Who was he?' Sean asked again.

'Another she. She was the Goddess of Darkness and Destruction. Tried to seduce him everywhere he went, and he kept rejecting her.'

'Was this the Skatha?'

'No. The *Morrigan* was evil in female form. Cuchullain was the good, if you like – the white to her black. Anyway, she wanted him and he was having none of it. She never got her hands on him in the end, no matter how she tempted him. Even tried to kill him off a few times. Never forgave him for cutting her hand off, I suppose.'

'Pretty gruesome stuff,' Siobhan said. She looked up at Sean, who stood at the bar, his eyes unfocused, as if he was staring into the far distance, deep in thought.

She was about to say something when he shook his head, as if batting away whatever thought had held him. Connarty, storyline forgotten, dragged Liz off to dance.

Sean turned to Siobhan. She saw a wary, almost tired expression flit across his face and then mellow out.

'Want to dance?' she asked.

'Sure.'

By this time there were a few other couples on the floor, while over by the fire, the two old fellows were tripping and hopping by themselves, each holding pints of dark beer in their free hands and miraculously failing to spill a drop. Sean led Siobhan into the middle of it and turned, inviting her close. She had walked in to him and snuggled against his chest. He had felt warm and strong against her as they swayed slowly to the music.

The old man's words kept coming back to her as she tried to fix her mind on the photographs and rubbings and, try as she might to push it away, they kept wriggling in there, disrupting her concentration. Outside, the rain hammered ever harder against the glass. Inside, if you ignored the wail of the wind, it was silent except from the muted sound of the radio from the room Theresa and Agnes shared, and occasionally the soft murmur of their conversation.

Siobhan got up and poured herself another coffee and turned back to the papers. She could see the old man, Niall Tully, earnestly staring at her from under grizzled white eyebrows, his mouth a little twisted to the left, the legacy of his stroke.

'The *witch*. The *Bav*. The *Shee*,' he'd said. 'They put her in *Bavcroo*.'

Siobhan remembered the small thrill of disquiet that had tripped through her when old Niall Tully had said that. She'd spent the past days working on the old scripts that had been carved so intricately on the face of the solid stone. And the words he had used were words she had recognised.

But it couldn't be that.

It simply couldn't be that. The old Celts had believed in the *Shee*, the *Morrigan*, the Goddess of Death who could take on any shape. She, the *Shee*, was part of mythology, and while, as a child, Siobhan had loved the old tales, that's where the *Shee* belonged.

It couldn't be that, she told herself again.

But if that was the case, why were the scaly fingers of uncertainty trailing up and down her spine? And was there more than just uncertainty in their scrabbly touch?

'*No king lies under that hill*,' old Niall had averred. '*That's where they buried the* Shee, *sure enough. And if you dig her up, then it'll be worse luck on you.*'

He'd seemed so certain, that old man who'd lived in Kilgallan longer than anybody else alive.

'*It wasn't Saint Patrick, and it wasn't snakes neither, sure as you're born. It was the snake. That's where they caught the* shee-serpent *and brought her down from the heights to put her under the ground.*'

Siobhan shook her head. There were always local fables, stories to scare the children.

But the trailing fingers didn't stop. In the spring, when she and Connarty and the whole bunch of students had first started digging, nobody was sure what they would find under that high mound. She'd worked on other, similar tors, peeling away the layers of soil that marked off the calendar of the ages, and found homesteads, daub-and-wattle walls, beakers, and even in one memorable case, a fine gold torc that was beautiful in its simplicity. On this dig, it hadn't been until they found the passageway that they knew it was a tomb of some sort, and it hadn't been until Terry Munster breached the inner chamber that they had found most of the carvings on the stone.

She was, Siobhan knew, the only person north of Galway with any knowledge of the old Ogham and Runic scripts and even *she* was having difficulty translating them.

So no-one else, apart from the team, knew that she'd seen the words *Baibh* – a terrible sight – and *Mor-righinn*, which could mean many things, including a serpent, or a great nymph. Yet old Niall Tully had spoken those words at her through his twisted mouth.

And there was more. He'd spoken of the curse.

'*She told them there would be no peace in Ireland for ever. She said there would be hunger and famine and disease and death, and she said that brothers would fight brothers for ever more.*'

How did he know about the curse? Siobhan had told the professor that the words she had pieced together sounded like a powerful warning, and he'd laughed. He'd told her that it was the best way to keep out grave-robbers.

Yet . . .

She remembered the feeling of *power* in the words.

A neverending geis be upon this place, where light has prevailed. A price on him who enters here, the serpent's lair. On him be the price of this land and the price is death.

And then the foreboding cadence of the rhyme cut in the stone:

> *Eternity holds the* Shee
> *Forever barred in light*
> *Desolation in her curse,*
> *Yet awakening is worse.*

Niall had told her: '*She called down a curse on them all.*'

Connarty believed he had at least the tomb of a king, though he hoped to find the final burying place of Maeve, the old Queen of Connacht. Yet Siobhan recalled the feeling that the inscription on the stones hailed no gallant deeds, no kingly triumphs, no queenly praise. It was written like a sing-song narrative, with great care, with that powerful sense of motivation. The words read like no epitaph she had ever read. There was only the grim feeling of *warning*.

Siobhan scattered the papers aside until she came up with the one on which she'd written the piece of translation. She held it up, letting the light of the lamp illuminate the words she'd printed in neat block capitals.

That's what the old man had called the *Shee*. The serpent. Banished, not by the beaten drum of the old evangelist, but driven into captivity by desperate, *terrified* people in skins and rough woollen cloaks thousands of years before the birth of Christ.

And there was more on the next page:

> *The sons of kings, to guard the sleep*
> *Five brave, to watch and promise keep*
> *Between the lands of men and youth*
> *Forever stand their watch.*

They had found one body, old and wrinkled and shrivelled, but still holding that strange weapon clenched in the dead grip of the bony hand. He had fallen from the niche in the wall. One of five that circled the chamber.

Why had he been buried there, standing upright, just as the carvings had said? It was as if he'd placed himself, weapon drawn, on guard, even in death.

Forever standing his watch? Against what?

Siobhan felt the cold fingers trail long nails down the length of her spine. There was something here that didn't fit, yet *did* fit so precisely it was uncanny.

Siobhan was not a superstitious person. She was twenty-eight years old and had a doctorate in archaeology and had spent most of her adult life in study. She did not believe in fairies and leprechauns or kelpies or warped warriors, though she knew of them from the legends. Her feet were firmly on the ground, her whole training dug deep into *real* history.

That was the truth of it. Yet when the wind gave a particularly hard blast, driving the rain to hammer against the glass and flaring the fire in the hearth into sudden brightness as it moaned down the chimney, she jumped, startled, and the fine auburn hairs on the back of her neck twitched and rose like hackles.

Sean McCullain was not asleep. Neither was Liz Cannon. They had come down the track, arm in arm, with Siobhan hanging on against the wind, and with much laughter had negotiated the cattle grid at the gate. Sean's trekker shoes were easily large enough to span the spars, but both Liz and Siobhan, buffeted by the rain-laden wind, slipped and floundered their way across, holding on to him for balance.

At the point where the path diverged, next to the cottage where Siobhan stayed with the two other girls, who had come back from Donovan's with them and the professor, Liz invited the archaeologist back for a nightcap, but she declined, telling them she wanted to have a look at the photographs.

As she turned towards the door, she swivelled and gave Liz a quick, friendly hug, then stood on her tip-toes to do the same to Sean. Playfully he lifted her off her feet and gave her a kiss on the lips.

Back at their cottage, they took off their coats and shook them out in front of the fire, spraying the raindrops to sizzle on the smouldering peats.

'Best night I've had in months,' Sean said.

'You looked as though you were enjoying yourself.'

'Sure was.'

'Especially when you were dancing,' Liz said. She was across at the dresser, where Sean had set the bottle of wine he'd bought earlier. He heard the pluck of the cork and the tinkle of glasses.

'Yeah, that was fun. I didn't stand on anybody's toes.'

'I wouldn't be too sure,' Liz said, turning round with both glasses in her hand. She handed one over to Sean, her expression flat.

'No, I would have heard the crunch,' he said.

Liz took a sip, then raised her eyes. There was a trace of the old truculence in them.

'I think she's taken a shine to you.'

'Who?'

'Siobhan. Who else?'

'Oh? You think so?'

'I thought it was fairly obvious.'

Sean seemed to think this over. He took a drink from the glass, standing with one hand on the warm stone of the mantel. Liz thought she could detect a smug, self-satisfied smile beginning to form, but he managed to keep his face straight.

'She's a fine-looking girl,' he said at last. 'Good dancer too.'

'Any closer and I'd have needed a bucket of water,' Liz muttered.

Sean took another drink, and this time the smile did break through. He shoved himself away from the fire and sauntered back to the dresser and jabbed a finger at the switch on top of the small pocket radio that stood beside the wine bottle. The tail end of an introduction faded away and an orchestrated version of 'Yesterday' started slowly.

'I didn't know you cared.'

'I don't, McCullain. You can dance with whoever you like.'

'All right. I'll dance with *you*.'

He crossed the room slowly, looking straight into her eyes, and she looked up at him. Immediately the memory of the kiss in the car came back to her and she felt her face suddenly flush. He took the glass out of her hand and put it on the mantelpiece, still looking straight into her eyes. He brought his hand back and put it lightly on her shoulder. Almost involuntarily she went straight into him and felt his arms enfold her. The music played and they moved with it.

Much later, about the same time as Siobhan Kane was startled by the blast of wind against the window, Sean was lying on his side beside Liz, listening to the mounting storm. She was facing away from him, her fair hair soft against his cheek. His arm was draped across the smoothness of her hip and he could hear the light susurration of her breathing, like soft sands on an ebb tide.

A jumble of thoughts kept him awake. They had danced slowly and he had felt her against him, warm and soft, and her arms had come up around his neck. Sometime during the dance she lifted her head and he bent his and they kissed, very softly. Then she put her hand behind his head and pulled him down to her hard, demanding, and he went with it.

They drifted towards his bedroom, still kissing, and when they got to the door she broke away from him, pushing him until he was at arms' length. He just looked at her, face impassive, not wanting to push it.

'Damn you, McCullain,' she said, and then came back into his arms. And with her free hand, she opened the door.

Now, in the darkness, flickering shadows of guilt played across his mind. He told himself that he hadn't started it; hadn't asked for it. He hadn't even made the first move. But he'd never been involved with a colleague before. He'd always avoided that because it worked against the professional side of the job.

Yet despite that, he was *glad* of it. Not just the physical part, which had been tempestuous, tumultuous when the dam between them finally broke. He hated to admit it, but Liz Cannon, despite a poor start, had got under his skin.

Later, he began to doze, snuggling beside her, and though the big storm was winding itself up to a fury outside, here it was warm and safe. Darkness closed in and Sean began to dream.

24

The six-foot bulge in the middle of the ocean had swelled to twenty feet by the time it hit the Continental shelf miles out off the west coast. Bracketed by the storm fronts and funnelled eastwards, it doubled in size to a forty-foot wall of water in the space of four miles, a wave travelling at a hundred and twenty miles an hour. The storm had reached its peak when Dezzie Lynch and Derry Conlin in their fishing smack were only a mile from the relative security of Westport haven, running so hard before the wind that the powerful Volvo diesel was almost redundant. The waves were so high that the propeller was out of the water half the time anyway.

The seismic shock wave of water came roaring in from the ocean with a force that made the earth shake from Galway Bay to Sligo. In the shallow water a mile from the shore a kelp field three miles wide and four deep was simply uprooted by one giant watery ploughshare and carried along on the vast current. A colony of seals on the seaward side of Stark Island were lifted bodily by the surge, carried four miles into and beyond Ballynakill Harbour, and dropped, when the wave crashed through the trees, into Kylemore Lough, where, a month later, the seven that survived the awesome transport were discovered by a perplexed water-bailiff, who found they'd wiped out the lough's entire stock of rainbow trout. Equally perplexing for crofters on the flat bogland of Ballycroy was the rotting body of a sperm whale that was found decaying in their peat diggings. Four miles to the south, a farmer with the unlikely name of Shaun-Shamus O'Shea wondered at the commotion in the pine plantation that bordered his steading, and when he went to have a look discovered two hundred seagulls and another seven species of carrion-eater feasting on the twenty-foot carcass of a basking shark that had become lodged in the branches of a stout Scots pine. The stench was awesome.

This was some time after the cataclysmic wall of water devastated the edges of the west coast. The main focus of damage was on the south side of Clew Bay, where the deeper water in the west allowed the wave to hit with more force before it broke itself on the headland. At the height of the storm, with winds rising to higher than ninety miles an hour, bolts of lightning were spanging back and forth between the earth and the towering clouds, ripping the air with their aweful power. The few remaining slates on the sagging roofs of the deserted village at the edge of Tallabaun Strand were whipped off like knives to embed themselves in the fields beyond or shatter against the stone dykes that lay empty on the lee side. The wave swelled higher, powered by the first shock and stoked on its narrow path by the immense anti-cyclone, to come rising out of the ocean like a runaway express train from hell, roaring its madness as it scoured the seabed. The bow-swell hit the mainland on Roonah Point at the kettles where the sea boomed through the fumaroles at high tide. On this black night, the shock of the bow-wave strike was so enormous that one of the sea caves literally exploded under the pressure, and pieces of rock, some weighing five tons, were blasted up into the air before being hammered down by the weight of the water and scoured across the ground for a quarter of a mile, leaving huge furrows feet deep in the tough soil.

On the far side of the bay, where the Coortslugan whirlpool milled at every rip tide, the wave roared past Clare Island and battered the lighthouse on Achillbeg with such a force that Milo Conn, the keeper, felt the whole tower move on its foundations. As it was, the stones that were whipped up from the seabed were thrown so hard from the cresting wave that they smashed through the toughened glass and shattered the light and its reflectors, leaving it blind for a week. Small pebbles were found dug into the concrete walls like bullets in the aftermath of a battle.

Gathering channelled force, like a roaring river that has been squeezed into a defile, the wave thundered into Clew Bay. Desmond Lynch and Derry Conlin saw the lights of Westport Harbour ahead of them, and both of them, now manhandling the wheel as a team, breathed a sigh of relief. Then suddenly the lights fell away. One second they were ahead in the distance, and the next, they were *below* the boat. The little smack was lifted sixty feet in the air and, by a miracle, held its course, riding the downslope like a forty-foot surfer. When the barrage of water hit the shallows in the throat of the bay, the little islands took much of the force, breaking up the wall. Still and all, the fishing boat kept on going. There were three farmhouses that were deluged, killing two occupants and all of the livestock except one lucky bull which was tethered to its stall that had been made out of railway sleepers. When the wall went, so did a ton of beef, bellowing fear, but bull and stall were carried for seven hundred yards and dumped in the garden of a retired publican, who subsequently refused to release the beast until he was compensated for the damage done to his rosebeds.

The fishing boat *flew* past the farmhouses on the turbulent crest and crashed, still upright, into a plantation of sitka spruce, carving a slipway through the thick foliage and scattering trunks like twigs. It ground to a halt, still miraculously intact, while the skipper and his mate, so frozen with abject terror that their hands were still locked on the wheel, screamed like frightened children on the last leg of their overland flight.

For thirty seconds they stared ahead, eyes almost popping out of their sockets, until finally Desmond's throat unlocked.

'Dear Jesus, Derry, I've shit my – '

Then the back-wave came tumbling behind them and flipped the boat right over in a complete somersault. Both skipper and mate were thrown out into the trees and landed fifty feet apart. Both of them instinctively held onto the branches whipping past, and the only damage they had was a couple of cracked ribs and a punctured testicle from a splinter that drove through Derry's oilskin overtrousers. Getting it out, even under a local anaesthetic the following day, was agony. Just as bad was the ignominy of having his oilskins removed and the young district nurse discovering that not only did he have a three-inch skelf of spruce transfixing his left ball, but that he, too, had voided breakfast, lunch and dinner in one easy movement that had all but filled his boots.

Down at Kilgallan, the wave hit with the force of a bomb, right along the coastline. Funnelled between Clare and Inshturk Islands, where the water is deep at first but then rises in a steep slope to only sixty feet, the vertical water precipice gained height and speed, still travelling at more than a hundred miles an hour.

The little quay where the two Irishmen had hauled their boxes into the van caved in under the onslaught. The mussel beds on Gallan Bay, a small inlet south of the town, were ripped up to form a vast dune of shellfish on the slopes of the small hills that abutted the high-tide edge. Careening on, the wave pumped its power into the mouth of the Roonah Water that was already swollen by the violent rains to three feet above its highest level in twenty years. The brown water was surging under the hump-backed bridge with only six inches to spare, hammering against the upstream side and scouring at the foundations. The sea water came sweeping in against the worn cliff rock on the north side of the stream, veering across the marshes in a black mountain of water. The downflow of the stream could not compete. Water hit the bridge with a sonic boom like the thunder down at the kettles at Roonah Point, and the whole bridge, built in an arch to take the downward pressure, was simply lifted off its pilings and twisted clockwise. When it came down again, ten feet further upstream, its back broke with an almighty crack and the two halves tilted drunkenly in mid-stream, bowing towards each other like exhausted synchronised swimmers.

Kilgallan itself, of all the coastal towns, was perhaps the least affected by the blast of the wave that had started out as a bulge two thousand miles out in the ocean. This was due to a fluke of nature, and the chance positioning of the village which, while right on the southern edge of the bight, was protected by the hills that enclosed Gallan Bay. Out in the broad inlet was an underground slope which diverted the thrust of the pulse northwards towards the jetty and beyond to the Roonah Water. Still and all, the towering water-wall crashed against the low hills. A swirl demolished Finn Finnerty's farm, tumbling the barn like a tin-can and flattening the byre under a thousand tons of water. Two old cottages at the end of the village, down the Killadoon road, sagged as the foundations gave way, but by and large the village was spared, though a big smooth piece of Connemara marble that had been lifted up from the bed of the sea and carried by the water for six miles was catapulted over the hill, where it flew a quarter of a mile and bulleted through the roof of Patsy McGavigan's house when the undertaker was fast asleep, causing him to wake with a yell in a stream of rain-water deluging from the hole in his ceiling.

The little defile between the hills leading down to Gallan Bay offered the least protection, and while the main force was diverted, there was enough power to send a surge roaring up the pass, filling the gully to the brim with forty feet of saltwater. If anyone had been there to see, it would have seemed the land had suddenly dropped and the black wall of water, capped with mucky white foam, had blasted into the vacuum. The water exploded against the tor with the sound of thunder and the back-wave flowed in behind, completely submerging the small hill. There was an explosion of noise as the bow-wave rammed into the passageway, compressing the air inside so tightly that there was a reverse explosion when the power of the wave was spent, and the water was spat out again in a huge cough.

To the left of the tor, the sea crashed through the stand of trees, uprooting elms and limes that had stood for a hundred years and more, and ripping away the hawthorn hedge in one tangled strip.

It was three o'clock in the morning when Doug Petersen stumbled out of his bed, awakened both by the thunderous roar of the wave as it hit the kettle-holes at the point, and by the internal pressure on his bladder. He grunted angrily when he stubbed his toe on the door as he opened it and lurched towards the bathroom. It took him maybe twenty seconds to empty himself loudly, and then he turned and went into the lounge. Through the curtains the lightning flashed and danced, sending an eerie glow into the room. Storms didn't bother the Australian. He'd spent the past two years on the exploration rig off the south coast and he'd weathered storms a-plenty, and they were *nothing* compared to the big Pacific typhoons back home that rammed the coast. He only hoped that this one would blow itself out and that they'd be able to take the dinghy out in the morning to try for the big cod off Clare Island.

He yawned, savouring the relief from the pressure, and scratched at the thick red hairs on his belly. He ambled towards the window and peered out into the gloom beyond the rivulets that streamed down the glass. There was a cataclysmic flash of lightning and an instantaneous peal of thunder that imprinted painful jagged lines on his retina and blinded him for several moments. When the afterimage faded, he pulled the curtain back again and squinted into the storm. The lightning flared again, but this time it was behind the house and he saw the whole of the scene suddenly lit in silver-blue. He stood for a second, open-mouthed, unable to comprehend what his eyes were telling him. He could see the trees and beyond them the black hump of the hill. Behind that there was another hill, equally black, yet strangely topped with white that was unbelievably *rising* behind the tor. Doug shook his head, as if to clear his vision, and looked out again. The new hill rose higher and higher, becoming a crazy black mountain and then it just seemed to *drop* down on the tor in a vast swoop. The blast of the strike could be *felt* as much as heard and the ground shook underfoot.

'Holy *fuck*,' Doug bellowed.

He stood at the window, transfixed by the vastness of the destruction, frozen into immobility for maybe five whole seconds. He watched the trees tumble under the onslaught, heard the tremendous *ripping* sounds of great taproots being torn out of the earth, heard the tortured cracking as trunks simply snapped under the weight of water. And beyond that, above that, even above the incessant peals of thunder that fell in a tight bombing pattern around Kilgallan, he heard the high-pitched howling scream that soared out from the *far* side of the wave in such a screech that he felt it riddle into the bones inside his ears.

He stood there, hands on the sill, with the curtain pulled to the side for another two seconds, and then saw one big elm trunk still falling, ahead of the rest and coming right towards him.

'Ohhh shiiii—' was all this man of words, backing away fast, could get out before the whole window imploded. The old elm hit the cottage with a thump that shook it to its foundations. A great leafy *arm* of a branch crashed through the pane and reached gnarled fingers towards him. Doug tripped over the chair next to the fire, and the deadly jabbing fingers passed over him, spearing into the room only two inches from his nose. Winded and unhurt, he managed to utter a litany of oaths without repeating himself once, and then the wave that had thrown the elm ahead of it followed through the window, cascading into the room in an explosion of water. Doug was bodily lifted off the floor, along with the armchair, and tumbled backwards. The force of the water blasted open the kitchen door and threw Doug and the chair through it, and they both ended up jammed under the sink. At this point the water was five feet high, but fortunately Doug had been winded by the fall and by the time he got his breath back he'd managed to pull himself out from under the sink and thrash his way to the surface, gasping for air. Apart from the fright and the soaking and the tumbling throw, there wasn't a mark on him.

The oilmen's cottage was the worst hit, but only one of the other six small buildings escaped the deluge.

Something in Sean McCullain's unconscious mind heard the blasts of thunder and was aware of the flickering stabs of lightning, and converted the sensations into his dreamscape.

He was back in the water, treading backwards, turning slowly in the shallows, feeling the slip and slide of rounded pebbles under his bare feet. On the far side he could see faces wavering in his strange vision and he could sense the muscles under his skin, the big ones on the back of his neck, the thick ones on his forearms, even the ones behind his eyes, shift and twist back to normality. The red hue that covered the world began to fade.

In the water, the body floated down, carried by the fierce current of the stream. Beyond it, the flow was tinged pink, and he felt the bleakness, the *sadness* replace the savage joy of the fight. In peripheral vision, far upstream, he glimpsed the ripple in the water that showed something swimming in the deep pool, something big heading for the willow trees that trailed down into the stream.

He waded out, hearing the cheers, seeing the faces that were at once familiar, yet strange. Tall men and broad, their hair matted with resin until it stood up in spikes, held clubs with polished stones fixed to shafts bound with leather thongs. Some men had tall spears; others had thick wooden bows that recurved on themselves, and these men bore quivers of arrows four feet long and viciously barbed. Each man was tattooed in whorls and circles. He could read the *force* of the markings, could sense their strength.

He came up onto the bank, letting the manic surge dissipate in his blood. Beyond the men there was a tall standing stone, like a tooth from the grass and on it perched a battlefield bird, black and glossy, lowering its head to let out its raucous cry for the dead. The bird leapt off the stone and he heard the *swoosh* of its broad wings as they beat the air. It jinked and flew in a circle, passing behind the stone. It did not reappear from the other side.

He walked past the throng of men, knowing he should respond to their hands on his shoulders, but the anger and sadness at losing his friend, losing his *geis-brother* prevented him from taking the joy of battle, the triumph of the kill. He walked on and stood before the stone, knowing that one day he would have to give himself back to the rock to find his own way to Tir na n'Og.

From behind the stone *she* came. And he knew her for what she was.

She was beautiful. Her skin was the colour of snow and her eyes were the black of night and her hair, which fell from under the dark hood, was the black-on-blue colour of the wings of the carrion bird. She came towards him, eyes burning on him, and he held up his spear against her, but she pushed it away with such grace and gentleness that he let her do it. Almost as tall as he, she was terrible in her beauty, and he knew it had been she who had tripped him in the water, who had brought on the battle fury that had warped him and caused him to kill his *geis-brother*. Yet she still came to him and put her hands on his chest. She leaned to kiss him and he could feel her silk-hair coil and twist in the wind against his cheek . . .

And then he smelled her again and his blood sizzled under the onslaught of her *scent*. It was a compelling thing, a *commanding* thing, a scent that could drive out thought and willpower and fill the head with swirls and clouds of need and lust. She put her head up to him, offering her lips to kiss.

The woman's face had *changed*. It had become the face of Liz Cannon, now sleeping beside him, breathing slow and deep. In his dream he had bent his head to return the kiss and the stench had hit him like a blow. Foul carrion, rotting bodies, pustular sores: that smell was shocking in its noisome filth. His lips had touched hers and he felt them crack and wither beneath him. He jerked back in revulsion, her face wrinkling and sagging and breaking up. The eyes shrank back into deep sockets, and the skin melted off the high cheekbones, and the long teeth, snaggled and yellow, grew downwards from shrivelling gums. Inside, he felt his heart stop dead in his chest and a dreadful gasp of horror escaped from him. The thing cackled gleefully and the shock of it woke him up. He came awake, a pounding in his temples and a sudden cold sweat trickling down his belly.

Sean lay in the darkness, listening to the thunder, aware of the flashes of lightning beyond the curtains, and felt the dreadful image recede from him. He turned onto his side and put his arm around Liz, who snuggled against him.

She mumbled something and turned sleepily. Sean could feel her warmth against his cold skin and he tried to stop the trembling of his hands. Still sleepy, Liz nuzzled against him. Outside, the lightning flashed and he could see her face, pale in the flickering light, her hair limned with it, and he kissed her softly on the lips. Immediately, her eyes opened and she smiled.

'McCullain, you're insatiable,' she whispered. She snuggled further in to him and tilted her chin to return the kiss.

And as she did so, her face *changed* as if blasted by a furnace. The skin shrivelled off it, leaving only twisted ropes of muscle, through which poked white bones. The jaw fell downwards, so far it almost rested on the withered breast-bone that jutted up through parchment skin.

'McCullain,' it said, and it was not Liz's voice. It was a low, growling snarl that dripped venom. Sean tried to back away, but the thing lunged at him and the shout that had been stoking inside him was suddenly released. His body shook with the force of it as all his breath was let out in one huge bellow of shock.

And then he did wake up. The scene winked out and he came awake sitting up, drenched in sweat, as he had *dreamed* he had done, but this time he knew he was really awake.

Beside him Liz had been startled by his sudden noise and was sitting up beside him, rubbing her eyes.

'What's the matter?' she asked groggily.

It took Sean a second or two to get his breath back and when he did his voice was still shaky.

'Nothing,' he said. 'Just a dream.'

She reached up a hand to touch his back. 'You're shivering and sweating,' she said. 'Are you all right?'

He turned round towards her and saw the concern in her eyes.

'Sure,' he said. 'It was just a dream. I'm fine now. Go back to sleep.' She nodded and gently pulled him back to lie beside her. She pulled the blankets up over both of them and snuggled against him, holding him tight. In his mind's eye he saw the horror vision again, saw her face dissolve and run, and he shucked the image away from him as hard as he could.

'I think you should get something done about those dreams,' she said.

'I think you might be right,' he replied.

She lifted her lips towards his and kissed him gently. She kissed him again and he held onto her tightly.

And it was just at that moment that the wave crashed against the wall of their cottage and broke the door open with a deafening roar.

The two of them almost fell out of bed, and by the time they got to the door, the water was surging through the living room and tumbling up the hallway, already two feet deep.

'What the hell's going on?' Liz shouted.

'Flood,' Sean called back, trying to make himself heard over the noise of the water.

'Oh hell. My cameras,' he yelled, and this time there was no difficulty in hearing him. He floundered up the little lake in the hallway towards the living room. The water was lapping just under the lip of the table. His gear was still intact. Behind him, Liz, still naked, waded like a water sprite. Finally she found her jacket on the hook next to the kitchen door and put it over her shoulders.

Sean turned to look at her. She was knee-deep in swirling water, wearing only the jacket that came down to her hips. She looked shocked and angry and bewildered, and very appealing.

'Well, Liz Cannon,' he said. 'Did the earth move for you or what?'

All the cottages except one were on the same level in the flat field.

Edward Laird and Hugh Sands were woken by the wave crashing against their gable wall, and they had a few seconds' grace, clambering into their clothes, before the water started pouring under the door.

Dr Connarty didn't hear a thing and Terry Munster was sound asleep when the wave hit and flooded their cottage. Terry was lying sprawled half out of bed, his head lolling off the mattress, when he woke to find himself drowning. He swallowed a lungful of water and went into a fit of coughing, and his frantic yells finally woke the professor, who leapt out of bed and began swimming.

Siobhan had fallen into a light sleep and woke instantly. She scrambled out of bed and roused the two girls, and then rushed about in the sodden room, picking up all the documents that she'd left scattered over the table.

Bridget Massey, Brian Cooney and the two new arrivals spent half an hour floundering around in the water, stacking their bags up as high as possible, before anyone noticed that Bridget was completely naked

257

except for a little nightdress that came down just far enough to cover her backside but which had become completely transparent with the water.

Seamus O'Farrell let out a long whistle of appreciation, which caused Bridget to blush furiously and Cooney to tell him to keep his mind on the job.

Tom and Nancy Ducain were asleep when the pounding on the door started. Tom stumbled out of bed and barked his shin on the edge of a chair before he turned the key in the lock. There was a fair crowd outside, all of them soaking wet and bedraggled-looking in the light cast through the doorway. Beyond them, in the eerie flashes of lightning, he saw a lake that he had never seen before. It stretched from ten yards in front of his cottage right across the field beyond the rest of the cottages. The other buildings stood out like islands.

'You'd better come in,' he finally said.

Up at Kilgallan, some of the men had gathered out on the road, as men tend to do whenever an emergency hits a village. Patsy McGavigan, normally the most reserved man in town due to the nature of his profession, was yelling blue murder to anybody who would listen that it must have been a volcano that threw the big piece of stone through his roof. Peter O'Neill the policeman managed to shut him up for a moment while he tried to get some organising done, though to tell the truth, he wasn't sure what organising was needed, or where. Finn Finnerty's barn was flattened, down at the far end of the village, and lay tangled in the middle of the street, a great mess of corrugated iron. There were slates all over the road; they had been blown off by the winds, though that was nothing unusual. Peter had thrown on his greatcoat and a big pair of rubber boots and was standing in the doorway of Donovan's bar, trying to make himself heard over the roaring of the wind.

Finally, unable to compete, he grabbed Declan Donovan by the shirt sleeve, which was now soaked through to the skin, and yelled in his ear: 'You'd best open her up just the now, Declan, or we'll freeze our arses off.'

'It's long past the closing time,' Donovan bawled back.

'Well, I'm declaring a state of emergency until we find out what the emergency is,' Peter overruled him. Donovan bent down and uncocked the hasp that shot the bolt into the stone step, and swung the heavy door inwards. Everybody jostled inside and stood in a group.

Out of the wind, Peter could make himself heard. 'Right now, everybody shush up for a minute till we find out what's about.'

'It was a volcano, I'm sure of it,' Patsy McGavigan piped up from the back of the group.

'Right, Patsy. We'll check that one, sure enough,' Peter said, and was about to go on when Danny Boyle, whose son Michael had been found drowned in the Roonah Water in the spring, said: 'It was the sea.'

There was a silence that fell like a weight in the room.

'It was the sea. I saw it,' Danny said. Everybody looked at him, and you could see all the colour was drained right out of his face, giving him a flat look, as if all his muscles had lost their strength.

'I couldn't sleep, what with the storm and all, and everything else,' Danny started. Everybody knew that Danny hadn't been the same since his boy died.

'I was sitting having a smoke and looking out at the storm from the top room. It looked like the whole sky was afire. Then I saw it.'

'Saw what, Danny?' Peter encouraged.

'The sea, man. The sea came right up through the gully down at the pier and it was as high as a hill. Didn't you see it? It lifted Finn's barn up like a tin-can, and next thing I saw it had gone. Then it came over, a huge mountain of ocean, and for the life of me, it took down half the trees at the back of the farm.'

'Right. We'd better have a look and see what the damage is,' Peter said. He pointed his finger into the crowd and gave out a couple of instructions. 'You, Padraigh, you run over and fetch the doctor and bring him down here. Mickey, you take some fellows down by Finnerty's place and see what's afoot. If there's any cattle roaming about, then tether them over at Feargal's place. If there's anybody hurt, bring them back here if they can be moved, and if they can't, just come running yourselves.'

Peter detailed another handful to go in the other direction to check out the bridge to make sure it was clear for the ambulances which would no doubt be speeding their way to Kilgallan in short order, and he sent another detail down to the cottages to check out how the incomers had fared. Finally he turned round and put his hands on the bar.

'You, Declan, have the most important job of them all,' he said.

'What would that be now, Peter?'

'Pour me a Guinness and a whiskey. Sure, I've a feeling this is going to be a long night.'

Declan did as he was told and poured for each of them. Peter, a heavy-set, red-faced Garda with a beer belly that told of a fine appetite for the dark stout, put the glass to his lips and didn't stop until he had drained the pint pot.

'I needed that,' he said, lifting his whiskey to chase the beer down.

Runners came back from where he'd sent them. There were two people trapped in the ruins of one of the cottages down at the far end beyond Finnerty's farm, and the men were shifting the rubble to get them out. They didn't seem badly hurt.

Two of the men who'd gone down to the cottages reported the track blocked off completely by fallen trees, but they were able to say for certain that all the cottages appeared to be intact, though the sea had flooded the field almost to window-ledge level.

Then from the north end came the message that the bridge was down. Peter and the rest of the men hurried up towards the Roonah to see for themselves and found the two halves of the bridge shifted off their pilings and slanted across the torrent. The whole of the marsh downstream was now a lake and the banking had been cut away by the enormous force of the water, changing for ever the contours of the stream.

'Now would you look at that,' Peter bawled. 'The whole thing's been shoved sideways. How will we get the ambulances through?'

'And look over there,' one of the men said. Everybody looked. Beyond the bridge, where the bank had been scoured away and widened by more than twenty feet, the stout post that carried the electricity supply into the village was teetering drunkenly as the ground on which it stood crumbled away. Matching it, the telephone pole on the other side of the road was swaying in unison.

'Everybody stay back,' Peter ordered, while he himself stepped forward and managed to get onto the nearest half of the bridge. 'We might be able to span something across here in the meantime, at least to let the emergency services through,' he shouted.

Just then there was a shout from the group of men who were huddling together against the wind, and Peter turned just in time to see the power pylon slowly topple from its position. The cables pulled it one way and then another, and they watched it dance back and forth for several seconds before it made up its mind to fall to the left.

All the men scuttled to the right, just in case, and it was as well they did. The pole toppled sideways and one of the seven cables snapped off it and whipped like a thin steel snake towards where they had been. The power line snaked around Peter's legs, and if he hadn't been wearing his thick rubber boots he'd likely have been fried on the spot. Instead, it simply threw him off balance and he fell into the space between the piece of bridge and the road. Even over the roaring of the torrent, the rest of the men heard his thighbone snap when he landed. The cable writhed in a jittery electric dance and finally sprang into the water, with a sizzling blue flash where it hit. The water steamed for a split second and then the sparks died.

The power pylon finally crashed against the telegraph pole on the far side of the water, and snapped it off a yard above the ground. The pole fell with a crash and the thin wires snapped in a rapid series of pinging sounds, but though the power pylon swayed, it miraculously remained standing, drunkenly listing over the road. The men piled down into the hole and hauled Peter out. He was yelling blue murder much more loudly than Patsy McGavigan had only half an hour before, and the reason was plain to see. The edge of the clean fracture had come right through the big muscles of his thigh, rammed through his heavy twill trousers and ripped its way out of the thick waterproof leggings to jut white and red in the torchlight.

By the time they got him back to the pub, Peter had fainted, which was good enough for Dr Tim O'Brien who found that the bone had missed the femoral artery by half an inch. He gave Peter a heavy shot and when the Garda woke up in the morning, the bone was set and splinted and the wound was stitched. Dr Tim ordered Peter to stay in his bed for at least a week, which infuriated the policeman. The biggest emergency of his life had come, and he was going to miss the lot of it. Worse, his leg was encased in a cast supplied by the local vet. It was the kind they used for horses.

25

The great black wave had hit the tor with a mighty explosion and rammed its way straight into the passageway. Up and over the tor it continued, throwing off the rocks that dotted its scarred surface and firing them like cannon-balls into the air.

Inside the chamber, the weight of water was so great that the air was compressed against the roof and only the incredible workmanship of artisans long dead prevented the whole top of the hillock from being blown off like the core of a volcano. When the first pulse had passed, the compression reversed itself in a counter-explosion as the air expanded and the sea water came out of the entrance in a seething torrent.

Cataclysmic noise rent the night as rocks and stones and roots and trunks were crashed together all around, and over that were the deafening explosions of real thunder as the storm that had whipped and channelled the wave from out in the ocean spent itself in a prodigal frenzy.

Yet beyond that there was another sound, the one that Doug Petersen heard only seconds before he was tumbled arse-for-elbow through the kitchen door and under the sink. It came ravening over the thunder and ripping through the devastating roar of the waves, high and ululating and inhumanly *ferocious*.

It was one great screech of triumph that soared high into the night, bringing its own madness to the mayhem.

The final *geis* had been broken.

And the thing that had waited in the infinite darkness came raving from its prison of stone, screaming its unearthly joy and its terrible fury as it swooped down the passageway and blasted out onto the scoured earth.

It stood there, a black, strangely twisting shape that seemed more shadow than substance as the water swirled around in a chaos of froth. The back-wave that had shot out of the chamber met the oncoming second surge, much smaller than the first seismic pulse, yet still a powerful wall of water. It came roaring inwards, towards the tor, and the thing stood, oblivious to any danger. The water soared high, tumbling over the back-flow, and crashed onto the dark shape. Again the high-pitched demonic laughter tore jaggedly at the air, and the wave passed on, leaving the dark thing still standing in its wake.

It swelled and twisted, defying *form* as if undecided. It elongated and contracted hideously for several minutes before it suddenly stretched upwards and launched itself into the air. The wind seemed to pick it up like a fluttering rag that swooped over the tangle of fallen trees, and then it was gone.

Down at the Tallabaun Inn, Mike O'Hara shambled along the narrow corridor. He was unshaven, his thin hair tousled. The white shirt was now grey with sweat and stained with the brandy that had dribbled down his chin. He was drunk, but not drunk *enough*.

Inside his head was a crazy jumble of thoughts and ideas that rolled and roiled around a central numbness. Mike O'Hara was not a bad man and he was not a violent man, and yet he had done something *terrible*. He knew it, but he didn't know what that awful thing was. He remembered nothing of what had happened since the previous morning. There was only the echo of the sizzling *compulsion* that had been in his head, which had shoved and pushed at him until he had *done* something.

Inside the numbness there was a great freezing fear, and a pint of brandy had done nothing to diminish that. For the compulsion was back again, dragging Mike to the outbuilding. The small part of his mind that had any volition left tried to make his limbs stop, but they refused to co-operate, and slowly, jerkily, he made his way along the passageway, the fear inside him swelling hugely. He could hear the beating of his heart behind his ears and it seemed very far away.

Marie was stretched on the bed, her plump legs down side by side and her hands still twisted to clamp on the old brass bedhead where they were tied to the metal. There was a smell of dried blood in the room. Mike stood at the door, taking in the scene, although what he was actually seeing hadn't registered. The expression on his face was flat calm, almost thoughtful, belying the jangled tumbling inside his head. The compulsion moved him forward two steps until he was at the side of the bed, looking down at the girl. Her head was contorted to the right, and the face was a mottled dark purple, the colour of a bruise. Brown flecks of blood were spattered around her mouth, and below that her neck was grotesquely narrowed. The dressing-gown cord had bitten so deeply that the flesh on either side had swelled around it, completely hiding it from view. Marie's eyes bulged out of their sockets, staring emptily up into the corner of the room. Mike O'Hara's eyes slowly swept up the length of her, the lucid part of his mind strangely aware of every detail: the little golden hairs that stood out on her legs, the red callous on the inside edge of her foot where it had rubbed against the ill-fitting shoes she'd worn. A wisp of mousy hair had tumbled down and plastered itself across her cheek. She had a small strawberry birthmark underneath her left breast.

O'Hara stood staring glassily for a few minutes more and the muted roaring sound, like an ebb tide on a distant shingle beach, started its susurration inside his head.

Very slowly he started to undress himself, hauling the dirty shirt over his head and then peeling the trousers down his skinny shanks. Again he felt the *heat* that had come over him before, and the pounding in his temples. The lucidity faded away to the jumbled numbness as he stepped closer, his movements jerky, his limbs forced against their will, and lay down beside the girl. His hand moved forward and touched the flesh, cold and damp and strangely unyielding. It was like touching a toadstool, clammy and rubbery. For a brief moment he tried to draw his hand away, and as he did so, he saw the girl's chest move slowly upwards, then fall down as if she had taken a breath. Even then, his sluggish mind did not react. It was as if something inside him had been closed down.

Mike O'Hara reached and undid the belt that bound her ankles together and then clambered on top of the body of the girl in the bed, clumsily hiking himself across until he lay on her cool length. His skin puckered and tingled at the contact with her coldness, but he was unable to prevent himself, driven as he was by the compulsion that had robbed him of all volition.

For several minutes, he lay prone, the roar in his head soaring louder and louder like an approaching storm.

Then suddenly the noise stopped and his mind was instantly released. The numbness disappeared in the space of one quick heartbeat, and as it went the realisation of the *wrong* thing, the *terrible* thing that he'd done, came flooding back to him.

He saw himself – yet *not* himself – grappling with the young girl who had frozen in fright. He watched the rerun across the front of his mind as he hauled at her hands until they were up behind her head, then lashed her ankles with his belt to the footboard. The memory showed him her pale blue terror-stricken innocent eyes rolling wildly. Then there was a frantic bucking of her soft warmth underneath him as he looped the cord round her neck and jerked himself savagely backwards, throwing his weight into the pull of the noose with such violence that, through the taut braid, he felt *something* inside give way. He remembered the heat behind his eyes and the terrible joy of the violence. He felt again her body jerk as the dying nerves pulsed their last frantic life. He saw his hands tighten and pull apart so hard that the knuckles stood out white against the skin and the tendons showed like cords on his own wrists. He relived that final spasm ripping through her – and through him – when the life was suddenly gone, but the nerves continued to jitter in the dance of death.

All this came back to him in one foul rush, and for many seconds O'Hara was frozen by the terrible impact of it. He lay there, still as death, his thoughts dazed with horror and guilt and revulsion, before he realised where he was and what he was doing.

'Oh . . . my . . . oh, God . . . oh no,' he mumbled incoherently. In that moment, his paralysis left him and he shoved himself off the stiff dead girl, his eyes fixed on her sightless ones.

And in that second the girl's mouth opened and she made a small croaking noise.

Mike stopped in mid-movement, unsure of what he'd heard. Then the girl's eyes, still bulging from the internal pressure, rolled down in the sockets and glared at him.

'Marie . . . girl. You're not dead . . . You're *not dead*,' he blabbered.

The eyes fixed on him and they *changed* from pale, watery blue, to purple and then pure black, like the eyes of a snake. Underneath him, he felt the deep pounding of a heart beating and knew it was not his own. From the side there was a movement and his eyes flicked towards it. One of her hands, curled around the bedhead, twisted away, pulled against the thick cord, then jerked forward with such speed that the cord broke with a cracking sound. The other hand twisted, and the binding gave way so quickly that it was thrown right across the room.

With the speed of a striking snake, the hands shot forward and grabbed O'Hara by the head. Hard fingers dug into his temple and he felt himself wrenched forward with such force that he *heard* the ligaments in his neck creak.

The hands hauled his face up close to hers. He tried to pull away but all the strength had drained out of him. He made a small gasping sound, and the girl looked at him.

'Marie . . .' he managed to say.

'Oh, Mr O'Hara,' she said, and while it sounded like her voice, it wasn't. He heard the undertone, the deathly *coldness* there.

'Oh, Mr O'Hara, you bad little man. You've taught me something I never knew before.'

He felt the pressure on his temples, his own eyes beginning to bulge. He tried to say something else but the terrible force of the hands on the side of his head prevented his jaw from moving.

'And you've given me a taste for it, so you have,' she continued in that soulless voice.

He tried to pull back again, but couldn't move against the enormous strength of her grip.

'I fancy another taste now,' she said, and then her blue lips peeled back to show her teeth, long, yellow-brown, the teeth of an old woman. His eyes fixed on the mouth, those teeth, and as he stared he saw the jaw open wide, wider, a terrible cavernous gape.

The hands that gripped his head suddenly jerked him forward, and this time the tendon at the side of his neck snapped with the sound of a branch breaking. The pain soared to an unbelievable high, and it was on the crest of that immense pain that Mike O'Hara died.

The thing that had moved into the dead space that had been young, innocent Marie Lally dragged O'Hara up to its jaws, and mantis-like, began to feed.

Before dawn, three miles out of Kilgallan, on the moors where the track wound its way round the black oily tarns, the peat diggers slumbered in an old drystane cattle shed. Protected on the west by an outcrop of rock, this part of the moor had been screened from the seismic wave of water. There were seven men in all, ranging in ages from a skinny teenager with a lantern jaw and dull eyes to a wizened old fellow in his sixties who had only one black tooth in his caved-in mouth and whose head was oddly foreshortened so that it seemed to come to a point. The peat cutters had gathered together before the storm, stumbling and shambling their way over the moor to shelter under the corrugated tin roof. Like hibernating animals, they had crawled into the corner while the rain drummed a tattoo over their heads, and slept in the damp, smelly shed.

After Mike O'Hara met his end in the Tallabaun Inn and after the doctor had put the patchwork of stitches into Peter O'Neill's thigh, something came fleeting across the moor on the face of the west wind, something black that tumbled like a ragged shadow over the barren expanse.

It appeared silently in the shelter and called to the men in words that were not spoken but wormed their way into the empty places in their poor, benighted heads. Slowly, like dull animals, they came awake, each one a twisted, ungainly parody of a human, each one malleable and biddable. They looked into the shadow that was the shape *Shee* had taken and cringed from the awesome power that emanated from her in black waves.

In words that were as old as the land she spoke directly into the strange, deformed parts of their minds.

'Guard me,' the words told them.

One by one, they got to their feet, went out of the old shed and sat in the lessening wind and rain while the thing slumbered and savoured the memory of the feast.

She slept for a while and her black mind went wandering over times past and revenge to come. And in her dreams she saw a face that was hazy in memory; even in sleep she felt the desire well up again in her. There was a *sense* of the presence, even now, a trace of it in the air, and she hungered for it.

But it could wait until she was ready. The shadow that was black on black in the dry corner of the shed seemed to twist and writhe as the terrible thing dreamed on.

Sleep came late for everyone in the crowded cottage that Tom and Nancy Ducain had hired for the week.

Tom had hauled the door open to find Siobhan and the two girls drenched to the skin. Siobhan had two bags, which she balanced on her shoulders, and Theresa and Agnes each had a rucksack with what they had managed to save from the flood. Behind them, Connarty was knee-deep in water and venting his fury on the storm in the most unacademic language. Terry Munster had the professor by the arm to help him to the higher ground, and even in the darkness you could see that he was enjoying the professor's discomfiture. Sean McCullain was laden with camera gear that he held high over his head as he waded towards them, along with Liz and the three oilmen, each cursing in his individual and highly colourful vernacular. From the right came the Irish couple with another pair of men that none of them had seen before, but on a night like this, when the whole field on which the cottages sat had become a lake, strangers were welcome to shelter. Edward Laird and Hugh Sands were last to arrive, with rucksacks on their heads.

'You'll never forget an Irish honeymoon, young fellow,' Connarty said as soon as he came through the door.

'You better believe it,' Tom said. 'The folks back home sure won't. What's happened?'

'We've been inundated, that's for certain,' the professor said. He was sitting on the kerb at the edge of the fire, peeling off a pair of thick woollen socks from which salt water simply poured onto the floor.

'That must have been some gale,' Sean ventured.

'I don't think it was the gale at all,' Connarty said.

'Then where did all the water come from?' asked a Northern Irish voice from the opposite corner. Everybody looked round to see the questioner. He was a young man in his twenties with a shock of Celtic red hair that was slicked into wet ringlets.

'I'd say, from all the damage, that we've just been hit by a tidal wave, though that's the wrong name for it.'

'What does that mean?' Tom asked.

'A *tsunami*,' Nancy told him.

'I saw one of them in Indonesia once,' Doug Petersen said. 'Wiped out a string of towns along a whole coastline.'

'I imagine there's a few towns hit tonight. But Nancy's right. A tidal wave has nothing to do with the tide, and there's never been a wind strong enough to lift the sea up so high as it has tonight. I think there's been some sort of seismic activity out at sea. An earthquake, most likely. What hit here, I'm sure, is the shock wave that follows.'

'Like the film *Krakatoa, East of Java*?' Tom asked.

'West of Java, but essentially the same,' Connarty said, wringing the legs of his trousers out by gripping them against his shins and running his hands down so that the water puddled at his pink bare feet.

'So what do we do now?' Frank Wysocki asked.

'That's up to our hosts, I imagine,' the professor said, cocking an eye at Tom, who was sitting on the arm of the chair with his own arm slung across Nancy's shoulder.

Tom shrugged. 'You're welcome, all of you. Nancy and me, we were kinda lonely anyway,' he said, nudging her.

'Very good of you. Once the wind dies down, we should check the road up to the village, just in case we have to move, but I think if there was going to be another wave, it would have arrived by now.'

Nancy got up from the chair and gingerly stepped through the crush of people dripping onto the floor. 'I'll put the kettle on, though I don't know if there's enough cups.'

Agnes and Theresa offered to help in the kitchen and followed her through. Connarty declined a coffee and instead produced, as if by magic, a bottle of Irish whiskey from the bag that he'd brought out from the flooded cottage.

'First thing I reached for as soon as I got out of my bed and into the water. The only two things a man needs are a bottle of whiskey and a dry change of clothes.'

'Oh, man, you're a lifesaver,' Frank Wysocki boomed, taking the proffered bottle after the professor had had a substantial swallow and rubbed the neck with the flat of his hand like a true gentleman.

The bottle passed round and almost everybody, including Liz, took a swig, letting the fire of the whiskey burn the cold out of their bodies.

'We've got a forty-ouncer back in our place,' Pete Coia mentioned brightly when the bottle finally arrived back in the professor's hands with only an inch or two left in the bottom.

'Yeah, but it's across a bloody lake,' Doug Petersen reminded him.

'To hell with that,' the wiry little Canadian told him. 'I'm wet as it is, and if it's going to be a long night, we might as well enjoy it. I'll go and check the road and then I'll get back over and bring our supplies. If there's any blankets still dry, I'll take them too.'

'I'll come along with you,' Sean said. 'I only managed to get my cameras. I want some dry clothes.'

There was a blast of cold air in the room when Sean and Pete Coia opened the door, and the embers flared in the fireplace. Nancy and the girls brought in a pot of coffee and every cup and jug they could find in the kitchen, and started pouring. The girl who had come in with the Irish fellows came across and asked if she needed any help.

'I'm Bridget Massey,' she said by way of introduction, 'but everybody calls me Bridie.'

'Nice to meet you,' Nancy said, 'though the circumstances could have been better.'

'They could that. The water poured right into my bedroom. I woke up swimming. You're dead lucky it didn't get your place. I've a fine suede jacket that my brother bought me and it's ruined. I'll never be able to wear it again.'

'As least you made it to dry land.'

'Yes, I suppose we should count our blessings.'

Bridget took four cups of coffee, spooned brown sugar into them all and carried them over to where her companions were sitting by the window. Outside, the wind was already dying and the thunder had stopped.

As usual, the professor was holding forth, giving them all a lecture on the nature of seismic waves, aided and abetted by the several large whiskies he'd poured down his throat. He only stopped when somebody pressed a small milk jug filled with coffee into his hands. With deft expertise he unscrewed the whiskey cap with his left hand

and poured the remainder into the jug. He bent forward, gnomish beside the fire, and took a sip.

'Now *that's* what I call a cup of coffee,' he said with a blissful sigh. 'There must be some of the old blood in you, Nancy, for only the Irish can make it just like this.'

'And you've made it a hundred proof,' Siobhan put in, and everybody, even the Irishmen by the window, had a laugh.

It took Sean McCullain and Pete Coia about fifteen minutes to come back. Again, both of them were drenched, but between them they had managed to bundle up a pile of blankets and duvets, wrapped in a sheet, along with a couple of bags filled with dry clothes.

'Storm's dying down,' Pete said. 'And I think the water's draining away somewhere. It's a foot lower than it was.'

'That lake'll be gone by morning,' Connarty said. 'The drainage ditch will carry it all down to the sea.'

Pete Coia bent over his bag and rummaged in its depths. There was a clink of glass and he produced the big bottle of Scotch. He handed it to the professor, whose eyes lit up with pleasure. A beatific smile creased his face.

'Sure, I took you for a gentleman the minute I laid eyes on you,' he said, and again everybody laughed.

Liz handed Sean a cup of coffee and he drank it gratefully, letting the steaming brew warm him inside.

'What's it like out there?' she asked.

'Wet. *Bloody* wet.'

'Now there's a surprise.'

'And the road is blocked, as far as I can tell without a light. There's half a dozen big trees down. I think it wouldn't be a good idea to go up to the village before morning.'

'Did you see what the dig's like?' Siobhan asked.

Sean shook his head. 'We didn't go that far. There's branches and trunks everywhere. You could break a leg.'

'We'll probably have to get a pump, if there's one to be had.'

'I'll bet they're like gold dust by the morning,' the professor said. 'I think the whole coast has been inundated. The place will be soaking and sodden for weeks.'

'Don't worry about the tor,' Terry said. 'Remember how unusual its design is? The passage goes upwards instead of descending. The water would come straight back out again, and the ground there's higher than it is here.'

Connarty thought for a moment, and then nodded in agreement.

'What is it you're digging for?' asked the red-haired young man with the Armagh accent. He gave his name as Seamus O'Farrell.

'It's an old tomb . . .' Connarty started right away, delighted to have found somebody else to expound to. The two newcomers seemed interested enough, though in a room crowded and beginning to steam with the heat of bodies and the mess of wet clothes, it was hard to tell. Still, the wave that had roared over the field where the cottages stood gave them all something in common, for the night anyway, so everybody listened, some for the third or fourth time, to what Connarty had to say.

When he came to describe the carvings on the rock, he told them about the warnings against grave-robbers.

'Who would want to rob an old coffin?' John Boyle, the other young Ulsterman asked.

'You'd be surprised. A lot of the kings and princes took their wealth with them when they went, and everybody knew it. There used to be a roaring trade in grave goods, but if it was known there was a curse on the place, then the folk would leave well alone. They were a superstitious lot. They believed there were things called up from the underworld that would come out of a grave and drag them back.'

'Like the *Shee*,' Siobhan said.

'What's that?' Nancy asked.

'She's an old Celtic figure. A sort of Goddess of Death and Destruction,' Siobhan told her. 'I was working on the inscriptions tonight. There's a great deal about her. The old Connacht folk believed she was the embodiment of all evil, so her name over the lintel of a tomb would be enough to scare people off. They called her the *Babd*, which means *abomination*, and the people believed she was a shape-shifter who could change her appearance at will. There seems to be a lot about her inside the chamber, which doesn't fit with the idea of an injunction against grave-robbers. I'm still working on it, but I get the impression that it's more of a defence *against* her than anything else.'

Siobhan paused for a minute, then went on. 'One thing's for certain. She was the most fearsome of all the Celtic supernatural forces, and they feared her because she could be a woman when she chose.'

'It's a fine tale, sure enough,' came a voice from the window, and everybody turned around. John Boyle, a sallow fellow in a big dark donkey jacket, looked back at them all. 'But Ireland doesn't need a *banshee* for death and destruction. Sure, we've got one already, and she comes from over the water and she's visited all that on our country for the past thousand years.'

Brian Cooney, still perched on the windowsill beside Bridget, put his hand on his arm and motioned him to be quiet. Boyle shut up and cast his eyes downward. There was no mistaking the smouldering anger in him that had forced out the words.

There was a silence for a moment and then Tom Ducain broke it as lightly as he could. 'All that stuff about graves and curses scares the hell out of me,' he said. 'I think the whole thing's creepy. What if there *was* something that came out?'

Connarty laughed, a high-pitched infectious chuckle that set everybody grinning. 'If there was, then there would be plenty of them after me. I've dug up about fifty of these things.'

'But all the bodies. Skeletons. I couldn't dig up graves.'

'Me neither,' Liz said. 'I'm claustrophobic. Even when I was in there, with you, and with the light on, I felt as if the walls were closing in on me. I don't know if I could go back in again.'

'Oh, we've all got phobias. And you'll never guess what mine is,' Connarty said, smacking his lips after taking another large drink of whiskey. He was not quite drunk, but getting merrier by the minute.

'Tell us then,' Nancy demanded.

'Well, believe it or not, I've a great fear of being buried. Me an archaeologist and all. I'm a discredit to the profession.'

'You're kidding,' Tom said.

'No, I'm not. When I'm gone, it's me for the gas jets. And sure, when they turn them on, the whole building will go up in a bang when all the whiskey in me catches afire. But no burial for me. I don't want the likes of myself poking around and raising my bones in years to come.'

Everybody laughed, but for a second, Connarty's merry red face went still and serious. The only person in the crowded room who saw the flicker of change was Sean McCullain.

'I hate spiders,' Siobhan said. 'Ever since I was a girl, I couldn't go into a room if there was a spider in it, and I've never got rid of that in all these years. That's the worst part of my job. There's always spiders everywhere and they give me the shivers. I think God made his own special curse for me the day he thought up spiders.'

The thing turned into the kind of game people who barely know each other play when they are thrown together by chance and adversity.

'It's heights for me,' Tom Ducain declared. 'Yesterday we had a picnic up on the moors and Nancy climbed the hill. I couldn't go with her because every time I go up any height I want to be sick. Hell, I stay in one of the best ski resorts in the whole US of A, and I'm the only man I know who has to stay on the low slopes.'

'Heights are nothing,' Doug Petersen drawled. 'It's not the fall that kills you, it's just the sudden stop at the very end.'

There was another tired chuckle.

'But what scares the living shit out of me, pardon the language, ladies, is sharks, and where I come from they scare *everybody*. I was up north swimming off the big reef when a white shark came in and took a mate of mine in his jaws. Nearly ripped the poor bloke in two. Only his wetsuit held him together. I was in the water at the time and I nearly died of fright, don't mind telling you. That's why the fishing here's so bloody good. No bloody sharks. I just don't like big fish with teeth.'

'I get the twitches in a swamp,' Pete Coia said. 'Went off the road down in Florida once and got lost in two minutes. Took me a day to find the road again. Twenty-four hours up to my armpits in crap. I never want to do that again.'

'How about you, Sean? Got a phobia?' Siobhan asked.

'Not a phobia,' Sean said, eyebrows coming down in a frown that shadowed his eyes. 'But I don't like the dark.'

Doug Petersen laughed aloud. 'Christ, mate, we're *all* scared of the dark.'

'That's odd for a photographer,' Siobhan probed.

Sean nodded. 'Spend half my time in the darkroom. Shouldn't bother me.'

Liz slipped her arm round Sean and softly rubbed his ribs. She was the only one who knew about his dreams. Siobhan caught the movement and came to a quick, if regretful, conclusion.

The bottle was passed round again. Some took a drink and the others stuck with coffee, and the game went on.

Tom Ducain said that what scared him almost as much as heights was the prospect of malpractice lawsuits, and Nancy told him there was little hope of that. Theresa Laughlin admitted that frogs and toads made her shudder, and Edward Laird, who had introduced himself and Sands as ornithologists, said he had a revulsion of snakes. This was not entirely true. Laird did have one great fear. A colleague of his had been blinded by flying glass in an explosion, and Laird had developed a pathological fear of losing his sight. But he was not prepared to tell this to a company of strangers.

Neither were some of the others in the room. Brian Cooney, on his first ever mission for the Republican Army, was petrified at the thought of interrogation and torture. He told the room that he only had a fear of God, being a good Catholic and all.

Young Seamus O'Farrell, not quite a hypochondriac, was afraid of disease. But he professed that what scared him most of all was the escalating price of Guinness, and this got a faint laugh from the rest. Hugh Sands declared himself concerned about the greenhouse effect, but in truth, he still suffered from nightmares about the four weeks he'd spent in a wheelchair after a rugby injury which had almost broken his back while still at school. The thought of paralysis, of being confined to a wheelchair, was what frightened him more than anything.

Some of the group did not voice their fears. Terry Munster, already more than half drunk, did not want to admit that he was afraid of fire. And Agnes Finnegan, who was only eighteen and still a virgin, would have died before letting everyone know that she said her prayers every night because the idea of sex repelled her and the thought of rape was a burning horror. Nancy Ducain, perhaps the most striking of all the women in that crowded room, cared not to admit that the prospect of disfigurement was her most closely held fear. Bridget Massey could be ill at the sight of maggots. Frank Wysocki, the hulking Polish-Canadian, would have surprised everyone if he had admitted that he avoided wide-open spaces. John Boyle, the other young Ulsterman, had survived his own worst phobia when he stepped off the heaving boat down at the quay. The whole trip had been a nightmare, especially in such heavy seas, for John Boyle was pathologically afraid of drowning. While Seamus had been rolling around on the floor, being sick over Desmond Lynch's boots, John had been flat beside him, fingers hooked around a metal pipe, and if his toes could have done so, they would have grasped on as well. John had been terrified for every minute of the journey.

Those fears remained unspoken, but the bearers of them made up facile replacements which either brought laughter or howls of mild derision. Eventually, aided by the whiskey, heads began to nod. Liz snuggled in beside Sean and fell asleep. Dr Connarty leaned back against the warm stone of the chimney breast and was snoring within minutes. A few hours before dawn, almost everything in the room was asleep.

The thing that had come out from the tor, freed by the breaking of the final curse, was awake. It had spread black wings and launched itself over the trees in the darkness, veering against the gale, far out over the moor, to alight, a shadow blacker than blackland, in a gully where a cleft in the rock led to a small cave. A vixen sheltering in the cave with her almost-grown cubs sensed the approach and snarled and bared sharp fangs. Something swooped into the cleft. The vixen, puzzled by a scent it could not identify, a shadow it could not see, crouched and prepared to spring past its yelping cubs. The shadow loomed, and from it came a devastating thought that blasted the vixen back against the wall of stone and crushed her young where they cowered. The black shape flowed into the cave, contracted into itself and was still. Alive and free, it hunched there and once again sent out the fingers of its mind across the moor.

It touched briefly warm minds in farmhouses and cottages, feeling the cracks and the flaws, savouring the small anguishes and fears and angers. It skirted past the undertaker's and gave Patsy McGavigan the worst nightmare he had ever dreamed. The old fellow woke up yelling, convinced, for a moment, that the coffins down in his parlour were filled and that now they were opening, and the long-dead were coming out to pay him another visit.

It sensed the presence of the other one, the old enemy, and warily probed for it. The touch stroked the minds of the people sitting in the crowded room of the cottage, a cold touch that made them shiver. It scraped across their fears and brought them, even the deep-hidden ones, to the surface, and tasted them, one by one. It found the mind of the one it sought. It was him, surely, but different. Still powerful and clean. It pulled away, not ready for the contact, but now aware of him as it had not been completely aware while trapped in the dark.

Greedily the *Shee* trailed her touch through the soft minds around him, sipping at their fears, teasing them out, before withdrawing. There was one warm, weary mind where she lingered. Here was one who knew something of her. But not enough. She probed just a little . . .

Siobhan, curled up beside Nancy Ducain, was dreaming. The conversation in the room, combined with the whiskey and the warmth, had made her drowsy. She had begun to doze off while the phobia tally was still in progress, and was soon sound asleep. In the dream she was walking up the passageway to the central chamber within the tor, scanning the carvings on the stone lintel which lined the corridor at head height as she continued. The passage seemed to go on and on and the strange writings flickered and writhed in the light of the lamp she was carrying in her hand. Finally she got to the chamber and walked slowly, silently towards the black bulk of the stone block in the centre. There was no noise, except for her breathing, and she laid the lantern on top of the stone and peered down at it. The intricate carvings covered every inch of space, and yet *beneath* she could sense something, as if the stone was somehow hollow, strangely translucent. In the dream it seemed as if the block of pure rock held something within it.

Siobhan leaned forward and again the carvings writhed and twisted, making no sense to her and then, quite abruptly, they seemed to merge into each other in an elaborate pattern. They coiled together and then separated, and the pattern was new. Almost like the photographic paper that she'd seen only the day before, the blankness changed and focused and suddenly it was there for her to see. In Siobhan's sleep, the conundrum that had puzzled her unravelled as her unconscious mind encompassed the *whole* pattern and accepted the concept.

Her mind's eye scanned the pattern, and the meaning of the words leapt out at her. Even in sleep, her fascination was intense. She *read* the words in the stone.

The whole story unfolded before her. How they had trapped the *Shee*, the one they called the *Babd*, the *Mor-righinn*, the great nymph. They had found her hiding place and burned the green sapwood of mountain ash and witch hazel, and they had bound their eyes and stopped their ears so they could not hear her voice nor look into her dead eyes. With their own song they had dragged her down the mountainside and they had put her *into* the stone that was the hub between the lands of the dead and the world of men, so that she would never return.

Siobhan, still dreaming, read on. The *Shee* cursed them and promised that this green land would be laid waste by blood and death and famine and disease. Brother would fight brother for ever more.

Yet there were the *geis*, the great bindings that were also carved into the stone. The Sons of the Five Kings had given themselves to stand guard for ever, and the Sword of the Son of Light was placed to bar her path to the Dead World and prevent her return to Tir na n'Og.

The words, even in sleep, held strange power. The *geis* said that the tomb must never be opened to allow the light inside. So long as the tomb was unopened, she would slumber; and so long as the guards stood, she would not wake. As long as the land stayed above the sea, she would remain in the dark between the worlds; and as long as the Sword of Light barred her path, there would be no escape from this world.

Siobhan's dreaming eyes scanned the stone. Her mind had translated the ancient language, yet it seemed the old script had unravelled its *own* meaning for her, and the story had simply leapt out at her. She felt her body move, walking slowly, so slowly, around the block, eyes still fixed on its strange surface, when abruptly she froze, and in the typical *twist* of a dream, she felt the atmosphere change and harden with the sensation of impending threat. She backed away. The monolith shimmered as if it had lost its rigidity, almost as if it had become a dark liquid. Siobhan's feet felt as if they had become part of the floor. She could only stand and watch, frozen into immobility as the flat top began to pulse and bulge.

Then, with astonishing abruptness, there came a rending noise that tore through the still air of the chamber and echoed thunderingly from the walls.

And out from within the stone, a black shadow swelled and grew into the dim light. At first there was no shape, just the impression of something impossibly black. It *drained* the light of the lantern that had toppled to the floor at the first movement, and then the darkness seemed to coalesce, to become solid.

The thing stopped, as if sensing, and then something that might have been a head swivelled, so slowly that the threat of it was magnified enormously, in her direction. Siobhan's lungs stopped working as her breath, even in the dream, backed up inside her and locked. The shape finished its slow turn, and in the blackness her heightened senses told her that huge eyes had flicked open and fastened upon her.

Suddenly her feet were unbound as the pressure snapped. She turned and dived for the entrance and ran down the tunnel. Behind her, she could sense the blackness following her, and she ran and ran and ran. Up ahead there was light, dim light, but enough to spur her on. The sound of her feet reverberated on the stones and pounded like a frightened heartbeat in her ears.

Then she was out into the daylight.

From behind, she heard a screech that sizzled and crackled through her like a rusty blade. Her momentum kept her going until she had reached the bottom of the hill. Sweat ran down her forehead, a cold, clammy sweat, and her heart was thudding so hard it was painful. Siobhan skidded to a halt and stopped at the entrance to the cottages, just before the cattle grid. She bent, as if she was about to be sick, then straightened and looked ahead of her, and her breath stopped again.

There was nothing in the field but smoking ruins where the cottages had been. And under her feet, the soil was red with blood.

She took a step backwards and her foot tripped over something hard that rolled away. She was falling, and from the corner of her eye, she saw what she'd fallen over. It was a human head, rolling in the dirt and covered with grit. A scream expanded in her throat and suddenly she woke up with such a start that Nancy, who had been curled next to her, fell into the vacant space.

'Whatsamatta?' she asked sleepily, but Siobhan, with her scream of fright still locked in her throat, was unable to speak.

26

The scale of the devastation became apparent after daylight broke on a strangely calm day in the west of Ireland. The storm had fizzled out quickly as it passed over the coast and headed inland.

In the cottage rented by Tom and Nancy Ducain the slumbering crush of people came awake slowly, though Siobhan Kane, launched out of the slumber by the force of the dream, had only managed to doze fitfully in the aftermath. Professor Connarty was last to wake, and he had to be shaken several times by a concerned Agnes until he finally came round. His bright blue leprechaun eyes had lost their sparkle and much of their colour. As soon as he opened them he screwed them closed again quickly and both hands went to his temples.

'Whatever it was I was drinking last night, I've given it up for good,' he moaned.

'Heard that a million times, and still we wait for the miracle,' Terry said, though he looked just as worse for wear.

Somebody opened the curtains, and the bright light of mid-morning bolted through. There was a muted moan from Connarty and some sniggers from the younger members of the motley group. A few crowded at the window and looked out. The lake that the field had been last night was gone, and the grass was back, though it was littered with stones and seaweed and mounds of flotsam deposited by the receding waters.

Sean was out of the cottage first, and he stopped, breathing in the cold salt air. 'What a mess,' he said, stretching the stiffness out of his limbs.

Siobhan, on his left, pointed to the jumble of logs and branches and tree-roots covering the track up to the village. 'Look at that,' she said. 'They've been lifted right out of the ground.'

'If it wasn't for them breaking the force of it, we wouldn't be here now,' Sean said. 'That must have been some wave.'

'Do you think it's just as bad all over?' Liz asked.

'Probably. Now you've got a real story to write about. Intrepid reporter survives tidal wave shock horror drama,' he said, and Liz gave him a dig in the ribs.

'Once you get your film back from the chemist's, of course,' she retorted.

The pair of them squelched across the track while Sean automatically unhitched his camera and started shooting frame after frame in every direction. Right in front of their cottage, Liz stumbled over the flopped carcass of a large cod that had been swept in on the wave and left to die flapping on the grass. Nearby, a small sapling that had withstood the rush of water was festooned with an odd red netting. It was only when Sean inspected it that he discovered the big jellyfish that had become ensnared in the branches, its tentacles trailing down from the tree onto the ground.

The damage in the cottage was less than they expected. The water had come up only a couple of feet, and while the floor was sodden and slick with mud, it was tiled and would eventually clean. The beds were sodden, and Sean hauled them out to the flagstones outside, propping them up on the wooden chairs to dry out in the breeze and the sun.

'We can't stay here,' Liz said when she saw what he was doing.

'Probably not,' he agreed. 'But everybody will be in the same boat. We might as well help. There's probably fifty places worse off than this, and there might be nowhere else to stay. I don't want to take the chance, and I do want to take pictures. We should make this place liveable just in case.'

Liz saw the logic and began to help.

Of all the cottages, the one the oilmen were using as a base for their fishing trip was perhaps the worst affected, but they seemed to care the least. Within minutes they had almost the whole of the building cleared, tables, chairs and all. Frank Wysocki found a hose that had been used in the summer for the flower-beds that separated the cottages, and was getting the mud from the floors and walls, while the other two brushed the muck and water out through the front door.

Once Sean and Liz were satisfied that they had done all they could, they opened all the doors and windows and let the strong breeze gust through. The peats were sodden, but there was so much wood about that had been scoured up from the shore, and from the broken-off branches of the trees that had been felled, that it didn't take long to get a fire blazing that soon began to warm the cottage. Once they'd done that, they managed to get the cooker going again and had a quick hot breakfast before Sean got his gear and went out to take pictures.

They walked down to the quay first and found nothing there, not even a trace of where the old stone construction had been. The wave had simply lifted it up and thrown it away. Sean clicked the shutter time and again, taking in the torn-up hedgerows and the high-tide mark that had left a dirty rim only feet from the top of the two hills that shouldered onto the bay. All around them seabirds were wheeling and screaming as they fought for the bounty of shellfish, crabs and other fish that had been left, a banquet for them on the land.

'You never stop,' Liz said eventually.

'Stop what?'

'Taking pictures. It's always the first thing you think of.'

'Sometimes the last thing I think of. Especially late at night,' he said, and grinned over at her. She blushed, and he was surprised how girlish it made her.

'But ever since I met you,' she continued, despite her momentary embarrassment, 'you've been taking pictures. You must have shot dozens.'

'About two hundred and twenty frames,' he said quickly. 'So far.'

'Why so many?'

'It's my job.'

'No. It's more than that.'

'Well, I told you already, it's my main interest as well. I work in light. That's my speciality. Just getting the light to draw pictures. There's magic in that. Never fades.'

It was not long after noon when they made their way up to the village. In daylight, it was not difficult to negotiate the obstacle course presented by the fallen trees and ripped-up hedges. At night it would have been dangerous, and even now, it would be impossible to get the car up the track.

Kilgallan was strangely quiet, although there was not much evidence of damage. There was a hole a yard wide in the roof over the funeral undertaker's parlour and the pavements were littered with shards of slates that had been whipped off the row of houses. Further down the road there was a red mess of crumpled metal where Finn Finnerty's barn had been flattened right across the street, but apart from that, the village had got off lightly.

They met one of the locals in the newsagent's shop that was open for business as usual. The cheery woman behind the counter welcomed them and volunteered that it had been a murderous night.

'Never seen a storm like it in my whole life, so I never,' she added. Sean agreed with her. He asked if she had any of the morning's papers left, though he had worked in the trade long enough to surmise that the freak wave had come too late for the morning editions.

'Not a one, and there won't be for a while, not with the bridge gone,' she said.

'What bridge?' Liz asked.

'Why the only one, dearie. The Roonah Bridge was washed away last night. They said it just broke itself in two halves and it took down the telephone lines as well, though we've still got the electric.'

'You mean the road's not there any more?'

'No road at all. Sure, and didn't Peter O'Neill break his leg up there last night in the middle of it all? My man was out there this morning and there was a Garda in a car on the other side of the stream with a loudspeaker, asking us if we were all right. Said Westport took a fair old hammering and all over the coast there's houses been knocked down. I was on my knees all of last night, and the Holy Mother answered all my prayers.'

All this was delivered in a rush in the woman's rolling west-coast brogue, as if she couldn't wait to tell somebody all her news.

'You'll be staying here for a while then,' she declared rather than asked, and Sean shrugged his shoulders.

'Not unless there's another road out of here.'

The woman shook her head. 'Only goes as far as old Tallabaun and down to the shore.'

'Then I think we should revise our estimates,' Sean said. He'd only bought a couple of packets of cigarettes. He picked up an empty carton from the floor and started picking tins of food from the shelves. When the box was brimming over, he paid the woman and the two of them left.

'That's enough for a week,' Liz said. 'We can't stay here that long.'

'We might have to,' he said.

'But what about the story? And the pictures? We have to get it out.'

'If I could, I would,' he said agreeably. 'But if the bridge is down and there's no other road, then there's not much we can do. Anyway, the story will still be valid when we do get out. In the meantime, every photographer in Ireland will be up in a helicopter taking pictures. If the whole coast got it, they'll declare a national emergency.'

Sean was right, as they discovered further along the street. Donovan's doors were wide open. The bar was filled with people, both locals and a number from the cottages.

The television set was blaring from a high shelf in the corner. All eyes were fixed upon it and occasionally one of the throng would let out an exclamation of wonder or awe.

'Look at that now, that's Newport, though you'd never know it.'

The cameraman, flying overhead in a helicopter, panned across a swathe of fallen trees and crushed buildings, then zoomed in close. The reporter kept up a running commentary, outlining the extent of the

282

damage, naming, in one sentence, more than half a dozen coastal villages that had been hit by the freak wave.

The scene flicked over to a studio, where an expert was asked what had caused it. He confirmed Professor Connarty's view that this had indeed been a massive surge of water caused by seismic activity far out in the ocean. Three stations had picked up the underground pulse and they were able to identify the epicentre of the underwater blast. A computer graphic was shown next to explain how the whole thing had been caused, and that did nobody in Donovan's bar any good. They had *been* there. Been in the middle of it, they said, though in truth they had been damned lucky that the full force of the wave had missed them. Kilgallan didn't even rate a mention on the news. That, and the luck, was about to change.

'Biggest story of my life, and I can't even get it out,' Liz complained when the news finally finished.

'You can write the film script,' Sean said jokingly.

Brian Cooney and his companions hadn't bothered to do more than let their cottage drain out, because they had been preparing to pull out long before dawn. It had been their intention to load the boxes into the van and drive off immediately, but the storm had prevented that. After hearing of the devastation along the coastal roads, they all agreed that not setting off in the middle of it had been the best thing. Their route north would have taken them along those same roads and they would have been caught in the monstrous surge of water. Still, the news that the road had been cut off was a blow.

'We're stuck here until they get the bridge back up,' Cooney said.

'But that could take weeks,' John Boyle retorted. 'We can't stay here with that lot for long,' he said with a jerk of his head to indicate the loft space. 'It's too risky. And we don't want anybody poking around here, that's for sure.'

'Nobody's likely to be doing that now. Everybody's in the same boat. Look at last night. They were all just pleased to be out of the wet.'

'Me as well,' John said. The memory of the trip in the small boat coming round the Point in a screaming gale was bad enough, but even worse was the recollection of waking in the middle of the night with water splashing over him as he lay in a sleeping bag on the living-room floor.

'We'll have to sit tight,' Bridget stated firmly. 'Sure, we can't even get the van up the road to the village for all them trees that came down. But nobody else is moving out either. We'll have to make the best of it.'

'Just as long as we get out as soon as we can,' John Boyle said. 'I want those things off my hands. I don't fancy twenty in the Maze.'

'None of us wants that, and it's not going to happen. Nobody knows a thing,' Cooney said reassuringly. 'Sure, even if we have to help ourselves, we'll clear those trees from the road, and I'll bet you they throw a couple of spans over that wee stream to make a crossing in no time. Remember, the whole place is cut off from the rest of the world, and when the baker's van can't get through it's amazing how quick they'll get things sorted out.'

'And it'll be even quicker when the beer truck gets stopped at the bridge,' Seamus said with a laugh. 'These fellows like their Guinness fine.'

'Right. There's no panic,' Cooney said. 'What do you think yourself, Bridie?'

'Same as you. As long as we're careful. John and Seamus better be my cousins just passing through and getting caught by the storm. I don't want anybody thinking anything odd's going on. I think most of the lot around here are harmless, though I'm not too comfortable around those birdwatchers. One of them scared the hell out of me round the back of the house the other night.'

'What was he doing round there?' Seamus O'Farrell asked.

'Looking for night birds. I heard a cough or something and there he was. Said there was a nightjar around. I heard the thing hooting, so he was probably telling the truth.'

'We'll keep an eye on them. The archaeologists are all right, and those Americans too, unless they've brought in the CIA,' Cooney said, and Boyle grinned at that one. 'I'm not sure about the three fellows who say they're here for the fishing.'

'Oh, come on now,' Bridget said. 'Weren't they all talking about the big flatfish they caught yesterday? They wouldn't be out there fishing if they were watching us, now would they?'

'I suppose not, but you can't be too careful.'

The three subjects of the conversation had made a good job of cleaning out their cottage, and there were two reasons for that. They were used to working together on the rigs in heavy weather, and muck and water never bothered them. Also, they had booked the cottage for another five days, and what they most wanted to do was to get back to their fishing.

Like Sean and Liz and the other inhabitants of the cottages, they had collected and stoked the fires up to blast as much heat through the rooms as possible, while putting on the back boilers at full vent until the radiators were almost red-hot. Around their cottage, their gear and bedding was hung on ropes or suspended from sticks of wood they'd driven into the soggy ground to drip dry in the fresh wind. Their perimeter looked like a boy scout camp that had been rained out, but for all that, the three of them were enjoying themselves. They reckoned that they'd be able to resume their fishing by the following morning.

Meanwhile, Nancy Ducain insisted on running a coffee service for everyone else because hers was the only place that didn't need to be wrung out. Despite the fact that she was on honeymoon, she too was enjoying the fun now that the emergency was over, and in any case, she was a practical girl who didn't mind mucking in with the rest.

Siobhan went with Professor Connarty and the rest of the team to inspect the damage at the tor. When they got there, the hillock and the diggings were a quagmire of mud, covered in fronds of dripping seaweed. They could see where the wave had come over the top of the man-made hill, because much of the turf had been scraped away, leaving raw earth-coloured wounds. The light had cut out, but Terry had his torch, and they all went up the corridor to look in the chamber. Halfway along the narrow passageway, Siobhan's dream suddenly came back to her in a powerful rush and she stopped dead in her tracks, instantly overcome with dread, with *déjà-vu*, but she struggled against it and shook her head to fling off the night shakes, and made her feet go on.

It was surprisingly dry inside the chamber. They could see where the wave had penetrated until it was a foot from the ceiling, and had gone no further. It was Terry who suggested that the weight of the water had compressed the air inside like an airgun. When the force of it was spent, the expansion had thrown the water right back down the tunnel again.

Siobhan made herself go right into the chamber and inspect the stone. Some wet bladders of dark wrack hung limply from its surface, but apart from that, there was no real evidence that the place had been inundated. She stood there beside the massive block and stared at the writings, again fighting *déjà-vu*. There, on the surface, were the lines of runes which she'd studied in the photographs and read in her dream. Somehow, in her sleep, her mind had played a game with the patterns and symbols, sorted them out, made sense of them. Now, as her eyes scanned the carvings, the meaning of them again leapt out at her as it had done in her dream, in sudden clear focus, easily legible.

It went in reverse order, from right to left, and her lips moved as she read the words again, this time seeing them for real.

She had been right after all.

There the story unfolded. The trapping of the *Shee*. The heroism of the five young men. The dreadful curse and the terrible warning. It was all there, carved in the stone, a powerful *geis*, a *taboo* against the breaking of the seal.

Immediately, her thoughts jumped back to the nightmare, and Siobhan backed away from the stone, as if expecting the surface to ripple and bulge; for some foul black shadow to heave its way out of the depths and into the chamber. But that didn't happen. Across on the other side, Terry, who had been scanning the flashlight over the four remaining niches to ensure they were still intact, caught the movement. He swung the beam onto Siobhan.

'What's the matter?' he asked.

'Nothing, Terry, I just slipped on some seaweed,' she said quickly. She didn't want to let them all know that she could read the meaning of the carvings. Not yet. She didn't know if she wanted to tell *anyone* what she'd read. That would take some careful thought.

One thing she did know was that this was no ordinary dig, no ordinary tomb.

In fact, and the realisation came upon her with the force of a blow in the back of her mind, this was no tomb at all. She now knew that for certain in an inexplicable, instinctive way. This was a prison, built to hold something ancient and terrible.

Overnight, Siobhan's faith in archaeology had been shaken to its roots. Last night she'd had a dream and she'd tried to shake off the insistent echoes of it all morning. But now a part of it had been confirmed.

Siobhan had heard all the tales of leprechauns and kelpies, of Cuchullain and the *Shee*, and she'd always put them down as the fanciful notions of the old primitive folk who lived in the bogs and huddled together against the dark night. Now it had all turned around inside her head. If they had built this place as a prison, then they'd believed in what they were doing.

Her eyes flicked towards the stone and gingerly she took two small steps until she was right before the stone block. There was no translucence now in its squat bulk. It was cold stone.

Yet the words incised on it, cut and carved to last for thousands of years, told what was here and how they had made it stay. They had put five men to guard it. So long as the tomb remained undefiled, she would sleep. As long as the land was above the sea, she would remain.

Abruptly Siobhan was rocked with another thought that almost took her breath away.

They *had* opened this place up to the light of day. And now, there were no longer *five* men to stand their dead vigil. Worse, for one appalling moment last night, this land had not been above the sea. The sea had risen up in a huge wave and covered the tor, drowned it with the ocean.

The stone was cold. There was no life in it. She stared at it, unable to drag her eyes away. There was no sense now, as there had been in her horrendous dream, of anything *inside* it.

The thought that kept hammering at the front of her brain, insistently thudding away like an alarm, was that whatever might have been in the stone, the *Babd*, the *Morrigan*, the *Shee*, whatever *had* been there, was no longer there.

For the most powerful *geis* she'd ever seen carved on a stone had been broken.

There was no evidence of it there, none that the eye, however trained, could see, but Siobhan suddenly knew with certainty, that something black and shadowy had come out of this stone. And she didn't know what on earth she was going to do about it.

27

All day long there had been the buzz of chainsaws and big two-handed whipsaws as men mucked in to clear the fallen trees. Out at the Roonah Bridge, broken-backed and upstream from where it had sat for centuries, some of the farmers had dragged straight trunks behind their tractors with the idea of making a temporary bridge over the now less-swollen stream. Finn Finnerty's crushed barn had been scraped off the main road by his neighbour, who simply hooked a hawser from barn to lorry and dragged, helped by another neighbour shoving from behind with the tines of the shit-shovelling scoop on his ancient red tractor. It made a noise like a pig-sticking party as the tangled metal scoured the road.

During the day there was the kind of camaraderie that always surfaces when there's emergency work to be done, and despite the damage to the roofs and some of the outlying houses, humour ran high, possibly because the television pictures showed villages much worse off than Kilgallan. Everybody had a story to tell about slates which narrowly missed folk in the street, the chimney-pot that came crashing through the roof and landed in the empty pram, and a couple of kids had a wonderful time chasing a large edible crab with a shell more than a foot wide that had been found, fully half a mile from the sea, scuttling along the road.

Old Milo Cullen, the parish priest, past retirement age and deafer than the old gravestones that stood aslant in the little churchyard, opened the doors for early mass in the morning, and looked out to find the whole town up and awake and clearing debris.

'Holy Mary and all the saints,' he called out to the only two parishioners who had bothered to turn up to the service. 'What the devil's been going on to make such a mess?'

The old soul had slept through the whole thing.

Peter O'Neill fretted in his bed, unable to move because of the massive plaster cast that encased him from ankle to hip, courtesy of Chris Brannigan the vet. Dr O'Brien had forced him to take painkillers and ordered him to stay where he was, threatening him with dire consequences of gangrene and amputation if he so much as tried to sit up.

The incomers living in the cottages were the centre of attention when it was discovered that the wave had actually reached them and flooded them out. There was no shortage of offers of drying and laundry work. Apart from the lock on the oilmen's door, which had snapped off with the weight of water, their cottage now looked the least affected, thanks to their teamwork. They wanted nothing further to spoil their fishing.

Professor Connarty had gone along to see Mike O'Hara at the Tallabaun Inn to try to get a room for the next couple of days because, of all the archaeologists, he least liked roughing it. There was no reply, and the professor recalled that the hotel was closing down for the winter season, so he thought nothing of it. Beside that, he was still flattened by a monumental hangover, and what he really wanted was to lie in a dry bed all day long and get rid of it. There was no respite for him, so, later on, he simply chose to combat it with more of the same medicine.

It was close to five o'clock when Fidelma Brogan, the cook, who had been visiting her sister's farm two miles over the moor, came back to the hotel, and another hour before she found what had happened to Mike O'Hara and young Marie Lally.

She had come bustling into the kitchen and clicked her tongue when she saw the oven was out and the fire cold in the grate. She knocked on O'Hara's office door and got no response, so she simply busied herself in putting her kitchen in order. At nine, there was still no sign of either of them and, with the big soup pot bubbling on the stove and a massive steak pie going crusty in the oven, she wandered through to the extension.

Through the big convex lenses that magnified her eyes to twice their normal size, Fidelma at first couldn't make out what she was seeing when she switched on the light. There was an odd metallic smell in the air and a jumble of things lying on the bed, and for an instant she thought that Marie, normally a tidy girl, had just dumped all her clothes on it. She clicked her tongue again, irritated, preparing to give the girl a piece of her mind, when she saw, sticking out whitely from the red-and-brown jumble, a leg that ended in a small foot.

Still unsurprised, she walked towards the bed, and the tangled mass leapt into focus, though it was another several long moments before Fidelma's brain registered what her eyes told her.

She stood there for almost half a minute, mouth opening and closing without any sound at all coming out, eyes bulging hugely behind the thick lenses, then slowly backed away until she finally came up against the wall. The sudden bump seemed to give her back the power of decision and she turned and grabbed the handle of the door that had swung closed. Her fingers slipped on the round brass knob, and when she pulled, the door refused to open.

That was when the scream made it out of her throat. For a second of pure terror, Fidelma imagined herself stuck in a locked room with the nightmare tangle of bodies on the bed, and her screech soared high enough to make the windows rattle in sympathy. Amazingly, the handle turned at her second frantic grab, and with a strength born of sheer fright, Fidelma wrenched it open so hard it slammed against the wall and the doorknob dug a half-inch hole in the plasterwork.

Still in her slippers, and with her paisley-pattern apron flapping in the night air, Fidelma came streaking down the middle of the road, a rotund little bundle, arms waving in front of her, and screaming fit to wake the dead. Doors opened, neighbours looked out of windows as she went screeching past their homes, running straight for the Garda station.

Tim O'Brien was there, checking upon the policeman when Fidelma burst in, wailing like a *banshee*, and flung her considerable weight on top of Peter O'Neill, who let out such a roar of surprise and pain that the doctor thought she'd broken the plaster cast and separated the broken ends of the bones. She hadn't. Dr O'Brien hauled her off the bawlng policeman and got her to her feet. She babbled incoherently for at least a minute before her eyes rolled up hugely behind the glasses and she fainted right away.

'Whatever's got into the woman?' he asked, while Peter groaned on the bed. 'Has she taken a sudden fancy to you or something, Peter?'

'Silly old bloody bitch,' the policeman said, quite uncharacteristically. With a massive effort he reached for the cabinet beside the made-up sofa bed and brought out a bottle of whiskey.

'I wouldn't take that with painkillers,' Tim said, as he bent down to the prostrate woman.

'Stuff your painkillers up your arse,' Peter said vehemently, and with a swift motion unscrewed the top, put the bottle to his lips, and didn't stop until he had taken three or four good swallows.

Dr O'Brien brought Fidelma round in the usual medical fashion, by slapping her face a couple of times with the flat of his hand, a method much appreciated by Peter, whose hip was pulsing objections to the old cook's collision. Finally the woman managed to get up to a sitting position and the doctor helped her to a chair. She seemed to be unaware of what was happening, and then her eyes flew open and she started screaming again.

'Oh, for mercy's sake, give her something to shut her gob,' Peter bawled. 'Can't she see I'm a sick man?'

It took more than fifteen minutes to get any sense at all from the old woman, but finally her hysterical babbling began to slow down and separate into individual words.

'Dead. The both of them. On the bed,' she told them.

'Who would that be now, Fidelma?' Dr O'Brien asked soothingly.

'It's Mr O'Hara, and the wee girl. Oh, Doctor. There's blood all over the place, and Mr O'Hara . . . his . . . his . . .'

Fidelma's eyes rolled up again until the whites filled the lenses and the blood drained right out of her face. The doctor eased her down into the soft chair and left her.

'There's been some sort of accident,' Peter said. 'Is that what she's saying?'

'Sounds like it. I'd better go and check.'

'Damn this gammy leg of mine. I've never had such bad luck in my whole life.'

'Don't move out of there,' Tim warned him sternly, snapping the hasp on his black bag. 'I'll be back as soon as I can.'

He went towards the door.

'What about her?' Peter asked, pointing at the old woman. 'You can't just leave her here with me.'

'She won't come to any harm.'

'Sure it's not her I'm worried about,' Peter bawled furiously. 'She nearly broke my other damned leg.'

Dr O'Brien smirked and left the room. From the front door, he called back: 'I'll get Agnes next door to come in and watch after the pair of you.'

The story buzzed around Donovan's bar less than an hour after that. The place was filled to overflowing, because, apart from the church hall, it was the biggest room in the village, and besides, nobody could get a drink at all off old Father Cullen. It seemed every man, and a few of the women, had gathered in the big bar just to exchange the news and views over the day's events.

Dr O'Brien had stopped a couple of the men who were working at clearing off the wreckage of Finn's farm and brought them along with him to the Tallabaun Inn, which was just a hundred yards or so along the road. He wasn't sure what to expect, though he thought it possible that Mike O'Hara or the girl, or possibly both, might have been injured by a falling roof or some other storm damage. Old Fidelma was too overwrought to have made any real sense, and probably didn't know what she was talking about in any case.

Nothing he had ever seen prepared him for what he stumbled into when he opened the door at the end of the narrow corridor.

For a medical man who had delivered half the village into the world and had carried out emergency surgery many a time on the usual range of farmhand wounds, Tim was confident he'd a strong stomach. It wasn't as strong as he imagined.

He stood there, much as Fidelma had done, staring at the mess on the bed, at first puzzled by the red-and-brown jumble, and then he realised what he was seeing.

Mike O'Hara, completely naked, was lying on top of the girl in a stiff parody of the missionary position. Her legs were curled up and around his hips, feet pressing into the small of his back, and her hands were clasped onto his head. The girl was almost in a sitting position, neck arched and head brought forward as if she was at the height of an orgasm. That was where the comparison with sexual congress ended. For the whole front of Mike O'Hara's head was gone. There was blood spattered all over them in such profusion that the pair were drenched in a thick, congealing mass that made them look as if they were rusted.

There was nothing left of O'Hara's frontal bone from below his eye sockets to the crown of his head. Instead there was a wide crater from which flesh and bone slivers and brains had dripped and oozed, and in the crater was Marie Lally's face, buried up to the cheeks. Her mouth was hugely agape, and filled, as Dr O'Brien discovered later, with what had been the front of O'Hara's head and most of his cerebral cortex. But what was even more horrifying – the thing that rocked O'Brien back in disgust and horror – was the fact that her eyes were open. They stared out of her, like the eyes of a ravening animal, wide and glaring, frozen in the dreadful act of feasting on the hotel owner.

Dr O'Brien backed out of the room and stumbled into the kitchen, where he was quickly and most violently sick into the sink. The two farmhands, who had wandered into the room from curiosity after the doctor shoved his way past them, soon came rolling along the narrow corridor in similar fashion and regurgitated their latest meals.

The doctor was finally able to go back into the room and begin a clinical examination. Within half an hour he was able to make a preliminary report to Peter O'Neill, and by this time, word had got right round the village.

The Garda wanted to send somebody into Westport, until it was pointed out that the bridge was still broken and the river too high to cross. The telephone lines that had come down when the electricity pylon crashed against the pole meant they couldn't telephone for the emergency services. Furious at his incapacity, Peter reached again for the whiskey bottle. This time Tim O'Brien didn't warn him about

292

drinking on top of painkillers. Instead he took the bottle from Peter's hand and, medical man that he was, didn't even wipe the neck with his hand before pouring a large amount of it down his own throat.

Nobody but the doctor and the policeman had any idea of exactly what had happened to the hotel owner and the girl, and even those two could hardly believe that Marie Lally had died of strangulation and that O'Hara had died because she had started to *eat* his head off.

But in Donovan's bar that night, the place was buzzing about how they'd been found naked on the bed and covered in blood, battered to death. There was some speculation that the girl's father had done it, though he lived twenty miles away, and if nobody could get out of the village, nobody could get *in* just to murder a couple of folk. There was a suggestion that there might be a jealous boyfriend, but since everybody in town knew everybody else's business, they couldn't come up with anybody who had been seeing the plump little chambermaid, and if they had, what on earth they would have to be insanely jealous about, nobody could figure out.

Both of the bodies had been carried out, under sheets, to Patsy McGavigan's undertaker's parlour, which was the only place to store bodies anyway, and left on the slab in the cold room. Dr O'Brien knew he'd have to do an autopsy with the facilities he had on hand and didn't relish it, but that was his duty. The pathologist down in Galway could do another one later. While everybody was picking over the bones of the story in Donovan's bar, Tim was picking over the opened cadavers in McGavigan's and wishing he had one of those hand-held recorders that they had in the movies. It took him a couple of hours, though he was no expert in this sort of thing, but he was able to ascertain the causes of death. That wasn't the puzzle. What he couldn't understand was *why* it had happened. Most of all, what his tired brain couldn't fathom out was how a sixteen-year-old girl could bite her way through the thick skull on the front of Mike O'Hara's head. Not only that, she had done so while he was *alive* as the amount of blood indicated . . . after she herself had been strangled. It seemed as if O'Hara had killed her . . . and *then* let her begin to feed on him.

There was nothing, Tim thought, in all the medical books that came anywhere close to explaining that. He thought he might have missed something, but he *knew* he hadn't. Finally, he turned and took off his white coat that was now as bloody as a butcher's apron. He scrubbed his hands until they were red and nipping from the carbolic soap and then left McGavigan's, after covering the bodies again with plastic sheeting.

He decided to go back down to the little police house and help Peter O'Neill finish the bottle.

Finally Donovan got his bar emptied, much later than usual, and everyone, many of them tired after the day's exertions, started to find their way home. The chainsaws had done a good job on the tangle that had blocked off the road down to the cottages, and as Sean, Liz and a few of the others strolled down, the pale circles on either side showed where trunks had been cut away to allow them to pass.

It was a cloudless night and the moon was high in the sky, only a shaving away from being full. Sean and Liz said goodnight to Tom and Nancy and then called over to where Terry Munster was wending his way, with the two Ulstermen he'd been drinking with in the bar, towards his cottage. Professor Connarty had gone home earlier, claiming he'd done enough damage to his liver. Siobhan and the other two girls hadn't even gone up to Donovan's that night.

The cottage still smelled of sea water, but was fairly dry. Sean had stuck a couple of large logs on the fire before they'd gone out and they were still crackling in the grate, sending out waves of heat. Liz made milky coffee and they both sat on the slate kerb by the fire, disdaining the still-damp armchairs, slowly sipping their drinks.

'What should we do?' Liz said finally

'I think we should go to bed,' Sean replied, turning to look at her.

'No, silly. What about getting out of here?'

'What's the rush?'

'Well, I want to file copy. We've two good stories.'

'Three, if you count what's supposed to have happened to that man at the hotel, and the girl.'

'Oh yes. And to think I wanted to stay there.' Liz gave a little shiver.

'Here it just gets wet,' Sean said.

'Seriously, we should contact the office. And I don't think I want to stay here any more. This place is beginning to give me the creeps.'

Sean looked at her over the edge of his cup. 'Really? Why?'

She shrugged her shoulders. 'Nothing in particular. It's just like . . .' She searched for the phrase. 'Like something out of *Harvest Home*.'

'I read that. Good book.'

'That's what this place reminds me of. Those men out on the moor. And last night. And now we're incommunicado. We can't even get out of here.'

'Not unless you want a swim and a long walk. But they're working on getting the bridge fixed up. It should only be a day or two.'

'I don't know. There's something *wrong* here.'

'Nonsense,' Sean said as confidently as he was able. Yet her words resonated with thoughts he himself had been trying to ignore.

The sensation of *not-right* had sneaked up on him and taken him by surprise from time to time in the past day or so. The dreams were part of it. They hadn't stopped at all; they had increased, and ever since he'd driven across the border and into the Republic, they'd been changing into weird fantasies, too. More and more, they left him drained and washed out and unable to sleep after he woke up in a sweat. And they left him with a feeling of foreboding, of prescience.

That was only part of it, of course. The rest, the *weirdness*, was something that was too vague to identify positively. But there was *something* in the air that only very recently had brought a new sense of *threat*.

'Just a day or two more, and then we're out of here,' he said.

He drained his cup and stood up, stretching, and took the other cup from Liz's hands. She got up from the kerb and put an arm around his waist.

'I still don't like it,' she said, bringing her other arm up to cuddle into him. 'I don't want to sleep by myself tonight.'

'Good idea,' Sean replied, bending to drop a kiss on the top of her head. 'I won't feel safe unless you're with me.'

She dropped a hand and dug him in the ribs. 'Cocky bastard,' she said. He left both cups on the mantelpiece and they made their way towards his room.

In a nearby cottage, Tom and Nancy Ducain cuddled into each other, still warm and perspiring after an energetic hour together.

Beyond, in the next little house, Siobhan was poring over the photographs of the inscriptions. She'd stayed in the cottage all afternoon and evening, writing out the translations. She still hadn't told the professor, and didn't know when she would. She drank cup after cup of coffee, knowing that she wouldn't sleep that night. In Siobhan, more than anyone, the feeling of foreboding was a dull, dark threat. No matter how she looked at the inscriptions, the translation was always the same. She *knew* she was right in this, knew it with absolute certainty. And another part of her, a part that perhaps had been inherited down through the generations in some sort of genetic memory, knew that there was something badly *wrong*, that they had opened something best left alone. Siobhan drank more coffee because she did not *want* to fall asleep. She was afraid of what the night might bring.

Out beyond the cottages, behind the stand of trees, Kilgallan started to fasten itself down for the night under the silvery glow of the nearly full moon. Doors were locked and barred, curtains were drawn and fires were banked up. Yet in every house, for a reason that no-one could have told, there was a vague unease. Here a child whimpered in its sleep. There an old man shivered against a cold draught that came from nowhere. In another place, a young wife jumped at a shadow, and in an attic room a farmhand got out of his bed and knelt against it to say his prayers, something he hadn't done since he was a boy.

The wind soughed under the eaves, and out of the moonlight dark shadows gathered and crowded in the corners and under the branches of the trees.

Kilgallan huddled against the night.

For some there would be no sleep.

Down at the west end of the village, between the Tallabaun Inn and the stone wall of Finn Finnerty's now deserted farm, Sinead Boyle was knitting by the side of the fire. Opposite, her husband was quietly trying to read a book, though both of them knew it was just a pretence. Upstairs, their burgeoning family were in their beds, and downstairs, between them, there was the other child. Not in person, for little Mickey was under the old churchyard, but Mickey was still *there*, an almost palpable presence in the space between them.

Sinead's needles clicked staccato as she made row after row of a pullover she was knitting for one of the girls. Her fingers worked automatically. Her mind was elsewhere, cuddled around the memory of her lost son. At times, she could *feel* him; and she saw him in the tilt of her husband's head, in the freckles that her other children had, in the eyes that stared back at her from the mirror. Sinead knitted late and Danny Boyle pretended to read, and little Mickey stood between them, forcing them away from each other, yet binding them together in the despair of it.

It was past midnight when the quiet knock came at the door. Danny looked up and glanced at the old brown clock that sat solidly on the fireplace.

'Who's that?' he asked.

Sinead had been far away in her thoughts. She looked up as though hardly aware that he had spoken, and the rap on the front door came again.

'Who can that be at this time of the night?' he asked. He laid his book on the mantelpiece and Sinead put down her knitting. She stood to go to the door, but he stepped in front of her and put a hand on her shoulder.

'I'll get it,' he said, and the way he said it told her that he should go to the door this late at night, especially after the terrible thing that had happened in the hotel.

She nodded, but followed him through to the dark little lobby. He slid back the bolt, turned the latch and pulled the door inwards. It was dark on the doorstep and Sinead put on the light. A beam was cast out into the small garden beyond.

An old woman stood there, hunched up in a shawl against the cold night air.

'Yes?' Danny said.

'Oh, bless you, son. I wonder if you could be helping me?' The woman looked frail and held a black headscarf tight, her scrawny hand clutching the ends of it near her neck. 'I can't get back home over the bridge, and I don't know what to do.'

Danny stood at the door, puzzled. He'd never seen the old woman before.

'I was visiting my sister's house, and it's gone. The sea took it away. And now I don't know what to do.'

'Oh, you poor soul,' Sinead said. If the old woman had come along the road, she could only have been at one of the outlying crofts down at the far end of the Killadoon road. And she must have walked for miles.

'What a terrible thing,' Sinead went on, almost pushing Danny out of the doorway. 'Come away in, now,' she said, putting an arm around the old woman's bony shoulders. She bustled back into the house, propelling her, from behind, into the kitchen, the room still warm from the heat of the old range where she'd cooked the family's meal.

She sat the woman down and put a kettle on to boil. 'You must be frozen stiff, coming all that way,' she said. 'And starving too, no doubt.'

Danny stood at the kitchen door for a moment then went to join them. 'You say the house is gone?'

The old woman nodded, her rheumy eyes filling with tears. 'I don't know where,' she wailed softly.

'And what's your name now, missus?'

The old woman looked up at him, the picture of misery, and her eyes took on a bewildered look.

'I . . . I . . . can't remember that,' she said. 'I can't remember anything but the long road here.'

'Oh, Daniel, she's had a terrible time, the poor woman has. You go and sit in the room and I'll fix her up something hot, and you can ask all the questions you want when we've some hot tea in her.'

Danny shrugged. It was odd to have anybody come knocking on the

297

door at this time, and an old, confused woman wandering on a cold night near wintertime was odder still. But she *was* old, and she *was* confused, and for a minute or two, he'd seen the empty look drain away from Sinead's face as her heart went out to somebody who might be suffering worse than herself. He went back into the room and sat by the fire. From the kitchen he could hear the sound of women's voices.

Sinead made tea, heated a couple of scones for a minute or two on the range, and poured two cups from the big black pot. She placed one down in front of the old woman and sat down next to her at the kitchen table.

'It's a terrible thing you're telling us,' she started off encouragingly. The visitor took the cup in both thin, arthritic-looking hands and drank gratefully. When she put the cup down she looked up at Sinead.

'Troubles. Only troubles wherever I go. But I'm fine now for the heat inside me, and grateful to yourself for a welcome on a cold night.'

'Don't you bother yourself about that, mother,' Sinead said. 'I'll be sending Danny down the road to fetch the doctor for you, for you'll be needing looking after.'

'No. I'll be fine now. It's yourself who needs a help, I'm thinking.'

Sinead sat back, surprised. The old woman fixed her with her watery eyes.

'You've had troubles yourself, I can tell,' the woman said in a high-pitched cracked voice. 'You've the sorrows written all over you, have you not? I can tell, for I've the sight.'

Sinead leaned forward. 'I don't understand what you're saying, missus.'

'Oh yes. You've had the sorrows, lady. You've lost a part of your heart and soul, have you not?'

Taken aback, Sinead merely nodded numbly.

'A wee boy, I'm feeling. A wee boy lost in the water?'

'Yes. I did. How did you know that?' Sinead's voice had descended to a shaky whisper.

'I've the sight, so I have. And I'm seeing that you'll have your boy back again.'

'No. That's not true,' Sinead whispered, drawing back from the old woman. The watery eyes fixed on her, looking right into her.

'Oh yes. You'll have your Mickey back again,' the woman said, her voice getting louder. There was something in the tone of the voice, in the look in the eyes, despite the fact that the tiny woman was ancient and frail. Suddenly threat seemed to stream out from her.

Sinead pushed her seat back. 'I want no more of this, old woman,' she said, her voice catching in her throat. 'You just drink your tea now and we'll be getting the doctor for you.'

She couldn't keep her eyes off the wizened face as she backed away out of the kitchen door. In the hall she turned and went into the living room.

'Danny, you'll have to go and get the doctor.'

'Why, what's happened?'

'Nothing, except I think she's a wee bit touched. A bit looney. She's talking a whole lot of nonsense and I don't want her here.'

'It was yourself who brought her in,' Danny protested.

'And it's myself who'll put her back out again if I have to. Get your coat on and get O'Brien.'

Danny slung his book down on the chair and turned to go to the door, and just as he did so, a voice came from the kitchen.

'*Mother*,' was the only word that was spoken, soft and plaintive, and it was enough to drill both of them through their hearts. Danny Boyle froze in mid-step; Sinead felt the blood drain out of her face.

'*Daddy*.'

Little Mickey's voice, almost a sob, came calling from the kitchen. The room spun about Sinead in a wave of dizziness that made her think she would faint, and Danny was frozen where he stood.

Simultaneously, they broke and ran for the door and along the short lobby to the kitchen, Danny ahead and Sinead, suddenly overwhelmed with a powerful dread, grabbing his shoulder, trying to pull him back.

Danny slammed the door open and stopped as if something had come up from the floor and thumped him a blow between the eyes. A little coughing noise came out of his opened mouth.

Mickey Boyle stood dripping onto the kitchen floor. He was naked, his hair was plastered to his forehead. He stood there pale, almost blue, and shivering. He looked exactly as he had done when Danny hauled him from the Roonah Water, except then he'd been limp and sightlesss. Now his face was pinched and distressed, while water dripped from his skinny frame.

Danny's mouth opened and closed several times while his son looked up at him, shivering. Finally Danny's voice escaped the lock on his throat.

'Mickey,' he breathed. He took a step forward, stopped, looked down at his boy. '*Mickey*.'

'Daddy, I'm *cold*,' the boy said. His voice came out in a sob again. Behind Danny, Sinead took all this in through wide, terrified eyes. The old woman was gone and now her son was here, alive and shaking with the cold. Her mind, as did her husband's, went into overload with the pain and shock and the frantic *need* to believe. Almost as one, without pausing to think, they moved forward in a rush. Danny scooped the boy up from the floor and clasped him in his arms, tightly hugging the little frame, clutching his son to his breast in an agony of *wanting*. Sinead reached for her boy and held on tight, pressing her warmth against his dread cold, willing her heat into him.

Their boy was here, and he was alive. It had all been some ghastly mistake, a terrible nightmare. They clutched and pawed at him, both shaking with the awesome force of the emotion, each unable to speak. Between them, the boy brought his arms up around his parents' shoulders, hugging them tight.

Tears streamed down Danny's face, tears of joy and bewilderment, tears of mad, soaring intoxication. He had his son back, and nothing else mattered, not even the mouldering smell that came off the child cradled between them. Sinead smelled it too, and for a second it cut into her blown-out consciousness. The odour of rotting meat was suddenly overpowering. She pulled back fractionally to gaze at her son, and in that instant her eyes widened and her mouth opened to scream.

She never got that far.

The child in their arms, the boy who was now holding on tightly to their necks, *changed*. The flesh cracked across his face and the shape of the skull twisted and writhed under the peeling dead skin. The weight between them was suddenly enormous, pulling them to the ground.

The arm around Sinead's neck grew hideously thick, clenched so tightly her breath was cut off. Danny blinked his tear-filled eyes, bewildered, and when his vision cleared he let out a sudden grunt of fear. Right next to his face, a loathsome apparition grinned at him from a narrow, pustular face that was dripping, not with water, but with rotting flesh. The arm around his neck squeezed tight and cut off sound before it started, and both the arms, now thick and gnarled like beech-tree roots, pulled together with astounding strength. Danny felt his feet being lifted clear off the ground as he was brought closer to the appalling face, then his face was pressed flat against Sinead's. For a mere second their mouths were forced together in an awful kiss, before the arms *flexed*. Danny Boyle and his wife were driven into each other. Their lips were forced back, their teeth clashed, and still the enormous pressure continued, grinding their skulls against one another. Sinead's nose popped and the bridge bone came through the skin: Danny's teeth broke off at the roots. Then a stupefying force cracked their skulls like eggshells. They were dead long before the motion stopped, their heads so completely merged that it looked as if there was only one crushed head serving two bodies.

The thing that had been the old woman and then the young boy, the *Shee* that had waited in the stone for an eternity, savoured the life force that drained from her victims, as she had savoured their grief and their fear, feasted on their horror. Finally she dropped them disdainfully to the floor and flitted out of the kitchen. She paused at the bottom of the stairs, considering whether to continue up and rampage among the hot life that she sensed there, slumbering in their huddle. Yet she stopped. Now was not the moment for that. She would banquet on the waves of terror and despair when they awoke to find what she had left cooling in the kitchen. And then, maybe another time, she would return when the harvest was ripe. The thing that looked like a shadow writhed and twisted and flowed out of the house and into the night. She stopped there under the moon and *sensed*, this way and that, before flicking off to the left like a fluttering black rag in the wind.

Maura Quinn was sleeping and dreaming. Beside her, Jack was snoring, but nobody heard it. Maura, cocooned in sleep, was smiling, for in her dream, she was lying in a warm field with the sunlight on her face, beside the banks of the tumbling Roonah Water.

Jack was somewhere near, throwing stones in the stream, while she was reclining against the bole of a tree with the baby nuzzling at her breast. She looked down at him, a little scrap of life, eyes tightly closed, with the shock of fine, silky dark hair spiked up where the slight breeze caught it. She was blissfully content in the safety of the dream where reality couldn't reach her. Here she was with her baby, warm and wanted, feeling his tiny gums suck on her nipple, sending waves of fulfilment shivering through her.

The dream went on and on until a cloud passed under the sun and sent a shadow fleeting over the field. The air grew chilly and she saw goose bumps coming out on her arms. The wind ruffled the baby's hair and he screwed his face up against the cold. The little mouth came away from her nipple with a soft popping sound and immediately opened to yell.

'Hush now, Jacky,' she crooned to him, and the wind blew colder. The clouds piled overhead and she knew it was going to rain.

The baby cried harder, struggling to find her nipple again. He started to scream and she cradled him close, rocking to hush his crying, but despite that, the tiny thing wailed even louder and louder until the noise filled the valley. Maura felt the panic rise up in her as the baby's screams, now sounding like screams of pain, built up until they hurt her ears.

Then she woke up in the bed. Jack had pulled the blankets off her in his sleep and her right side was goose-bumped with the cold. She pulled them back over her and turned on her side, careful not to crush the baby who was nuzzling at her breast. She cuddled down, with the child between her and her sleeping husband, and began to doze off again, dreamily enjoying the suckling.

Then she awoke with such a start she was sitting up before she knew it. Beside her, Jack grunted and rolled over.

Maura looked down, gasping with alarm. Her nightdress had been pulled down past her rounded breast, and the baby was greedily clamped on to her, his face red and his little jaws moving up and down. She could feel the pressure of his hungry suck.

Her arm was holding the tiny thing in to herself, as in the dream, and the feeling was the same, the same as the dream and the same as she had felt when she had fed Jacky before . . . *before* . . .

Maura's wail of anguish woke Jack instantly.

'What's wrong?' he asked sleepily. Ever since Maura had come back from the hospital, only a month before, she'd often woken in the middle of the night, sobbing in the aftermath of the dreams that beset her. He turned to face her, and froze when he saw the baby nuzzling at her breast.

'What on earth. . . ?' was all he managed to get out, twisting to kneel up and free himself from the sheets that entangled him, before Maura's scream suddenly rent the air. He jerked back, startled and Maura also threw herself backwards, hitting her head on the wall behind the bed. She was shoving at the thing at her breast, pushing at it, and all the while her screaming was terrifying.

The baby was suckling no longer. The tiny mouth had opened up in a gape and a double row of spiked teeth had clamped themselves right over her breast. And the baby had changed. No longer a small pink thing, it had changed colour to a dull, wet grey. Its skin was covered in warty lumps and it seemed to squirm and slide of its own volition. Great black hungry eyes rolled in the flattened head that was now fastened onto Maura's left breast, and in the split second that it took for Jack to turn and look, a stream of blood suddenly flowed from where they were clamped. '*Get it off me. Oh, GET IT OFF ME!*' Maura screeched as her legs and arms thrashed frantically. Her eyes were wide open and staring in a face contorted with shock and pain. Jack rolled himself across the bed, unable to take in what was happening, but instinctively grabbing at the horrible wriggling thing that was chewing at his wife, gurgling hungrily, and snorting from two wide nostrils between the flat, dead black eyes. He got two hands on its narrow, froglike hips and jerked at it, feeling the repulsive skin slip under his grip. He grasped tighter and, spurred by Maura's screams of agony, he heaved backwards.

There was a ghastly *tearing* sound and Jack tumbled, landing with a thud on the floor. The thing twisted in a slippery curling motion, squirming itself out of his hands, and scuttered up his arms. Its wide jaws were still chomping, a froth of red outlining the thick wide lips, and then it gulped something down its throat. In that instant, Jack saw its scrawny neck swell hugely and then subside as whatever it had swallowed was squeezed down by some dreadful peristalsis. He jerked back and the thing clambered in a blur up his arms and onto his shoulders. He saw the mouth gape as the dreadful flat face lunged at him, and he threw his head back from the jagged red teeth. As he did so, the thing dived again, this time for his neck. He felt no pain, just a dreadful squeezing pressure under his jaw. He heard a ringing in his ears and then a popping sound, followed by a far-off liquid hiss that quickly faded away.

Maura was consumed with pain. When her husband had pulled at the hellish thing, its jaws had clamped even tighter and she had felt the mandibles move from side to side, *sawing* the teeth into her skin. Her blood had splashed out from her chest when the nightmare creature was plucked away from her, and she had fallen, striking her head on the wall for a second time. The pain was an intense flare shooting up in a continuous stream from her chest and she cupped her hand to her breast.

She looked down, through glazing eyes, when her hand disappeared into a warm, wet crater. She screamed again, high and loud, in sheer horror. Her whole breast had gone.

The blood poured from the wound, drenching her torn nightdress, and pooled thickly between her legs. Dimly she was aware of Jack scuffling with the thing on the floor. Weakly she eased herself to the edge of the bed, just in time to see the grotesque creature scuttling up Jack's arms and the flat, bony head lunging for his neck. She heard the snap of jaws and the sudden pop, and stared as the life drained out of her husband's eyes.

She fell back, the room spinning around her. From down on the floor, beyond her line of vision, she heard snuffling, gobbling sounds and tried to raise herself in a desperate effort to fight for her man. But the effort was too great and the loss of blood too devastating. She slowly crumpled back on the wet bed and the room faded. The last thing she was aware of was the shocking gulping sounds as the thing swallowed.

28

The second day dawned cold and bright, with not a cloud in the sky, yet there was an odd silence about the place. It wasn't until just after dawn, when Pete Coia and Doug Petersen went down to the inlet from which the Roonah Water fed itself into the bay, that they realised the reason for the silence.

The tide was well out, leaving the expanse of mudflats exposed. Every day, when they had come here to dig rag and lugworms for bait, the flats had teemed with wading birds gorging themselves on the life that abounded in the silt exposed by the ebb. The two of them stood on the shingle beach and stared out across the bay. There was not a bird to be seen, either on the ground or in the air. It was as if there had been a sudden mass migration. The birds had simply left.

'Never seen anything like it,' Pete said.

'Too true, but it leaves more for us,' Doug replied. 'They've been robbing us blind every morning.'

The shingle and mussel beds gave onto a sandy shoreline where the swirl of the tides had formed a bar at the south of the inlet. Beyond the low sandbank the mudflats spread out for half a mile or more, dappled with the casts of silt-feeding creatures and empty oyster shells carried in on the rip. Doug and Pete dug for half an hour, collecting the fat black-and-red lugworms that filtered the sand for microscopic food and piled them in a slowly writhing mound in their bucket. Down at Gallan Bay they clambered over a tumble of stones, all that was left of the little jetty, and made their way out to the Point where the shoreline plunged down into deep green water.

They set up their beachcasters, skewered the fat worms onto hooks and then swung the rods to let the seven-ounce lead weights soar over the calm water and splash nearly two hundred yards out. Doug Petersen, taller than Pete by half a head, was able to cast a fair distance further, into even deeper water. The results of this extra distance became apparent only twenty minutes later when the Australian's rod started to quiver and then slowly bend forward as a sizeable cod took the hook and swam with it. He grabbed the butt and hauled away, cranking slowly at the multiplier reel at the end of every heave. Soon the fish was dragged through bladderwrack and fronds of kelp, and Doug hauled it, flapping and gulping, onto the beach.

'Five pounds easy,' he declared. 'I'll bet Frank won't match that.'

'I don't think he'll get anything down at Tallabaun Strand,' Pete said, though his own rod had shown no movement. 'Reckon the seabass will have shifted with that wave.'

'The big Polack thinks otherwise. He says the shit stirred up by the back-flow will have them there in droves. Don't believe it myself.'

Doug cast out again as soon as he had baited the hook, and within another few minutes he was heaving on the rod again.

Pete looked on enviously. Nothing was touching his bait. After an hour which saw his fellow angler bring in another two fish, he decided he'd have to change tactics.

'Lugs aren't working where I'm reaching,' he said.

'Why not try a bit to the left? I think it gets deeper.'

'Naw. It's the bait. You're getting to the cod, but nothing closer in wants lugs. I think they'll take ragworms.'

'Did we get any?'

'No. But it won't take me long to get enough.'

Pete wound in his line and left his rod standing wedged between two rocks on the shore. He clambered back to where the path was and picked up the large garden fork that he'd left sticking into the ground. On the way up the path that would take him round towards the flats, he looked back, just in time to see Doug's rod bend almost double as another fish took the bait.

'Bastard,' he said jealously.

Beyond the sandbar the flats were exactly that: flat, black and almost featureless, spreading and oozing out way beyond the north end of the inlet and far into the bay. Pete turned up the tops of his rubber boots and started out, using the fork for balance as the thick sludge made walking difficult.

About two hundred yards out from shore, he started to dig in a likely spot, covered with worm casts. Fishing is an odd game. You can catch dozens of fish one day and the next, when you use the same bait, you can get nothing. Pete, like every other angler since the sport began, knew that fish simply, and inexplicably, went off one kind of food.

The first forkful of mud and mussel shells exposed two big ragworms, each more than a foot long and as thick as a finger. They coiled and looped, their oily colours changing from red to purple and back again in a weird doppler refraction as their hundreds of cilia-like legs powered them through the silt. Pete picked up one and dropped it

306

into the bucket and then grabbed the other. It squirmed muscularly between his fingers and he watched while its head unfolded from within, like the eye of a snail, turning inside out. Finally the mouth was exposed and the two pincers on either side opened wide and then snapped together with a faint click as it tried to defend itself against capture.

'Feisty little bugger, aintcha?' Pete said, chuckling as he dropped this one into the bucket, where it immediately squirmed round and bit its neighbour.

He found two more a yard away, and then walked on to the next promising patch, digging at random and leaving behind a trail of small molehill-sized mounds that slowly subsided back into the featureless flats. The whole of the tidal plain was strangely quiet, devoid of life, and there was hardly a breath of wind. The slight mist that had drawn gauzy curtains over the bay when he and Doug arrived had dissipated under the morning sun, and far out he could see the sheen of the water twinkling lazily.

It was not until after half an hour of digging that Pete realised how far he'd walked out onto the expanse of mud. He turned and looked behind him and saw his footsteps, deep tracks in the mud, for a dozen or so yards behind him. The earlier ones had simply filled in, quickly oozing closed, leaving no trace of his passage. He hefted the bucket in his hand, estimating the weight, and guessed he had enough bait to last him through the day and well into the evening. Ragworms were a good taker. They were fat and had a strong, oily smell which attracted fish over a distance, and down in the depths where the sunlight never reached they had a natural luminescence that made them shine in the gloom. He might not be able to cast out as far as the Australian, Pete thought, but with the right bait, he wouldn't have to.

Pete started to retrace his few remaining bootprints and when he got to where they disappeared, he looked over at the sandbar, working out the best direction. The flats, while featureless on the surface, were far from uniform underfoot. In the tidal swirls, mussel shells and gravel were deposited in pockets, overlaid by the oozing sediment. In other places there was only mud, filling holes and depressions. Twice on the way out, Pete had sunk up to almost the top of his boots and he had had to haul at them with his hands to make sure they came out *with* his foot, instead of being left behind. He got about twenty yards when he felt the gravel under the slick give way to a mud hole and backed out to the left, only to find another depression sucking at his boots. He used the fork to probe and it went down right to the handle, and when he drew it out it was black with slimy mud.

Pete followed the narrow gravel bar, looking for a safe place to cross and cursing himself for coming out so far. He probed again and again, and almost everywhere he dug the tines in, they kept on going. Somehow he had lost the track and instead of fruitlessly trying to find a place where he could get through, he retraced his steps to try to find solid ground underfoot. He got about five yards when the underlay simply disappeared. It caved under his weight like thin ice and he felt his right leg plunge into the mud up to the hip. The fork dropped out of his hand and skittered on the surface slick as his momentum carried him forward, off balance, his arms pinwheeling. His left foot dug into the mud, plying for purchase and finding none. In a second he was up to his crotch in a morass of cold ooze.

'Fuckit,' Pete spat, heaving his torso left and right in a bid to screw himself out of the grip of the mud. He reached across the top and managed to get his fingers around the handle of the fork and pulled it towards him. The slime, built up over years by sediment and decaying plankton, smelled oily and stagnant as trapped gases escaped to the surface, dislodged by his movements. He pulled his right foot upwards and felt it slip out of the boot. He tried to slide it back in before it filled with mud, but the pressure on either side closed it and instead of getting the boot back on, he succeeded only in pushing it further down into the mud beneath him.

There seemed to be no bottom to the mud hole, and that thought jangled an alarm through him.

I'm sinking! The alarm flashed through his mind.

He hauled the fork back, grabbed the handle with both hands and tried to prod for firmer ground. But the tines simply plunged into the deep mud without making contact. Pete leaned forward. There was a sucking sound as the mud behind him tugged at his waterproof jacket and he sank an inch or two.

'Oh shit,' he squawked, his voice a full octave higher than normal, as the first wave of panic washed through him. With a wild effort, he managed to twist himself round so that he could face the shoreline. It was deserted. Beyond the low rocky hill that separated the inlet from Gallan Bay, Doug Petersen was fishing, probably hauling them in. They were separated by only half a mile, but it could have been a hundred for all the difference it made.

'Doug!' Pete bawled at the top of his voice. The shout rang out across the still flats, carried on the clear air with nothing to bar its progress. Nothing but the rocky hillock.

'Doug! For Christ's sake!'

The only response was the faint echo of his words bouncing back off the rocks.

Pete hauled again at the clinging mud. His other foot slipped out of his trapped boot, and this too was trampled down into the ooze below. There was another sucking sound and he slipped down another few inches until he was stuck up to his waist, and the buzz of panic inside him became a jittery whine.

Pete Coia *hated* swamps. He'd even admitted it to everybody the other night. A bit of mud a few inches deep on hard gravel was no problem, but this was no little bit of mud.

He was sinking.

He quickly looked at his diver's watch, scraping its muddied face against his shoulder to clear the dial, checking on the state of the tide, for the suddenly awesome thought had struck him that if he didn't get out of this mess, the sea would soon come rolling in. That realisation made him redouble his efforts, but hampered by heavy clothing that trapped the ooze within the fabric, he succeeded only in sinking further. The mud slowly and surely came up to the level of his ribs, and still his feet could find no bottom.

Pete called for help again. He shouted for his friend, hoping that Petersen would run out of bait and come looking for him . . . But he knew this would not happen. They had dug up enough lugworms to last them the full day, and once his friend had started catching fish, then the rest of the world could go to hell in a basket before he would even *notice*. The mud dragged him down inexorably, and as it reached his chest, compressing his ribs and adding to the effort of breathing, Pete Coia started to bawl for help. He called to God to help him. He sobbed for somebody to come and get him out of there, but nobody came.

A few feet away from him, on the surface, his bait bucket had overturned and the ragworms were escaping into the mud, while he, a million miles up the evolutionary ladder, couldn't escape *from* it.

Pete's frantic yelling went unheard and the more he panicked and thrashed, the more he sank. The mud was creeping up to his collar bone when he felt the first movement under his foot, and for one glorious moment he thought he'd touched the base of the pan. Once he stopped sinking, no matter how much effort it took, he could dig himself out and then, if necessary *crawl* back to the shore, and he'd *never*, not *ever* come out onto the mudflats again. The relief of something solid under him washed over him like a cool balm.

In an instant, the relief vanished.

Under his foot, the solid *moved*. He felt it through his thick fishermen's socks and for a moment he thought he'd simply trodden on his boot and shoved it further down. He probed again and felt a mass hump upwards under his toes, pressing against the flat of his foot. Instant fear rippled through him. The movement came again, stronger, and then something *slid* itself underneath his foot, a slimy forward motion. He jerked his knee upwards, canting himself to the side. At thigh level, it pressed against him and forced past, rubbing itself along his flank. Without thinking, Pete Coia twisted away.

Something eased itself sinuously out of the mud.

It was purplish-red and on either side thick, six-inch-long frills rippled in unison. The snout was long and wormlike and the snaky body more than nine inches across. There was a familiar bitter smell emanating from its skin and as Pete stared, riven with fear, the worm head unfolded, turning itself inside out, the front peeling back in an alien, boneless unsheathing, until finally the pincers appeared, curving like eight-inch scythes and wide open.

They snapped together with a loud, chitinous crack and the monstrous anelid worm swung towards him. Pete jerked back from it, eyes wide with terror, and felt another weight twist against him at shoulder level. He spun his head round and saw another colossal ragworm loop out from the surface. The frills on either side flagellated synchronously like the legs of a vast centipede. Even as panic vaulted inside him Pete could make out the rhythmic pulses down each segment of the long body that set them in motion. Beside it, the mud erupted and another rubbery blind head nosed out and peeled back to display the scimitar mandibles. The one nearest him nosed the air as if sensing him, *smelling* him, then swivelled and with heart-stopping speed lunged at him.

In the slow-motion clarity of the adrenaline burst, Pete saw it all happen in minute detail. The black jaws sprang open more than a foot wide. Behind them the mouth was just a mess of pulpy red frills ringed by bands of muscle. His head moved back about three inches in the time the thing moved three feet and he saw the jaws start on their clamping movement. There was nothing he could do to avoid them. One pincer dug into his forehead and the other took him at the back of his skull. Instant pain bored like a hot drill between the two points of contact. It felt as if his head was locked in the jaws of a jagged vice and squeezed under great pressure.

His scream, loud and high, soared into the empty air and across the flats. In the mud something snapped against his side and fire erupted under his ribs. The worm that had clamped his head was shaking from

310

side to side, oozing itself back into the mud with its prey. Down under the surface, at his side, another was dragging him to the right. Then another nosed upwards in between his legs and that pain drove the others into the distance. The scream that followed could have been heard from the lighthouse on Achillbeg Island to the far side of the bay.

Pete Coia's mad bellows of pain and terror continued to rip into the air as the vast, sinewy creatures pulled him inexorably downwards, ripping into jerking flesh until only his face was visible pointing to the sky as the worms' pincers dragged him backwards.

There was one final screech and then the mud filled his mouth, cutting it off to a ragged gurgle, and Pete Coia disappeared from view. A coiling motion rippled the surface and then there was nothing, no sign that anyone had been here, except for the empty bait box from which the final small ragworm crawled to freedom.

Down on the rocks, Doug Petersen heard the far-off shrieking of a seabird and raised his eyes to the sky, but there was nothing to be seen. He had just dragged in his fourth big cod and laid it beside the other three on the thick carpet of seaweed. Like many sea-anglers, he was of the persuasion that it was best to let them die naturally in the air, rather than bruise the flesh. He'd caught more than all three of them could eat, but Donovan would take every fish they brought, though what he did with them, nobody knew. Doug was in his element. On the rig on the south coast, they had four weeks on and two off, and there was no point in going back to Brisbane every few weeks. He preferred to save his money to really enjoy himself when he went home. The two Canadians were of the same opinion, and their savings were mounting steadily. The locals might complain about the price of beer, but hell, a fishing holiday here cost next to nothing, and if you had good mates to fish with, then it was little short of paradise, especially when they were biting like today.

The high-pitched scream came from out in the bay again, but still there were no birds to be seen. Normally the air was a tumult of their cries as vast flocks of them wheeled in over the water to feed on the flats. Doug shrugged, wondered briefly when Pete was coming back without even realising how long he'd been gone, and grinned at the thought of big Frank Wysocki heaving his line out on the sands of Tallabaun Strand while he was hauling them in hand over fist not half a mile from the cottage. They had kept a running tally, with a tenner every fishing day on who had the biggest catch. So far, Doug's holiday really *had* cost next to nothing.

311

He cast out again, bending his body, powering the fourteen feet of carbon fibre to sling the big lead slug in a gleaming arc over the water. It went so far he couldn't even hear the splash, though he could see the brief sparkle as the sun caught the spray where the slug hit the surface. He jammed the rod upright and went to sit on a flat stone beside the small fire of driftwood where his blackened tea-can was on the boil.

He waited by the fire until the tea was ready and poured a spot of milk into the stewed brew. He ignored the heat from the tea-can as he picked it up from the fire and put it to his lips, enjoying the scald and the strong smoky aroma.

'Only worthwhile thing the poms ever gave us,' he said to himself, smacking his lips.

The tip of his rod bent itself right over on a tight arc.

'You beaut,' Doug shouted aloud, hurriedly placing the can on the flat rock and scrambling to where the big beachcaster was doubled over and jerking madly. The clear, monofilament line was hissing through the water as the big fish – *and from the curve on the rod it* was *a belter* – fought against the strain.

Doug grabbed the butt of the rod, lifted it free from the rock wedge and immediately braced himself against the powerful strain. He leaned back, bringing the tip up, and then quickly dropped it again and cranked vigorously at the reel spindle, feeling the powerful jerking pull of the fish.

'A bloody *monster*,' he whooped. 'Beat this one, Wysocki, you *bastard*.'

Cheerfully cursing, he hauled at the line, hearing it sizzle across the surface as it was dragged through the water. The strain was enormous, exhilarating. Through the line and down the curve of the rod, the frantic thrashings of the fish were telegraphed to his hands, like an electric shock connecting fish and fisherman in a final struggle.

Doug dropped the rod's tip and was about to heave back again, drawing the fish in another few yards, now speculating on the size and weight that could put such a pull on the line, when instead *he* was jerked forward on the slippery stones, caught off balance by the force of the pull, until he was knee-deep in the water.

'Bloody *hell*,' he yelled vehemently. 'Jesus bloody *Christ* what a *beauty*.'

He stumbled, still unbalanced yet still trying to pull the rod back, when another mighty jerk on the line dragged him forward, this time pulling him down a shingly slope under the water until he was standing waist-deep in the bay. Doug hardly even noticed the cold water as it filled his waders. His mind was fixed on the fish at the end of the line, concentrating so hard that nothing else mattered but bringing it to the shore. He found his footing and pistoned the reel, holding the rod high. It was curved round in a fine arch and the strain on the line caused it to sing a high-pitched note. Doug pulled back and saw the line angle towards him, cutting a vee shape in the surface and gaining a few yards on the fish.

'Got you, you bloody *whale*,' he sang out. 'Got you *now*!'

He pulled again and cranked, dragging the bucking weight further in towards shore, and bent for another haul that would bring the fish over the kelp bed and into the shallows. He took a step back, gingerly finding his balance on the smooth stones, when again there was a huge tug on the line. It spilled him forward with such force that suddenly he was up to his neck. The battle was *monumental*. Another tug pulled him further and the bottom slid away from his feet. He coughed in water, managed to find the rocks and threw himself backwards, still valiantly holding onto the line. He managed to get his head clear of the surface and took two stumbling steps, fighting the weight of the water that clogged him, and got himself back to waist depth. Just then he caught a glimpse of a shadow a few yards in front.

It was *huge*, a long dark sinuous shape, black against the light green of the kelp fronds. He saw the taut line cut again on the surface, this time not jerking right or left, but sizzling in *towards* him.

In that instant, all thoughts of valiant battle against the great fish fled. In its place came the freezing vision of a huge shark under the water. If Doug had stopped to think, he would have recalled that in these waters there were no sharks except the big toothless baskers off Achillbeg Island that fed on plankton and couldn't bite if they tried. In his mind's eye he saw *shark*; fins and teeth on a living torpedo. And with that thought came the utter terror that made his stomach sink like a stone and his bladder simply open to send a hot jet into his waterproof trousers.

With an incoherent grunt, he stumbled backwards. The long shape darted towards him so swiftly it covered the twenty yards in three seconds. Those three seconds were enough for Doug to scramble, scuttling on his backside and his heels and his hands, out of the water and onto the rocks. He didn't stop until he was ten feet from the brink. The ominous shape jetted in to the edge, causing a bow-wave to hump the surface of the water above, and turned away only feet from where the rocks met the bay. At that, the rod was simply whipped out of Doug's hand, despite the spastic grip that had clenched his fingers on the butt. It went flying high into the air, and reached the furthest point of its arc. The line snapped with a noise like a whipcrack, and the rod continued to sail over the bay, landing almost a hundred yards off in deep water.

A head came up out of the water.

From his safe vantage, Doug saw that it was no shark, but an immense conger eel, with a long flat head and a lower jaw that protruded like a pike's mouth. A black, flat eye rolled and a dead gaze swept over him as the head turned violently and disappeared under the water again with a splash that drenched the rocks for yards around. The bow-wave shot out from the water's edge as the colossal eel dived into the depths and disappeared.

Doug sat there, heart thudding and eyes still wide with panic, trying to make his lungs work again. Finally he breathed out in a huge relieved sigh, not caring a jot that he had pissed in his pants and down into his boots.

'Strewth,' he breathed, with great feeling. 'Nearly a flippin' gonner there.'

After a few long minutes, the shaking in his legs and hands subsided, though when he stood up, his knees threatened to give way and dump him back down on the rock where he'd sat transfixed.

He finally made it to his feet and from his vantage point, six feet above the level of the water, looked out over the kelp bed. There was no sign of the monster eel.

After his struggle and the dreadful horror of being caught by the incredible eel, Doug was almost light-hearted with relief. His rod was gone, but he had another, and it was much better, he thought, that the rod was out there in the bay rather than him. He just couldn't believe the *size* of the thing that he'd battled with, that had finally turned to attack him. Congers just didn't grow that big, unless there were some monsters out in the deep that had been washed into the bay by the great wave. It might not have been a shark, but it made no difference. It was immense, swam under the sea and had huge jaws with teeth in them. That was enough to make Doug realise that he'd barely got away with his life. And one thing was certain, he assured himself. He was going to stay away from the deep water from now on.

He gingerly turned on the rocks, made his way to the fire and picked up the tea-can. It was still scalding hot, which showed him how short the duration of his match with the fish had been, though it seemed as if he'd battled for *hours*. Gratefully he drank the brew down a throat that, tight and dry, began to loosen. He looked out at the water, peering through the surface glare to the kelp, searching for the beast, but there was no dark shadow in the water. Doug walked a few steps down the shingle to where the four sizeable cod – all of which could have been swallowed in one gulp by the eel – were lying in a row, a couple of feet from bladderwrack floating in the shallows to the left of the rocks.

He bent and picked up two of them by their tails to carry them up to the grassy bank beyond, when the carpet of floating seaweed simply exploded.

A black blur shot through it and out of the water at the edge of the shingle. Still pumped up with adrenaline, Doug's reflexes were remarkably quick. He dived in the opposite direction, dropping the fish, and hit the ground eight feet ahead of where he had been standing. He *felt* the thump of the large body hit the shingle. Without even looking back he scrambled up the slope on hands and knees, frantically trying to get to his feet.

He made another two yards when something grabbed him by the heel of his boot with an audible snap. The force of it twisted him round until he was lying on his back, and he saw the huge eel's vicious jaw fastened to his foot. There was no pain, for the teeth were driven right into either side of the thick rubber heel, and as he jerked back the boot slid off. Despite his terror, the relief that he was getting away came like a white surge through him. Using his hands and feet and backside again, he scuttered backwards, eyes fixed on the monstrous jaws that opened, snapped at the green rubber boot, swallowed it down with a gulp.

He made another couple of yards and stopped, watching the long head cast left and right and the flat black expressionless eyes that seemed almost blind out of the water. But Doug had forgotten the essential difference between eels and sharks. Sharks never come out of the water until they're caught. Thinking he had moved far enough up the shingle, Doug, though still terrified, thought he was safe.

The eel cast right and left again and then with a sudden snakelike motion it came slithering towards him so fast he didn't even have time to move. The jaws opened wide very quickly and snapped shut even quicker on his knee. He felt the thud of it, but there was no pain. It seemed, in a dreamy way, to be happening to someone else. The long slimy body, more than a foot broad and so long that its tail was still in the water, flexed, and Doug was dragged in one quick movement down to the water's edge. The creature twisted and he felt the joint in his thigh pop out of its socket as he was spun round into the bay. There was a coolness as the water closed over his head and he was dragged down into the dark.

On the rocks, the fire burned itself out. Later on, by the time darkness fell, the tide came in and washed away the two fishing bags that had lain side by side on the jumbled stones. The other rod, still standing where Pete Coia had left it when he went to gather bait, tumbled into the deeper water and slid down into the bay.

Tom and Nancy Ducain had walked a couple of miles from the kettles at Emlagh Point down to the top of Tallabaun Strand. Despite the road east being cut off, they were in no hurry, although, like Liz, Nancy was beginning to find the area oppressive and unnerving. She would never have said so to Tom, because she didn't want to spoil his holiday, and besides, until they put a span over the bridge, there was nothing they could do about it. Nancy was a pragmatist.

They avoided the deserted village where the strange men had tried to rape her, but she wanted to see again the impressive vista of the great strand as it stretched down the coast in the direction of Connemara. From the rocks at Emlagh, silent now that the tide was out, the sands, lost in the distant haze, went on, it seemed, for ever.

'It's beautiful,' Nancy said. 'It makes me feel like a heroine in a book. Now I know why they write poetry about this place. It's bleak and hard, and yet it's so stirring.'

They made their way down the narrow track and onto the hard-packed sand, following the edge of the water as they beachcombed. In at the corner of the Point, where the sands butted against hard rock, there was a tumble of flotsam mixed in with smooth green rounded stones that had been scraped up from the seabed. Nancy picked up a piece that was big enough to cup in her hand and held it up to the sky. The sunlight shone through from one polished side to the other.

'I'm keeping this for a souvenir,' she said.

'I'll get you a bigger piece,' Tom said, rooting around the logs and branches that had been cast above the high-tide line.

'No. This one will do. It fits. It's a magical stone from the bottom of the sea.'

'Now you're *talking* like a heroine in a novel,' Tom said, and put his hand affectionately round her shoulders. They walked on by the edge, picking up scallop shells and fragments of odd coiled whelks and pieces of pinkish coral as they followed the waterline down into the strand.

They had gone about a mile, sauntering slowly, when Nancy shaded her eyes against the sun. She pointed further along the shore.

'What's that?'

Tom followed the line of her arm. Way in the distance, there was a shape lying on the sand, dark against the flat buff colour.

'Could be a dolphin or something.'

'Let's go have a look,' Nancy said.

The others had dismissed the notion, but Frank Wysocki knew he was right. The big wave that had come in would have scraped up the bottom of the sea in front of Tallabaun Strand and swept the burrowing things on the seabed into the free water. If there was ever a time to catch bass, this was it, he'd told them. They'd disagreed, opting for the cod off the rocks at the harbour, but Frank had caught cod aplenty in the past week and bass, he explained, that was a *fighting* fish.

At his height, he had the advantage over both of them, because he could hurl his bait out even further than Doug Petersen, and on a flat sand beach, distance counted for a lot. He looked forward to the electric juddering of the line as silver bass took the bait and ran with it.

He parked their car at the deserted village and came down the path and onto the sands. The tide was well out, which meant there was a chance of good fishing on the turn. He started walking on the flat, rod on his shoulder and bag banging against his hip. The sand was firm and hard-packed, which made the going easy as he made his way out to the edge. He walked for fifteen minutes, whistling as he went, and then stopped to look ahead at the water.

It seemed no nearer.

'Can't be still running out, surely?' he said to the empty air.

He turned and looked behind. The car, a white station wagon, was only a white dot in the distance, up above the start of the sands where the road petered out. He had walked a good mile, and yet, oddly, from his perspective down on the strand, he looked no closer to the water. He shrugged and walked on, though in truth he felt uneasy. He wished the other guys had come, for he'd feel a great deal better in this flat place with others with him.

Frank did not like open spaces. He didn't know why. He could remember nothing from his childhood that could have traumatised him. But flat, empty spaces made him nervous and a little nauseous. Fortunately, there were rocks to the north, and behind him, beyond the car, the tall hills that had helped save Kilgallan from the great wave gave him a sense of enclosure. He walked on, feet rasping on the hard sand.

Another fifteen minutes later, the little buzz of apprehension gained a notch when Frank stopped again to look ahead.

There was something *wrong*.

The more he walked, the further the sea seemed to get. And those rocks at the north, they seemed to be *behind* where he was standing, though, from the angling map, he knew they should be further out than the sand itself. He turned to look at the mountains and his breath caught.

The beach stretched away into *infinity*.

The hills that had towered up behind him when he left the car were low mounds in the hazy distance. They looked a hundred miles away.

Frank found himself on a vast flat expanse, and even as he stood, the rocks to the north receded, shrinking away from him as, before his eyes, the strand *expanded*, leaving him completely exposed on the featureless plain.

He spun round and the sea drained away as he watched, exposing mile after mile of sand that went on and on and on as far as his bewildered eyes could see.

There was no rationality to Frank Wysocki's fear of open spaces, but that counted for nothing. His mind could not take in what he was seeing. The sudden shock was enough to set up such a dreadful panic within him that his vision spun in and out of focus. The world around him, the vast, flat *empty* world, whirled like a planetary centrifuge, leaving him with no reference point, no sense of place.

Frank Wysocki had never screamed since his early infancy yet he did now, and the scream, had anyone heard it, would have been pitiful. It came up from inside him, the dreadful wail of a man in despair. He was lost and alone in the middle of nowhere and his mind, completely disoriented, collapsed under sudden and enormous pressure. Frank took eighteen steps, no three in the same direction as the previous three, while his mind simply shut itself down. The wail of sheer terror cut off, and at last the giant Canadian toppled to the sand, where he twitched for a few minutes, snuffling like an animal, and was still.

Tom and Nancy drew closer to the shape, and when they were less than a hundred yards away, Tom stopped and grasped Nancy's arm.

'I don't think it's a dolphin,' he said quietly. 'Looks like a body.'

'We'd better have a look.'

'No. Wait here. I'll have a look,' Tom said, but Nancy shook his hand off.

'I've seen bodies before. Let's both go.'

She stared at him levelly until he finally nodded. They both went, walking slowly, approaching with caution.

They found Frank Wysocki lying on the sand, face up to the sun and eyes wide open. At first they were sure he was dead, but Nancy knelt down, put a hand to his neck and felt the pulse, very slowly beating, under the skin.

'He's alive,' she pronounced.

'What the hell happened to him?' Tom asked.

Nancy shrugged. 'Pitched a fit, maybe. I don't know. We'll have to get him out of here.'

'If we can. He must weigh three hundred pounds.'

'We can't just leave him here,' Nancy stated firmly. 'If we go for help, the tide will come in before we get back.'

'I never thought of that,' Tom admitted. He knelt down, got an arm under Frank's armpit, and grunted with the effort of hauling him up to a sitting position. Tom revised his estimates. The big man must have been three hundred and fifty. Between them, they got him to his feet, holding him upright, and miraculously, when they moved forward, Frank Wysocki's feet walked too.

Together, they slowly made for the head of the beach, while Frank stumbled, childlike, between them, his face a complete blank. His mind had shut down with such force that there was no sight in the pale blue eyes. Frank Wysocki was no longer stuck out in a vast emptiness. He was inside the warm dark. And nothing, no miracle of modern medicine or science, would ever make him come out again.

29

Darkness fell swiftly on the second night after the flood, and the moon rose full and white, casting silver on the silent waters of the bay and long shadows on the strangely hushed land.

A peculiar sense of anticipation settled over Kilgallan. For some it was an inexplicable shiver of nervous expectancy, though of what they could not have said. For some few others, it was more than that. It was the realisation that something had *begun*, and with that came a deep foreboding of wrong.

No-one knew that anything had happened to Doug Petersen and Pete Coia, and as yet, the stiffened, bloodstained bodies of Maura and Jack Quinn lay undiscovered in the bedroom of their small house. Frank Wysocki was lying flat out and unresponsive on the low couch in Tim O'Brien's front room, eyes still open but focused far into the distance.

The children of Sinead and Danny Boyle were crowded into the sitting room of the parish priest's house, being tended by his housekeeper, though there was little she could do for them. Their white, blank faces bore mute testament to the devastating discovery they had made on the floor of their kitchen.

Tim O'Brien had been run ragged that afternoon. The grotesquely conjoined bodies had been taken to Patsy McGavigan, whose tiny parlour was now full. The cause of death had been apparent, but just *how* Sinead and Danny had been crushed together with such force that their skulls had smashed like soft pears, was not.

Despite his broken leg and his furious frustration, Peter O'Neill was able to make some decisions. Firstly he insisted that the farm labourers work flat out on getting the Roonan Water spanned with the logs of trees which had come down in the deluge, and already the makeshift bridge was coming along nicely. Peter also insisted that two of the more able young fellows crossed the water and made their way along the road. The television had mentioned that the village was cut off, as were six other towns on the west coast which had suffered even more damage than Kilgallan, and from the aerial pictures, taken from a helicopter that had buzzed the coastline, it was known that the road to Westport had caved in on two stretches. It was not passable by car, but it could be walked.

The policeman also deputised a group to round up the peat cutters and bring them in. He'd heard the stories from the two visiting women, and while he was reluctant to consider that the odd, *touched* men who spent their days digging on the moors were anything more than harmless defectives, he decided to take no chances. But the men returned after scouring the moor. There was no sign of the peat cutters.

Somebody had killed four people in Kilgallan, terribly, violently, *mindlessly*. Peter wanted no more of that in his village.

Sean and Liz joined Siobhan Kane in the Ducains' cottage. They had met the archaeologist on her way from the tor and walked along with her.

'Pictures any help?' Sean asked, and Siobhan nodded. She looked preoccupied.

'I've done a translation,' Siobhan said.

'Good for you,' Liz told her. 'So did you find out why the place was built?'

'I think so.'

'You don't seem too happy about it,' Liz said. 'Wasn't it somebody important?'

'It wasn't a king, if that's what you mean. And I think we've made a mistake.'

'How so?' Sean asked, but Siobhan just shook her head.

'I can't say.'

Just then, Tom and Nancy came down the road in their car and stopped just beyond the cattle grid. Nancy rolled down her window and called them over.

'There's been another murder,' she told them breathlessly. 'Come on over to the house.'

Inside, Tom explained how they'd found the big Canadian down at the beach and then, when they'd brought him to the doctor's, all hell had broken out.

'A man and his wife – Doyle or something, they're called. Their kids found them killed in their own kitchen. Place was covered in blood.'

He stopped and looked at the three of them. Siobhan's face had lost its colour and had gone so pale it looked white.

'Hey, is this place weird or what?' Tom asked. 'I think we should think about getting the hell out of here.'

'Oh God,' Siobhan whispered. Sean cast a look in her direction. He didn't get a chance to say anything, for Liz immediately started asking Tom what had happened.

'They don't know yet. Could have been some animal. They said they'd been crushed together like gnats. Weird, huh?'

Siobhan's face grew even paler. She steadied herself against the table, sat down slowly. Then she put her head in her hands and a little moan escaped her.

'What's wrong?' Liz asked.

'We shouldn't have done it.'

'What's she talking about?' Tom asked.

Sean shrugged. He sat down beside Siobhan and put his hand on her shoulder. 'Tell us what you mean,' he said softly.

'The chamber. It wasn't a grave. It says so in the carvings on the stone.'

'What's that got to do with anything?' Tom asked, and Nancy, standing behind him, squeezed his shoulder tight, urging him to silence.

'They didn't bury anyone there. They *trapped* something,' Siobhan said, her voice almost a whisper. 'I didn't believe it at first, but now I have to. They trapped something and now I think it's out. We *let* it out.'

'What's out?' Sean asked.

'The *Shee*. That's what they called her. The stone tells the whole story. They caught her and put her inside the stone. They put five guards there so she'd never get out.'

'The *Shee*? What the hell's that?' Tom ignored Nancy's grip.

'It's hard to explain. She was like a force, a conscious, malevolent force – the most evil thing the old folk could think of. There's lots of legends about her. I don't know whether she was always there, or whether she was just conjured up out of superstitious fears. I always thought it was a fairy story, just like the leprechauns, but these people believed it utterly. They called her the *Morrigan*, and for them she was the apotheosis of all evil. She was a kind of vampire, they said. She fed on their fears and terrors and she fed on *them* too.'

Tom looked over the table at Sean and gave him an incredulous look which also conveyed that he thought Siobhan might just be a little bit crazy. Sean didn't react.

'That's what the words in the stone say,' Siobhan went on. 'They trapped her and put her there and laid a curse on the place – what they call a *geis*, which was a powerful spell. I don't know how they did it, but we've broken it.'

She looked up at them and her face was pinched with worry. 'I think the *Shee* is *out*.'

'You really believe all this?' Nancy asked.

'I didn't, but I do now. I think she's got out and I think she's started to kill people.'

'What, some sort of Irish *gorgon* for chrissakes? You have to be kidding,' Tom exploded.

Nancy hit him on the shoulder. 'Shut up, Tom,' she said firmly.

'What makes you think that?' Sean asked.

'I studied your pictures and then the meaning just jumped out at me. It's all there. They wrote that she'd sleep as long as the five men still stood there. But we took one away. And they wrote that she'd stay there until the sea covered the land.' She looked around. 'Can't you see that when the wave hit, the tor was *under* the sea? That was the last spell. And there was a curse on anyone who broke open the chamber. That's clear.'

Sean looked at her for a long moment. He couldn't explain why, but what Siobhan said had set off an echo in his own mind. It was not yet a conscious thought, but it was working its way up to it.

'This *Shee* thing,' he said. 'What was it like?'

'They called her the serpent, but she took on human form. She was female, like some sort of queen of death. They said she came from the Land of the Young . . . that's what they called the underworld. Some called it the Dead Lands.'

'They might have believed in it then, but that was a long time ago. They believed in fairies and goblins too, didn't they?'

Siobhan nodded. 'But this is different. I can *feel* it. It's more than coincidence that the tidal wave hit here, and just after that Mr O'Hara and the girl were killed.' Siobhan paused, her face slack. 'Now those poor folk are dead, and I think it's because we opened the chamber.'

'Hey, you believe any of this?' Tom asked, looking around at the others. 'Witches and fairies?'

'I don't know,' Nancy said. 'I've got a weird feeling too.'

'Aw, come on,' he said, exasperated.

'I don't know about any of that,' Liz interjected. 'But there's something odd going on around here.'

Sean was silent and the girls looked at him.

'How about you?' Liz asked.

For a moment, he looked as if he was lost in a daydream, but Siobhan's words thrummed in his mind like a guitar string vibrating in sympathy with a twin note. Sean was recollecting the dreams that beset him, the ones that changed from the horror of Belfast to the strange *fantasy* scene and then abruptly tumbled into the horror when the thing *changed*.

'Could this thing change its shape?' he asked.

'She could be anything she wanted, so they say, but took human form only at night. She was a dark princess, or a young girl, or an ancient hag. But during the day, she could only take the form of an animal.'

'Like a crow?'

'Like anything.'

Sean went silent for a moment and everybody watched him, wondering what he was leading up to.

'I think I've seen her.'

'Where?' Nancy said.

'I mean, I've *dreamt* about her. I get these nightmares. And then they change. It's from something I saw last year, wakes me up at night. But since I came here, they've been *different*. I'm standing at a stream, no, *in* a stream and I've been fighting somebody.'

Sean went on, almost in a monotone, describing his dreams. He told them about the woman in the dream, who changed from a dark-haired smouldering beauty to a withered crone in a dreadful metamorphosis from fearsome *devastating* comeliness to monstrous ugliness.

'It started in the car,' Liz said. 'I remember. You shouted out at me to look where I was going and I almost crashed.'

'That's right. I was calling to someone in the dream. I think it was "Luke". That was just after I killed the man in the water. It was someone I knew, and I was *angry*.'

'Do you remember who you killed?'

'It's strange. It was my brother. I remember thinking that. His name . . .' Sean closed his eyes to concentrate. 'I remember shouting it out after the fish, a big eel or something, tripped me up. Fergus or something. Maybe Feargal.'

'*Ferdia*. Was that it?' Siobhan asked, almost whispering.

'That's it!' Sean seemed to snap out of his recollection. 'That's it. How did you know?'

'I've heard the story before. It's from the *Legend of the Brown Bull*. How did you kill the man?'

'With a sword. I hit him with it, then I used a spear with a stone blade. I *kicked* the spear at him and it hit him in the chest.'

'The *gae bolg*. They sang songs about it.'

'What's that?'

'It was how the Skatha taught Cuchullain to kill.'

'I've heard of her before. Didn't the professor say something about her living in Skye?'

'Yes. She taught Cuchullain to fight and he killed his blood brother

324

Ferdia at a ford in a river. The *Shee* turned herself into an eel and tried to trip him up and the champion was so angry he went into his battle rage. His body warped and he killed Ferdia.'

'And who is Luke?'

'Not Luke, though it sounded like that. It was Lugh, the God of Light and Day.'

'So what did he have to do with it?'

'He was Cuchullain's father,' Siobhan said finally.

They sat in silence for a minute until Tom finally spoke up.

'Sounds great, but what's that got to do with this place?'

'Quiet, Tom,' Nancy said again.

'Well, if you think about it,' Siobhan said, 'it's an incredible coincidence. We've just opened a chamber the professor thinks is nearly five thousand years old and the words in the stone say that it was used to trap an entity that was the embodiment of destruction, and Sean here has been having dreams about her. The old Irish Celts believed in dreams. And what's more, that's how I really learned to translate the words. I was dreaming about Sean's pictures being developed and when they were, the words just came into focus. I remember thinking it was just like the geneticist who worked out the double-helix shape of chromosomes. He dreamed of two snakes coiling around each other. I just saw all the words come together and I could read them. When I woke up, I checked the prints, and I could *still* read them. Somehow my brain did all the work when I was sleeping.'

'Do you believe what you're saying?' Nancy asked her.

'I don't want to, but I do. I don't know why, but I think we have let something loose.'

'How about you, Tom?'

'You kidding?'

'Sean?'

'I don't know. I only know about the dreams. I've never heard the legend. All I've read is a few history books and some of Yeats's poetry. But I think there *is* something strange about this place.'

There was another silence, then Nancy turned to Liz. 'How about you?'

'I think Sean's right. And I can't say Siobhan's wrong. It's a hard thing to take in, but if she *is* right, what do we do about it?'

'I don't know if there is anything to do about it.'

'If you tell somebody else, they'll say you're section eight,' Tom said.

Siobhan looked at him, puzzled.

'He means crazy,' Nancy translated.

Night was falling. Nancy made bacon sandwiches and coffee. Siobhan brought out the pictures Sean had taken of the carvings, and took them through the story that had been cut into the stones three thousand years before the birth of Christ. The more she read, the more it merged with Sean's strange dreams and the more Liz and Nancy shuddered.

Maeve Donovan wasn't behind the bar that night, much to Terry's disappointment. The other two fishermen hadn't returned from their trip, so were still to be told about the strange affliction – a stroke or something similar, everybody reasoned – that had overcome their friend down on Tallabaun Strand. Professor Connarty, unable to face a third session after the abuse his kidneys had taken on the previous two, had stayed in the cottage, vowing to go to bed early. Unlike the night before, Donovan's big bar was almost empty. Most of the locals, concerned maybe for their families after the discovery of Sinead and Danny Boyle, just after the finding of Mike O'Hara and the girl, had decided to stay at home. The Roonah Water was not yet spanned.

The two young men from Ulster were leaning against the bar, and Terry joined them amiably, offering them a pint, glad of the company. They were close to his age, in their early twenties, and since Terry had studied in Belfast and knew most of the drinking places, they had enough in common for a friendly blether.

They stayed, matching each other pint for pint, until John Boyle decided he'd had enough and shoved himself off the bar.

'Oh, stay for a nightcap,' Seamus O'Farrell insisted.

'I'm swilling about as it is, and we could have an early start in the morning.'

'They won't have that water bridged by tomorrow, that's for sure. We'll be here another day, I'm telling you.'

Boyle shook his head, turned up the collar of his donkey jacket and lumbered unsteadily out of the door.

'Never could hold his drink, nor his water,' Seamus said. 'Should have seen him on the boat.'

'You fish as well?' Terry asked, and Seamus put a finger to his lips.

'Not me,' he said conspiratorially.

Terry bought him another beer, and when they sank that Seamus bought another. They had a third, taking their tally well over the gallon, when Donovan looked up from the end of the bar, where he was stacking glasses, and told them they might as well drink up now.

'It was open until midnight last night,' Terry objected.

'And it was worthwhile keeping it open and all,' Donovan replied. 'Some of us have our beds to get to.'

The young men drained their beer glasses and called it a night. Outside, the moon was high and clear and the air was cold. Terry shivered, zipped up the front of his windcheater, dug his hands in his pockets. Seamus, his face flushed with drink, strolled down beside him.

They were halfway down the narrow road, avoiding, with some difficulty, the pot-holes that cratered the gravel, when Terry moved to the side, to a space between two tall elms. Behind he heard footsteps. Seamus followed him into the shade.

'Always the same. In one end and out the other,' he said.

Terry pissed against the dark trunk of a tree. After all the beer, the relief was enormous, and he heard Seamus give a sigh of satisfaction as he emptied himself against a bush.

Unknown to either of them, Hugh Sands was only forty yards away, sprawled behind the cover of a clump of honeysuckle, taking in the scene through a pair of night sights. The infra-red binoculars picked out the shapes of the two men, and in the monochrome image, the twin streams of urine were like bright curved rods of light. They winked out as the men finished and zipped themselves up.

Terry turned away from the tree, still fumbling with the front of his trousers, when he stopped abruptly.

'What was that?' he asked.

'What?'

'I heard something.'

'It wasn't me. I only had a pee,' Seamus said with a chuckle.

Then the sound that had stopped Terry came again, very softly, through the trees. It sounded like laughter.

'There it goes again,' he said.

'I heard it myself,' Seamus agreed. They both stood, listening. Tinkling, girlish laughter, this time closer and louder. A shape slipped out from the trees.

'Who's there?' Terry called out. Seamus had come up alongside him and was peering into the shadows.

The laughter came again, now very close, a high, *delighted* sound, and the shape came towards them and stopped less than ten yards away.

Terry strained to see, and the shape took form. In front of them, Maeve Donovan stood in the small clearing, bare feet planted apart. Through the tall branches moonlight dappled her, illuminating the fine, silky shift that came down only to her knees. Her black hair threw back the blue sheen of ravens' wings, limned with silver.

She smiled at Terry and he felt his heart thud in his chest. She was *beautiful*.

Standing there in the moonlight, she was not the pretty, shy girl who lowered her eyes when Terry spoke to her in her father's bar as she washed the glasses. Here, alone in the trees, she looked like a nymph, a fairy. She was simply heartstoppingly lovely.

She beckoned to him, turned and flitted away from them. Terry took a step forward. The scent hit him.

It was a sweet smell, yet sharp, and when he breathed it in he felt his senses reel. At the first taste of it, he felt a heat build. The dark stand of trees around him took on a reddish hue, and on the peak of that heat came overwhelming desire.

Something hit him from behind.

Seamus O'Farrell had smelled the scent too; lust sizzled in his veins. He was overwhelmed by hunger for the girl, a hunger that swelled so suddenly it felt like a *rage*. He shoved Terry out of the way with a blow on the back of his neck and walked forward into the moonlit glade, wide eyes fixed on the fleeting pale form.

Terry staggered a few steps, recovered his balance and turned on the other young man. He drew his fist back and hit Seamus a mighty punch on the back of the head, and felt a distant satisfaction as he sprawled into the undergrowth. He'd just *hit* as hard as he could. Seamus fell, rolled and came up like a snarling tiger. Terry saw the man's lips peeled back over clenched teeth and heard the manic gurgle in his throat as Seamus launched himself.

Neither of them stopped to think about what they were doing. Their bodies only reacted to the irresistible imperative that seized them when they breathed in the musky, bitter-sweet scent of the woman. Her high-pitched mocking laughter drifted back to them from the shadows. Seamus snarled and grabbed Terry's neck, clenching his fingertips on the windpipe. Terry brought his knee up and drove it into the other's testicles, but despite the blow, despite the grip, neither of them was aware of pain. All they felt was screaming lust and roaring anger that surged inside them. In the course of a second, they had become ravening animals.

All this Hugh Sands saw from his vantage point behind the honeysuckle, baffled by the inexplicable turn of events.

Seamus flexed his biceps, almost driving his fingers *through* the skin of Terry's neck, and it was only the fact that his opponent fell to the side that he failed to do so. Terry tumbled to the ground and Seamus ignored him. Driven by the scent, he lumbered through the bracken towards where the girl had disappeared.

The *want* of her was burning high at the front of his brain, clouding his vision, and the smell of her was a screaming *need* in his blood. So fixed was he on his intent that he didn't even hear Terry roll in the crackling leaf-litter and come staggering up behind him. The log in Terry's hand swung high in the air and came down with a thud that even Sands heard, forty yards away. If the dead branch hadn't been waterlogged and pulpy, the strike would have taken Seamus's head off at his shoulders. Even so, the blow was so vicious that the young Ulsterman crumpled to the ground without a sound.

Terry dropped the club and ran forward. He lumbered between two trunks and stopped.

There she stood, smiling at him, beckoning him with her hand. He went to her. She stood, eyes reflecting silver, and opened her arms. He went into her embrace like a drowning sailor reaching the shore.

He felt her hands on him, unfastening his clothes, and the smell of her was driving him mad with desire. He heard the zip of his trousers tear and there was a coolness as she pushed the waistband down over his thighs. He was hugely, almost painfully erect. When she had freed him she stepped back, and with one movement she shucked off the silky shift and stood there, silently eyeing him, her face pale, yet bright with a hunger that made him lust even more. She came towards him and put her hands around his neck, pulling him down on the ground, in the same movement bending her knees and arching her back. He felt her thighs reach up and round him and she brought his face onto hers. When their mouths met, he tasted the bitterness of her that drove his desire to a frenzy. He felt her open and almost *pull* him inside: he drove forward in a violent jerk. The feeling was indescribably wonderful as he slid inside the slick warmth. She held onto the back of his head and forced his face into hers, winding her tongue around his, and he felt her heave under him, dragging him into her. He heard her grunt passionately and he drove again, hard, and again and again.

She shoved his head to the side so strongly that he could not resist. Her body twisted and she flipped him over in an easy movement and was astride him. He was lying on the leaf litter, with the girl crouched over him, bucking on his heaving pelvis, and the smell was in his nose and in his brain and everything except the lust and the movement fled.

From his concealed position, Hugh Sands watched, mouth agape. The night sights showed everything. He had sneaked forward to the edge of the clearing. He couldn't take his eyes off what was happening. The man and the girl were coupling frantically, both of them making low, growling sounds with every thrust of their bodies. The girl was on top and she was violently screwing herself onto the man. The moonlight flashed off her pale body as it flexed and bucked. Sands realised the effect it was having on him: he had to adjust his own trousers to relieve the uncomfortable pressure on his crotch. He licked his lips, feeling the vicarious thrill, the flagrant eroticism of the copulation. He watched, fascinated, his breath shallow and quick. The woman arched herself up from the man and, still bucking, stretched her hands into the air. As she did so, she turned her head slowly and stared right into the lens. Her face split into a wide grin.

Sands made to jerk back, out of sight, when he froze.

The face *changed*. The grin widened in a white arc that pulled her cheeks back. And then it kept going, the skin puckering right round her face. Then the mouth opened and he could see, green on the sight screen, an impossible row of jagged teeth.

The snub, narrow nose stretched itself out of the front of the face and flashing eyes sank behind a bulging ridge across the brow. Right in front of him, the face was *twisting* into something grotesque. The raised arms elongated and withered until every stringy muscle appeared to writhe and knot under wrinkled skin. From the hollows under the ridges, the eyes stared at him, burning with a smouldering fire.

The thing that had been a girl still moved and the man underneath heaved and grunted.

It stared at him, still grinning that huge, jagged-toothed grimace, and then turned away. Sands, shaking, was unable to draw his eyes away, despite the deep *fear* of the thing looking at him. It had been a devastating look, of challenge and scorn and glee.

The head went down and arms reached to the man's head. The thing that was no longer a girl put her face on the young man's, as if to kiss him, and then the arms stiffened. The jaws opened and even across the distance, he heard the crunch of bones. The thing's head came up and in its terrible mouth were pieces of dripping, raglike flesh.

'Aaah,' was the only sound Sands managed to make. He felt his stomach heave violently. But he wasn't sick. Not then. He swallowed involuntarily. The obscene creature's hands, wide and clawlike on the ends of the long, stick-thin arms, flexed, and there was a wrenching, *rending* sound.

Terry Munster's head came ripping off his shoulders in one ghastly motion. The thing that sat astride him, almost spider-like, with its long knees bent up almost to the level of its deformed shoulders, pulled the head forward and took a casual bite out of it.

That was not the worst.

Underneath the loathsome thing, the body of the headless man, dead from the instant his neck was broken, even before his head had been torn away, was still bucking frantically. Copulating with the thing that had killed it. Still driven, even in death, by the waves of black desire that flooded off the thing.

Sands felt the blood drain so quickly that he thought he was going to faint. The trees spun and a mist swooped in to cloud his vision, but the idea, if he did faint, that he'd be completely powerless against that creature was enough to bring him back from the edge. He swallowed hard against his heaving stomach, and failed. He vomited with such force his dinner splattered on the tree six feet away from him.

When his breath came back again, he was already gibbering with fear and he turned, scrambling on all fours until he got to his feet and ran between the trees towards where Seamus O'Farrell lay felled. He made thirty yards, eyes still smarting and mind reeling, then ran smack into the trunk of a tree, the impact bouncing him back to land on his backside. He dazedly got to his feet, scrambling for the night sight, riven with fear.

There was a small click beside his head and he froze.

A voice, low and soft, muttered in his ear in an accent that was bred up north in Armagh.

'I hope you know some fuckin' prayers.'

30

Siobhan had the papers and prints spread out in front of her while the rest sat around the table.

'This piece here,' she said, jabbing a finger at a line of curvilinear notches that to the others looked just like squiggles. '*Never free, the high-born kings, brothers' hearts rent asunder. See death soar on famine's wings, see war's havoc, dread plague plunder.*'

'What's that mean?' Tom asked.

'That's what the *Shee* promised. That was her curse. Her prophecy,' Siobhan said bleakly.

'And it's come true, hasn't it?' Liz said.

'She predicted the famine?' Sean asked.

'And the troubles that have been Ireland's lot for thousands of years. Brother fights brother, and the five kings of Ireland are long gone. It's all come true.'

Siobhan put her chin on her hands and bent to look again at the photographs.

'It said there is a curse and death on whoever opens the chamber and sets the *Shee* free.'

'And is there anything in all that that would give a clue about putting the thing back, assuming that it did get out?'

Siobhan shook her head slowly, despondently, then stopped in mid-motion. 'Hold on a minute. There was something, on the top of the stone.'

She riffled through the stack of prints, scattering them apart as she searched for something. Finally she slipped one out of the scatter and held it up.

'Here, in the *geis* it says something. Just after the part about the land standing above the sea.' She paused, frowning in concentration.

'Go on,' Nancy encouraged.

'Yes. I've got it. *As long as the guards stand she will not wake. As long as the Sword of Light bars her path, she will stay.*'

'What's the Sword of Light?'

'Haven't a clue,' Siobhan said. 'But there was something like it on the other side.'

She scrabbled in the papers again and drew another out.

'Another reference. It says here, translated as best I can: *Should she be free, naught but the sword, in the hands of the Son of Light will stand against her and send her away forever.*'

'Who's he then?'

'I don't know. It's possibly a reference to Lugh, the God of Light, who was the direct opposite to the *Shee*.'

'So now we got to find a god and ask him to be Rambo for us?' Tom's sarcasm was heavy.

'I don't know what we've got to do.'

'I don't buy any of this. You get a couple of people killed and you say it's all to do with a million-year-old pile of *rocks*? My money's on those retards who tried to rape Nancy.' Tom broke off, got up from the table and went to the cabinet. He jerked the door open and brought out a bottle and a single glass. He knocked back a drink in one angry gulp.

There was a momentary silence, and then Nancy spoke up. 'I think she's right, Tom. I can't shake off this feeling.'

'Me too,' Liz said. 'I don't want to stay here any more.'

'Then you can leave if you want to,' Tom said irritably.

'No, I mean I don't want to stay *here*. In Kilgallan. It's giving me the creeps.'

'I'll go along with that,' Sean said. 'I think we should maybe move out tomorrow.'

'So you believe what I'm saying?' Siobhan asked.

'I don't know what to believe,' Sean said. His voice was low and bleak.

The kitchen door came crashing inwards, sending shards of wood spinning away from the doorpost. Edward Laird, hunched at the table over the innards of his radio, whirled to dive his hand beneath the jacket hanging on the back of the chair. A harsh metal rattle froze him.

'Now there's a good Englishman,' a deep voice said. 'You just keep both of your hands on the top of that table, or I'll put a big hole in the back of your head.'

Laird kept his voice steady.

'I'm not moving,' he said, without turning. 'Just take whatever you want.'

Footsteps sounded behind him. He tensed for the blow, still estimating the distance and the speed at which he could reach his gun. Something very cold jammed hard under the curve of his jaw, just below his ear.

'Don't be thinking any foolish thoughts now,' the voice said, so quietly and calmly that the menace behind it was chillingly magnified. 'We'll take what we want, sure enough, and then we'll be gone,' the man said, and Laird felt a soaring relief mingled with the unreasonable hope that the man was just here to rob them.

'We'll take you, for starters,' the voice went on, and the hope dropped like a stone.

Laird did as he was told and put his hands behind him, all the time waiting for the crash on the back of his head and the oblivion to follow. Hands grabbed his and he found his wrists being lashed with thin twine that was pulled so tightly it cut his skin. Then he was bound so strongly he couldn't even move his arms. His shoulders, pulled back too far, began to ache.

The man who had tied his arms kept his hands on Laird's shoulders, gripping his fingers into the muscle to prevent any movement. The other one came sauntering round the other side of the table. Laird looked up into his eyes, dark glitters behind the holes of a black balaclava.

'What should I call you now? Sergeant? Maybe even Captain?'

'I don't know what you're talking about,' Laird said quickly, his eyes darting to the dark circle at the end of the gun's muzzle. He recognised the deadly Armalite. The bullet would go through his skull and probably through the wall behind him.

'Of course you don't,' Cooney said. 'You're a birdwatcher.'

'That's right.'

'Aye, a birdwatcher with a field radio.'

Cooney strolled round the table, keeping the rifle pointed at Laird's head. He reached out and flicked the jacket off the back of the seat, revealing the shoulder holster dangling on its harness.

'And with a Browning and all,' Cooney said, chuckling. 'Now there's one thing a birdwatcher should know, for it's a thing I know, having been brought up on the farm.'

'What's that?' Laird felt the quaver in his voice and was ashamed of it.

'Nightjars. They don't hoot. Owls do that.'

On the west of the village, at Roonah Water, shapes moved, graceless and ungainly, from the shadows of the trees bordering the road. They made no sound but for their snuffling breathing as they lumbered onto the road beside the still-high stream running dark under the moon.

By day the men of Kilgallan had worked hard to build their makeshift bridge, now halfway across the flow. The trunks that had come down at the copse near Bavcroo had been cut and laid over the broken back of the bridge, then lashed together. Stones were placed on the broken masonry to level it to take the platform. By the side of the road, the rest of the timber lay waiting for dawn, and the men to complete the task. The bridge would be strong enough, when it was finished, to take traffic for a short while until a real bridge could be built.

The shadowy figures came out in a group, loping forward to stand together on the bank, looking at what had been built. Their odd shapes cast odder shadows on the road behind them as they shuffled, as if undecided. Then, as one, they lurched forward. Each picked up a piece of stone and started to saw at the strong ropes that bound the logs together. It took them some time to grind their way through the tough fibres until at last the bindings fell away. The logs, loosened, began to separate. On the downstream side, where the bank shelved away sharply into the deep pool, one of the things that had come out of the trees bent a skinny, strangely off-centre frame. It wrapped long arms around the first log, braced its legs, and heaved. Animal sounds carried low in the night. With a grinding sound, the log started to lift.

The grinding noise became a screech of stone against timber: the log lifted from the bracket until the shadowy thing had it at chest-height. Then, with a quick jerk and another, deeper grunt, it twisted and let the trunk fall. There was a thud as it bounced on the bank, a vibration deep in the ground, and then a loud splash. The water was deep enough there for it to plunge straight down before its own buoyancy carried it back, rearing out of the dark pool, then falling with a lesser splash to float on its side. The fast current swept it away down the stream and out of sight. Beside the shadowy creature its neighbour bent to shift the next, and in a series of heaves and jerks and grunts, the bridge was methodically dismantled and slung into the water. This done, they turned lurching, like a pack of hyaenas.

The moonlight shone down and briefly lit their twisted faces. The peat cutters had come down off the hills, no longer the poor unfortunates employed by the small community of farmers and villagers. They had become something else. Their deformities had become more exaggerated, their bodies more twisted. Their faces were now bestial, grotesquely animal.

The goblin-like group shuffled and snuffled, as if scenting the air, before beginning to walk forward towards Kilgallan.

Not even a nightbird called from the shadows.

'It's a bit of a tall tale for me to swallow in the one gulp,' Professor Connarty said. 'I've been on too many digs to start believing in old Irish fairy tales.'

'I'm very scared,' Siobhan said flatly, simply.

'It'll all look different on the morrow,' Connarty told her. 'I'm pleased you've got the key to the translation, but I think you must have mixed things up a little bit.'

'I wish I had. But I don't think so.'

Sean and Liz, seeing how disturbed she was, had walked Siobhan to her own cottage. They found the professor talking to Theresa and Agnes. Siobhan decided there and then to tell him what she thought she'd discovered.

'Things will look a bit different in the morning. It's not as if we can go anywhere, even if we wanted to,' he said. 'And I'm sure there will be another explanation in the carvings if we look hard enough.'

Edward Laird was manhandled in through the back door of the cottage, arms still tightly bound behind him and an ache knifing into his shoulders. He only got a brief glimpse of Sands, slumped in a chair and tied equally efficiently, his face and eyelids swollen and blue-black with bruises. A trickle of blood ran from each nostril.

They dragged him into the next room and forced him into a seat.

'Your friend there nearly killed our young fella,' Cooney said in a low voice. Over at the window, Bridget Massey looked on impassively. Beside her, the young red-haired man had a bandage wrapped round his head.

'You've got a lot of explaining to do,' Cooney went on.

'But I—'

Cooney spun on his heel and brought his foot up in a tight arc. The heavy boot connected with the side of Laird's head, and stars exploded.

'Let's start again. Special Branch, or Intelligence.'

Laird, dazed, shook his head in mute denial.

'All right now, no more mister nice fella,' Cooney said.

In the kitchen, Sands, groggy from the terrible beating he'd received, was slowly coming round, and the first thing he heard were the moans of pain coming from the other room. He knew what was happening, for it had already happened to him. They had stuffed a sock in Laird's mouth and were systematically beating him. It had been easier, to a certain extent, for Sands. He was still in a state of stunned horror, his mind beaten flat by what he had seen in the viewfinder of his night sight. He had tried to speak, but his voice refused to come out. Even the pain of the beating, a terrible series of agonising blows to his head and face, had been far off, as if happening to somebody else. No matter what they did to him, all he could see in his mind's eye was that *thing* in the forest changing shape and then pulling the man's head off his shoulders. He still saw, in a continuous playback, with every detail imprinted, *seared*, onto his memory, the body of the dead man bucking in sexual frenzy while the loathsome thing feasted on his face.

He couldn't raise the mental acuity to think much about Laird. His partner's agony continued to filter through.

Cooney and Boyle were systematically using the butt of Laird's Browning automatic and their hands and fists to beat Laird into submission. He felt the blows rocking his body from side to side, felt the bridge of his nose crack and a terrible pressure inside his ear, which soared to a crescendo and then suddenly stopped. He felt a warm trickle pulse out from it and flow down his neck.

Only one eye was open now. He was gasping for breath through a plug of blood and mucous in his nostrils while trying frantically to shove the sock out of his mouth. His eye caught the movement of an upraised hand and his whole body cringed in expectation of the blow, when a loud thud banged out to his right.

Everybody froze and the noise came again, twice. A sharp hammering at the door: silence; and then knocking, a fast rap beaten out.

'Lights!' Cooney barked, and somebody hit the switch. The room went dark except for the mute glow of the peat fire.

'Who the fuck's that?' Boyle whispered.

'Shut up,' Cooney whispered back.

The knocking came again, hard and fast and urgent.

'Stand back. Get yourselves ready,' Cooney hissed, and slowly made for the door. He stood at the wall beside the handle, the pistol beside his face, then shot his hand out, pulled the door in with a violent heave, twisting to crouch low, his gun-hand jammed into the black void outside.

No-one there. He swung the gun quickly left and right, a movement he'd picked up not from any military training, of which he'd had none, but from American cops-and-robbers films. He slowly raised himself to his feet. Behind him, Bridget Massey and John Boyle crowded through the door.

'Who was it?' John asked.

'Don't know. But we'd better find out.' He stepped out onto the path and caught in his peripheral vision a movement at the side of the cottage. He swung and saw a shadow flicking out of sight.

'Right. Get the guns. There's another of them,' he said.

Bridget dashed inside and came out within seconds, trailing Seamus O'Farrell, whose bandage shone white in the moonlight. Each of them carried one of the deadly rifles that they'd broken out of the boxes only two hours before.

They followed Cooney and Boyle to the space between the cottages. Beyond that, the barrier of trees loomed dark. Cooney didn't pause and the rest of them followed as he pursued the sound of footsteps along the edge of the wood, where the trees had escaped the force of the monstrous wave.

Inside, Laird struggled against his bonds and the nausea that looped up from his stomach. He felt as if he'd been hit by a truck and he couldn't find a part of him from the waist up that wasn't pulsing urgent pain messages. He twisted right and left, trying to find a looseness in his bonds, still trying to call out, though all that came from his blocked mouth was a series of muffled grunts.

In the kitchen, still unable to speak properly, Sands backed his chair against the sink and managed to get his hands up against the chipped edge of the work surface, sharp enough to saw through the nylon monofilament fishing line wrapped around his wrists.

After a few moments see-sawing, he heard a satisfying *ping* as the first strand parted. Spurred on, he rubbed frantically at the edge until more of them gave away, and he was eventually able to jiggle the rest of them, loosening the bonds with every moment.

Laird was having no success. The more he pulled, the more the nylon line cut into his skin, and the pain shooting from his wrists was a hot fire. He gasped with the effort and opened his eye, which had been screwed shut in concentration. There was a movement in front of him and his heart sank, and then leapt. A girl stood in the open doorway, small and slight, her pale face open with question.

'Is there anything wrong, sir?' she asked in a soft, shy, west-coast accent.

'Hmmph,' Laird said uselessly. He worked his jaws, almost choking, to get the sock out and failed to budge it.

The girl came forward, almost timorously, and stopped in front of him. He could see a smattering of freckles against the pale skin. She had an air of innocence, and her face seemed somehow familiar.

'You want this out?' she asked, and without waiting for the muffled, incomprehensible answer, she reached out for the toe of the black sock, and pulled. He felt the material rough against the inside of his cheeks, and then it was gone. Laird inhaled almost desperately, drawing air into

338

his hot lungs. Finally, when he'd taken several deep breaths, he was able to gasp out his thanks.

'Could you untie me, miss. We have to get out of here,' he said quickly. 'We're all in great danger.'

The girl stared at him, almost solemnly, and took a step backwards.

'Come on, girl. Be quick,' Laird snapped. He was in a panic to get out of there before the Ulstermen returned.

Just then, Sands came stumbling out of the kitchen, head down, rubbing his wrists. His face was almost unrecognisable under its camouflage of bruising and swelling.

'Thank Christ for that!' Laird said vehemently, and Sands looked up.

Laird saw his eyes widen and his jaw open and close several times. Sands looked like a man who was choking.

'What's the matter, man?' he rasped. 'Get me loose before those bastards come back.'

Sands sounded as if he'd taken a stroke. There, standing only feet from his bound partner, was the same girl he'd seen in the clearing. His mouth continued to open and close and the words still refused to come. The girl's form started to flow and alter itself. Her body elongated and bent and her arms stretched out, seeming to *grow* out on either side, lengthening into wizened, *spidery* pinions that seemed to have too many joints. The back hunched up and the knobs of the spine could be seen poking up between the shoulderblades. The heart-shaped face seemed to droop and sag and *stretch* while the smooth skin wrinkled and shrivelled.

The thing that had been the girl jerkily hunkered down like some appalling four-legged *insect*. The legs bent and stretched until the knees, scaly and warty, were at shoulder-height. There were two skinny horns of bone where the gnarled hips protruded. Her pointed backside grew outwards, curving like a black tail until it looped up over the shoulders.

Laird, in an agony of desperation and frustration, twisted in his seat towards the girl.

A hag, a pustular, loathsome parody of a woman. Ancient tits, wrinkled and warted, swinging low over a slatted ribcage. Long, skinny legs, twisted and bowed. The bones protruded through the grey flesh. Between the stick-like thighs Laird could see the wrinkled, diseased sexual organs, and even in his terror he saw them twitch and pulse.

'Oh God,' he said with feeling, revulsion flinging him back from the sight of her. Eyes smouldered red from deep within bony crevices on

339

either side of her hag face. They bored into him hungrily for a few long, *dreadfully long* seconds, then her gaze swept away and he felt a blessed relief, as if he'd turned from a burning fire.

Sands couldn't move as the creature turned. A black shape like a monstrous scorpion reared up and then, with an impossible pistoning of arms and legs, came for him. Hands with long, crooked fingers and multiple joints grabbed him: he could feel the thumbs on his breastbone and the fingers in the middle of his back. The grip was *enormous*. The tail-like protrusion swung up. Huge red eyes blared like headlights.

The curved tail came down behind his shoulders.

Something stabbed deep into his spine. He felt a hard *pulse* and then a terrible pressure as pure fire was pumped into his body.

The pain was so big, so unbelievably *colossal*. A whistle of air came from his throat, and another small sound. Molten agony . . . His paralysed legs collapsed beneath him and he toppled to the floor.

Laird struggled against the fishing line as the thing turned towards him. He felt violence transmitted like a pulse of energy across the intervening space. His fear was so great that from somewhere came a spasm of strength. His shoulder muscles flexed so strongly that two of the strands parted like violin strings snapping. He wriggled his wrists together desperately, not caring about the pain, and felt the coils slowly slide off. His hands suddenly came free. He lurched out of the chair.

The grotesque hag, a few matted hairs on either side of her loathsome head, shambled towards him. He backed off, eyeing the distance between himself and the door.

So fast it was a blur, the thing pounced. Two skinny hands grabbed him by the neck. He kicked at it. His toe hit something that felt like solid stone. He turned, dropped his weight, tried to throw the thing off-balance.

Sands, on the floor in a searing cauldron of pain, could only watch as the paralysis crept through his muscles. He saw Laird's desperate, hopeless fight. He heard his screams as the hands clamped on the side of his head. He heard a liquid snap as the bones broke. And a dull thud as Laird's body fell, twitching, to the hard floor.

Laird's foot jittered.

Sands closed his eyes, waiting for it to return to him, to start *feeding* on him, to yank his head off his shoulders. A tear of pain and anger and horror bubbled up in his eyes. He couldn't even blink it away.

The three men and the girl had followed the line of trees, still convinced they could hear something blundering ahead of them, when the noise stopped. Cooney held up a hand, pale in the light of the moon, and they stopped behind him. Everybody held their breath, straining to hear, but the sounds had gone.

'Who was it?' John Boyle finally asked.

'I don't know, but we'd better find out. Let's go back.'

They followed him along the line of darkened cottages, coming to the third from their own, when a dark shape flitted out from the corner and scurried away from them in the opposite direction.

'There's the bastard!' Cooney bawled, and without thinking he squeezed the trigger of the Browning. There was a flash and a deafening *crack* and the gun bucked powerfully in his hand, jarring the wrist. The report rolled out across the field.

'Bloody hell, Brian, you'll wake the town,' Seamus said, but Cooney was already running fast, paralleling the tangle of fallen branches, trying to get a sight of the shadow ahead.

The dark shape jinked and tumbled ahead, just beyond the range of his night vision, and darted over the low stone wall that separated the field from the track. He ran and scrambled across the barricade in pursuit, barking his shin on a protruding stone and ignoring the blossom of pain.

He caught a blur of motion ahead. The others joined him on the track.

'That way,' he pointed, indicating the dark hump of the tor against the velvet sky. Ahead, sounds of movement again. They followed, emboldened by the powerful rifles and the automatic pistol, and went running across the flat, muddy diggings where the turf had been scraped away. Up ahead there was a rasping noise from near the entrance to the tunnel and they ran towards it. From inside the rectangular opening, a dim light shone.

'We've got the bastard now,' Cooney said, and strode forward.

Bridget Massey put her hand on his arm to stop him. 'What if he's got a gun as well?'

Cooney stopped to think for a minute and the other two darted nervous glances up the tunnel.

'Nah. If he'd a gun, he'd have fired instead of running. Anyway, we've got four.'

He looked at the three of them. 'Listen. We have to get him. We don't know what he saw, but that doesn't matter.' He was speaking in a harsh whisper. 'He knows enough to put us in the shit, that's for certain.' He stopped, gathering his breath, and the others could hear the tension in the fast pant of his lungs.

341

'We have to go in.'

'Don't be a fool, man.' Bridget Massey's voice was low and quick and hard. 'Look at it. The first one of us in there is a sitting target. You can't see a bloody thing.'

'Well, what do you suggest? We wait him out?'

She shook her head.

'Four guns to his one. I'll go first. Low down. Seamus and John take the right and left sides for cover. Anything moves, put all you've got into it, over the top of me. And for fuck sake, do it fast.'

Boyle nodded, grinning.

'Bridget,' Cooney went on, 'you come in after me. Even if he's got a gun, he'll have to know that as soon as he fires it he's a dead man.'

Cooney didn't wait for another objection. He turned and stepped silently to the black hole in the side of the hill, edging up against the stone, gun held tight against himself, barrel pointing to the dark sky. With his right hand he motioned the others into position. Seamus O'Farrell jinked quickly across the entrance, with only a small scuffle of his boots against the gravel. No shot rang out.

When he was in place, Brian Cooney eased himself onto one knee, then lowered his body until his head was less than two feet above the ground. Gingerly he pressed himself against the stone and edged his face round so that only one eye was looking down into the blackness. Even if there had been movement, it would have been impossible for him to see it. He drew back, lowered himself until he was flat on the gravel, then, using elbow and knees, he scuttled inside. The others watched as he disappeared into the gloom.

Once Cooney was inside the passageway he was suddenly alone. Up ahead was dead darkness. It could have been a million miles wide and a million miles long: there was no point of reference for his eyes to fix on. And down there, somewhere ahead of him in the narrow confines of the stone corridor, a gun could be aimed straight at his head. The hairs on the back of his neck shifted and crawled. Sweat oozed out of the pores on his back, cold and clammy.

He hauled himself forward, feeling his elbows scrape on the stone, every minute expecting to see the flash, hear the thunder, of gunfire. He was more scared than he had ever been in his life, yet still, despite his fear, he hauled himself along the floor.

A touch on his ankle almost made him cry out aloud with sheer fright, before he realised, with a blessed cool wash of relief, that it was Bridget Massey following behind. His breath came out in a long, shaky sigh. Despite the danger ahead, a danger he could now *feel* as a presence,

342

having her behind him diminished it just a little. He crawled on, gun pointing ahead, foot by foot into the swallowing dark.

He heard the others move in behind him, and he hoped that one of them was still high on the entrance, ready to spray heavy calibre over their heads.

His eyes detected light. At first he thought he was getting accustomed to the gloom, using the minute trace of moonlight at the entrance, but the further he crawled, the brighter it got until he could make out the edges of the stones that formed the corridor.

Another ten feet and the strange glow, which seemed to have no source, was bright enough to let him see ahead. A weird, purple-green light that seemed to come from within the stones themselves. Whatever it was, it gave their four guns more advantage. In the semi-dark, he grinned.

He came to the hole that led into the chamber, and hauled himself against the wall, facing the way he had come, until Bridget crawled up to him. Seamus O'Farrell came next, then they had to wait a full minute until John Boyle made it slowly to where they crouched.

Bridget could sense the wound-up tension in them all, could feel fingers of apprehension walking up and down her spine. Inside the chamber, the glow was feeble. And there was something *else*. Bridget could feel pure *threat*, an overwhelming *bad feeling*. For some reason that she could not identify, her whole being wanted to leap up and run from this place. She had to grab it and tie it down. It wasn't the danger of gunfire, though that was real enough. There was something *other*. It was as if a part of her had reached ahead and come into contact with something cold and foul and powerful.

The fear wound up within her. Her fingers clenched on the stock of the gun.

Cooney turned to the hole in the wall and very slowly, very carefully peered ahead. The wide chamber was dimly lit like a luminous bruise. His eyes flicked left and right, taking in the stone, instinctively noting the lack of cover. No sign of anyone.

'Hey, you in there,' he called out, the final *there* echoing in a quick succession of syllables up the corridor. Diminishing.

'There's four of us, and four fucking guns. Just put your hands on the top of your head and come out slow as you like.' His loud, reverberating voice faded away.

From the chamber, there was silence.

'I'm going to count to ten, then we're going to spray this place. You've got ten seconds to think about it, so think fast.'

He motioned to the others with his free hand, telegraphing his intention, easing himself to his feet even as he started counting.

'*One*.' He flattened himself against the wall.

'*Two*.' He slipped his finger into the trigger guard, bringing the gun up tight.

'*Three*.' Cooney leapt forward, twisting to the right to throw himself flat on the floor up against the wall. John Boyle dived into the chamber, taking the left side. Bridget Massey and Seamus O'Farrell launched themselves low across the floor to crouch behind the massive stone. Around them the dismal, poisonous light writhed, casting strange shadows into the chamber.

Their movement stopped and silence fell like a blanket.

Dark shadows crawled on the walls all around them. Bridget could feel threat expand in a wave of pressure. Inside her mind a voice was screaming at her to get out of there, make a run for it, just *go*.

There was something here.

She could feel it. She could *sense* it.

Bridget saw, out of the corner of her eye, Cooney rising to his feet, gun forward, ready to shoot. Boyle and Cooney got up very slowly, and finally she forced her muscles to lift her.

Cooney stepped forward, eyes fixed on the big square stone, and the others spread out on either side. Cooney came round behind the stone, checked the shadow, stepped forward and turned, keeping the gun extended. No-one was there. He stood up, baffled. There was no other hiding place.

The light flared brighter and Seamus O'Farrell started to say something. Then he stopped abruptly. He was staring at his hand, clenched around the rifle's forward grip, and the forearm below the turned-up sleeve of his heavy shirt. Lumps had appeared: large dark swellings that became ever larger, visibly growing up from the skin like bubbles.

'What the hell is that?' Cooney asked, his voice sharp with alarm.

'I don't – Oh shite, that *hurts* . . .' His voice trailed off into a pained gasp.

'Seamus. Your face. What's that stuff?' John Boyle hissed in alarm, stepping back from the man next to him.

The red-haired man took his hand off the stock and lifted it to his cheek, his expression bewildered and panicky. Under his fingers he felt the lumps beneath his skin swelling so quickly the spaces between them were crowded out. The lumps grew as if inflated from within, and he could feel his skin stretch tautly under the pressure. For a few seconds they itched badly and then the pulsations behind them started, rising up in a swoop beyond the threshold of pain until his entire face was throbbing. Under his shirt, he felt them grow on his skin, forcing their way up through the subcutaneous layers, stretching his skin so much it felt as if it would burst.

'Brian! John!' O'Farrell wailed. '*What's happening to me?*'

Cooney took a step forward and his face wrinkled in disgust. The pustules bubbling over O'Farrell's skin were *audibly* expanding.

O'Farrell let out a wail and started twisting. He dropped the gun to the floor with a clatter and tried to drag his shirt off. Just then, a huge lump on his forehead burst. Cooney felt his gorge rise in abrupt reaction. Another one burst, and the skin, bellowed out under pressure, sagged back in a poisonous-looking crater. The young man spun round. To their horror, they could see fresh lumps growing underneath his hair. It made him look as if his carroty mop was *alive*.

Seamus screamed aloud, a desperate hoarse cry that just wouldn't stop. He collapsed to the ground, and the bubbles on his skin rose up in the crater where another had burst only seconds before, until there was nothing left but a mass of ragged holes.

John Boyle watched Seamus O'Farrell collapse to the floor, his face a bursting ruin, and then, under his own feet, the solid floor gave way. Before he could even shoot out his arms for balance, he was falling, tumbling and sliding down the steep face as the floor tilted. He let out a yell that echoed up and away from him, reverberating off smooth walls, and he kept sliding on a surface that gave no purchase. The gun fell from his hands and skittered down the face beside him, and it felt as if he was falling *for ever*, until suddenly he hit cold water. His breath was dashed out of him and he struggled to the surface, gasping for air. He didn't know what had happened. He trod the black water, groped for the edge, and found it. The edge was almost sheer and it was smooth as glass. He paddled round it, trying to find a handhold, but there was none. The pool he had fallen into was round and cold and deep, and there was no way out. Panic swelled within like a black bubble, choking his breath back. There was *no way out*.

His worst nightmares swamped him. He was in a black pit, a freezing pool of water and he could not escape. Then something under the water reached and took his ankle in a strong, almost soft grip. The fear exploded within him. Insistently and slowly, he was pulled down. John Boyle bellowed his fear up the well, hearing his voice echo in the vast chamber until the sound was cut off. Black water poured into his mouth and flooded his lungs.

Bridget Massey felt a movement at her feet and she jerked back. Coming from holes between the flagstones, insects, a *mass of insects* swarmed. Some of them were white, glistening pulpy maggots: others scuttered on scratchy feet. They seethed out of the cracks in an upsurge of crawling life, a carpet of chitinous bodies that swarmed up her feet and legs. For an instant she was frozen in terror, then she too started to scream. The mass of chittering things raced up her thighs and the maggots were under the legs of her jeans. She could feel tiny jaws nip and hard legs scrape on her skin, and then she was moving, frantically jerking away from them. She stamped her feet and heard the bodies crack and splutter as she squashed them by the dozen, by the hundred. But more and more kept pouring out of the cracks, racing up her legs.

Bridget Massey was the only one who acted on sheer instinct. She had lived with her fear of insects a long time. She turned, raced out of the chamber and up the tunnel. She ran for her life.

Brian Cooney did not see her go. He had turned away from Seamus O'Farrell's wriggling *destroyed* body, fighting down the waves of nausea and fear. Something came out of a niche in the wall and fastened great red eyes on him. The Browning fell from his hand. The eyes had him in their grip and something *foul* slipped into his mind. He stood, paralysed in the darkness, as the blackness drilled into him, burning its way behind his eyes and into his brain. Then the pain started. Its touch was poison. Nerves shrivelled and burned out; dendrites sparked, sending out waves of agony. Synapses burst and died as pain ripped through them, arcing from one connection to another, sizzling flesh, boiling blood.

Driven by sheer panic, Bridget Massey fled for her life, for her *sanity*, out into the night. She tripped on a stone six feet from the entrance, rolled in the mud and came up running. The dry-stone dyke was perhaps four feet high at the side of the road. She cleared it like a champion hurdler and landed, still running on the short grass and did not stop until she ran straight into Sean McCullain who was coming round from the side of her cottage. The impact knocked her off her feet.

'Are you all right? I didn't see you there.' He bent to pick her up.

She didn't even seem to notice him. As soon as she was on her feet she started running again. Only with difficulty could Sean hold her back.

'Wait a minute,' he said. 'Bridget, isn't it?'

She struggled to break free and he merely held her tighter, wrapping his arms around her in a hug until her movements stopped. One minute she was all struggle and the next she just went limp.

Sean held on to her for a few more moments, then let go. Bridget started falling and he caught her, swung her up in his arms in the same movement and walked into the cottage. Inside, the archaeologists crowded the living room. Sean laid the girl on the sofa. Her eyes darted. She was shaking and her chest was heaving spasmodically.

'What in the good name's wrong with the girl?' Connarty said. 'Sure she looks as if all the devils in hell have taken after her.'

'Something in that cave,' the girl blurted out. 'It got Seamus. His skin fell off him. Oh, my *God*. And the flies. They were all *over* me.'

Siobhan sat down beside the girl. She lifted a hand to gently brush away a strand of hair that was sticking to beads of sweat.

'There now, Bridget,' she said soothingly. 'You just take your time and tell us what's happened.'

Eventually, they were able to piece the story together. Bridget hadn't seen what had happened to John Boyle, but she *had* seen the thing come out of the niche, although, at the height of her terror, she hadn't even been aware that she *had* seen anything. But the memory of it came looping back to her in a rush. Just as she had spun for the doorway, her eyes had swept the chamber and registered the movement. Even now, even though the glimpse had been for a fraction of a second, the image of what she had seen was enough to freeze the words in her throat. It had been a *loathsome* creature. And what was worse, though it did not look human, she knew, knew it on the instinctive level, that it had been *female*.

'I told you,' Siobhan said.

Everybody stood and looked at her in a huddle of silence.

'Told them what?' Bridget asked.

31

'They can't expect us to believe any of that,' Tom said. He'd poured himself a drink and was sitting at the edge of the fireplace kerb where Professor Connarty had been ensconced on the night of the flood. The stone was warm from the absorbed heat of the glowing peats.

'I mean, I know half of the place is back in the Middle Ages, but that's only for us tourists.'

'I think there's something wrong here,' Nancy countered. She was on the settee, knees drawn up to her chin, sitting still, brow furrowed. 'I can't say exactly why I think that. It's just a feeling. I had it before Siobhan said anything.'

'Is that some kind of feminine intuition?' Tom asked.

'Sarcasm's not your strong suit, Tom.'

'Yeah, maybe not. But jumping at shadows isn't like you either.'

Nancy shot him a look, but he was sitting with his head against the wall, eyes shut. She looked away.

They had heard sharp retorts of gunfire earlier and Tom had gone to the window.

'Must be shooting rabbits,' he'd said.

'At this time of night? I don't think so.'

'You can never tell in this godforsaken country. I think they're all on a different wavelength from the rest of the world. We should have stayed in Paris.'

'I thought you liked it here.'

'Sure did. But we've had a tidal wave, and then some inbred retards, and that Polish Canuck zonked out of his brains down on the beach, and a couple of folk torn to pieces. Sure. It's a *wonderful* country.'

'That's what gives me the shivers,' Nancy said. 'It's all *wrong*.'

Outside, there were more sounds: the muffled thuds of running feet, and after that, a high-pitched noise that sounded like the scream of an animal in pain.

'I'm going to see what the hell they're playing at,' Tom said angrily, but immediately Nancy sat up and shook her head.

'No. I don't care what it is. Stay here,' she said, sharply. Tom looked over at her and saw the determination on her face. He shrugged and sat back.

Tom got up and poured himself another whiskey. Nancy shook her head when he asked if she wanted a drink. She was remembering what Siobhan had told them. Despite the absurdity of the tale, that something dead, something *paranormal* could come alive after five thousand years or more to haunt a place, Siobhan had *believed* what she had said. That much Nancy had been convinced of, even though Tom thought the whole story was nonsense.

Tom turned, glass in hand, and as he did, Nancy thought she heard a muffled noise from the back of the house.

'What was that?' she said, turning on the two-seater.

'Hmmm?'

'I thought I heard something,' Nancy said, her voice low and quick.

Tom stopped and listened. There was silence. He took two steps towards her and Nancy heard it again, a muted bump, coming down the narrow hallway from the direction of the bedroom.

'There it is again. Like a thump.'

Tom looked across at her and smiled. 'This place has really got to you, hasn't it?' he said, and for a moment Nancy hated the patronising look on his face.

'I definitely heard a noise,' she told him. 'Back there in the bedroom.'

'All right,' he said, putting his glass down on the dresser. 'I'll go look see. I give you ten to one there's nothing there.'

He grinned again at her and sauntered off down the hall, whistling tunelessly. Nancy sat and listened, apprehensive and tense.

Tom opened the bedroom door and felt the draught immediately. The curtain at the window was billowing inwards on an eddy of cold air and he looked at it for a moment, puzzled. He hadn't opened it and, in fact, was sure it had been closed when he'd come into the room earlier on. Then he shrugged. Possibly Nancy had swung the window open to air the room.

'It's all right,' he called back, walking towards the sill. 'Just an open window knocking on the frame.'

He reached for the handle, pulled the window shut and heard the catch click. The draught stopped immediately. Outside, it was dark, but the full moon silvered everything in view. It was a still night. Tom looked at the pale disc high in the velvet sky and then shivered with the cold. He took a step back from the pane, and as he did, the temperature in the room suddenly *plummeted*. It was as if he'd stepped backwards into winter. In front of him, inexplicably, his breath clouded out, and as it touched the glass it froze onto the surface, crystallising in delicate ice-leaves on the glass.

He watched the patterns grow out, frowning in puzzlement, and then a noise to his left, in the corner of the room, made him jump. He spun round, peering into the dark corner. Something came out of the shadows. He jumped back, stifling a cry, and his heart hit his breastbone with a hard thump.

The shape passed by the window, and the moonlight caught smooth skin and long dark hair. Tom's fear evaporated as quickly as it had come.

The woman was stunningly beautiful.

She stood before him, stock still, like a marble statue in the moonbeam, dark eyes seeming to swell and swallow him.

'How did you get. . . ?' he started to say, when she held a long, slender finger up to her lips. The words dried up in his throat. She raised her other hand and touched his mouth with a finger, slowly sliding it across his lips.

The smell hit him like a blow. It came wafting up from her hand in a cloud of perfume. Instantly his vision blurred and every nerve in his body flared with heat. Even as the scent jolted into his nervous system, Tom had a single clear image of fluttering butterflies. He had seen a wildlife programme about butterflies which could attract a mate from miles away by the power of their scent, and strangely, in that moment, when he felt as if he'd been plugged into a devastating current that was surging with raw power, the image came back to him.

It was the last clear thought he had. Under his skin, he felt as if his blood was suddenly sizzling with heat. A pulse of intense, irresistible desire flooded into him and he was dimly aware of the urgent, almost painful pressure on his jeans. The hand slipped away from his face and crawled down his chest and belly. There was a slight wrench and a ripping sound and he was instantly free. The woman raised her head and shook her dark mane back over her shoulders and he saw her shape, naked in the pale light. Tom lurched forward, driven by the intensity of the raw hunger, and bore her backwards onto the bed.

In the living room, Nancy heard the window close and the quiet squeal of the handle locking it and then, a moment later, Tom muttering to himself. There was a silence for a while and she listened intently, alert for any sound. The apprehension welled up abruptly. Suddenly she felt terribly *afraid*.

'Tom,' she called. 'Is there anything there?' Her voice was cracked with tension.

She moved towards the hallway and looked up it, at the bedroom door. It was closed. Silence. Still the fine hairs on her arms were standing on edge, a matte of pale gold. She stood, debating whether to go forward, or backwards – and right out of the cottage – as the unaccountable fear burgeoned within.

Then the door opened. She saw the handle turn down and darkness widen behind the door. She took a step backwards, her heart beating fast, feeling as if she was running out of air.

Tom stepped out of the dark space. He stood for a second, then looked back into the room, before closing the door behind him and turning down the corridor.

'Just the window,' he said, strolling down the hallway. 'Nothing to worry about. The catch must have come off and the wind blew it open.'

Relief flooded through her. She could feel the anxiety drain away in a cold wash. Nancy let out a slow sigh.

She went back into the living room and Tom followed her through. He took his drink to the fireplace, where he hunkered down in front of the embers and drew out the poker to stoke them into glowing life again.

'You shouldn't get yourself upset,' he said, his back to her. She could see his shoulder moving as he poked the iron rod into the depths of the fire. 'All those old wives' tales are for the Irish, and the tourists they're screwing.'

Nancy felt sheepish. She'd listened to Siobhan's translation and her explanation, and she had absorbed it almost completely. Now she felt a bit ridiculous. She could admit and accept that there had been odd things happening. *Terrible* things. But each of them, she knew, could have a natural explanation. It was just that when she'd heard the archaeologist speak in such flat, almost despairing tones, she had empathised with Siobhan. She'd felt the stuttering crawl of apprehension, and it had all seemed to *fit*.

Tom continued poking at the fire.

'I still feel as if we should move on,' she said.

'No problem. As soon as the hicks throw a couple of logs over the creek, we're out of here. We'll find a five-star place down at Shannon, with room service and telephones and TV, for God's sake, even if it is in ould Oirish accents.'

She nodded and he turned to face her. The poker in his hand was red about six inches from the end, lightening to a yellow-orange near the tip, where it had been dug into the fire. Even from two yards away she could feel the heat it threw out.

'They're still back in the Dark Ages here. They don't even have freeways. And I hate to think what their orthodontists are like. Half the men up in the bar have only two teeth.'

He laughed, a little sharply. 'Compared to us, they're barbarians. No wonder they believe in all that hogwash. You have to remember, we come from the most progressive society that ever existed. We've the best schools and the best communications and technology and the best health care in the world.'

He slowly got to his feet, still holding the poker, and came towards her. She could see the rosy glow on the metal.

She looked up at him and saw his eyes on her. He was smiling, a slow, soft smile. There was something about it that struck her as odd, but she couldn't pin it down.

She smiled back.

The thought she'd been chasing suddenly focused clearly in her mind. Tom's teeth. His teeth were uneven when he smiled, snaggled and discoloured.

'*Not Tom*,' her mind's voice bawled urgently. '*NOT TOM!*'

And then his eyes changed.

They went from light brown to black and then to a dull red that almost matched the glow of the hot metal. She drew back, rocked by the force of the shock. The tip of the poker came swinging in towards her. If she hadn't wrenched away, the hot tip would have gone straight into her eye, but her motion, backwards and sideways, saved her. The edge of the metal came down on her shoulder, seared through her shirt, hissed onto her skin with a sound like water dropped into hot fat. Pain bucked like a mad horse into her neck and down her arm. She twisted away, rolling over on the couch and landing on her backside on the floor with such a thump her teeth snapped on her tongue. A metallic taste flooded her mouth. Her nostrils were filled with the acrid smell of singed flesh and her eyes blurred.

A shape loomed over her and she shoved herself backwards, blinking the tears away rapidly.

Tom – *not Tom!* the internal voice yelled at her – took a step towards her and he looked *insane*. His grin split his face in a jagged-toothed grimace and his eyes were sunk way back into their sockets, glowing red.

He swung the poker at her and she rolled again. It whacked onto the upholstery of the couch and burned a score in the fabric. Nancy, all rational thought fleeing, instinctively kicked out with her foot and hit him with her heel in the groin. There was a satisfying soft crunch as she hit bone and he grunted, falling backwards, the poker tumbling with a metallic jangle to the floor. Nancy completed her roll, got to her knees and then her feet and scuttled to the hallway, grabbing the poker as she did. Behind her she heard a snarling roar and *felt* him lurch after her, without seeing it actually happen. Her awareness was right down in the long nerves in her spine.

Utter fear gripped her.

She sped up the short corridor and into their room. The moonlight shot through the pane, giving enough light to see by. Nancy slammed the door shut behind her, knowing that the key would tumble from the lock, not believing her luck when it didn't. Her shoulder was awash with pain from the burn, but she ignored it. The key turned and she backed away from the door. The fine line of light between the door and the floor faded instantly to black. She waited, hearing the snuffling growl rise up only feet from where she was standing. The door buckled inwards with a screech of splintering wood and then sagged back. Nancy wailed in fright, expecting the door simply to crash inwards and the *thing* that Tom had become to spring on her and kill her. She could see all this in mental preview. Blood dripped out of her mouth from where she had bitten into her tongue. All around there was a strange smell, cloying and thick in the air.

The darkness under the door seemed to thicken, to coalesce.

She moved back, trembling, heart hammering wildly, and saw the darkness come *through* the space. In the wink of an eye it separated into two shadowy columns that solidified as she watched, and became long, emaciated arms. The ends spread out, separated, became many-jointed fingers that ended in long ragged black nails.

Nancy let out a little involuntary wail and was backing away when she felt the weight in her hand. Without real thought, she jumped forward and drove the still-hot tip of the poker into one of the scrabbling hands that were searching on the floor beyond the door on lengthening arms. There was a pressure and then a pop as the hot metal went right into the skin, burned its way between bones and came out the other side into the floor. Beyond the door, noise erupted as if a tiger had been let loose to fight another of its kind.

Nancy didn't wait, she almost fell over the corner of the bed as she leapt for the window, forced the catch up, and then banged on the frame so hard the window flew open wide enough to crash against the outer wall. The glass shattered loudly and Nancy clambered over the sill and out onto the grass. The screeching shivered the door. Nancy saw the frame buckle in again and then drew her eyes away. As she did, she caught sight of something on the bed. A dark, slumped shape that she couldn't make out. All around it, the bed and the walls were dark and reflecting light oddly.

From behind her a cold howl came, drilling through the air, soaring, a screech of wrath and thwarted *fury*.

It wasn't until she was halfway across the grass, heading for Sean's cottage, *feeling* the frenzied scream in the bones of her skull that she realised what she had seen. The shape on the bed, just a blur in the moonlight, impossible to delineate, sprang into focus in her mind, like one of those optical illusions where a pattern leaps into view from a jumble of lines.

Tom.

Nancy ran on, so riven by the horror of it that she couldn't even scream.

Inside the cottage something crawled, snarling, past the wet heap that had been Tom Ducain. It shot towards the window, clambered, hopped onto the roof. The black thing twisted and turned under the moonlight, sniffing like a hunting dog. Then it turned, spread tenebrous pinions like the giant wings of a carrion bird, and soared towards the village.

The full moon dropped behind the hills of Killadoon and the land was plunged into darkness.

From out of the shadows, figures that had once been human loped in ungainly strides into the street. Streetlamps cast their glow up the length of the main road. Here and there, a chink in a curtain cast a narrow beam onto a pavement or wall. It was as if Kilgallan crouched in apprehension.

One of the creatures that had been almost man, but now was a twisted scarecrow with long, oddly jointed limbs, stood at the side of the road, beside the thick resiny pole that carried the power cables from Westport to the town. The pylon towered forty feet above the misshapen head. At twice the height of a man was a three-strand barrier of barbed wire circling the post, a precaution against the foolhardy. The creature looked up, mind a blank, eyes dull as if pondering a great mystery. Then, jerkily, it moved forward and gripped the pole in both hands. Its fingers, splayed out and now *stretched*, curled round the thick post and gripped. Driven by a force it could not comprehend, it began to climb quickly and surely, moving with more grace than it had on the road. It reached the barbs and ploughed through them. Little metal spikes snagged and tore at its skin. It was through, more tattered than before, dripping blood, and continued its climb. At the top was a metal crossbar, three feet in either direction from the pole, each end of which bore a heavy three-ring porcelain insulator. Another one in the centre of the cross-bar completed the supports for the first three braided high-tension cables.

The creature clambered up on the crossbar and stood for a moment, like a tattered ape on a tree branch. Through the wires the power hummed a low and deadly song. The few remaining hairs on the unhuman head twitched and stood erect in the powerful electrical field.

The thing flipped off the bar, spreadeagled itself and landed across the cables.

Its large feet hooked over the furthest wire, its elbows catching the nearest, it hit with a *crack* like a tree snapping in a gale. Blue sparks raced up and down the body: there was a blast of pink flame that burst from inside the jerking, twisting man. All the lights in the village went out. For a few seconds more, the shape on the wires danced frenetically as power surged through it, boiling its cells, burning off scorched flesh, before there was a loud bang. Still twitching, it landed with a thud on the roadside.

In Kilgallan, the lights stayed off.

Doors opened and people spilled out in twos and threes. Some had flashlights, others carried oil-lamps. From a distance it looked like a dance of fireflies.

'What's happened now?' Donovan's bullhorn voice called from the doorway of his bar. 'All the lights have gone.'

'I heard an explosion along the way,' somebody called back.

'There was a flash like a bomb going off,' Patsy McGavigan said. He was peering out from behind the green door of the parlour, wearing his frock coat over a pair of grey long johns.

'I think the wires are down.'

'I thought I heard gunfire a minute or two ago,' another voice from behind a flashlight said.

The men gathered in the streets, undecided, puzzled.

'There's something bloody wrong going on around here,' Donovan said at last. 'Where's Peter O'Neill?'

'Sure he's laid up with a broken leg, is he not?'

'Never mind. We'll go and see him,' the big man said, and strode off, swinging his lamp, down the road. A half-dozen or so followed him.

Peter O'Neill had been reading a detective novel when the lights went out. He reached over to put his glass down on the table, and missed. His whiskey spilled to the floor.

He swore under his breath and tried to haul himself out of bed, but the plaster that encased him to the waist held him back.

There was a loud thump on the door.

'Come on in, whoever it is, for I can't get up to answer,' Peter yelled impatiently.

Donovan came in, along with the rest of the men, crowding into the small front room of the station's house where Peter's bed had been set up on a pull-out sofa. Lights flared and flashed in his eyes.

'Swing them out of my face, for the love of Christ. Can't a fellow get healing in peace?'

There were muttered apologies and the torches swung away. Patsy McGavigan wandered forward, holding up his oil-lamp until there was enough light to see by.

'All right, boys. What's going on out there? Sounds like the troubles have come down to us from Ulster.'

'The power's down. We heard an explosion and there's been gunshots down at the quay.'

'I heard the bang when the power went off,' Peter said. 'Made me spill a good whiskey.'

Somebody sniggered and Peter shot him a look.

'So what's happening? Has somebody been along the road to check?'

Donovan shook his head.

'Well, that might be a good idea. It might be nothing but the aftermath of the storm, but if there's been shooting, we'd better be careful. This place is going to the dogs, if you ask me. Get the women and the wee ones into the church, just to be on the safe side.'

Donovan nodded. He turned to go out and the rest of them followed.

'And don't forget to come and tell me what the devil's going on,' Peter bawled after them.

Patsy McGavigan left his lamp, so Peter had light. He picked up his book, found that he'd dropped it in a puddle of whiskey, and threw the sodden paperback into a corner. There was nothing he could do, so he poured himself another whiskey, listening to the diminishing sound of the men as they went up the road.

A couple of minutes later there was a muffled sound outside the door. Peter looked up. The handle turned with a small, rasping noise.

'Who is it?' he asked. There was no reply. Instead, the door swung open slowly and something stood in the frame. Peter couldn't make out who it was in the dim light. He screwed up his eyes, trying to recognise his visitor.

'Come on in, man, where I can see you,' he ordered.

356

There was a low sound, almost like laughter and then the thing lurched clumsily into the room. Peter drew back against the pillows as it scuttled towards him, short and squat and *twisted*-looking, as if its arms and legs were all different lengths. The face was man-like, but squashed out of shape, the features distorted beyond recognition. It grunted loudly.

'What in the name of God is. . . ?'

An arm swung up high and came crashing down with such speed that Peter didn't even have a chance to blink. The rough half-brick in the creature's grip hit him on the side of the head. He tried to call out but all he managed was a series of choking coughs. He turned to face the thing but the sight in his left eye had blurred with instant tears. He saw a movement, and then the light, which had been sitting on the table, swung away and up. There was a crash and then darkness. Then light started to return.

The goblin-like thing gurgled again, and then scuttled out of the room, slamming the door behind it. Still dazed, Peter slumped back on the pillows, not quite aware of what was happening. The light flared beside the bed as the puddled oil from the lamp began to burn.

Tongues of flame ran up the curtains and the sheets, trailed on the floor. When the first awareness of burning touched him, Peter tried to get away from the flames, but the plaster cast trapped him. He couldn't move. He couldn't escape.

A few seconds later Peter O'Neill began to scream.

In Kilgallan a wave of apprehension surged from house to cottage. Everybody in those houses felt it, a touch of cold, a touch of dark.

Even if the pounding of the explosions had not rattled the windows in their frames and shivered the doors, even if sharp and savage cracks of gunfire had not rippled out, they would still have felt it.

Something terribly *wrong* had touched the night. Something terribly *bad* was moving out of the shadows. There was still enough of the old blood in the veins of the men and women and children of Kilgallan to feel the touch of something even older.

Dread and fear leapt from house to house. Unspoken panic began to soar.

At the chapel house, the door shook on its hinges with the urgent pounding of its heavy brass knocker.

The chapel house stood apart from the church itself and its little graveyard. In the doorway, old Father Cullen blinked in the light of the torches and lamps. He was perhaps the only individual who hadn't heard any of the commotion. He only came to the door because his housekeeper spent several minutes shaking him awake. Even then, Dermid Mullen had to shout at the top of his voice.

Eventually Dermid, a big beefy fellow with a red face, simply grabbed the elderly, deaf priest by the arm and propelled him, dressing gown, carpet slippers and all, down the path towards the church. Mrs Patry, hair in tight grey rolls and face still covered with a death mask of cream, trotted behind with the big brass key.

They opened the double doors and the men hustled the women and half-awake children inside. The whole exercise had taken less than fifteen minutes. Nobody knew what was going on, but when you had explosions and gunfire, even in this far corner of Ireland, the church was the place to head for. The little chapel could take two hundred souls, at a squeeze. Kilgallan had half that. They filed into the pews, some of the women kneeling and crossing themselves as they did every Sunday. A few crying small children were hushed by bewildered mothers. The older kids looked around, wide-eyed, scared, wondering what they were doing in the church in the dead of night.

Donovan's party had gone out on the road east, following the lines. A couple of the fellows had gone and rooted out their old shotguns, though the big landlord had warned them to keep the catches on, just in case of accidents. He was the tallest of the lot, and the easiest target for goose-shot.

They found the charred body only four hundred yards away, lying half on the road, charred feet stretched onto the grass.

'What in the name is *that*?' one of the men asked.

Donovan bent down as flashlights played over the still-smouldering heap. He nudged it with a toe. A burned piece crumpled away and flaked onto the road. There was a smell of cooked meat, singed hair. He gave the thing a shove and it rolled over with a crackling sound.

'Jesus Christ, what *is* that thing?' The voice came again from the huddle of men.

'It's a fellow, sure enough,' somebody else said.

'Like no fellow I've ever seen,' Donovan said. He drew the beam of the torch across the twisted face. The eyes were gone and the skin had melted off the bones. There was a black, crusty tongue. The hands were drawn up towards the face, hooked like claws. The skull looked as if it had been twisted until it came to a point.

'It's a monster,' one of the farmhands said.

358

'It's a goblin,' an old man's voice piped up. Everybody looked up to see Niall Tully pushing his way to crouch beside it. 'This *was* a man, the poor unfortunate. And now he's been changed into something else.'

The farmhand spoke up. 'Talk sense, you daft old bugger.'

'Listen to sense, young feller. This was never any bomb-thrower, you can be sure of that. I don't know who he was before, but he's been *changed* into something else. And I'll tell you more. It's because of those fools digging in that hill down at Bavcroo Field. There's a curse on that place, and that's the cause of it, sure as I'm standing here.'

He pushed himself away from the remains, wrinkling his nose against the smell. 'If I was you lot, I'd get going with me to the chapel house. That's where I'll be staying this night. There's bad about in the air. I can *smell* it.'

The flashlights played over him as he walked off, limping and listing to the left, dragging his dead leg.

'What's the old fool talking about?' asked the farmhand. There was a general muttering. They stood and looked at the body, flickering the flashlights hither and yon, before deciding there was nothing for it but to go back to the village and tell Peter O'Neill.

They turned away from the ruined shape and walked. They reached the turn between the trees, when one of the men stopped suddenly and the man behind bumped into him, letting out a gasp of surprise.

'There, on the road,' the first man said.

The torch beams played like searchlights, pinpointing something else on the rough surface, lying spreadeagled on the asphalt. Warily they walked forward until they were a few feet away.

'It's the old fellow,' Donovan said in a low, booming voice. 'He must have fallen down with that bad leg of his.'

He walked forward, already bending at the waist to give the old man a hand when something launched itself at him from the trees. Thin hands clasped around his throat. Surprise made him drop the torch. It bounced on the road then rolled onto the verge, where it lay angled up into the black night.

Donovan whirled, bringing his hands up to grip skinny wrists that felt just gristle and bone. The hands on his neck were squeezing so tightly that his air was cut off. He couldn't even yell.

The men saw the tattered shape clinging to the big man. They got a glimpse of an emaciated, grotesquely *flattened* face with eyes that bulged idiotically from their sockets. The thing, in the flicker of light, looked more reptilian than human. Declan Donovan swung his body from side to side, feeling the long nails try to burrow through his skin.

From the side of the road, there was a crash of bracken and another dark shape launched itself out. It landed on the back of the garrulous farmhand. Then, behind them, there was a scuttling noise and two more raggedy shapes loped out from the shadows of the verge. Suddenly the whole group were battling with the night things that had ambushed them. Donovan managed to get his grip on the wrists of the thing that was choking him and groaned under the enormous strain in his broad shoulders as he prised the arms apart. He felt as if his own arms were coming out of their sockets: then there was a sudden *snap* and he knew he had broken both of the thing's arms.

Without a scream of pain, without hesitation, the creature that had been a man and was now just a warped parody, a poor human invaded by the terrible power of the *Babd*, lunged its head forward, opening its jaws wide to rip into Declan Donovan's throat. He jerked back and heard the snap of the teeth that had missed him by a millimetre. Without thinking he swung his arms backwards, with the wrists still clenched in his grip and the useless hands flapping from them, and at the same instant, brought his head forward and smashed the creature with his forehead. There was a satisfying *crunch* as the flattened face crumpled under the impact and an almost instantaneous *crack* as the head whipped backwards. The scrawny neck simply broke from the whiplash effect. Donovan dropped the thing onto the road. Dead, it continued to move. The head lolled preposterously to the side and the hands dangled, but still it crawled towards him as if intent on coming after him to fight again. Donovan took a step forward, swivelled his hips and swung a boot into its lolling face. The head whipped back again, but now, with no bone to anchor it, came flying away from the shoulders with a sick ripping sound and tumbled into the trees. The tattered thing flopped to the ground and lay still.

Donovan turned round just as one of the shotguns roared. There was a screech of mindless pain as one of the things, this one crazily elongated and mantis-like, spun off into the shadows. Another barrel bellowed and a squat creature, like a human-shaped frog, did a backward flip, landed on broad feet to launch itself at the man with the twelve-bore. The two of them spun off into the shadows. To the left Donovan saw a farmhand on the road, shrieking in fright and pain as one of the things drove at him with a pitchfork. The big landlord could hear the prongs puncture jacket and skin again and again. He leapt forward and grabbed the fork on the backswing, twisting it out of a powerful grip, reversed it and lunged the tines into the thing's eyes. There was a popping sound and the creature dropped like a sack. Down on the road, the young farmhand squirmed and squealed in a spreading dark puddle.

All around was noise and movement and turmoil. Donovan went into the edge of the trees, where the man who had dropped his shotgun was underneath a grotesque thing screeching and clawing at him. He drove the pitchfork into the thing's back and felt the prongs dig into the humped backbone, twisting on the haft as he did so. Down the handle he felt the force of the dying creature throw itself this way and that, its nerves kicking and bucking. Donovan drew the fork out and drove it into the neck. There was a high-pitched hiss as it pierced the great artery and blood fountained out. Underneath the dying thing, the man who had dropped the gun was dead. There was nothing left of his throat.

Back out on the road there was only one creature left, though there were four broken men's bodies lying crumpled at the sides. Two of the farmers were struggling with a wizened troll-like thing on whose head a tattered hat still sat. Donovan ran forward, bellowing to the men. They turned to see his shadow racing towards them, thought it was another attacker and dropped the one they were struggling with. It hit the ground with a thump, shook its head, and Donovan's mad dive with the pitchfork took it in the middle of the chest. Such was the momentum that it was driven along the road on its arse for twenty feet, twitching and writhing, until the landlord skidded to a stop. By that time, whatever it was, whatever it had *been*, was well and truly dead.

Declan Donovan and the two survivors stood and looked at it for a moment until one of the men plucked at his sleeve.

'What's that?' he asked urgently, pointing along the road.

Donovan raised his head. In the west, in the direction of the village, there was a glow of fire.

'Oh Christ,' Donovan shouted. He started running towards Kilgallan.

Peter O'Neill's house was well ablaze by the time the three of them got there. There was nothing they could do. The flames were so hot, none of them could get within twenty feet of the door. Despite that, despite the gunfire and the roaring of the flames from the Garda's blazing house, the streets were empty.

Just at that moment, an unknown technician way across in Westport flipped a switch after inserting a new breaker and immediately the street lights came back on in Kilgallan. They blared on a deserted village.

Donovan felt his heart sink. The town looked dead. 'Where is everybody?'

'Sure, didn't they go into the chapel?' Jim Toner reminded him. Jim was the nephew of Toomey Toner who had been stepping out with Rita Burke until she crashed her car off Tiraun Point the same day that little Michael Boyle had been found drowned in Roonah Water. That seemed like a lifetime away.

They made their way to the church and banged on the locked door until they were let in. Inside, a fearful crowd, who had heard in the distance shots and shouts and the screams of dying men, huddled together. Old Father Cullen was up in the pulpit, while Dr O'Brien was down at the front, facing the congregation.

Donovan went down the aisle and stood beside him, and Jim Toner followed, standing off, a little abashed, to the side. Donovan searched the faces, saw his daughter sitting with two of her friends and felt a pang of relief. As his eyes swept the crowd, he saw the faces of the women whose husbands he'd seen lying crumpled at the side of the road after their fearsome battle with the devilish things that had come from the trees.

He didn't know what to say. He drew Dr O'Brien off to the side, to explain what had happened, and an expectant hush settled on the people in the rows of pews. Finally the incredulous doctor accepted what he'd been told, nodded, and went back to the front.

'It seems it would be better if we stayed here for a while,' he said calmly. 'There's been a bit of trouble, and we don't know the details, but there are some strangers about. We don't know who they are, or what they want, but it's safer on us all if we stay together.'

One of the women wailed softly and somebody beside her put an arm around her. A baby cried. Everybody seemed to draw closer together.

'I wonder if you'd say a prayer for us, Father?'

'What's that, Tim? Speak up, man,' the old priest said.

'A prayer, Father.'

'Oh. Surely. That's what I'm here for.'

The elderly cleric came down from the pulpit and went towards the altar. He lit the candles on either side and got the vestments that were laid over the table at the side, carefully putting them on as everyone watched. Finally he turned to them all.

'I will go unto the altar of God,' he said, and began to say Mass.

Two of the young men came forward and knelt on either side to assist. Father Cullen mounted the steps to the altar and brought out the small key which opened the tabernacle. He clicked the lock and swung open the two small brass doors. He reached in for the chalice, brought it out, and then was thrown back ten feet.

362

A huge blast of freezing air exploded from the tabernacle, slamming the doors hard back against the marble sides. The shock of cold wind blew out most of the candles around the walls, leaving the place in dimness. There was a cry. Father Cullen gave a little groan and somebody went to help him to his feet; and then everybody froze.

Out of the tabernacle, the little alcove set into the wall, a black shape was extruding itself onto the altar. It heaved itself out from the tiny enclosure, expanding as it did, *growing* into the air in front of the pews. Finally something shapeless clambered off the altar and stood on the steps. Red eyes glared out ferally and burned across the huddle of people. The shape twisted, writhed, elongated and then stood up, and yet it was still impossible to define. There was a harsh sound like ragged breathing.

Father Cullen turned, saw the shape in front of him and immediately made the sign of the cross. The thing's mouth opened and a sound like laughter down a deep tunnel emerged in a raucous croak. The *Shee* stood there, a ravaged hag with a seamed and cracked face that was drawn back in a leering snarl.

The old priest held up the crucifix that hung from his cassock and raised it to the foul thing that stood swinging its head to and fro.

It slowly reached out a hand and gently took his in scaly fingers. He was too surprised to resist. It bent its head and pursed its lips obscenely, about to kiss the cross. There was a deathly hush. Even the babies were frozen to silence by the appalling presence of the thing.

Then its mouth opened and there was a crunching *snap*. The head came back up. Father Cullen staggered back, wide eyes fixed on the stump at the end of his arm.

A woman at the front fainted. The thing turned its head, and everybody saw the chomping movement of its jaws and then the tilt of the head as it gulped. A lump swelled in the scrawny neck as it swallowed and then it stood still.

A child screamed, and with terrifying speed the thing flicked from where it stood to halfway up the aisle. A long arm reached like a striking snake, grabbed the baby by the head before the mother had time to blink, and brought it up to its face. A man on the other side rushed to grab the baby back and the *Shee* grabbed *his* head with lightning speed. Long, insectile fingers tensed and everybody heard the skull crack. The man flopped to the floor. The thing turned and slung the baby away. It hit a wall on the far side, about ten feet up, and dropped to the floor with a little thud.

Out from the tabernacle the sudden raging wind blasted and the rest of the candles were snuffed out. Women screamed and children wailed as everybody made for the door. A few of the men turned to face the thing, Declan Donovan and Chris Brannigan among them. In the darkness no-one could see. Something smashed into the vet and caved in every rib on his left side. A shard of bone went through his heart and he took five steps before his body realised it was dead. Jim Toner felt something grab his groin. A huge pressure pain squeezed him into rigidity. Then he was ripped upwards, lifted off his feet by the clawing blow.

Somebody got the doors open, and the light from the streetlamp flooded into the front of the church. Everybody scattered, screaming and crying into the night. Behind them, the sound of the fight blasted out from the church, and above it, high and ripping, the laughter of the thing that had hauled itself out of the tabernacle. The women, children and men of Kilgallan who had sheltered for sanctuary in the chapel now fled for their lives.

32

'I think we have to go back to the chamber,' Siobhan said in a dull voice. Her face was drawn and bloodless.

'Whatever for?' Connarty asked. 'I think we should stay here.'

'Me too,' Theresa said. Agnes held on to her arm girlishly, fingers clutched at the baggy sleeve of the jumper.

'There's two reasons. I want to get a clear look at the carvings on the top end.'

'But why?' Connarty asked. He clearly wanted to stay put, with the door shut firmly behind him, and preferably with half a bottle of old Bushmill inside him. He had heard Siobhan's story earlier and had nodded sagely and thought to himself that the poor girl might be needing a holiday.

Then Bridget had been carried through the door in a state of near collapse and had babbled the most unbelievable story. Whether it was true remained to be seen, but for certain, if Connarty was the judge of anything, the girl *believed* it to be true. She had seen something and it had scared her out of her wits. The professor was now prepared to go along with the idea that something was amiss. There had been gunshots, and if Bridget admitted that she and the others had been firing guns, then that was all right by him, so long as there were no guns fired in his direction.

Nancy's story was something else entirely. She had been in as great a state of terror as Bridget, but she was more lucid. Startlingly so.

She had sat down and told them, very clearly and simply, what had happened.

'It wasn't Tom. It looked like him, and it talked like him, but it wasn't Tom. I *know*.'

Nancy had drunk a man-sized brandy in one long swallow, with neither a shiver nor a cough. She looked as if she could keep drinking all night and never show it. Her mind had been *slammed rigid* by what she had seen, and no amount of mere alcohol was going to be able to fuzz down that impact for a long time.

She described how the *Tom* thing had turned towards her with the red-hot poker and swung it at her face.

'It *knew* I was scared of being disfigured. I have been, ever since I was

365

little. A friend of mine was burned by hot fat and her face was all wrinkled and melted. I've always been terrified of that happening to me. And it knew it.'

'What was it?' Siobhan asked.

'*It was female!*' Nancy said so loudly that Theresa and Agnes both flinched. Bridget, sitting on the other side of the table, hands trembling, simply nodded her head.

'It looked right at me. Looked right *into* me and I could *feel* it. That's how I knew it wasn't Tom. Its teeth, first of all, and then its eyes were different. I just kicked out and ran to the room. I could feel it change into something else. It was still in my *mind*. It was like being touched with sickness. It tried to come through the door. But it couldn't, *not as Tom*, so it changed again. It was *real*. I saw it.'

They listened as Nancy finished the story. She told of how she looked back and saw the shape on the bed, dimly illuminated by moonlight, and knew it was her husband. Knew he was dead.

As she spoke, Sean felt a surge of admiration for her. She had told them all this without a tremble, as if her brain had floated up to some icy calm state where all thought was clear and unconfused.

'I know he's dead and I know there's nothing I can do,' she said. 'Nothing except kill that bitch. I'm going to *destroy* her.'

'We all are,' Siobhan said softly, but so definitely that the words fell like thuds.

'How?' Liz asked. She had listened to both tales and she had felt rising fear as she pictured the scenes that these two women had witnessed. She could *sense* the evil of the thing.

'I have to get back to the tor. Remember I told you in the rhyme there was something about how she could be put away for ever?'

'Something about a sword,' Sean said.

'Yes, I didn't get all of that,' Siobhan said. 'I need another look at it. But there was something about the sword barring her way to Tir na n'Og.'

'I didn't see any sword,' Connarty said. 'Not unless you count that club in the warrior's hand.'

'No, that's not it,' Siobhan said definitely, precluding argument. 'It's the Sword of the Son of Light. It's Cuchullain's sword.'

'Oh, that's only a legend.'

'That's true,' Siobhan retorted, almost angrily. 'The same as the legend of the *Morrigan*. We should have read the words before we broke the wall down.'

'Do you think it's there?' Liz asked.

'Somewhere,' Siobhan replied.

'I don't want to go,' Agnes said in a small voice from the other side of the room. She was pale and trembling. Siobhan wished she and Theresa hadn't been here. She wished *she herself* had never come here.

'I'll go with you,' Nancy said firmly.

Bridget just looked at her hands. They were shaking so badly they looked like bird's wings. 'I'll stay here,' she said.

Connarty went with them. He wasn't really afraid yet, but he was curious. His academic mind was at war with itself, for as an archaeologist, he knew the legends, understood there was a kernel of truth in all of them. But, first and foremost, for Connarty artefacts were empiric tools.

Liz took the small torch, though its batteries were fading. When it was switched on outside, it threw out only a weak cone of light. Sean lugged his camera, strap around his neck, flashgun whining as it charged. Out in the night, he felt exposed. He felt his skin crawl with apprehension and the sensation that something *familiar* was waiting for him. At the back of his mind, the image from his dreams jostled through the other thoughts, teasing him, before dancing away. Sean admitted to himself that he was scared. He tried to convince Liz to stay with the others, but she blankly refused, though he wished she had remained in the comparative safety of the cottage. Warily they went down the path towards the cattle grid, through the gate and took the left turn up the dark track to where the black mound of the tor stood out against the dark sky.

The mouth of the passageway yawned. Siobhan stopped in front of it. She looked into the black hole and asked Liz for the torch. She passed it forward and Siobhan, very warily, very hesitantly, stepped inside. Sean followed, with Liz and Nancy behind, and Connarty bringing up the rear. No-one spoke and the sound of their footfalls echoed ahead of them.

The loud knock on the door startled Bridget so much that she dropped the glass onto the table, where it bounced, sprinkling the surface with the small amount of brandy still in the bottom.

'Who's that?' Agnes whispered. Theresa looked at her, her face a pale mask.

The knock came again, twice, quite sharp.

'Are you all right in there?' a man's voice called out.

'Who is it?' Bridget called back. She sat frozen, not even looking at the door.

'It's meself. O'Neill the Garda. Are you all right in there? What's been going on down here?'

A wave of relief powered Agnes to the door. Before anyone could stop her, she had unhitched the latch and swung it wide. The big, red-faced policeman stood in the doorway.

'Evening to you all,' he said, touching the tip of his flat cap. 'And a fine night for having none of all this fuss and bother, eh?'

'Come in, officer,' Agnes said, pulling the policeman inside by the arm.

'Surely. And it's just the three of you here, then?'

Bridget nodded.

'And what's been happening down here that's kept the whole town awake?' he asked, smiling all the while. Theresa and Agnes visibly relaxed. For some reason, Bridget did not. It may have been the fact that he was a policeman, and she'd tried to avoid contact with policemen over the past two weeks, but there was *something* in her mind that made her feel even more uneasy. It was like the night she'd stumbled across the Englishman outside of the house and heard the coughing sound. It was only when she was telling the others about it later that exactly what the sound was had come clear.

Agnes blurted out some of the story and the policeman listened, his big homely face bland and understanding. At the end of Agnes's tale, he held his hand up.

'I don't know what to make of this at all. But you say there's people dead?' He turned and looked at Bridget.

'At least four. Maybe more,' she said.

'Well, the first thing I should do is take a look around, just to be on the safe side.'

He got to his feet and turned to Agnes. 'You can show me around, dearie. Let me know where things are.'

Agnes nodded, giving him a faltering smile. She opened the kitchen door and the policeman looked in, nodded, and came back out again.

'And the rest of the place?'

'This way,' Agnes said, and walked down the narrow corridor. The other two sat, looking at each other, listening to the voices diminish as the walls cut them off.

In the bedroom Agnes shared with Theresa, the policeman crossed to the window and checked the latch. He moved back. His big hand shot out and clamped over Agnes's mouth.

With enormous strength he lifted her right off the ground. She could feel the muscles in her neck creak in protest. Fright and panic simply exploded within her. With his right hand, he casually took hold of the collar of her blouse and ripped it downwards. She felt the shock of the cold air as she was exposed. Another movement and her slacks were torn off cleanly, leaving her dangling, naked in his monstrous grip. She felt as if her jaw-bone was breaking and she could feel the joint under her ear about to give under the pressure.

He turned, still holding her with one hand, and lowered her to a sitting position on the bed.

Agnes felt her consciousness fade in and out as fear overloaded her brain. Her heart was thumping against her ribs, each beat like a rapid punch, and she dimly realised that her bladder had let go, soaking the blankets.

In front of her bulging eyes, the policeman began to *change*.

The uniform seemed to shrivel and melt on the skin, subsumed by the distorting shape of his body. Knotted muscles bunched under ridged and wrinkled grey skin. Her head, still in that vice-grip, was forcefully held still so that she would see the horrible metamorphosis. From between the legs a monstrously swollen thing drove forward, pulsating threateningly, as if it was alive, knotted and gnarled and grotesquely jerking.

Agnes had lived a sheltered life. She knew what a penis was, from reading, not from experience. She had never seen one or touched one. They were parts of the anatomy that she, a good Catholic girl who had been taught in a convent, shoved away from her mind as soon as the thought intruded. Yet she knew what it was, and instinctively she knew that it should be *nothing* like this swollen monstrosity that reared in front of her.

The thing that had been a policeman swivelled her face upwards and she looked into its eyes and almost collapsed with the shock of it.

It had a *woman's* face. It was long, with high cheekbones and arched eyebrows. Straggly hair cascaded on either side, writhing with a life of its own. She was the *gorgon*, the epitome of evil in dreadful female form. Below the face, a pair of breasts bulged, and below them four others drooped like pigs' dugs, shrivelled teated sacks.

Red eyes fixed on her and glared right inside her and she felt the *pain* of that stare lance into her. She felt as if her mind was being sucked out.

And then, down between her legs, she felt the monstrous probing, and one vast bolt of pain.

A scream forced itself up from the bottom of her lungs and was squeezed off by the force of the grip on her neck. The long, silent

369

scream built up inside her as the unbelievable pain soared. Very soon, everything faded into darkness.

In the living room, Theresa was talking to Bridget in a hushed voice as if the very act of talking out loud would attract more danger.

'Do you think he'll take us out of here?'

Bridget shrugged. Her brow frowned in concentration.

'It'll be better up in the village,' Theresa went on. 'The Garda won't let anything happen to us.'

Just then Bridget held up her hand quickly. It wasn't shaking any more. 'Quiet!' she hissed.

'What—' Theresa began to say, but Bridget reached over and grasped her elbow, squeezing it hard.

From down the corridor there was a muffled sound, as if something was being dragged.

Instantly, Bridget was on her feet and heading for the bedroom. She halted at the door, hand half-outstretched towards the handle. Theresa followed her, though she had heard nothing. She just didn't want to be left alone.

Bridget listened intently, and then she heard the noise again. It was a low, rasping sound. She reached and turned the handle. The door swung open and both women looked inside.

There was movement on the bed and at first their eyes couldn't make out the shapes in the darkened room.

Then Theresa shrieked.

Agnes's legs were spread on either side of the thing crouched over her flopped body. It was long and emaciated and the knobs of its spine showed clearly against the shrivelled skin. Dark hair cascaded down either side of the sharp shoulders, wriggling and writhing with a life of its own.

Bridget backed off and bumped into Theresa, who seemed paralysed. She let out a gasp of fright and the thing that was sitting, spiderlike, on Agnes turned with a quick, snake-like movement. There was a ripping sound as it separated from the girl's body and turned to face the two women.

'Oh no,' Theresa moaned so softly it could hardly be heard.

And then the thing's face split open in a hungry grin. The row of discoloured sharp teeth caught the dim light from the hallway and flashed venomously. The mouth gaped like a cavern, and from inside, from the depths, came a howl of vile laughter that rattled around the room.

Bridget turned and in the same movement grabbed the door handle

370

and shoved Theresa backwards. She slammed the door on the apparition and bolted down the hallway, dragging the petrified girl along with her.

Behind them the thing shrieked demonically in a voice like the howl of a rabid animal. The skin on Bridget's back puckered and tightened in fear. It took them only seconds to get from one end of the hallway to the other and into the living room, but the time stretched to infinity, as if the girls were running through quicksand. And for every subjective second of that journey, Bridget was convinced that the bedroom door would explode outwards and the thing that had killed Agnes would come raging down the hallway and pounce on them with its foul spidery arms outstretched.

They made it to the front door and scrambled out into the cold night. The field was dark. Theresa simply ran for the trees. Bridget lost her in seconds as darkness swallowed the girl. She stopped, legs a-tremble, chest heaving, and then veered to the left, heading for her own cottage.

She scurried in through the open door and into her own bedroom. The boxes they'd brought down from the loft were still there. She hefted one of the rifles and dropped it back in the box with a clatter. The vicious-looking guns hadn't worked against the thing the last time. She clambered to the other side of the room and threw open the metal lid of the fourth container.

Inside, packed neatly in foam rubber, was a long grey-green metal tube. Bridget hoisted it from its packing and turned it around in her hands. There were two hinged appendages which she snapped down quickly, as she'd seen her brother do, and flicked up the car-badge sight at the front end. In the packing on either side of the indentation where the tube had been fixed, there were twelve metallic things like odd-shaped bottles. She hauled them out one by one and slid the first, quite expertly, into the aperture, which closed softly with the *snick* of precision engineering. The rest she placed side by side in the rucksack that lay on the bed, and slipped it over her shoulder. It was heavy and awkward, but she could carry it with some effort. She got to her feet and hauled the pipe onto the other shoulder, holding the rear grip tightly, with her finger over the red plastic trigger, and cautiously moved towards the door.

In the living room, she saw the two Englishmen for the first time. They hadn't even registered in her mind when she'd raced through towards the bedroom. Sands was sprawled on his back, while in the corner, arched over a fallen chair, Laird was bent backwards, his head on the floor. She couldn't see his face, but it looked as if his spine had been violently contorted. His hands were raied up in front of him, fingers hooked, frozen in the appalling act of death.

That was not all.

There was something odd about the bodies. At first Bridget couldn't fathom it. She took a step back, staring at the nearest splayed-out form, before her mind registered what her eyes were telling her. At first it looked as if the skin on Sands's face was moving, as if he was alive, yet strangely fuzzy and ill-defined. Then she realised that what was moving on his face wasn't made up of skin and muscle. His face was crawling with insects. A coating of scurrying, leggy things. Faintly, the chitinous noise of wing casings and gnawing chaellae filtered through the pounding of her heartbeat, and again, just as she had in the tor when the swarms of crawling things surged out of the cracks between the flagstones, Bridget felt the room begin to spin around her.

She took a step to the right, and her shin barked against the edge of the chair. The flash of sharp pain bought her back to reality. She gave a little cry that was as much panic and backed away, holding on desperately to the pulse of pain from below her knee, her only grip on normality.

She watched the mass of insects creep like a moving mat over the two bodies, then began to back off, breath tight in locked lungs. She made it to the door, eyes still fixed on the dreadful scene, and, still walking backwards, got halfway across the field. The door was still wide open and the light inside cast an oblong glow on the stones of the pathway in front of the cottage.

Bridget's mind was yammering at her, telling her to run. She could even feel the nervous twitches in her legs as they tried to obey, but she battled it down, forced herself to stand still. Finally her lungs unlocked and she took a deep breath of night air. She let the strap of her bag slip from her shoulder and lowered the weight to the ground. She brought her free hand up to clasp the forward handle on the tube and swivelled until the fore sight was centred on the light rectangle. In her mind, she could still *hear* the scurrying noises of the loathsome insects as they crawled and chewed at the corpses. She had to fight waves of panic and nausea.

Slowly she squeezed the trigger. There was a whooshing sound right behind her and a slight thrum on her shoulder and against her cheek; a brief flare as the mortar streaked forward like a firework rocket, white in the night and then, almost instantaneously, a wonderful explosion of red flame as it struck the wall at the far end of the room. The noise was *immense*. Both of the front windows billowed out like fragmented bubbles and the blast punched a hundred slates off the roof, shooting them upwards like flipped coins. The chimney pot with the metallic covering to keep the rain out simply took off into the air, tumbling and twisting in its flight. It landed fifty feet beyond the cottage, in the stand of trees, with a muffled crash.

Bridget felt the heat of the blast and staggered backwards as the shock-wave wind tugged at her, but kept her feet. Inside, she felt a wild surge of glee at the terrible destruction she had caused with one small finger movement. In an instant, her mind cleared. No longer could she hear the scuttering of insectile bodies. That sound was now replaced by the memory of the dreadful shriek of the thing that had destroyed Agnes on the bed in the other cottage. And competing with that sound was the strange ringing of excitement brought on by the surge of adrenaline. Quickly Bridget slammed another mortar into the aperture and clicked the cover. She hauled the bag up onto her shoulder, feeling the weight bump against her hip and walked towards the cottage from which she'd fled in a blind panic. Now she was not blind. She was armed.

Theresa reached the edge of the copse and plunged inside, ignoring the wild bramble thorns that snagged her shirt and ripped her slacks.

Behind her she could still hear the animal cackling of the thing in the bedroom, and all she wanted to do was run until she could hear it no longer.

Breath rasping in her throat, and almost on the point of collapse with fear-induced exhaustion, she reached a small clearing and slumped against the bole of an old oak tree. Her knees were shaking so hard they threatened to give way. Theresa just let herself slip to the ground, where she lay, eyes wide and panting like a frightened animal, on the moss.

She shivered with the cold. The perspiration from the effort of running was evaporating and her skin was puckered into goose flesh. It was dark down here in the trees. Above her, few stars glinted between the leafless branches. All around her was darkness and shade. It was so quiet that her own ragged breathing sounded abnormally loud.

She was alone in the trees. She huddled, shivering, curled into herself like a rabbit that has gone to earth and still hears the fox in the bracken. She could hear the poisonous screech of the terrible thing reverberate in an echo-loop in her mind. It went on and on for ever and she couldn't cast it out. Her brain still rang with the *banshee* wailing. Theresa tried to make herself as small as possible, yet all around it seemed as if she was being watched from the darkness. Occasionally she jerked her head to the left or right at some imagined sound. She wished she'd stayed with Bridget, for although she hardly knew the other woman, she wanted her, wanted anyone, to be with her in the dark.

Far off to the right there was a loud *whump* of sound and the distant crash of glass. The noise was followed by a staccato rattle that Theresa took for machine-gun fire, but was in fact the flipped-off slates cascading back onto the ruined roof. She cringed back against the tree, not knowing what was happening, when under her back she felt a slight movement. At first she thought it was a twig and shifted her body away.

Then it moved again and she froze. Something twitched against her spine. She unfroze and rolled away from the tree, eyes wide, staring down at the moss. In the darkness, she could only see movement. The thick carpet of moss bulged upwards and then ripped apart. From underneath it, something hauled itself out with an ungainly, clambering motion. Beside it the mossy carpet bulged and humped and tore open and then, to her left, the leaf-litter crackled and rustled with subterranean movement. A flat head shoved itself up and out and a mouth opened and closed with a leathery *snap*. Two dark eyes glistened on either side of the mouth. They blinked closed and sank below the level of the skull. There was a soft, gulping sound and the eyes popped open again. A toad. Indistinct in the deep shadows, it was still a toad, huge and warty, its rough skin knobbed with pustules.

Theresa thought she would die on the spot. Gibbering unintelligibly with frantic fear, she crawled backwards, away from the thing, and put her hand right onto the cold, fat body of another of the beasts that had dug its way out from the carpet of leaves. She felt the thing squash underneath her hand in a disgusting jelly-like way, and then the bubbles on its skin burst like ripe pods. Instant excruciating pain seared her palm. It was as if she'd thrust her whole hand into a bed of bright coals. The glass-slivers of agony shot upwards into her arm, and as she jerked away, she lost her balance and tumbled, rolling to the ground. She flattened another of the immense toads and in an instant of clarity she felt the horrid popping again just at her side, and this time the pain simply flooded into her. She cupped her other hand against her side, and her heart leapt into her throat. Her hand went right *into* a great sodden hole in her side. The skin and muscle had been eaten away as if concentrated acid had been poured onto her body.

Theresa flopped to the ground again, twitching madly, feet drumming so hard on the leaf-litter that they sent leaves and twigs flying into the air. Her eyes glazed: everything but pain receded from her. The hurt of it wormed its way between her ribs and burrowed into her abdomen, burning fire as it did so. She was hardly aware of the truly immense toad that clawed its way from under the moss right in front of her and came clambering on squat, thick legs. The great black eyes closed and it gulped, then scuttered a few steps more and crawled onto her face. She felt its skin against her cheek, cold and clammy. As it moved, it rubbed the pustules against her. The foetid poison streamed over her skin. Her face melted.

Theresa's voice finally came back for the last few seconds of her life. The sickening hurt was so unbelievably *consuming* that all she could do was scream, on and on, ringing high and clear through the trees into the night air until finally the screams cut off sharply, leaving the forest in silence.

For a moment, all was still. Then the monstrous toads that had burrowed their way upwards came together, clambering towards each other until they joined in a tangle of rough limbs and flat heads. Then they *merged*, flowing into each other until they were an amorphous mass of grey, putrid flesh. For a few moments the loathsome mound pulsed and twitched, and then it *changed* again. In the dark, something stood up and sensed the air and then began to flit silently towards the field.

33

'What in the name of God was that?' Connarty exclaimed when the sound of the explosion rammed up the passageway into the chamber. Under their feet the flagstones trembled with the shockwave.

'Sounds like a bomb,' McCullain said absently. The light from Siobhan's torch was failing too rapidly for her to read the inscription, so Sean had put his camera onto the infra-red automatic focusing to get the last of the inscriptions from the head of the stone. What good that would do, he didn't know. He wasn't sure if he'd even manage to get the film processed in his portable darkroom, but he went along with it anyway.

Sean McCullain was not a superstitious man. He'd been a press photographer too long for that. Yet he now *believed* everything that Siobhan had said. He could not explain why. He could just *feel* the rightness of it within him.

Something deep in his head had simply unlocked. Something *clicked* within him, and the whole pattern of it jumped into focus. He completely accepted what was happening and why it was happening.

Sean McCullain knew that he was going to face something monstrous. He *knew*. He did not know if he would survive it, but there was no avoiding it.

The clear knowledge seared him through. The dreams were only part of it. They had changed when he and Liz had left the north and headed into the old kingdom of Connacht, presaging what was to come, echoing what had *been*. The dreams had been a *preparation*.

Past and present swooped in on Sean McCullain. His dreams had shown him the face of the thing that was stalking the night around Kilgallan. He had *seen* her. Seen the *Shee*.

And he knew *her*.

He felt the old bond between them, the *Yin-Yang* connection of opposites, the light and the dark. He felt the vast age of her, and he sensed in himself something that went back through the ages, something that had shaken him when Siobhan had told the tales of the death faerie, the battles of Cuchullain and the lust of the *Shee* for him, the son of the Lord of Light.

Coming to old Ireland, the ancient part of the old kingdom, had opened something within him, letting the light of the far past blaze through the forgotten generations. Now he was *here*. Now he knew that within him there was more than Sean McCullain.

Underneath the tension, behind the fear, he felt heat build, the awesome white fire in his dreams when he had raised his battle arm and leapt into the fight.

Here was a terrible danger that Sean McCullain had to face. It would be faced tonight. He did not know yet if he *could*. Only that he must.

Liz had been violently sick when Siobhan flicked the torch around the chamber, confirming much of what Bridget had told them. O'Farrell was lying on the floor. They could tell it was him by the strands of red hair that poked through the peeling bubbled skin. There were craters the size of grapes all over him, overlapping each other where huge blisters had swelled and burst and others had taken their place. The pus from them was still slowly dribbling to the stone floor. Liz Cannon had taken one look and turned away retching.

Brian Cooney was crumpled against the far wall. His face was contorted, frozen in the final agony. His eyes were burst open and blood was streaming from the sockets as if some devastating internal explosion had taken place inside his head. His tongue, black and swollen, protruded from caked lips, and rivulets of blood from his ears were slowly congealing on his shoulders. Of John Boyle, there was no sign.

'If it can do this, what else can it do?' Connarty asked.

'We have to stop it before it does anything more,' Siobhan said forcefully, though her voice was shaking. She sounded as if she was working hard at keeping a grip on herself, and Sean felt another wave of admiration for her.

'I go along with that,' Nancy said resolutely. 'I don't care what it takes.' Despite what she had come through in the past hour, her voice was firm.

'How do you kill the *Shee*?' the professor asked. 'There's nothing in all the books that tells us that.'

'So you finally believe me?' Siobhan asked, and unaccountably laughed.

'I can't kid myself now, Siobhan. If there's evidence, then I'll believe it. There's evidence here.'

'So now *you* tell us what to do.'

'I want to hear what the final inscription says. You say there's something about a sword?'

'Yes. But I haven't got it all. It describes the Sword of Light that bars her way to the Land of the Dead. And there's something about the Son of Light.'

'That would be Cuchullain. He was the son of Lugh, the God of Light. And he's been long gone from these parts, even in the legends. He had a great battle with the *Shee*, so the songs say. He was the only mortal she could not kill.'

'Is that the hero you were telling us about? The one from Skye?'

Connarty turned to McCullain. 'The very one. Unfortunately, he's not with us, more's the pity.'

There was another huge explosion of noise from outside.

Bridget levelled the mortar at the cottage she'd fled with Theresa. The door had banged shut behind them, but she didn't aim for that. Instead she zeroed the sight on the window of the bedroom where the appalling thing had glowered over the girl's pale and flaccid body. She fired. The cottage erupted in a yellow fireball that lit the entire field.

She turned her back against the blast. A couple of small shards of glass zipped through her jacket and stung her skin. She ignored them.

Bridget crossed to the middle of the field, heading for the gate, when a shape flitted at the corner of the furthest cottage. Another joined it in the shadows, then a third. They loped in front of the house, shambling towards her. She clicked the shell in, raised the tube and fired low. The projectile hit the ground a yard in front of the door. She saw it bounce, go right through the frame and explode with a deafening *punch* of sound. The shapes skittered for the cover of the next building. Bridget calmly stood her ground and reloaded. By the time they reached the other cottage, she sent off another mortar that clipped the edge of the building and took out a ten-foot section of the corner. The whole cottage sagged downwards and burst into flames.

Bridget was working on automatic. All the fear and pain was gone. Her mind was now high and clear. She loaded, clicked and trailed the tube on the one remaining figure running in ungainly strides towards the other building. The circle at the end of the cylinder centred on the thing and she swivelled the barrel to the left, leading him by about two feet. She depressed the trigger, watched the flare and saw the missile take the misshapen figure high on the chest. He was thrown right back off his feet and slammed into the wall, and then disappeared in a roaring flash. Behind him the front wall of the cottage crumpled and the roof collapsed. Again, fire began to burn brightly. ◂

She reloaded and stood, waiting, knowing it was not over. In her

378

peripheral vision, something dark moved, and she swivelled and fired, almost casually, at the shapes that bobbed into view from the shelter of the building furthest from the one she'd just hit. This was the one where the professor and the young archaeologist had been staying since the summer. It disintegrated in a fireball and she noted with a grin of grim satisfaction that the odd-shaped things that had scuttled into her field of fire were gone, roasted in the flames. All around her was fire and flame, and the roar and crackle was deafening. Bridget didn't care. She'd hit *back*.

She slammed another shell into the loader and locked it. Planting her feet wide apart, she stood in the centre, now fighting mad.

The dark shape came screaming out at her from the space between the one remaining cottage and the stand of trees. It hurtled, screeching ferociously, across the open space like an express train. Without thinking, she raised the mortar, aimed and fired. The firework trail sparked a line of light as she followed the trajectory. It raced towards the dark shape like a burning arrow – and then, unbelievably, the thing reached out and batted it away. The mortar spun out of control. It skittered up into the air, twisting and turning like a burning stick, and hit the roof of the final cottage, where it thumped a huge hole in the slates.

The dark shape did not stop. It came at her so fast that Bridget didn't even have time to blink. One clawed hand hit her with such blurring speed the girl's head came spinning off her shoulders. For a split second, her decapitated body stood there, beside the almost empty bag of mortar shells, still with the tube slung over her shoulder. The thing screeched past: another long arm reached out and ripped Bridget's body downwards, opening her from the neck to the navel in one foul swipe. Its terrible flight did not stop. It was past, fleeting like a black shadow, and over the dyke by the time Bridget's twitching body hit the ground. Twenty yards away, her head stopped rolling. The look on the face was astonishment: its mouth hung open to the sky.

The series of explosions made the ground shake under their feet.

'What's happening out there?' Connarty asked, and Sean shrugged.

'Want to go and have a look?' he asked.

'Not really, but I think one of us should,' the professor said. 'I'll be back in a moment.' He turned and walked out warily, his arms spread to feel his way.

'I think we should all go,' Sean said. 'We should stay together.'

'I'm all for that,' Connarty said, the relief evident in his voice. They all followed him slowly along the long narrow passageway.

He was near the opening when the smell hit him like a blow, and he almost lost his footing. Another tremendous vibration shook the ground. Connarty sank to his knees, and the stones that made up the wall on his right simply peeled off and crashed on top of him. He cried out once and then his voice was choked off by dust and silt.

'Back, everybody,' Sean bawled as soon as he saw the wall start to go. For yards down from the tunnel mouth, boulders and flat stones were dropping off and tumbling to roll in the passageway. He turned and herded them back a few feet while the tremors continued under their feet. Dust billowed in a choking cloud.

'I think that was an earthquake,' said Sean.

Up at the end, Connarty shook his head and spat out the dirt from his mouth. That was all he could do, for his arms and legs were trapped under the rubble that had fallen on him. He could feel pain where the falling stones had cut and bashed him, but he wasn't seriously hurt. It was hard to breathe with the weight on top of him and the professor could only move his head slightly. The dense sweet smell cloyed his nostrils and made him gag. He sneezed and his eyes swam. When he blinked them clear he saw someone standing in front of him. At first he thought it was Siobhan, but he couldn't turn his head to see.

'Help me out of here before I choke to death,' he called out. The figure that was just outside his vision said nothing. He swivelled his eyes as far as they would turn in their sockets, though without his glasses, things were just a blur. He thought he saw a pair of small bare feet on the passageway floor ahead of him.

'Come on, *quick now*. Get me out from under this. It's breaking my ribs.'

The shape moved towards him and the strange, sweet smell engulfed him. He could feel his heart race. He tried to turn, but couldn't and panic welled up inside.

A face loomed towards him out of the darkness and he saw the woman. Her skin was pure white and her hair glossy and black. Her eyes were huge and luminous. She stared at him vacantly, and then smiled. When she did so, for some reason, Connarty was *riveted* with fear. The woman said nothing, but as she stared a picture flitted through his mind, slowing down, freezing, then gradually starting to unreel. He saw himself trapped in the tunnel, only his head showing. No-one came to help him and he screamed and cried out but there was no-one to hear. He saw his tongue turn black and his head loll when he finally died. His skin shrivelled and maggots started eating until there was nothing left but a raggedy skull.

But that was not the worst. Loosened rocks and boulders tumbled onto his rotting body, covering it completely. Dust sifted down, then built up in mounds, and the door to the passageway eroded, crumbled, caved in. Grass started growing on the mound of the earth, leaving it as it had been, but with his body buried inside it.

Connarty saw all this in the space of a few seconds as the woman stared into his eyes, and terror welled up inside him. He didn't want to die here, but more than that, he was dreadfully afraid of being *buried*.

The woman smiled again, a gleeful, hungry smile. Connarty started to scream.

A hand came close to his face. And it *changed*. The fingers spread, elongated, grew scaly. They gripped: Connarty's screams climbed higher as the nails bit. Then they gurgled and finally cut off: slowly, slowly, the hand pulled his head from his shoulders.

Down in the chamber they heard his pitiful wailing. Sean started towards the sound.

'Jesus Christ. He's alive!'

Suddenly Siobhan cried out in alarm. Both Sean and Liz turned to see her doing a crazy little dance at the other side of the chamber. The torch, now sadly fading, was dancing in her hand as she lifted her feet, stamped down, battered at her legs with her hands. Her screams were eerie and high. Her body thrashed and jerked as if she was being attacked by a swarm of wasps.

It was not wasps. Siobhan had turned round when Connarty's wail came echoing down to them, and an immense spider, big as her hand and with a fat, pendulous body, leapt off the wall and landed on her face. She had swiped it off and moved away. Another one had scuttered up her jeans. She could feel the grip of its legs on her knee and then on her thigh, and she almost fainted with the horror of it. She tried to bat it of, and another one, the size of a rat and covered in bristly hair, came out from the corner, racing on eight thick legs, and *leapt* onto her. Another dropped from the ceiling to land on her head. She could feel its legs tangle in her hair. She started to scream.

Sean moved towards her. There was a gasp from behind. He spun round and saw Liz. Her hands were splayed, her elbows bent as if pushing something away on either side.

In her mind, she *was*. Liz had looked at the strange dance that Siobhan was performing and then, without a sound, without warning, the walls had suddenly closed in around her. One second she'd been standing in the cavernous chamber, and the next the walls had contracted, crushing her. She raised her hands to push them back and had felt the enormous pressure. An involuntary gasp had escaped her and she felt the muscles in her elbows and shoulders stretch with the effort.

Sean looked at Liz, standing with her eyes squeezed shut, frozen like a statue. Her face was a mask of horror. Bewildered, he turned to Siobhan, who was hopping around as if she'd been jolted with a high-voltage current and screaming like a mad thing.

And then the lights went out, catapulting Sean McCullain into his own private hell.

It was pitch-black. The darkness swooped down and smothered him in dreadful folds. He felt his breath catch in his throat and when he tried to haul air inside his lungs it felt as if he was drowning. He wheezed asthmatically, completely disoriented in the infinite darkness – and then, in his mind, the dream started again. He was back in the crowd again, but he was not watching. He was the man who was about to die. He saw, in terrible slow motion, the contorted face in front of him. Saw the tyre lever come crashing down. Felt the crunch of metal on bone. Heard someone call his name from far away.

Nancy froze on the other side of the stone block. Something had stepped out of the niche in the wall, slowly, fluidly. Tom's ruined face turned towards her and his arms moved up. She was frozen into immobility. The hands reached and cupped her face. Tom leaned in to her. His head was oddly thin: his eyes bulged out of their sockets. For a second, she couldn't get her mind to explain the strange shape of his head, and then it struck her. It had been *squashed* in at the temples, as if he'd been put in a vice and some powerful hand had turned the winding handle until his skull elongated and cracked. The appalling apparition stood before her and she could feel the clammy touch of his dead fingers on her face. The fingertips moved up her cheeks and squeezed . . . It was as if something had taken control of all her nerve impulses and cut off their power. Inside, she felt a scream building.

Tom's icy fingers clenched and she felt his nails go right into the skin of her cheek. It was curiously painless. There was a tearing sound, like wet paper giving under pressure, and she felt his fingers hook and pull. The soft, pulpy rip continued and she sensed skin and muscle peeling away.

No!

Not Tom! NOT TOM!

The mental shout came bawling at her from the bottom of her mind, rupturing the paralysis.

The *Tom* thing, with its weird, squashed head, looked at her. The hand it held up clasped a wet, stringy thing that dribbled through the fingers. And then the whole apparition winked out. Nancy's breath came back again in a rush and she turned away, gasping. She felt as if she was going to faint and doubled over, holding onto the stone block. She breathed in hard, filling her lungs, and raised her head to see the shadow in front of Sean McCullain.

A whispery voice tickled her ear. The shape, in the dimness of the chamber, was fixed on McCullain, slowly gliding towards him like a creature stalking its prey.

It was *crooning*. She couldn't understand what it said, but she *felt* it, felt its twisted sick lust. Its pale hands reached out towards him.

Then the foetid emanation of the thing struck her and she reacted.

Her warning shout came as she leapt towards him and dragged him backwards just as the white hands were about to close on his head.

In the dark, Sean heard a cry that drowned out the hypnotic voice calling to him and he stumbled back. He lifted his hand in an instinctive motion, and for some reason that he could not fathom, *not ever*, his fingers triggered the camera.

A searing white flash blasted the chamber.

In front of Sean something warped and black and *obscene* shrieked. He pressed the flash again. And again. The walls shook. Stones shot out, erupting under the immense sound from the creature. It shuddered in agony and threw itself, its course more desperate than true, out of the chamber. Flagstones buckled and cracked in its wake as the power of its mind lashed out. Siobhan was knocked to the floor. Liz Cannon was flung against the walls, scraping her forehead badly enough to break skin. Only McCullain and Nancy Ducain managed to remain standing.

The wail of the thing reverberated up the tunnel, magnified in the confined space to a bone-shaking screech until its flight carried it outside and the sound faded away in the distance, like the bellow of a night train travelling *fast*.

Sean opened his eyes and saw light again.

Still shaking, he turned towards Liz. She was getting to her feet, using the wall for balance. On the other side, Siobhan was on her knees, moving slowly, dazed.

'It's gone,' Sean said.

'They've gone,' Siobhan corrected him. 'The spiders.'

'I didn't see any spiders. I just saw the walls coming in. But now they're back to where they were,' Liz told her.

'I saw the thing,' Sean said flatly. 'I hit the flash of the camera and I saw it. Nancy shoved me away.'

'It was reaching for you. I couldn't let it get you.' Nancy did not tell the others what she had seen in her paralysis.

'I saw a woman,' Sean said. 'But there was something else. I only got a flash of her, but it was as if I could see *through* her face to something behind her. She's female, but she's not a woman.'

'We know that. She's a *demon*,' Siobhan said. Her eyes were still darting about, making sure there were no more spiders.

'She wants me,' he said. 'She wants to *mate* with me. Christ, it's vile.' He turned to Nancy and put his hand on her shoulder. 'Thanks,' he said, sincerely. She shrugged.

'What do we do now?' Liz asked. She had come closer to Sean; Siobhan had brought the torch over. The four of them stood, close enough to touch, huddling.

'We can hurt her. I don't know how we can kill the thing,' Sean said.

Suddenly Siobhan cried, 'It *is* the light. Remember in the carvings? The Sword of the Son of Light could bar her way. They must have meant that light can harm her. If we get enough of it, maybe we can kill her like that.'

'How do we do that?' Liz asked.

'I've got the equipment,' Sean said simply. 'But we'll have to bring her back here.'

'I don't think that's a good idea,' Liz said.

'It's the only idea I've got.'

Siobhan turned away from them, arms wrapped around herself as if she was cold, and then stopped. 'Look at that now,' she said in a voice that was almost a whisper.

The others turned. Siobhan was pointing at the massive stone that stood in the centre of the chamber. A huge fissure ran diagonally across it: half the block had simply shattered. Siobhan played the torch over it. The fissure ran the length of the stone and down into the floor. Inside, below actual floor level, something reflected the light back at them.

Sean bent into the space and felt around. His fingers clenched on something hard and smooth and he drew it out.

'Holy mother, it *is* a sword,' Siobhan said under her breath.

'Never seen a sword like this,' Sean said.

It had a short blade, no more than two feet long. As it turned in his grip, the torchlight spangled off its black surface. It was a wonderfully crafted object of simple lines and deadly grace, carved and polished from one piece of stone. The blade grew out of a handle that fitted Sean's hand exactly, as if it had been designed for him.

'It's obsidian. Elven tears, they call it,' Siobhan said, reaching gently to touch the blade.

'Is this what the carvings meant?' Sean asked.

Siobhan nodded. 'Must be. Cuchullain's sword. Lying all this time under the rock.'

'It doesn't look much to me,' Liz said. 'It's just a piece of carved stone.'

'That's not the point,' Siobhan said, but there was no spite in her voice. 'If the legends are true, then the sword can be used.'

Everybody looked at her in silence.

'We'll have to do what we can to survive this,' Siobhan said.

34

The field was a mass of red and orange light from the burning cottages. Flames towered high into the night sky and sparks floated upwards on the billowing grey smoke. Sean's heart had sunk like a stone when they'd stepped out from the tor into a scene that reminded him of the aftermath of a guerilla attack in a far-off war he'd once covered.

Their cottage was well ablaze. Three others were almost completely gone and the rest were afire.

'Come on,' he yelled. 'We might be too late.'

He sprinted ahead and Liz and Siobhan trailed after him, running hard to keep up. Nancy paced him every step of the way without effort. Sean raced over the cattle grid and up the pathway to the cottage. All around was heat and noise. Timbers snapped and cracked. Glass shattered, masonry tumbled, and heat blasted out all around, searing the ground, singeing the grass.

They got to within twenty yards of the burning building and stopped, waiting for the others to catch up with them. The left side of the cottage was an inferno of heat, but the fire hadn't quite spread to the far end.

'What are you going to do?' Liz asked.

'I need my camera case,' Sean shouted over the roaring of the flames.

'You can't go in there!' Liz's face was a picture of disbelief.

'It'll be all right, if I can get to the bedroom,' he told her. He turned to Nancy. 'Here. Hold this.'

Sean gave her the sword by the handle, strangely reluctant to let it out of his hand.

'Don't cut yourself,' he said, and grinned. He reached out and ruffled her hair, then, in the same movement, brought her in to him and kissed the top of her head.

'You too,' he said to Siobhan. 'Be here when I come back.'

He gave her a hug and a quick peck and turned to Liz. She put her hands round his shoulders. He held her tight against him before turning towards the building.

The three women stood and watched as he approached the door.

386

The wall on the left was a mass of flame. As soon as Sean opened the door, the inrush of air fanned it to a blowtorch blast. Sean backed out far enough to take a big breath of air, filled his lungs and just threw himself between the doorposts and into the inferno.

Liz felt her heart drop inside her like a dead weight.

Inside, the smoke was blinding. Almost immediately a pungent smell assailed his nostrils and he realised it was the stubble on his jawline withering and shrivelling. He made it to the bedroom without opening his eyes or letting his breath out. The camera case was still lying opened on the bed. He felt around, using the years of experience to identify all his equipment and then quickly, but with a deadly calm, snapped the case closed, making sure the catches snicked home. Just then, from the living room there was an almighty crash as the roof caved in. A river of flame shot up the corridor and into the bedroom, and it was only by the luck that seems to spare small children and the crazy that Sean wasn't standing in its path. The pressure rammed into the room and blew the window out, complete with its frame. Sean dragged his case across to it and hauled himself over the sill, to the back of the cottage. Behind him the rest of the roof collapsed with a mighty roar and the gable walls fell in towards each other. White-hot sparks erupted in a volcano-blow.

Sean was far enough away to escape the heat that blew out. He came strolling round to the front with his case slung over his shoulder. Out on the grass, Siobhan and Liz stood with their arms round each other, shoulders heaving. Nancy stood a few feet away, eyes fixed on the inferno.

'Got it,' he said. The three of them jumped like startled cats. Nancy whirled and crouched with the sword outstretched, its black blade flickering in the light.

'Oh, you bastard, McCullain!' Liz wailed when she got her voice back after standing mutely with her mouth opening and closing like a stranded fish. Then she simply fell into his arms. He could feel her wet tears on his neck.

Out beyond the ring of fire, in the depths of the copse, not far from where the destroyed body of Theresa Laughlin still seeped into the damp earth, the *Shee* crouched in the shadows. Fire still burned in her eyes, and her face was contorted in a furious frown that squeezed eyelids shut over monstrous eyes. A dark liquid dripped out on either side of the hooked, beaklike nose and ran down over high, sharp cheekbones. Her head was sunken down below the level of the humped and pointed shoulderblades, right down on the narrow chest from which the array of shrivelled teats swung with a motion of their own.

Gradually the pain dissipated, and as it did, the anger grew, along with the appalling *need* that sizzled through her black, changing *self*.

She had been caught by surprise, just when she had *him* in her grasp.

Yes HIM. The thought came to her. *He* was *the one*.

She remembered him from back before the dead time. In him was the power of the one she had sought and harried and tempted. Her mind flew, rolling back the dark aeons of entrapment, to the days of light and hunger and destruction. It – *Shee* – had wanted him then, and he had spurned her. She had come to him in the night and he had turned his face away. She had swum around him in the river, blind with fury at his rejection, and he had come after her with that terrible sword and cut off her hand. She had grown it back, but the pain of that echoed down the corridor of time to pulse in her strangely jointed wrist that ended in what sometimes looked like a claw and sometimes like a shrivelled, many-fingered, distorted human hand.

As the fury twisted and squeezed within her, so the other urgency grew inside.

Shee was the only one left. She had been solitary before, for so long, after the great battle that had seen the creatures she ruled driven to the edge of the sea and down into the cold grey waters. That was in the days when there had been *power* in the earth, in the days when the first *men* had come to the west to drain the power out and to deny its very existence. Then, *oh then*, there had been power in the stones and the sons of gods had walked.

And he, Cuchullain, the white to her black, had been the only one who could have fulfilled her.

Now, in the dark of the copse, *Shee* hunkered in the fork of a great truncated oak, letting the burning pain drip and flow from her eyes, and her being pulsed with the imperative that drove her on.

She would have this one and she would spawn.

And her power would return a thousandfold in this barren land.

They made it back to the tor. Sean lugged his heavy metal case, careful not to crack it against the stone sides of the narrow tunnel. The pale wash of light from Siobhan's torch was enough, briefly, to illuminate the staring eyes of Dr Connarty's upside-down head on the mound of rubble, and the stringy tendons and torn flesh under – but now above – his jaw. Siobhan quickly moved the flashlight beam away before Liz or Nancy saw the appalling sight, but not quickly enough for Sean to miss it. The head registered briefly in his mind, but he closed himself off with an effort of will.

In the chamber, Sean dumped his case on the unbroken section of the block. Deftly he thumbed the catches. They sprung open with a loud click. The three women seemed to be holding their breath. Nancy stood with her back to the rest, facing up the tunnel, holding the smooth stone blade out in front of her. She looked tense, every cell of her body on the alert for the first sign of the thing's return. Sean cast her a quick glance as he quickly removed equipment from the case. She looked like a *Valkyrie* he thought. Like the *Skatha* in the legend Connarty had told, the female warrior who battled on the sweeping mountains of Skye. The faint torchlight caught her outline, straight, legs apart, back ramrod straight. It limned her mane of blonde hair. The woman, Sean thought, in the part of his mind that wasn't focused on his sensitive camera gear, was amazing. Her husband had died – and right horribly – bare hours before, but it was as if she had closed it off, shut it out. Or perhaps she had gripped it so tightly none of it could seep through. And everything about her proclaimed that she would meet head-on the thing that had stolen her new husband, meet it face to face, and *fight*.

Liz helped him while Siobhan held the torch in hands that only trembled slightly. All three of them were in an agony of expectation, knowing that what they were doing had to be done carefully and slowly, yet also aware that it had to be done with all possible speed.

Nancy lined up the remote units in a row on the flat slab while Sean worked the light sensitive diodes on the ends of their short wires. There were ten of the things, which had worked well when he had been taking the wide-angle pictures of the chamber for the archaeologists. Then, there had been plenty of light from the bulbs strung on the wire. Now there was only the pallid light from the weakening batteries of the torch.

'We can't have them on the floor,' Sean said. 'That was all right for the last time, but I need a clear field. They all have to go off at once and beam inwards.'

'Aren't you afraid?' Liz asked.

'Shitting myself,' Sean said, and then he chuckled. 'This is the best cure for constipation I've ever had.'

He looked up briefly and saw that both Siobhan and Liz were grinning. That made him feel good. Over at the exit, Nancy stood as if she was carved from stone. From way out, beyond the tunnel mouth, a howl came echoing across the field and down the passageway. It started off deep and soared quickly to a harsh shriek, still far off. Everyone heard it.

Sean took the first slave unit over to the wall nearest the empty niche and reached up, feeling for a crack where he could hang the little hooklet that jutted from the back of the cigarette-packet-sized box. The holes where the stones had burst out were much too large, and too low down.

'Damn,' he breathed.

'What's wrong?' Siobhan asked.

'Nothing to hang this on.'

He felt around above head height. Under his fingers the stone was smooth, without jutting angles. He reached down quickly and fumbled in the pockets of his jerkin, shoving aside keys and coins that jangled metallically in the silence. Finally he drew out a box of Bluebell matches that he'd carried with him from Levenford on Clydeside. He handed the unit to Siobhan, opened the box and spilled its contents into his hand.

'Keep your fingers crossed that these will take the weight.'

He picked a match and then groped upwards. The workmanship of men dead for thousands of years, labouring without steel saws and carborundum cutters, was incredible. Each stone fitted against its neighbour with such precision that there was hardly a hair's-breadth of space between them. The wall up there had taken the shock-pulse of the tidal wave and had been strong enough to resist the huge pressure.

Sean closed his eyes and let his fingertips talk back to him. He drew the outline of stone, traced the edge and followed the narrow crack until he felt a tiny space. He raised the match and prodded around until the butt end slipped into the little fissure, then used the pressure of his hand to screw the sliver of wood in as far as it would go until it jammed tight. He took the unit from Siobhan and angled it this way and that until the hook slipped over the inch-long protruding end of the match. He drew his hand away and the little slave unit pendulumed for a moment, threatened to fall and then hung there. Sean let his breath out, unaware that he'd been holding it.

It took him fifteen long minutes to fit the rest of the equipment in a rough circle around the walls. They were spaced as evenly as they could be, allowing for the few natural crevices in the stone, but finally they were all in place, though some of them hung more by the effort of their combined will than anything else.

Sean crossed to the stone and brought out the big Nikon, hefting it in his hands the way he'd done for half his life. He slotted the umbilicus from the battery charger on the handle of the flash, which was pinioned on a bracket so it stood out in a salute from the camera body. He thumbed the switch at the head. There was an insectile buzzing as soon as the charging light came on, a tickling mosquito hum that quickly rose up the scale beyond human hearing.

'I think that's us now,' Sean said. Liz and Siobhan nodded dumbly. Sean felt apprehension grip his stomach, but knew he could show no fear in front of them. It was all down to him now.

'Well . . .' he began.

'Let's get that fucking bitch,' Nancy said clearly from the end of the passageway. Her voice was ice in the darkness.

Yes,' Sean agreed with a short nod. 'Let's get the fucking bitch.' He handed the camera to Liz.

'This is idiotproof,' he said with a lightness he did not feel. Fragments of his dream were trying to intrude on him, taking shape in the shadows beyond the guttering light.

'I'll get you back for that, McCullain,' Liz said. He could hear her making an effort to keep her voice steady. 'Anybody can push buttons.'

'That's a union secret,' he told her, and smiled tightly. 'Just point and press and close your eyes.'

He walked over to the narrow doorway where Nancy stood. 'Right. I'll get her in here. Just don't stick me with that when I come back. Remember, I won't be taking a stroll. The first thing that comes barrelling down that tunnel will be me.'

'No it won't,' Nancy said flatly.

'Well, if it's not, the same rules apply. Stand aside, let the lights get it, and do what you can. If that thing comes first, they've got my picture on file for the obituary.'

'No,' Nancy said. Her face was set, stunning in the shadows, but firm. Her eyes were fixed on his. He could feel the power of her determination arc across the small space between them. 'No. It won't be you. It has to be *me*.'

Sean shook his head and made to pass her by, but she held up the stone sword, almost threateningly, in front of him.

'Don't be a fool,' Nancy told him. The two others looked across at them silently. 'It *has* to be me. Don't you understand? You have to stay here and get it. You can't be out of breath. I won't.'

Sean looked at her quizzically.

'Listen, I run six miles a day. I'm fit. I can outrun that thing any day of the week and I won't be doing anything just hanging around here.'

'But this is the safest place,' Sean said, though he was beginning to see her logic.

'Only until that thing comes back. I can *do* it, believe me. It got Tom and now I want to get it. I have to do something, and I'm the one who can do this best.'

Sean knew she was right, but every cell of him fought against it. In his mind's eye he saw himself out there in the open, calling to her, drawing her in. The muscles down the length of his backbone had twitched and shivered and the skin had started crawling on his arms. Already his balls had hoisted themselves right up and he could feel the up-tempo beat of his heart. He knew she was right, but the *man* in him told him it was wrong.

'But . . .' he began, then stopped.

Nancy held up her hand. 'No, Sean. This is for me.'

She stood up and touched his cheek softly with her free hand. 'I'll bring it in,' she said. She reached her hand out, like a gladiator making peace. 'Here, you take this. It'll just weigh me down.'

Sean grasped the proffered handle of the sword and immediately felt the tingle as his fingers clenched the smooth grip. It was as if the strange obsidian weapon *melded* itself to fit. He drew it in towards himself, feeling the weird *flow* of sensation ripple up his arm, into his shoulder, down the length of his spine. A *charge* from the smooth volcanic blade had flowed into him.

Without warning, the blade flared briefly with white wavery lines that shot up and down the two-foot length, blaring its radiance into the chamber. All at once the slave units fired themselves, punching the light of the sun into their eyes.

Sean jerked back, fingers automatically clenching on the grip. There was a brief, teeth-jarring hum as the light flowed up and down the blade again before it faded down and paled to darkness. The whole effect had taken less than a second.

Sean breathed out a long, wondering sigh.

'Luke Skywalker lives, for Christ's sake,' he finally said.

Everybody looked at him.

'May the force be with you,' Nancy said from the doorway, and without warning she burst into laughter. Despite what she'd been through, despite the terrors and the horrors, her laugh was loud and natural, with no sign of hysteria. The three of them looked at her for a moment and then the laughter affected them all. Only Siobhan, who hadn't seen the film, wondered what the joke was, but in that moment the laughter was so infectious, so wonderful and life-proclaiming, that she couldn't help but be swept up on it. The chamber rang to the sound.

Then Nancy strode out into the tunnel. Her back faded into the darkness and the laughter died instantly. In Sean's hand the sword still tingled its weird life, and his body responded. He could feel the muscles in his thighs and shoulders twist and turn, as if in preparation. Silence descended and they stood and waited.

The great eyes slowly opened. Wrinkled reptilian lids hoisted themselves apart over black orbs that sucked away the faint light of the moon
filtering into the coppice. The thing that crouched in the fork of the
spreading oak blinked twice, dark rivulets trickling down its nightmare
face. It turned its head, swivelling to stare this way and that. Off beyond
the trees there was the brief, scurrying sound of a small creature that
had awoken in its nest, shaken from hibernation by the bleak force that
juddered through the air. The head swivelled with the striking speed of
a snake and the eyes blared into the darkness. The scurrying sound
stopped instantly.

Jaws opened in the thin, rabid face and snapped shut. The sound
carried through the trees, ricocheting from the trunks until it faded.
The shadow in the fork of the old, moss-covered tree moved slowly. An
arm stretched out to clasp a lower branch. There was the hard scrape of
a claw on rough bark. Slowly, like a stalking mantis, it reached the
ground and then drew itself up high, *sensing* around. The head
swivelled and a snuffling, animal sound filled the glade. The head
turned again and then froze.

Something was coming.

The *Shee* stretched out her long, thin arms once again. Her fingers
elongated and attenuated slowly, and between them a fine, black
membrane stretched. The great wings spread and flexed once with such
power that small saplings bent under the rush of air. She stretched the
wings and folded them around her, and her hunched form slowly
stalked out from the oak tree on spindly legs.

Nancy Ducain walked out of the tunnel and into the night. The moon
had fallen in a velvet sky to the west, and now hid beyond the hills. A
pale glow, reflected from the clouds, cast little light. To her right, the
cottages were still ablaze. She could smell the scorched wood, and the
roaring of the fires and crackling of the ruined timbers came blaring out
from the field. Even from a hundred yards away, the heat was intense.
In a few seconds, her cheek was ruddy. A part of her mind was aware of
the surrealism of the scene. Here, seven cottages were ablaze, quickly
burning to ruin, yet there was no-one but her to see it. There were no

flashing lights, no sirens blaring into the night, no crowd of rubber-neckers gasping as a roof caved in here, a gable wall fell with a crash there.

She gave it little thought. Her mind was fixed on *beyond* the fires, out there in the darkness.

She moved slowly but steadily on, past the edge of the field until the heat was at her back. For a moment, she stopped. She stood there, eyes fixed on the shadows within a coppice of trees, and then called out.

'Come on, you bitch. Come and get me.' Her voice soared up and over the crackling of the flames.

In her mind a cruel picture of Tom came back to her. Tom, the serious, yet in some ways childlike man she'd met and fallen in love with. Tom, whose eyes shone when he looked at her, who wanted to protect her and nurse her through life, though it was often he who needed the protection and nursing. In the series of pictures that conjured themselves up unexpectedly, she saw him turn and smile that boyish, slanted grin. She saw the dark hairs on the back of his neck as he slept beside her. Then, in one grotesque instant, she saw the slumped, *slick* mass on the bed in the cottage and her heart froze. Despair and sorrow crowded in, but her anger, her *fury* leapt up from within to smother it back and close it down.

'Get out here, you fucking *animal*. Come out and fight, you cunt *bitch*!'

Nancy *hated* that word. Tom had used it once in her presence and she'd rounded on him so ferociously that he'd never used it again. But now it fitted, it expressed how she felt. The thing was female. It was a crawling, loathsome *abomination*.

'Get out here, you *fucking whore*,' Nancy bawled. 'Come out where I can see you, you filthy *bastard*!' All Nancy's fury came spewing out of her in a wonderful torrent of meaningful insults.

Finally she stopped, gasping for breath, and stood waiting. Ahead of her the forest was dark; yet Nancy *strained* herself forward, feeling for the presence of the thing she challenged. She stopped, now facing directly into the coppice where the shadows crowded.

There!

She could suddenly *feel* the poison of the thing in the depths beyond the thick black trunks. She forced her mind out, like a radar, and *felt* the presence of pure evil. Her mind touched the thing, and for a brief instant recoiled, and then probed again.

The sensation was disgusting. It was an *offence*.

She felt the thing's putrid consciousness swivel towards her, focus on her. She called out as much with her mind as with her voice.

'I'm waiting for you, *cunt bitch*. Come and get me.' She stood there, hands on hips, body thrust forward, like a madwoman in the night.

'I'm going to *KILL YOU!*' Nancy screamed.

Deep in the coppice the blackness *erupted* like a depth charge in a sea of night. A huge scream of rage came blistering out from the trees like a stone-saw rasping through granite, a sound that spanked the air like a blow and vibrated the very ground. There was a violent crashing as saplings snapped and small trees were simply uprooted in the insane rush of the *Shee* in its frenzy to attack the taunter.

It came screaming from the glade, battering the undergrowth aside in its mad lunge, the great wings churning the air when there was space for them to spread and splintering the trees when there was not.

Nancy felt its rushing approach like a black tornado and moved back into the open, eyes still peering forward, every nerve stretched taut.

The dimness among the trees right in front of her got suddenly blacker, impossibly black, and she skipped back even further.

Then it came out from the trees, spitting hate and screaming fury. Huge wings powered down to slap the ground. Between them a thin, contorted body sat on spindly legs that ended in clawed feet which scraped the ground and sent up divots of earth to spatter behind it. The *Shee* came powering out of the forest and skidded to a halt just beyond the trees. The gargoyle head craned forward on the end of the skinny articulated vulture's neck and the mouth opened. A tongue like a lizard's flickered out and cracked like a whip. Gobbets of sizzling liquid flew off and sparked on the ground in front of it, shrivelling instantly the short grass of the field. Where they landed, black, poisoned patches spread like inkstains.

Nancy's breath stopped in mid-gasp. The obscene *presence* of the thing emanated off it in powerful, putrid waves that made her shudder.

The screaming went on and on, great pulses of alien sound that jittered through the bones in her skull and rattled her teeth.

Nancy felt no fear. The sight of the thing was *appalling*. Her mind and soul revolted against the obscenity of it, yet still she was not afraid. Her own anger was a cold stone inside her.

'You're *dead, BITCH*!' she called out. The eyes fixed on her in a frightful glare, but Nancy turned her own mind away from their power.

Then she plunged her clenched hand into the crook of her elbow and brought her fist up, middle finger erect, in a salute. She did not know why she did that, but when she did, a savage joy burst her cold anger asunder. It was childish, it was cheeky, it was *wonderful*.

396

Suddenly laughter bubbled up inside her and came out in a wild whoop. She turned, still rocked by it, and took off across the grass.

Her thighs pumped, driving her feet into the soft earth and Nancy *flew* across the field, hair streaming behind her. She ran with wonderful fluid grace, powering herself past the burning cottages on the left, feeling the heat against her face and tasting the soot in the air she breathed. Beyond that the air was cold and her lungs dragged in oxygen, forcing it into her bloodstream. Nancy ran like the wind, ran like a goddess, ran like lightning. She felt that savage joy build up inside her. It was behind her, the *Shee* was racing after her, a black, powerful sensation of evil, a screaming, wailing screeching thing with wings that whipped the air in their mad rush from the trees. But Nancy was *alive* and running. Inside her the feeling of life leapt and soared and exulted and she ran with it as if she could run forever.

She reached the wall and went over it in a graceful glide that brought her to the narrow road and then it was gone in two strides. She was on the track that led up to the tor; behind her the air shattered and cracked with the screaming fury of the blighted thing in pursuit. It was closer and closer. Nancy could feel it like a touch of death, but the life in her ignored it. Fifty yards away the entrance to the tor yawned like a dark mouth and she veered towards it, thighs burning, feet thudding on the dirt, lungs hauling, racing for sanctuary.

Behind her the thing spat poison. Its jaws opened in an impossible gape, then row upon row of dripping snake-like fangs snapped shut with the sound of stone shattering. The pinions whipped the air as it came on, powered by the hunger and the hate. It screeched again, blistering the air, and lunged forward, mad with fury.

Nancy felt the blast on the back of her neck like a punch but kept going. Fifteen yards and it was closing. Ten yards and it was on her heels. Five and it was breathing down her neck.

And then she was *inside*. There was no hesitation. The doorway loomed and she went straight into it. Scooting down the tunnel, heart bursting with triumph.

The thing saw that it would not be fast enough. Even as it powered through the air it could see that the mortal would reach the tunnel first. It snarled in frustration, but even as it did so, it started to *change*. The great membrane wings drew in on themselves and as they did its clawed feet hit the ground. It couldn't *fly* down the tunnel. The wings shrivelled and the arms shortened and by the time it reached the entrance, its metamorphosis was almost complete. The shape twisted and writhed, even as it continued, a fluid, noisome thing that followed

397

Nancy down the narrow confines towards the chamber like a demented night train.

Nancy made it with a split second to spare.

She came up the incline of the corridor, bawling all the time.

'It's me. Sean! It's me . . .' she yelled. 'Watch out it's *COMING!*'

Her feet thundered on the flagstones. She could feel the thing right behind her and she came to the narrow chamber opening and skittered almost to a halt.

Just as she did so a black, clawed hand on the end of an appallingly long arm struck out in a savage swipe.

Nancy's sensory perception, stretched to its utmost, was flooded with the unseen threat. She jerked forward, not seeing but *knowing* she was about to be ripped open from shoulders to pelvis. The hooked claw, at the end of one grotesque finger, missed her back: instead it snagged in the belt of her jeans and snapped it in two. Grabbing downwards, sideways, it simply lifted her off her feet. Nancy had a nauseating glimpse of the floor and then the ceiling as she tumbled into the air, cartwheeling, and then hit the wall with a sickening crash. Light flared and then darkness swamped it out.

Sean was turning towards the stone, reaching instinctively for the camera and flashgun instead of the obsidian blade that lay flat on the plinth. Siobhan was on the other side of the cracked block and Liz was beside her, nearest the doorway.

It had happened sooner than expected. Nancy's frantic yell had come clamouring down the passageway, magnified by the walls of the tunnel almost before they'd had time to move. Siobhan was on the point of swinging the flashlight around. The weak circle of light trailed across the wall of the cavern and then Nancy had come bounding down the flagstones and leapt into the room, her eyes wide and mouth open. A shattering scream came buffeting down the narrow confines, shivering the stones.

Sean saw it in the slow motion of heightened awareness. There was mud on her running shoes and a strand of hair was caught across her face. He saw her take a step and then the girl arched her back as she threw herself forward. Something black blurred behind her and Nancy tumbled into the air flipping over as she went past him. He heard the thud as she hit the wall to his right.

Blackness rushed into the chamber, formless and massive. Something reached out from within its depths, something long and hooked and moving at such speed that even in Sean's slowed down time scale it was just a flicker of black. It hit Siobhan on the chest and smacked her

398

down. There was a wet, crushing sound like an apple being squashed and Siobhan flopped to the floor. On the other side of the ferocious shape an arm reached out and took Liz by the neck. She had no time even to gulp as the claws on the end of the elongated arm gripped her by the throat and jerked her into the air.

The savage screech soared to an ear-splitting crescendo. Rocks cracked and shattered. One of the slave units tumbled to the floor and smashed.

Sean was frozen into immobility. It had all happened so *fast*. His hand was still outstretched to lift the camera when the *pulse* of thought hit him in the centre of his brain.

'*NO!*'

'This is what you want, *hero*,' the thought came at him. It scraped against his mind like clawed fingers. The flashlight had fallen to the floor and its feeble beam had guttered so low that he could hardly make out more than shadows. Liz was in front of him, a dead weight in the black extrusion that held her. He could see her eyes bulging and her tongue protruding from her gaping mouth.

Sean tried to speak but the words wouldn't come. The paralysis held him, bound his hands and feet.

'This is what you want, this weak thing,' the scraping *alien* voice whispered in his head.

The scaled fingers squeezed on Liz's neck and he heard a choked gulping sound come from her. Her head lolled to the left. A bubble of blood expanded between her lips and burst wetly.

'This is *nothing*, Cuchullain. *Nothing!*'

The mental blast of the thing was like a drill biting into his brain. He recoiled from it, squirming within himself under the onslaught.

'*No!*' he managed to get out past clenched teeth. '*Stop . . .*'

Then the smell hit him. It was a sweet, sickly odour that flooded over him and swamped him. Underneath the sweetness was a foul bitterness, a scent of decaying flesh and suppurating foetor, yet it was overwhelming, *overpowering*.

His heart punched hard in his chest, powering itself up, accelerating like a turbine flooded with fuel. His nerves twitched under his skin and all down his back the muscles jittered and danced.

In front of his eyes, the darkness started to reform, twisting and writhing. An arm still reached out to clench Liz by the throat, but the mass of the thing was changing, narrowing down. Huge eyes suddenly glared at him, then shrank in size. What might have been a head narrowed and shortened, growing paler and paler.

There was a flicker and the *Shee* stood in front of him. She was *terrible* in her beauty. The smell of her engulfed him and her perfection seared his vision.

Her arm was still stretched out, pale and smooth, holding Liz in a relentless grip as she drew him in towards her. Sean felt his feet move and was powerless to stop it.

The desire for her welled up like a gusher, boiling hot.

'*Yes, Cuchullain.*' The voice came at him again, and this time it was clear and soft. It was the voice of *woman*. '*I am what you want. I am that which you need.*

'*Come to me!*' it commanded.

She was naked. Her skin was so white. He could see the perfect swell of her breasts and the red buds of her nipples. Her hips curved from a narrow waist: he followed them down to where they became smooth pale thighs. Between them a mass of dark hair glistened as the hips undulated slowly.

He could feel an enormous pressure in his head, as if his blood was racing so fast all his veins and arteries were pumped up to bursting point. His entire awareness was focused on the woman in front of him and he *wanted* her. She drew him in with a scent that invaded every cell of him. *Need* powered within him like a bolt of raw energy.

The *Shee* crooned to him, bringing him closer.

On the floor, Nancy stirred and opened her eyes slowly. Her head felt as if a maniac was swinging a hammer on the inside of her skull. There was a wet trickle behind her ear. She could smell her own blood. As soon as she'd come out of her daze, Nancy had instinctively remained still. Just within her line of sight as she lay against the wall, she saw a movement and slowly let her eyes swivel.

Sean McCullain was slowly walking across the floor towards it.

Tall as Sean and grey-black, its spine reared up and out between its shoulders, showing every knob of its distorted backbone. The neck was wrinkled and shrivelled and covered with flapping wattles that looked like the blotchy skin of a toad. One arm was stretched out to the right, hugely elongated and with more joints in it than was possible. Liz was suspended in the grip of a strangling claw-hand.

The thing's chest was slatted with crooked ribs: down their length flapped a double row of withered teats. The pelvis stuck out on either side and scaly legs braced the weight in a hunkering crouch, splayed wide.

The hips bucked slowly backwards and forwards in anticipation.

Sean was walking into its embrace.

Her muscles unlocked and she *rolled*. In one flowing movement she was on her feet, took two quick steps and then launched herself, *kicking* with all the force of her body. The contact was like hitting a live power cable. A jolt of power spanged into her and threw her backwards: she arced, hit the ground with her hands, flowed with it and landed feet apart on the far side.

An almighty bellow of rage battered the chamber.

As if someone had thrown a switch, cutting off the current of unearthly power between them, Sean snapped out of his hypnotised state. He staggered. Nancy's powerful kick had shoved it to the side, and the thing had dropped Liz, who lay crumpled on the floor beside Siobhan. Liz coughed twice, then gasped in great whoops of breath as her lungs desperately sucked for air. He saw Nancy raise her head, the side of her face a ruin of cuts.

Sean's mind recoiled from the thing that now stood there. It was not a woman. He saw it in its true shape, the mottled and lumpy dugs that swung down the length of the narrow abdomen, the squatting, splayed legs and, worst of all, the swollen sex organs that pouted obscenely and twitched with muscular pulses.

The thing swung its hideous head round to glare at Nancy. Its scream of rage was reverberating off the walls so loudly that shards of stone started to flake off. It turned towards the girl who stood near the wall, feet planted firmly, body bent protectively.

Sean didn't hesitate. He took two steps forward, drawing his hand back as he did, and punched the thing on the side of the head. He felt warty skin under his knuckles and the creature's head snapped back. His momentum carried him forward and he dived for the block of stone. As he did so, he was aware of a movement to the left, right beside him.

Liz had hauled herself to her knees and was grabbing for the camera.

'Sword,' she gasped. '*Use the sword!*'

Sean hauled himself round the block of stone, reaching out with his right hand. He was inches from the handle when the flashgun went off right in his eyes. Immediately the nine remaining slave units threw out their glaring light, pinioning everyone in a flash of stark brilliance, searing the whole scene in their eyes.

The roar of rage from the dreadful thing became a shriek of pain so loud the stone block resonated with the vibration. The *Shee* blasted the air with its agonised howl.

Orange circles danced in Sean's eyes, fading to violet. He blinked

401

hard, trying to regain his vision. As he did so, the flash went off again and the unearthly roar thundered. The walls shook and three of the slave-units tumbled to the floor.

Sean's hand clasped the handle of the sword. A jolt drove right up his arm and through his body. He twisted, bringing the sword up, rolling across the stone to land in a crouch, facing the thing. Its jaw was agape and its lizard tongue flicked out, whipping the air and sending driplets of poisonous saliva scattering. Some of it landed across Sean's cheek and he felt his skin bubble even as the burning pain registered.

The thing's eyes were blind. They steamed and sizzled, dripping foetid liquid, yet it still reached out its two twisted and jointed arms to claw at him with whip-like speed. He ducked below them and swung his body upright.

In his hand, the sword suddenly bucked and twisted, turning itself towards the thing. Sean looked up and saw the creature writhe and *change* again. It swelled monstrously, stretching itself out. The legs thickened and the chest expanded as muscles seemed to *grow* under the skin over the slatted ribs. The screaming roar soared in a mind-splitting crescendo.

And as Sean faced the thing, he felt *himself* change. His shoulders twisted and widened, his arms broadened. Great veins pumped themselves up along the ropes of muscle that expanded down to the wrists. His torso distorted and his chest bucked upwards. His eyes widened until they were huge in his head and his dark hair spiked itself up in a mane. All he could hear in his head was Professor Connarty's words: '*The* warped *warrior.*'

The thing, blind though it was, reached out for him. Liz hit the button of the camera . . . and nothing happened. She tried again and the camera clicked, but the flash refused to operate. An immense, clawed hand hit Sean on the shoulder and tumbled him sideways. He rolled and came bounding to his feet, his face now a contorted, almost inhuman mask. He could feel his blood singing. His senses soared in exultation. A fierce anger swept through him and it was bright and hot. He opened his mouth and he roared a song in strange words that had great meaning and he stepped forward.

The *Shee*, the *Mor-righinn*, the great serpent, reached for him again and he swivelled. As the claws passed, he noted with satisfaction that the hand was a lighter colour than the grey-black length of the distorted forearm. The hand he had cut off in his dreams had grown back again. He could see the puckered line where his sword had bitten and he bellowed terrible laughter. The sword sizzled and flared into light.

402

Shards of white lightning raced up and down the length of the blade, searing the chamber with an intensity that made the light of the flashgun and all the slave units pale by comparison.

The light was awesome. As he held the sword up he could feel the river of power cascade from himself into the obsidian blade and jolt back into him, growing as it did.

The *Shee* screamed in agony. Its eyes burst in their sockets, splattering the walls with foul, sizzling liquid. It tried to *change* again but its skin only flowed and twisted sluggishly. The claw-hands were up to its face, protecting its head from the light, but to no avail.

Sean, now distorted almost beyond recognition, leapt forward and swung the Sword of the Son of Light in a wide arc. It caught the thing on the side and bit deep into the ribs. There was a crunch and a hissing sound as the light burned into the flesh and through bones. The creature reared in writhing agony, but Sean did not falter. He braced himself, tugged the sword out of it and swung again, bringing the weapon down through a circle onto the thing's shoulder. The scaly arm bounced right away from the body. It flew over the stone block and landed on the floor, still clenching and flexing. The black blood that flooded out in a stream eroded pot-holes in the hard basalt.

Sean twisted again and cut at the crown of the thing's head. The sword sliced through the bony carapace and down between the puckered, melted eyes. He pulled and cut in at the throat and the dreadful, gurgling scream was cut off instantly. The foul, mutilated thing flopped to the ground. Its great legs were spread wide, still undulating, as its ghastly instinct to reproduce continued even as its alien, *un-life* drained away.

Sean braced, took the Sword of the Son of Light in both hands and rammed it through the leathery skin up to the hilt. The fire of the light burned the skin away. He could feel the power cauterise everything inside. In his mind, the shrieks of the un-formed, unborn within the creature scrabbled at him, but he ignored their death-blasts. The fire burned everything. From the gaping hole, yellow steam blasted out, and then the whole of the thing's abdomen collapsed in on itself. Immediately, the flesh started to melt off the hideous bones and ran into the cracks in the stone. Before his eyes, the creature that had come into the world before history had begun, dissolved and flowed and crumpled until there was nothing left but a stinking puddle of foul sluggish liquid which finally evaporated in noxious clouds.

Sean turned towards Liz and Nancy, feeling his blood still sing in his veins. Their faces were blank and white, eyes wide in fear.

At once, he realised they were afraid of *him* and that realisation made him start to *change*. The reversal happened as quickly as the first distortion that had overtaken him. He felt his muscles ripple and slide and his bones locked and unlocked as they found their previous positions. His spiked mane subsided and the great strength, the strength of the battle-fury flowed out and away from him.

A few moments later, he stood near the centre of the chamber breathing heavily. The sword was still in his hands, but its light had gone out. There was no power in it. It was black.

He turned towards the girls, feeling as though he'd been hit by a train.

'It's all right,' he said, letting out his breath in a long sigh. 'It's me again.'

36

Between them they managed to carry Siobhan out of the tunnel and into the pale light of the dawn that was just breaking beyond the sweeping sides of Croagh Patrick in the east.

Siobhan was still breathing, though her breath was ragged and shallow. Sean laid her on the ground, which was still damp and dew-covered, and stripped away the torn threads of the jumper. The ribs on her right side had been caved in. The imprint of a splayed, clawed hand was there in the depression of broken bone. The jagged ends of two of the ribs had ripped through the skin and pectoral muscle in a gaping wound. Claw lines gouged deeply between her breasts, in ploughed furrows almost to her navel. *But Siobhan was still breathing*. A trickle of blood from her mouth told them that her lung had been punctured, through how badly, none of them could tell.

Sean got two of the marker poles, both about six-feet long two by twos of unfinished wood and managed to sling the tarpaulin that covered the ruined generator between them to make a stretcher. They gently lowered Siobhan into it and stood for a moment, listening to the laboured breathing. Liz had an enormous bruise that covered her whole neck and ran from her jawline down to the top of her chest. Her voice was hoarse and husky and it hurt her to move her head. Nancy's shoulders were stiff from the collision with the wall. Her cheek was a mass of abrasions and she had a deep, three-inch cut that curved across her cheekbone, giving her a fierce look. Sean still felt as if he'd fallen from a moving train.

He took the fore end and Liz and Nancy took a pole each. They eased Siobhan off the ground and slowly moved away from the tor towards the village. They went past the field where the cottages still smouldered. There was a singed, scorched smell on the still air. When they reached the cattle-grid on the track, Siobhan moaned and turned her head. They all stopped and Sean twisted himself around.

Siobhan opened her eyes and looked up at him. She smiled painfully.

'Is it gone?' she asked in a ragged whisper.

Sean nodded and Siobhan smiled again, though it looked as if it took a great effort.

When they finally made it to the village there were few people to be seen. The church door had been blasted off its hinges and lay on either side of the bare opening like two halves of a clam shell. Several of the houses on the left side of the road were gutted and smouldering. Beyond the church, in the space on the far side of the little cemetery, was a small crowd of people around a grey-green truck. On the grass, there was a line of plastic-covered heaps. Immediately Sean knew they were bodies. Some of them looked awfully small.

Dr Tim O'Brien nodded to them from the side of the truck. He and Donovan and a couple of the others were standing in a small huddle, while a team of strangers worked on the line of injured under makeshift canvas shelters. The side of Donovan's face was a purple, abraded mess and swollen out, giving him a lop-sided appearance. His arm was in a sling and he looked as if he'd been in the wars.

The doctor came over when he saw the makeshift stretcher and called to the newcomers. They carefully hoisted Siobhan into the back of the truck just as another heavy vehicle came trundling along the road. Two men in white coats started working on her immediately, jabbing a fluid drip needle into the vein in the back of her hand and carefully washing the wound and packing it in pads.

'They saw the fires and came this morning,' Dr O'Brien said. 'They got a span over the river.'

'They're a bit late,' Sean replied.

'Will she be all right?' he asked, nodding to the truck that was edging out of the space.

'Will any of us?' O'Brien asked back.

Liz and Nancy came closer and both slipped their arms around Sean. For a moment the three of them stood in silence. Then they turned away.

Liz never wrote the story. They were finally able to drive down to Limerick to catch a morning flight. Both of them waited first until Nancy boarded the jumbo that would wing her across the Atlantic.

The scar was quickly healing and did nothing to mar her beauty. The night before, the shock of it all had finally hit her. She had held out since the moment that the thing, the obscenity in the form of her husband, had stalked her. She had sought it out and challenged it and had *fought* it. If Nancy hadn't been there, hadn't been brave, then none of them would have walked away. And the village would have been devoured when night fell again. Nancy kept it all tight within her, until the night before her flight a full seven days after they had stumbled out into the dawn.

Sean and Liz hadn't let her out of their sight. They had taken adjoining rooms in the hotel and they were with her every minute. They hardly spoke about what had happened until Nancy went into the bathroom to wash for dinner and both of them had heard her suddenly burst into tears.

Liz rushed in and found her sitting on the floor, knees down under her chin, curled in a tight little ball, weeping. Both of them sat down with her and held her tight for a long time until the sobbing began to diminish.

Next day her plane took off for Boston and they watched in silence, just able to make out her pale face in the window, three from the front. She waved and then the plane shot forward and she was gone.

No. Their story was never written. When they had got down to Galway on the first night afterwards, Sean had opened up the back of the camera to take out the film. But when the case opened, he found the whole inside of the camera had melted down to a blistered pool of metal and plastic. He'd laughed ruefully at that. The next morning, just before dawn, they agreed that their part in what happened should never be told.

The night after that, Liz awoke with a start in the dead of the small hours. She reached across to the other side of the bed. The blankets were thrown back and the sheets were cooling. Sean was not there.

She raised herself sleepily, not alarmed yet, and slipped into her dressing gown. Quietly she went down the hallway and into the kitchen. In the dim light from a streetlamp outside, she could make out Sean's silhouette. He was hunched over the table, naked except for a pair of skimpy briefs, turning something over in his hands.

Liz stopped at the doorway, about to speak, when a movement caught her eye. In the shadow, she thought she saw the muscles at the top of Sean's shoulders twist and writhe and expand under his skin. She gave a startled gasp and he whirled quickly. The sword was in his hands and she thought she saw a flicker of light run in a quick stream up the length of the blade before it turned dark again. Sean's eyes were black in the shadows under his brows. He seemed to glare at her and then his face softened. He leaned forward enough to let the light catch his face. His eyes were gentle, sleepy, and he was smiling.

'Are you all right?' Liz asked.

'Yes. I woke up. I was having a dream.'

'A bad one?'

'No. A good one this time.'

Liz smiled and walked towards him, lifting her hands to hold his head against her.

'Okay, Cuchullain. Let's go back to bed.'